HOPEPUNK

JIMMY PATTERSON BOOKS FOR YOUNG ADULT READERS

JAMES PATTERSON PRESENTS

Stalking Jack the Ripper by Kerri Maniscalco
Hunting Prince Dracula by Kerri Maniscalco
Escaping from Houdini by Kerri Maniscalco
Becoming the Dark Prince by Kerri Maniscalco
Capturing the Devil by Kerri Maniscalco
Kingdom of the Wicked by Kerri Maniscalco
Kingdom of the Cursed by Kerri Maniscalco
Gunslinger Girl by Lyndsay Ely
Twelve Steps to Normal by Farrah Penn
Campfire by Shawn Sarles
When We Were Lost by Kevin Wignall
Swipe Right for Murder by Derek Milman
Once & Future by A. R. Capetta and Cory McCarthy
Sword in the Stars by A. R. Capetta and Cory McCarthy
Girls of Paper and Fire by Natasha Ngan
Girls of Storm and Shadow by Natasha Ngan
Girls of Fate and Fury by Natasha Ngan
You're Next by Kylie Schachte
Daughter of Sparta by Claire M. Andrews
It Ends in Fire by Andrew Shvarts
Tides of Mutiny by Rebecca Rode
Freewater by Amina Luqman Dawson

CONFESSIONS

Confessions of a Murder Suspect
Confessions: The Private School Murders
Confessions: The Paris Mysteries
Confessions: The Murder of an Angel

CRAZY HOUSE

Crazy House
The Fall of Crazy House

MAXIMUM RIDE

The Angel Experiment
School's Out—Forever
Saving the World and Other Extreme Sports
The Final Warning
MAX
FANG
ANGEL
Nevermore
Maximum Ride Forever
Hawk
City of the Dead

WITCH & WIZARD

Witch & Wizard
The Gift
The Fire
The Kiss
The Lost

Cradle and All
First Love
Homeroom Diaries
Med Head
Sophia, Princess Among Beasts
The Injustice

For exclusives, trailers, and other information, visit jimmypatterson.org.

HOPEPUNK

PRESTON NORTON

JIMMY PATTERSON BOOKS
LITTLE, BROWN AND COMPANY
New York Boston London

JIMMY Patterson Books / Little, Brown and Company
Hachette Book Group
1290 Avenue of the Americas, New York, NY 10104
JimmyPatterson.org

First Edition: January 2022

JIMMY Patterson Books is an imprint of Little, Brown and Company, a division of Hachette Book Group, Inc. The Little, Brown name and logo are trademarks of Hachette Book Group, Inc. The JIMMY Patterson Books® name and logo are trademarks of JBP Business, LLC.

The publisher is not responsible for websites (or their content) that are not owned by the publisher.

Library of Congress Cataloging-in-Publication Data
Names: Norton, Preston, 1985– author.
Title: Hopepunk / Preston Norton.
Description: First edition. | New York : Little, Brown and Company, 2022. | "Jimmy Patterson Books." | Audience: Ages 14 & up. | Summary: "After her sister runs away, teenager Hope Cassidy rebels against her conservative family by starting a rock band with her former crush, Danny, who is kicked out of his house when he comes out to his family."—Provided by publisher.
Identifiers: LCCN 2021016156 | ISBN 9781368057851 (hardcover) | ISBN 9780316335140 (ebook)
Subjects: CYAC: Bands (Music)—Fiction. | Homosexuality—Fiction. | Social action—Fiction. | Family life—Wyoming—Fiction. | High schools—Fiction. | Schools—Fiction. | Wyoming—Fiction.
Classification: LCC PZ7.N8253 Ho 2022 | DDC [Fic]—dc23
LC record available at https://lccn.loc.gov/2021016156

ISBNs: 978-1-368-05785-1 (hardcover), 978-0-316-33514-0 (ebook)

Printed in the United States of America

LSC-C

Printing 1, 2021

To 45,
That your walls may fall,
That your cages may crumble,
That we may rise from the ashes you've left
stronger than ever before.

—ONE—

FAITH WAS HERE

THE GRAFFITI WALL HAD EXISTED FOR AS LONG as human thought. Or at least as far back as Mom and Dad had attended Sundance High. It had clearly been expanded upon in the two decades since. The thought was, if we let kids deface one wall as much as they want, they'll leave the rest of SHS property alone. There were, of course, certain prohibitions—no swears, no genitalia, no blasphemy (it was anyone's guess what a "blasphemy" looked like)—but otherwise, free game. And it worked! I mean, there was the occasional "867-5309 call for a good time" carved on the inside of a bathroom stall, but even those were relatively clean, content-wise.

Maybe it was just me, but I thought the graffiti wall was high art.

It was a mosaic of identity, generations on top of generations. Images and colors and emotions splashed together into a psychedelic, face-melting kaleidoscope. Words like "DOOM" and "EUPHORIA" filled incredible amounts of space, painted like monuments. Phrases like "Be Someone" and "Don't Wait" offered simple advice that had probably affected countless souls. There were images of staggering tree silhouettes with sprawling roots that wove into an invisible Earth. Black cats slinking by. Birds soaring. An impressive Chinese dragon, red with gold spines and whiskers, winding in and around the graffiti wall like a ribbon, tying the whole thing together.

At the very bottom corner, scribbled in thick black Sharpie, practically faded, someone had written "Faith was here." It read like a metaphor. The power of past tense. Faith *was* here but no longer.

Unfortunately, Faith, in this case, was a very real person.

I was there when she wrote it.

I had joked about how tacky it looked next to everyone else's art. I wasn't trying to be mean. I was just joking.

Faith had shrugged sheepishly and said, "Yeah, but my existence is all I have to offer."

Looking back, now that she has left, these are the words that haunt me most.

What a cruel way for the universe to show me how much her existence meant.

♩ ♫ ♪

I was born full of swear words.

This was what I told people when they asked me when it was, exactly, that I started swearing like a character in *South Park*. They always seemed curious, considering I was born into the most blisteringly Christian family this side of the Black Hills. I certainly didn't start *verbally* swearing until maybe a month before my sixteenth birthday. But as far as my inner monologue was concerned, I felt like I was nothing *but* swear words. Swear words and this vast, consuming emptiness devouring me from the inside. I heard the word "fuck" once, and suddenly, it was the only word in the English language that made any sense. I held on to it like a life preserver in the middle of an endless ocean.

I'm not saying there was anything inherently meaningful about the f-word. But sometimes, in a world that I completely failed to understand, it felt like the only word that understood *me.* All I really knew was that the God I had been taught to believe in since I was little had a real fucked-up way of doing things, and I wasn't sure I believed in that Holy Shithead anymore. And once you've allowed yourself to pull *that* spiritual rug out from beneath your feet, all equilibrium goes out the window. I was left reeling for balance in a world that didn't seem to make sense anymore.

Anyway, I'm getting ahead of myself. Let me tell you about Faith.

Faith was my older sister. Faith was my best friend. Faith was the coolest person I ever met.

When I say "coolest," I mean that in a more genuine, intimate sense of the word. Faith was a nerd and a total introvert weirdo. By some fake fashion magazine standard, she was like the exact opposite of cool. Outside of one-on-one conversations, she wasn't eloquent, she wasn't TV-definition attractive, and her sense of style didn't extend beyond understanding the difference between shirts and pants. But she was gleefully, recklessly, 100 percent *herself,* and if that isn't cool, then fuck. I don't know what is.

Faith's one true love was science fiction. She gobbled up all the subgenres—hard sci-fi, soft sci-fi, apocalyptic, postapocalyptic, space opera, space western, dystopia, alien invasion, dying Earth, Afrofuturism, steampunk, biopunk, nanopunk (there were seriously way too many "punks")—but her favorite was the granddaddy of the "punk" subgenres: cyberpunk. From books (*Neuromancer*, *Snow Crash*), to movies (*Blade Runner*, *The Matrix*) to anime and manga (*Akira*, *Ghost in the Shell*, *Battle Angel Alita*), she was hardcore for this shit. And that was just the classics. She had *plenty* of room for modern Netflix mindfucks like *Black Mirror* or *Altered Carbon*. She loved stories with artificial intelligence, virtual realities, hackers, and megacorporations, juxtaposed against a radical change in the social order. When I tried to pry into her obsession, she explained that at their core these stories were about one person making a monumental difference. At their beating heart, these stories were about what it meant to be human.

For as long as I can remember, our family used to go to this megachurch (Faith liked to call it "MAGAchurch"—not a compliment) in Gillette, the next big city from our town. We were there every single Sunday. It was called Traditional Family of Christ, and it looked like a sports stadium and a rock concert got baptized, married, and had good, old-fashioned marital sex. At the time, I didn't even realize how problematic the title was. But Faith would always nudge me in the side and whisper her commentary into my ear. Like when Pastor Raines instructed his congregation of thousands, filled to the rafters, to not do *anything* without first consulting the Lord in prayer.

"Because God forbid we learn to make rational, independent choices for ourselves," said Faith.

Or when Pastor Fulco said that all good is the product of Jesus and that all evil is the product of Satan.

"It's a good thing the world is so black and white," said Faith. "Can you imagine if there was a gray area? We'd be screwed!"

Or when Pastor Brighton said that the Bible is the inerrant, infallible word of God. It is flawless and incapable of error.

"Like when those kids call Elisha 'bald head,' so he curses them, and two bears come out of the woods and eat the little bastards—Second Kings, Two Twenty-Three?" (This was tragically and hilariously her favorite scripture and probably the only one she could cite off the top of her head.) "Like, screw those kids! Male pattern baldness is serious."

If you're wondering how I kept a straight face through all of this, I didn't. It almost always resulted in me snorting, barely stifling my laughter, and—when assailed by homicidal looks from both parents—pretending I was just so totally moved by the word of God, praise him. **wipes away rapture-filled tear**

When Pastor Raines went on an incredible rant about the "eternal nature" of gender, and homosexuality being a "direct attack" on the family unit—that anything outside of this was unnatural and wrong—I expected her to have an entire comedy skit. These guys didn't get to go on crazy rants like this without some tasty riffing from Faith.

But Faith was perfectly still. Perfectly silent.

She was like that the entire drive home.

It wasn't until later that evening that Faith knocked on my bedroom door and peeked inside.

"Hey," she said.

"Hey," I said. "You okay?"

Faith nodded her head. Then shook her head.

"What's wrong?" I asked.

Faith stepped inside and shut the door behind her. "Can I tell you something?"

"You can tell me anything." I thought this was a given, but I scooted across the bed, tucked my legs in, and patted the open space in front of me. I even moved my favorite stuffed animal, Loafy—who was technically a plush loaf of bread with a smiley-winky face—and placed him in my lap, at attention. When we were in elementary school, Faith once told me that she watched the movie *Flashdance* at a friend's house, and Loafy and I had kept that secret thus far, and we intended to keep it to the grave.

Faith sat on the edge of my bed, her hands balled tightly in her lap. She was staring at my wall. She couldn't even look at me.

"I'm lesbian," she said.

She was fifteen when she told me this. I was thirteen. What you have to understand is that we were essentially the Flanders family from *The Simpsons*. I had never met a real-life lesbian—at least not one who was publicly out—and the only famous queer woman I was consciously aware of was Kristen Stewart.

So I wasn't *deliberately* being an ass when I said, "What, like Kristen Stewart?"

Faith paused to consider this. "I think she's bisexual? But yeah, I guess?"

I nodded slowly. "I like Kristen Stewart."

Faith started crying. Her face just completely broke apart.

"Whoa, hey," I said, panicking. I dropped Loafy, scooched forward on the bed, and hugged her. "Hey, hey, hey. I love you, okay? Thank you for telling me that."

"You're not going to tell everyone, are you?"

"Do you *want* me to tell everyone?" I asked.

Faith shook her head violently. "No. Not yet. I think Mom would murder me."

I wanted to tell her that Mom *wouldn't* murder her, but honestly, in my thirteen-year-old brain, I wasn't entirely sure that was accurate. So instead, I just hugged her tighter. "Your secret is safe with me. Safe as *Flashdance*."

Faith started crying even harder. When she finally hugged me, I thought I might snap in half. She hugged me like I was the only thing in the world she had to hold on to. Now that I think about it, I probably was.

I don't remember that hug ever ending. That memory was pure hug. Pure love.

Faith and I were already close, but from that moment on, we were unbreakable. Our relationship was one of intimate understanding, sacred trust, and fierce loyalty. Because I knew about her sexuality, I felt the need to tell her my deepest, darkest secrets—which were honestly about as deep and dark as an Oprah Cinnamon Chai Frappuccino with extra whipped cream. They consisted mostly of the fact that I was developing a deep, abiding, possibly sexual love for punk rock.

I was also in love with a boy, but someone else was in on that secret.

♩ ♫ ♪

My name was Hope, and her name was Faith, so obviously we had a little sister named Charity. I guess my parents lucked out, having three girls in a row. We were all cesarean sections, each of us spaced roughly two years apart, and the doctor made it explicitly clear you don't have more than three of those bad boys if you're keen on the miracle of life staying that way. Can you imagine if Mom wasted that last C-section on a boy? Faith, Hope, and... Charlie? What a disgrace. Bullet dodged.

Charity and I used to be super close, the way that young children often are. The beautiful thing about being a kid is that boredom and the insatiable need to have fun 24/7 often superseded any differences you had. If Faith was the nerd, and I was the wild child (by conservative Christian standards), Charity was the romantic. Eons before puberty, she loved to pick dandelions and wildflowers and make scraggly bouquets out of them; she'd hold Barbie and Ken wedding ceremonies; sometimes she would even try to write love letters to Jesus whom she legitimately wanted to marry—and I did *all* this shit with her. During the Barbie wedding ceremonies, I usually played Ken, who happened to be an FBI agent well versed in the art of karate. When she "wrote" her love letters to Jesus, she usually recited while I transcribed. The deal was, if I played her games, she would play mine, and my favorite game was The Floor Is Lava. You know the game. We would jump around the living room from furniture to furniture, and if you touched the floor, you were dead. We would play this until we broke something, or Charity's clumsy ass fell and hurt herself, or, the most common endgame, Mom came in, saw us jumping on her West Elm Hamilton leather sofa, and had a full-blown conniption. It was great.

This all makes Charity sound like a simple-minded rube, but she was weirdly a prodigy, at least when it came to key-based instruments. Charity was taking piano lessons before she even learned where babies came from. The story goes that she found Dad's old

Moog Minimoog synthesizer from his high school days, when he was in a band called the Trash Can'ts—he had since cleaned up and found Jesus—and she taught herself a version of Moby's "God Moving Over the Face of the Waters," which she had discovered on the internet and mistaken for a gospel song, although that's not to say that it was anything short of a spiritual experience for her. When Mom found out, she had no moral choice but to take out a mortgage and purchase a proper piano (because let's be honest, Mom hated the Minimoog and everything it stood for). However, rather than becoming the next Sergey Rachmaninoff, which Charity seemed fully capable of, she opted to dedicate her keyboard skills to Jesus instead, playing both piano and organ for the church choir. The Minimoog was exiled to the attic.

It was only recently, when she thought no one was listening, that she would get scandalous and tap out a little Marshmello or deadmau5 on the ol' Steinway or—if she was feeling particularly rave-y—lock herself in her bedroom, slip on a pair of fat noise-canceling headphones (hand-me-downs from yours truly), and get funky with whatever DAW (digital audio workstation) she could get her hands on. I shit you not, Charity was a closet electronica/EDM junkie and an aspiring DJ—the sort who feels the need to have a giant robot helmet and a secret DJ identity, à la Daft Punk—but I wouldn't find this out until later, much later. I'm only telling you now so that you'll believe me when it does happen.

Anyway, when Charity and I were still young and naive and in love with life—trading off things like sloppy makeovers and talking about boys for backyard parkour—there was this playground at City Park, close to our house, where I "invented" this new game called Wyoming Ninja Warrior. That was when I first laid eyes on Danny Roger. Charity was maybe seven years old at the time, meaning I must have been about nine and in the early throes of puberty, because lemme tell ya what: *hubba hubba!*

The concept of "sexual attraction" had never registered in my brain until that moment. He was the sexiest boy-creature I had ever seen! During those summer months, he wore tank tops that exposed his long, ropey arms, and he smiled in this way that gave me a stomachache, and I just wanted to, like, *grab* him. I didn't know what I wanted to do after the grabbing, probably explore the texture and absurd lankiness with my fingertips, but believe you me, the desire to grabby-grab was idolatrous, almost pagan.

Danny also had a twin brother, Dylan, but Dylan was the whinier, more annoying version of an otherwise perfect model. They came to the park to play sports, all sports, literally any and every sport ever invented, and more often than not, I found myself losing Wyoming Ninja Warrior to Charity because she was in the throes of a growth spurt, and I was too busy making googly eyes. When I informed Charity that I was in love with the boy-creature called Danny, she and I made low-key plans to marry the Danny and Dylan Roger package. (Charity now knew she wasn't allowed to marry the Messiah—and she hadn't yet discovered Calvin Harris—so she lowered her standards to Dylan.) That way we could move into the same house together, and our kids would be best friends, and we could all play The Floor Is Lava together, and it would be great. Sometimes we squared away the details while hanging upside down from the monkey bars.

I thought Charity was less in it for Dylan and more in it for me.

♩ ♫ ♪

Dad jokingly called electric guitar the "devil's banjo," but I think it was one of those jokes that was actually serious because in the Cassidy household, there were effectively only four music genres: country, gospel, classical, and show tunes. The funny thing was that—like Charity with the Minimoog—it was his fault I wandered down this treacherous, sinful road of rock and roll.

It all started a year after Faith came out to me. Mom, Faith, and Charity were away one Saturday morning for some women-and-girls-only church activity. I think it involved "arts and crafts." Not important. What was important was that I had caught a nasty stomach flu and spent the previous night relocating my insides to my outside. (I barfed.) So, no arts and crafts for me.

Before they left, Mom tucked me in bed, put a hot compress on my head for the concaving headache, and was even so kind as to put her favorite big mixing bowl by my bed so I could just roll over and vom, should the need arise.

"No TV," Mom instructed. "Only sleeping."

She didn't need to tell me twice. Last night's pukefest was the ab workout of a lifetime. I should have had a six-pack at this point. If I even tried to sit up, I might have died.

And so I lay there, drifting in and out of consciousness for the better part of an hour. It was around then that my actual dreams melted away into this fever-dream reality where the most rock and roll thing I had ever heard in my entire fourteen baptized years on Earth was blasting from the garage.

I thought I was imagining it. It wasn't hard to see why. The sound was experimental, almost hallucinatory, like jazz on hard drugs. Drums chanted out shamanic rituals. A guitarlike sound drifted spectrally through walls and dimensions. (The guitar sound was actually an electronic instrument called a theremin, I would later learn.) The lead singer, meanwhile, was moaning like he was in the throes of sin. The culmination of the sound was a mountain of pure madness.

I sat upright—even as my achy abdominal muscles screamed in existential terror. I crawled out of bed. Draped a blanket around my shoulders like a shawl. Wandered down the hall in a foggy daze. The music was definitely coming from the garage. As I drew near, the song's hallucinations reeled into a singular vision: the singer's voice.

From his lyrics clear down to the fabric of his voice, this dude was pure sex.

The guitars—real guitars—riffed and rolled like storm clouds filled with thunder and noise. The lead singer screamed, "My, my, my, my!" Possessive? Yes. Hot? You better believe it.

I reached the door leading from the house into the garage. I could feel the rock and roll thrumming against its surface. Silently, I peeled the door open.

The sound and the fury washed over me like floodwater.

The old stereo was front and center on Dad's workshop counter. The garage door was closed, and the hood of the Honda CR-V was open. Dad was leaning over the exposed engine, singing into the monkey wrench in his hand—faintly, so as not to ruin it with his tone-deaf pitch.

"*Shake for me girl,*" said Dad. "*I wanna be your backdoor man.*"

"Dad?" I said.

Dad might as well have been caught in the very act of adultery. He was a big man, with a big, square face and a haircut that only seemed to emphasize the bigness and squareness. So when he whipped upright, he hit his cinder-block skull on the hood of the car with such force that the hood rod was knocked loose, and the hood slammed shut. It only barely missed his meatloaf fingers.

"*Aaaaauuuoooohh!*" Dad and the lead singer screamed in stunning unison.

I gasped. "Dad, are you okay?"

Dad offered a wincing smile and gave a crooked thumbs-up. He seemed more concerned with the "devil's banjo" blasting from his stereo than any possible head injury he might have incurred.

"Yeah, I'm—" he stammered, rubbing his head. "Lemme just—"

He couldn't seem to finish a thought. So he shuffled to his workshop stereo and fumbled to shut the music off. When it ended, the absence was like a hole.

"I liked it," I said.

Dad stopped. Looked at me. His face was a paradigm of pure confusion.

"What was that?" I said.

"Uh," said Dad. "Led Zeppelin?"

Sweet Jesus. Even the name was sexy.

"It's cool," I said.

The wall of awkwardness separating me from Dad slowly crumbled. I saw the validation in the curl of his smile, in the way he nodded. "Yeah! It is cool, isn't it?" Dad glanced left, then right. His hand brushed across the wood surface of the counter, grabbing a CD case. "It's off their second album. Song's called 'Whole Lotta Love.' "

"Can you play me more of it?"

As the father of three daughters—let alone husband of the most religious woman in all Wyoming—I'm sure Dad never thought this day would come. For a second, he seemed to question whether this was real life. Or some sort of trap.

But it was only a second. The next instant he was grinning with abandon.

We plopped down on the floor, leaning against the workshop counter with the stereo between us. Track by track, Dad took me on a stroll through rock and roll history. This was what I learned:

1. That sexy man on vocals was Robert Plant. Not to worship false idols or anything, but Dad called him "the god of rock and roll," and I was inclined to agree.

2. John Bonham was, bar none, the greatest drummer of all time. Case in point: "Moby Dick." The entire track was instrumental and basically a showcase for his drum-soloing madness. Fucking madness, I say! It made Ahab look sane by comparison. It made that whale look like a goldfish!

3. Jimmy Page was a samurai, and the guitar was his katana. He slayed with poetry and honor.

4. Last but not least, John Paul Jones. Primarily on bass and keyboards, but he was also known to dabble on the mandolin, violin, cello, banjo, keytar, sitar, ukulele, harp, autoharp, koto, clavinet, mellotron, and the recorder. To name a few.

At the end of the day, my favorite song was "Ramble On." Not only because Page achieved violinlike Zen on his Les Paul or because JPJ's rolling bass line was as smooth as ice cream or because, according to legend, Bonham was banging on a plastic trash can. But because the song also served as damning evidence that these four grown-ass men were total nerds. The entire thing was a lyrical tribute to *The Lord of the Rings*. Robert Plant went so far as to name-drop Mordor and Gollum. The line between nerdom and badassery was left in a fiery, guitar-screeching haze. By the end of it, I was dumbfounded.

"Wow," I said.

"Right?" said Dad.

"That was epic."

"Right?!"

"How come you never listen to this around the house?"

Even as I said it, I knew the answer. I knew Dad knew that I knew. I guess I was just perplexed and frustrated that secrets were necessary for coexistence. That sometimes the key to acceptance was to not be your true self.

"Oh, you know," said Dad, meanderingly. "Your mother...she's a very spiritual woman. She's sensitive to things that interfere with her relationship with God. I knew that when I married her. Sometimes, when you love someone, you have to make sacrifices for them."

I knew what he was trying to say. And I didn't not agree with it, not completely. It was about selflessness. But this conversation was about more than just rock and roll. It was about Faith. It was about who she was. And it went so much deeper than music preferences.

"But doesn't she love you?" I said. "Shouldn't she have to make sacrifices for you too?"

"She does. She gave me three beautiful daughters. And every day, she helps me raise you. It's more than I could ever ask for."

I bit my lip and hugged Dad. He hugged me back. The sort of enfolding, bearlike embrace that makes hard things endurable. The unfairness was still there, but it dissolved in the moment. Love had the power to do that sometimes.

"Just so you know," said Dad, "I'm not saying you're not allowed to listen to whatever music you want to."

I stared at Dad.

"Just so long as your mother doesn't find out," he said. "And it has a guitar solo that melts faces."

He winked.

My eyes widened with a rush of criminal adrenaline.

"There's this record store downtown," he said. "It's been there since I was a kid. It's been through a few different owners and name changes since then, but it's basically the same store. That's where I discovered all my favorite bands. Last I checked, they still have headphones where you can listen to stuff before you buy it."

Dad tilted left and removed the wallet from his back pocket.

"When you get over this bug, have Faith walk you down there sometime. Find a piece of music that speaks to your soul."

He slipped out a twenty-dollar bill, crisp as an autumn leaf, and handed it to me.

Well, he tried to. I didn't grab it. I stared at that shit like drug money.

"Dad," I said, deadly serious. "Are you telling me it's okay to keep secrets from Mom?"

Dad chuckled. "I think there are two types of secrets, Hope. Secrets that hurt people and secrets that protect people. I'd like to think this is the sort that protects. Nothing strengthens the soul like music that speaks to it—especially when you find it on your own. I think there's power in that."

He gently nudged the twenty-dollar bill closer.

I know Dad didn't know Faith's secret. I *know* that. But somehow, it felt like he did.

Like he was telling me that everything was going to be okay.

♩ ♫ ♪

It was now called Ralph Records: New and Used CD + Vinyl. Faith took me without question, partly because we were best friends, but also maybe partly because of Mavis Mackley, the supercool, pink-haired, sixteen-year-old girl who Faith was acutely aware worked there. According to legend, she played the drums. The moment I saw Faith eyeing her like candy—or worse, like some dorky manga—I knew what was up. Birds and bees and shit. I didn't want to cockblock or whatever the lesbian equivalent was, so I nonchalantly perused. Left Faith to mentally recite pickup lines or whatever.

That's when I saw it. The Strokes' debut album, *Is This It*. The cover was a hypnotic alien atlas of yellow and blue. I later learned it was an image of subatomic particle tracks in a bubble chamber. It sounds naive to suggest that it was love at first sight—that I knew this album was The One before I even listened to the damn thing—all I'm saying is that something karmic was at work here. It was a used copy, and just as Dad promised, all used copies were unsealed and available to sample on various players throughout the store. So I popped it in, clamped a pair of fat, noise-canceling headphones over my unpierced, virgin ears, and entered the voice of Julian Casablancas and his title track, "Is This It."

It was a spiritual awakening. I was not okay. I had been infected by a sound, and I needed more of it, stat.

By the second track, "The Modern Age," I was ready to fork over my music spending money.

By "Last Nite," I was what you would call "obsessed."

By the end of "Take It or Leave It," I was ready to get a tattoo, smoke a cigarette, start a garage band, and move to New York City. I was a changed girl. No. A changed *woman*. Over the space of forty or so minutes, I had accumulated a wealth of life experiences. I was no longer Hope Cassidy. I was someone new, someone cooler, someone who seriously needed to get her fucking ears pierced already. I used to be afraid of needles, but I was pretty sure I could take it now.

Apparently, I wasn't the only one who had discovered themselves at Ralph Records: New and Used CD + Vinyl. Faith and Mavis really hit it off. Ralph Records became a regular trip for us. I was on a conquest to feed an insatiable hunger for the sound that infected me, and Faith was falling in love.

I guess I was falling in love too, but you know what I mean. It was different.

♩ ♫ ♪

We were walking back from Ralph Records one particularly sunny afternoon, and in typical Faith fashion, she was lost in the stratosphere of her thoughts. I just figured she was thinking about Mavis. Or maybe the plot to the modern Netflix mindfuck *Russian Doll.* Normal stuff. At least until she turned to look at me and point-blank asked me:

"Have you ever thought about writing a book?"

I had not, in fact, *ever* thought about writing a book. It was times like this when I realized what completely different people Faith and I were. I had thought *plenty* of times about starting a rock band—but first I would probably have to learn how to read music or play a badass instrument. Musically speaking, I guess you could say I was sort of illiterate.

"Nuh-uh," I said. "Have *you* ever thought about writing a book?"

Faith nodded emphatically. Of course she had.

"What sort of book?"

"Well, it has to be sci-fi, obviously," said Faith. "But also, maybe a love story."

Faith was trying not to smile, which of course made her smile even more than she normally would if she just let herself smile, which in turn caused *me* to smile, and you know how that situation goes. It was a smiling crisis.

"Stop it!" said Faith.

"Stop what?" I said. "I'm just smiling. You're the one in *loooooove.*"

"I am not in love!"

Neither of us looked like we believed her for a second. Faith was smiling so much, it hurt just to look at her.

"Besides, it's not *just* a love story," said Faith. "I think at its core, thematically speaking, the story will be about identity."

I nodded like I understood what any of that meant. Which I didn't. Not contextually, anyway.

Faith seemed to notice that she had lost me, so she added,

"The main character's name is Andromeda." Finally, a bone I could fucking chew on.

"Ooh, that's a cool name."

"It is, isn't it?"

"Andromeda," I repeated, testing the name on my tongue. "An-dro-me-da."

"I think Andromeda has to run away from home," said Faith.

"An-*drah*-me—wait, what?"

I blinked and looked at Faith. For the first time in this entire conversation, she wasn't smiling.

"Why?" I said—probably a little too seriously.

"She just has to," said Faith, matching my seriousness. "Because she's going to be trapped forever if she doesn't."

"Trapped?"

"She's afraid of what will happen if she *doesn't* run away. Because literally every possibility feels like the scariest thing ever."

I opened my mouth, but the right thing to say eluded me. What were we even talking about anymore? This conversation was slipping rapidly away from me.

"She's afraid of people finding out who she really is, and what then?" said Faith. "What if something really bad happens to her?"

"But...," I said, "what if everyone just learns to love and accept her for who she is?"

"That's not going to happen," said Faith.

The edge to her voice was so sharp, I felt the cut. The blood pooling at the wound.

I stopped walking. Faith took several steps past me before she stopped and turned around.

I was weeping silently.

"What are we talking about?" I said.

Faith frowned.

"We're just talking about your book, right?" I said. "It's just a book. *Right?*"

"Oh, Hope." Now Faith's eyes were watering. She took three tremendous strides and wrapped her long arms around me. "It's just a book."

I hugged her back. Ferociously. Possessively. I refused to let her go until I had some sort of assurance she would never leave me.

That's when Faith chose to hit me with possibly the strangest and coolest assortment of words strung together I had ever heard in my life.

"Andromeda and Tanks Through Space and Time," said Faith.

"*Hunghh?*" I said, sniffing violently.

"That's the name of my book."

"Whoa." I sniffed again. "That's a really cool name."

"Heck yeah, it is."

There wasn't an inch of her that doubted it.

I finally dared to let go of her.

"Tanks, huh?" I said, forcing a weepy grin. "Does she have *pink hair*?"

"Oh my *Godddddd*," said Faith, pushing me away. "You are the worst. Please go away."

But she was smiling.

That smile was all I needed.

Andromeda descended from a long line of four-dimensional beings.

That is to say, technically, they were three-point-five-dimensional beings because being a literal four-dimensional being would make you some sort of god. The Dresdorians, however, were a proud, regal race, too good for decimals. They rounded up. So four-dimensional beings it was!

What this meant—being an entity of more than three dimensions—was that from the moment of Andromeda's conception, her consciousness was a tesseract with a panoramic view from birth until death. Her memory extended in both directions, a perfectly straight line, the sort that only exists in mathematical abstractions, not reality itself. The line was a tunnel, and she saw the light at the end, dying in the arms of her lover, a vaguely immortal being. In her infant brain, barely capable of motor function, she knew she would marry Tanks, and Tanks hadn't even been born yet. Or rather, constructed. Tanks was a manufactured, synthetic being, property of Ixion Inc.

This romance was apparently forbidden. Or at least heavily frowned upon by Dresdorian standards, to say nothing of the Church of Time.

To be clear, Andromeda's knowledge of what the future held wasn't a picture-perfect understanding. It was more like an aggressive, premature sense of déjà vu. It was like "knowing" yourself, in the limited sense that you are yourself, yet completely failing to understand who you are on the existential level. Why you do the things you do, say the things you say, behave the way you behave. Why are you the way you are? Existence was a largely irrational thing. Seeing the end didn't necessarily help you understand it.

So even though Andromeda "knew" that on her seventeenth birthday Allfather Odyss was going to sit her down and give her The Ultimatum, she didn't necessarily know what that meant.

Even though she knew she would be exiled from Dresdore and have her third eye clipped, she hadn't quite registered what a terrible thing that was.

* * *

—Andromeda and Tanks Through Space and Time,
ÆonQ

-TWO-

AN ACCESSORY TO LESBIANISM

I DON'T WANT TO SAY THAT FAITH COMING OUT to me drove a wedge in my relationship with Charity, but well, it kind of did. Faith needed me more than Charity did. At least that was the way I saw it.

When our Ralph Records trips became a tradition, Charity often begged Faith and me to tag along. I would look at Faith, and she would shake her head, and I would politely tell Charity to shove off. Our excuses for why she wasn't invited varied, but her uninvitedness did not.

Honestly, I felt bad for her, but what could I do? We couldn't very well bring her along. She would rat us out in a heartbeat! Charity *loved* church. She gobbled up anything any pastor ever said, no questions asked. Jesus was her first love, her one true love, and even when she got married, her husband would have to accept that he was number two.

At first, we got real creative with excuses. And when that got tiring, we got real stoic with just saying no. She was not invited.

Charity was resentful, but we could live with that.

This went on for about a year. Because I was in my own world discovering new-for-me music, I was a little clueless about how visible Faith and Mavis's relationship had become.

As the story goes, Charity's friend Brianna saw Faith kissing a girl through the store window.

Brianna told Charity.

Charity prayed desperately for direction, asking God what she should do, and God said, "Rat her out." So that's what she did.

♩ ♫ ♪

The thing about Mom was that she was gorgeous. Easily prettier than her three daughters, although Charity was a close second place. She had that wide Cameron Diaz smile, an indisputably perfect nose, and her hair was this unreal, spun-out-of-pure-gold blond that looked like *surely* it had been dyed, but no, Mom was just that pretty. To top it all off, she always made a prodigious effort with the makeup, walking the tightrope between glam and all-natural so effortlessly that it was difficult to look at her and not hate your own face.

When she found out about Faith, all that gorgeousness fossilized and hardened into something stony, impenetrable, and kind of scary.

Charity and I were ordered to go to our rooms, but *No no no, Faith, not you, you have to stay.*

On the way to our rooms, I looked at Charity like *What the fuck?* And Charity looked at me like she was singing that old German hymn "Be Still, My Soul" in the amphitheater of her heart. That's when I knew something was really wrong, and I was the only one not in on it.

Charity and I opened our respective bedroom doors.

Charity went into hers and closed the door.

I closed my door but stayed in the hallway.

Clinging to the wall like one of those sucker fish that eats the gunk off of aquarium glass, I slinked to the edge of the shadows and peered covertly around the corner into the living room.

Mom was sitting on one recliner, and Dad was sitting on the other recliner, and Faith occupied a very small space in the dead center of the sofa, softly imploding on herself. This was her tribunal.

Dad was there more for decorative purposes. In this hearing, Mom was judge, jury, and executioner.

"Honey, do you know what sexual sin is?" said Mom.

What a question. How do you even respond to something like that? Faith certainly didn't know because she opened her mouth, but nothing came out. It just gaped, frozen in horror.

"Sex is a very special gift that God has given us," said Mom. "It was given so that a husband and wife can show love to one another, but more importantly, it was given for the very sacred and special purpose of creating life. When a husband and wife create life within the bonds of marriage, they are doing the work of God. There is literally no more important work on this Earth than giving birth to God's children and raising them in a God-loving home. So I want you to tell me, Faith: Why is it wrong that you were seen kissing a girl inside that record store?"

Faith was mortified. She looked to be balanced on a very precarious point. On one side she was erupting into tears, and on the other she was throwing up, but the internal ducts were all backed up, leaving her looking sad and sick.

Dad didn't look much better. His silence spoke as loud as Faith's. Maybe even louder.

"This isn't the end of the world," said Mom. "In fact, this was the very reason Jesus died. He knew we would make mistakes, but lucky for us, he's *already died for them*. All that's left for us to do is to accept him into our hearts, and he can heal us. Also, you're never allowed to see Mavis Mackley ever again. Obviously."

"What?" said Faith, brokenly.

"It's for your own good. An important part of the repentance process is to make an effort to avoid temptation. Mavis is a temptation and a bad influence, and, quite frankly, a bit of a harlot. The very least you can do is stay as far away from her as humanly possible. That's the very least thing you can do."

"Mama, please!"

"Don't 'mama, please' me. Do you accept Jesus into your heart or don't you?"

Faith's silence spanned eons.

"I asked you a question, Faith. Do you accept Jesus into your heart or don't—"

"I don't know," said Faith so quietly that it could have easily gone unnoticed.

But it didn't.

"I'm sorry?" said Mom, in that way that is the exact opposite of sorry.

Faith probably could have pretended that she didn't say anything, and Mom would have moved on, the way a bulldozer moves on.

But she didn't.

"I don't know if I believe the same things that you believe," said Faith. "I'm not sure that there's anything wrong with me."

Mom snapped like a delicate twig.

♩ ♫ ♪

Faith was grounded indefinitely.

Not that Faith went anywhere except to Mavis's job and back. But the extent of her punishment was a little more intense than not being able to go anywhere or do anything. Mom ransacked all of Faith's belongings. Combed through anything and everything that could be considered "lesbian in nature." So the surprising amount of female nudity in her anime and manga collection was a problem. In fact, the sheer amount of R-rated material Faith owned was kind of miraculous. Faith was such a nerd, I guess Mom never suspected her of smuggling in "sexual paraphernalia." (By the way, "lesbian in nature," "sexual paraphernalia"—these were actual fucking terms Mom was using.) Even relatively clean movies like *The Matrix* got the boot. Mom took one look at Trinity in that tight black leather outfit and threw her outta there.

Mom took all of Faith's belongings, stuffed them in a Hefty black trash bag, threw it in the back of the Honda CR-V, and drove off. When she came back, the trash bag was gone—in a storage unit (unlikely), a Goodwill bin (more likely), or some random dumpster (most likely). For all I knew, she could have gone full sociopath and dissolved it in a tub of hydrochloric acid. Every day that passed with Faith's sexuality out in the open was a day Mom grew just a little more unhinged.

Faith didn't fight it. She didn't say a single word in protest. Faith usually spent that time occupying as little space as possible, probably hoping she'd go invisible or maybe just disappear entirely. She still had her laptop, which seemed to be the one place she could retreat to, but Mom had somehow disabled her access to the internet, so God knows what she was doing. Writing a book, probably.

I somehow escaped punishment. Neither Mom nor Dad asked if I knew about Mavis, and I didn't tell. I think Dad may have come to my rescue on this one. Ralph Records was, technically, his fault.

I hated how relieved I was.

I should have kept better tabs on Faith. There's this Bible phrase, "my brother's keeper," which comes up sort of ironically when Cain kills his brother Abel, but after that, it's sort of implied that being your brother's keeper is a good thing. It indicates a certain togetherness, a responsibility to have one another's back, blood relation or otherwise. Faith may have been older and smarter, but she also had a secret that made her more vulnerable, and in that sense, I guess that made me my sister's keeper. It was my responsibility to keep her safe, and I fucked up big-time.

Our house became a psychological minefield. I tiptoed around conversations and interactions, and I kept my head low. I wish I could tell you that I was there for Faith, but I wasn't. I didn't offer a single word in her defense. I didn't even talk to her. She was in ideological quarantine, and Mom was the CDC. The best I could do was offer Faith heartbroken eye contact at dinner while prodding my mashed potatoes with a fork.

It was at dinner the next week that Mom made her announcement.

"Faith is going to be leaving us for a little bit," she said.

I dropped my fork completely in the mashed potatoes. I glanced down as the handle sank slowly into a well of gravy. Then I glanced at Mom. Then at Faith. Mom looked like she was riding a spiritual high. It was the happiest and healthiest she'd looked all week. There was color in her cheeks and a visible weightlessness to her conscience. She was smiling.

Faith was staring at the contours of her creamy garlic chicken like they were fortune-telling tea leaves telling her she was fucked.

"What?" I said.

Mom had no problem looking directly at me. In fact, she was about to deliver this entire fucking spiel to me. I may have escaped punishment, thanks to Dad, but Mom knew better. By her moral compass, I was complicit. An accessory to lesbianism. For all she knew, this shit was contagious.

"There's a wonderful camp in the area that helps children who've lost their way," Mom explained, fingers interlocked, smiling broadly. "They're called Change Through Grace. They're not far from here. What they do is help young people like Faith re-center themselves by learning to love and know the one person who loves and knows them better than they know themselves: Jesus Christ. He's already paid the price; Faith only needs to accept him. Satan wants us to think that we can be born a certain way, that we can't change, but that's simply not true. Faith's eternal destiny is to be a wife, to be a mother like me, and to start a family just like ours. She may not know it, but someday she's going to meet some handsome young man who will make her heart flutter, and together they will make the one thing that threatens Satan's kingdom more than anything else: a righteous, God-loving family."

I looked at Faith to confirm she was hearing this shit. Faith looked like she was about to be tangibly sick on her creamy garlic chicken and mashed potatoes.

"Faith and I have already talked about this," Mom said (translation: *Stop looking at your sister*). "She realizes she's made a mistake. She's ready to do her part to repent, and to heal, and to become the young woman our Lord and Savior wants her to be. This is her decision. How long it takes depends solely on how ready she is to give her heart and soul over to God."

There were a lot of things I wanted to ask, *What the actual fuck?* being at the forefront. But putting my incredulousness into words was next to impossible. All I could manage was a feeble "When?"

"Tomorrow morning," said Mom. "I've already spoken extensively with the chief therapist. They'll have a room prepared for her first thing. The paperwork's done, I've already paid for the first six weeks—"

"Six weeks?" said Faith.

Two words from Faith was all it took to completely disrupt and unsettle Mom's peaceful countenance. Mom unweaved her interlocked hands and pressed them flat against the table, like she was squashing a bug.

"Faith," she said, not even looking at her, walking a tightrope between calm and dangerous. "We've talked about this."

"You didn't say it was six weeks," Faith protested.

"*At least* six weeks," Mom corrected harshly. "As long as it takes."

Faith was already shaking her head—although it was less an act of defiance than a state of crisis. She was in the throes of falling apart.

Mom's nostrils flared indignantly. "Charity, Hope, go to your rooms."

♩ ♫ ♪

Going to our rooms was a formality. Even when I buried my head under my pillow, I could hear every word because they were either being hurled like projectiles or drenched in choking sobs.

These were the sounds I fell asleep to. How I even fell asleep, I will never understand.

I was fifteen then. The same age Faith was when she came out to me.

Andromeda and Allfather Odyss met at the airbus stop on Negative Fifth and Main, where they were intended to meet. They arrived at precisely the same time, sat down, and stared straight ahead. Both looked indignant about the predestination of this conversation.

"We both know how this is supposed to go," said Allfather Odyss. "I'm asking you to change your timeline. You can do that, you know. We have a facility for changing timelines."

The sky was greenish, and the air was salty, almost acidic. The skyline scraped across fat clouds, engorged with actual acid rain. Dresdorians had evolved to endure even the most acidic storms. Their physical makeup was so complex that the acid was incapable of reacting with it. They built their cities with similar impervious compounds. Regardless, a bad storm was coming. Andromeda might have thought it poetic, were she not so upset.

"I love her," said Andromeda.

And it was true. She hadn't met Tanks, and yet she loved her with all three of her hearts. Figuratively speaking. The literal purpose of her hearts, even the smaller accessory ones, was to pump blood to the siphuncle organ living mollusklike within the high-spired shell mounted to her forehead like a horn. Her third eye. It acted like an antenna for her pineal gland. These were the organs that told her this feeling was love, and it was insurmountable.

"It's not even a her," said Allfather Odyss. "It's a machine. A simulation of a life-form. It's not even capable of love."

"She is a her, and she loves me more than you've ever loved anything," Andromeda snapped. "Just because you don't understand it—"

"AND YOU DO?" said Allfather Odyss. He was standing now. Ah, yes. This was the part when he got upset. It was foreseen. Every muscle was a knot beneath his orange skin. His mouth vanished beneath the intense furling of his violently red beard. "You're just a naive little girl who's about to ruin her life, her future, and the reputation of her family, and over what? An unholy crush?"

"It's not unholy, and it's not a crush." Andromeda wanted to sound mad, but she was crying.

"You're right. Any non-Dresdorian relationship is unholy. This is an abomination."

"Fuck you."

"And I suppose it's not technically a crush if it's directed at a soulless imitation of a life-form. An obsession, maybe?"

"Fucking—fuck you!"

"This is your last chance," he said. "Come to the timeline facility with me. All I need is a word, a single word. Say yes. Predestination is only as immovable as the resolve of your faith. You can change, Andromeda. If you fail to do so, you know the consequences. And let me just say, the physical pain that comes from being clipped is nothing compared to the blindness. Exiled Dresdorians have killed themselves over it."

Andromeda stood up as well. Tall. Defiant. Her eyes may not have been level with his—she only stood a meager six feet tall to his eight and a half—but boldness elevated her. Her jaw was rigid, and she spoke through her teeth.

"I choose my timeline," she said. "I choose Tanks."

Of course, this moment was already part of the Church of Time's timeline. The Cardinal Guards, who observed the intervention from a respectable distance, proceeded to move in.

—Andromeda and Tanks Through Space and Time,
Æon Q

—THREE—

HOW TO DISAPPEAR COMPLETELY

I AWOKE THE NEXT MORNING TO MOM SHAKING me. She looked distressed—which wasn't exactly a new look on her, but this was different. More primal. She looked genuinely scared.

"Hope! Wake up, Hope. Where's your sister?"

I stared at her blankly. Blinking slowly. Still waking up. *Where was my... sister?*

The fear on Mom's face finally registered. That fear injected straight into my bloodstream. I staggered out of bed—almost tripping on my own blankets—without answering her. Made a jagged line for Faith's room.

"Hope!" said Mom, frantically. "Hope, if you know where she is... Hope! I need you to tell me whatever you know!"

I exploded into Faith's room. It was ransacked, but in a sad, crisply clean sort of way. Mostly, this was due to Mom emptying it of personality, but I spotted a few key indicators that it was missing more. Such as her humble, sticker-covered laptop, where she dabbled in creative writing that she showed to *no one*, not even me.

Her favorite pair of Chuck Taylor low tops. A few choice outfits that favored functionality over fashion. Her backpack.

Her bed was made with such careful precision, it was as if she never intended to sleep in it again.

"No," I said.

Mom grabbed me by the shoulders. "Baby, if you know anything, I need you to *tell me*."

Her voice quivered on those last words, but I couldn't spare a thought her way. I callously shook her hands free of my shoulders. "No, no, no!"

I ran out of Faith's room.

And right into Charity.

Charity had Mom's blond hair but cut into bangs, she wore thick-framed glasses (she was blind without them) that had sort of a hipster vibe but mostly made her look like she was cosplaying as a thirteen-year-old Zooey Deschanel, and she now stood an inch taller than me, which made me want to commit violent crimes. Or maybe that was just Charity's presence in general. All I had to do was look at her, and I was suddenly nauseous and furious and full of death.

Now here she was, standing in the hallway between my room and Faith's, just blank and hopeless like the dumbfuck that she was. Like she had a right to feel anything after what she did. Oh my God, I *hated* her!

I not so gently planted my palm in the center of Charity's chest, then *shoved* her into the wall as I passed. Mom saw it happen; she couldn't even utter a word in protest. I think she was malfunctioning.

Dad was walking in circles in the living room with his tiny

rectangular phone pressed delicately to his giant rectangular head. His beady eyes looked like they were barely holding back tears.

"I don't know, sometime last night," said Dad. "I thought I heard something, but I never checked... I never checked *her room*. Uh-huh. Uh-huh. She's, um, she's seventeen, still a minor, so—"

Dad saw me pause on my way to the front door.

"Sorry, officer, hold on a sec." Dad pulled the phone away and looked at me. "Sweetie, wait, I need to talk to you—"

I was out the door before he could even finish. And whether out of panic, anger, or just too much adrenaline, I slammed the door behind me.

I started running.

Not aimlessly. I was on an aggressive trajectory to Ralph Records: New and Used CD + Vinyl. I was halfway down the street when I realized I was barefoot. Unfortunately, it had been ages since last summer when I built up the calluses on my feet, and they were now soft as the butt cheeks on a ripe peach. I clenched my teeth through the pain. Ripping the soles off my feet sprinting on hard, sandpapery cement was literally my last concern. I would keep running until my feet wore off to the bloody nubs of my ankles. Fuck feet.

A Honda CR-V pulled up beside me with Dad in the driver's seat. The passenger-side window hummed down.

"Get in, Hope! We'll get there faster!"

I took one look at Dad, violently shook my head, and ran faster. Or I tried to. My body was starting to shake. I think I was going into shock.

"Please!" said Dad. He was crying for real now. "I'm not sending your sister anywhere."

I looked at Dad. Or I tried to. I was being blinded by my own tears and the ugly thing my face had contorted into.

"Just help me find her, Hope, and I swear to God that I will not send Faith anywhere. I promise. Your mom will have to kick me out first."

That was good enough for me. I barreled into the passenger seat. Dad floored it.

"Why would she leave without telling me?" I cried. "Does she hate me?"

"Oh baby. She doesn't hate you. This has nothing to do with you."

"But what if she d-d-does?"

I was a weeping, irrational, inconsolable mess.

"Then we'll just have to find her and hug her and tell her how much we love her just the way she is. Okay?"

I stared at Dad—long and hard, through the tears and the snot—just to make sure he wasn't bullshitting me. Everything in his countenance told me he was not. Brent Cassidy was 100 percent motherfucking serious.

"O-o-okay," I said, sniffling.

When we arrived at Ralph Records: New and Used CD + Vinyl, I didn't even allow Dad the chance to park crookedly, which he ended up doing anyway. I was out the door in the middle of a wide turn.

"Whoa, Hope, wait—"

I dashed across the sidewalk to the store, and thank God, thank actual Jesus Christ, I saw Mavis Mackley putting money in the register. I tried to open the door, but it only gave about half an inch before it resisted with a metallic *clank*. It was locked.

Mavis's normal reaction would have been to ignore the

customer trying to get in before store hours, glancing up only reflexively when she heard the *clank*, before returning her focus to the register. Then she did a double take.

Her reaction to seeing me came in fluctuating shades—from friendly to alarmed to downright scared. It became painfully obvious that she was not thrilled to see me.

"Hope, we open at nine."

I slammed my palm repeatedly on the glass—*BAM BAM BAM BAM BAM BAM!*

"Jesus Christ," I heard her mutter. She jumped the counter, fumbled with her keys, and opened the door maybe two inches. "What the hell are you—?"

I shoved my way into those two inches of open door like I had no bones.

"Hope, what the fuck!" said Mavis.

"FAITH!" I screamed, barging inside. The entry bell gave a cordial *ding*. "Faith, are you in here?"

I scoured the aisles. Heaved myself over the register counter. Searched the back room, which was honestly no bigger than a closet. If Faith was here, she was either hiding in the ceiling or in a secret underground hatch, both of which I was beginning to doubt.

Mavis watched me raid Ralph Records like the most gold-hearted but clueless member of a totalitarian secret police. She looked confused, and also sick to her stomach.

"Mavis, do you know where Faith is?" I asked.

"Isn't she at . . . ?"

She couldn't bring herself to say "Change Through Grace" or any of its uglier, more accurate monikers. Those ugly words seemed to be stuck in her throat.

There was a second *ding*, and Dad came in, lumbering and awkward. "Hello. Um. I'm Brent Cassidy. Um, Faith's dad. Look, Faith is missing, and we were hoping you might have some idea where she might, um . . . be?"

Mavis appeared visibly aghast that one of Faith's parents—one of the people who intended to send her to Camp Gay Away—was now asking her girlfriend for pro tips on where to find her. At least, that's how I interpreted it. She looked completely mindfucked.

I grabbed Mavis's shoulders. I just wanted her to look me in the eyes. To know how sincere I was.

"Just tell me," I said. "Don't worry about him. Just me. I promise you, nothing will happen to her. I just want to know she's okay."

Dad nodded eagerly and took a step backward. He seemed willing to go back to the car if it would get us Faith's location.

"I'm sorry," said Mavis, "but I don't know anything."

"Please, Mavis, you can trust me," I said, and the proof began to run down my cheeks again. "I love her, Mavis. She's my best friend. Please, please, please—"

"I know you do. But I swear, Hope, I don't know anything. She hasn't even talked to me since. And . . . didn't your mom confiscate her phone? All her online passwords? Hope, I'm telling you the one hundred percent truth when I say she hasn't spoken a single word to me in the past two or three days. And I don't think she's going to."

"No," I said, shaking my head. I was pure denial.

"I think she's afraid of being caught and sent away." Mavis nervously tucked a pink lock of hair behind her ear, avoiding eye contact with me. "Look, I don't want to freak you out but . . . she said some really scary stuff in her last text to me."

♩ ♫ ♪

Faith ran away from home on May 4. In nerd circles it was known as Star Wars Day. (May the Fourth be with you.) I don't *think* Faith did that on purpose. But from that day on, *Star Wars* would fill me with an irrational sense of dread.

Later that evening, I found Faith's phone. It was in Mom's purse. I searched her texts with Mavis, and sure enough, the last thing she sent was mere moments after Mom's intervention. This is what it said:

> Oh my God, Mav, my mom knows about us. I'm so scared. She's on the phone with one of those conversion therapy places.

And then:

> I don't know what to do. I just want to disappear.

And finally:

> I don't want to exist anymore.

Mavis sent about a dozen texts in response, but Faith never replied to any of them.

Andromeda was feeling two types of pain. The first pain was like a hole had been drilled into the center of her head, and it had been filled with white hot liquid metal. The sedatives were wearing off, and her pineal nerve was a raw, severed, bleeding limb that had been set on fire.

The second pain was somehow worse. It was like someone had violated her consciousness and pilfered her memories. What had once been so clear was now a great empty hole in her identity. Her first date with Tanks, their wedding, her beautiful, quiet death like a sunset. It was all gone. Like it had never even happened.

It hadn't happened, of course—not yet—but try explaining that to a four-dimensional being.

She couldn't see Tanks's face. She could remember it, sure, but she couldn't see it. That was terrifying.

This was what they called the blindness.

Andromeda was sprawled in the bed of a hover cart, being driven outside the Wall. The Wall separated Dresdore and the Dresdorians from the lesser life-forms of the planet, Dearth. The Wall had consumed many tax dollars. Dresdorians loved their fucking Wall.

A great sweeping shadow fell over Andromeda, lying corpselike in the bed of the vehicle. Her drugged eyes shifted, watching the Wall eclipse the sky.

The hover cart stopped. Andromeda heard the *beep beep boop* of the driver typing the code. A chirp of success. The growling, hydraulic crank of the drawbridge as it lowered its greedy jaw. Andromeda felt the slow, heavy impact in her bones.

The hover cart drove through—drove quite a ways, actually, deep into the rambling emptiness of the Southland Barrens—and then stopped.

A pair of Cardinal Guards—tall, gangly thugs draped in red—exited the vehicle. If you were to remove their robes, you'd find their bodies emaciated from fasting and tattooed in Holy Writ. It was the Holy Writ that sustained them, apparently, because these poor bastards were on the brink of self-inflicted starvation. The only thing they were physically capable of guarding Dresdore against was sin.

They approached Andromeda from either side and slid her out by her arms and legs. She was way too drugged to offer resistance and too devastated to think it made any difference.

They set her gently on the hard, acid-corroded crust of the ground. The guard holding her wrists let go. Reached into his pocket and pulled out what looked like a severed horn but was, in fact, an organ coiled up in a spired shell. A dead nub of pineal cord hung from the bottom.

Her third eye.

The guard set it softly—sympathetically—on the ground in front of her face.

"It can't be reattached, so don't waste your time," he said. "The eye is dead. Sell it to a pawn shop. Accept anything less than ten thousand points, you're being ripped off."

Andromeda wished he was being nice, but this was all technically part of the clipping exile ceremony.

With that, the Cardinal Guards climbed back into their craft and hummed across the barrens, into the open maw of the Wall. The drawbridge closed its mouth behind them. Sealed shut with a thunderous boom.

—Andromeda and Tanks through Space and Time,
Æon Q

—FOUR—

WHAT HAPPENS WHEN YOU RUN OUT OF HANDS

KIDS GET BULLIED FOR ALL SORTS OF REASONS and nonreasons. I was bullied because of the way I talk. More specifically, because of the way *my voice sounds.* I had accumulated a menagerie of nicknames over the years: Froggy, Gravel Breath, Chainsmoker, Lung Cancer, and, last but not least, Emma Stone. But the joke was on them because Emma Stone was glamorous as fuck, so thank you for the compliment, *you fucking assholes.*

I wasn't bullied ruthlessly. Just enough so that I was acutely self-conscious of my verbal ability to communicate the English language and therefore generally made an effort not to talk to anyone, ever. There was an awful period in fifth grade when my teacher, Ms. Whetten, would take the roll, and when she would say my name, and I said "here," the boy behind me would mimic me, croaking "here" like some froggy bog monster from the Black Lagoon, and the entire fucking class would laugh like he was Dave fucking Chappelle. From that moment on, when Ms. Whetten called my name, I simply raised my hand.

I used to be one of those kids who sang along to the car radio, but boy oh boy, fifth grade cured that.

For the record, I hadn't even smoked that one cigarette I vowed to smoke after listening to the Strokes. I would smoke it, believe you me, I would, just the once. It was an event that would occur after I got the tattoo, but before I started a garage band and moved to New York City. (There was an order to these things.) But that wasn't why I sounded like this. I didn't know why I sounded like this. I just did. It was simply a part of who I was.

The important thing to keep in mind, however, was that all this tough game I talked—all the swearing and the anger and the rebellion—I kept it all in my head. Sort of like how Faith kept who she was on the inside. It was different, obviously, but you know what I mean. On the outside, I was still what you'd call a "good Christian girl." The fact of the matter was that I was, and probably always would be, too socially awkward for things like "sex" and "drugs," and my love for "rock and roll" was a secret buried so deep that it was probably enjoying the view of my chakras.

Losing Faith was my snapping point. Days became weeks, and weeks became months, and there was still no word from the police on Faith's whereabouts. I wanted to rebel. I wanted to *break things*, preferably rules. I didn't want to break *all* the rules. But I sure as shit wanted to break *a* rule, maybe even a big one. To top it all off, today was Faith's eighteenth birthday, meaning that her running away from home was no longer illegal. Spending the day with my family just sounded like the fucking worst. Like an antibirthday. Like the degradation of it all might turn her sixteen instead.

So anyway, to celebrate Faith's birthday, and also to speed up the predestination of things, I got a tattoo.

Of course, it was technically illegal to get a tattoo if you're under eighteen (I turned sixteen that next month), so I had to find ulterior tattooing avenues. That's what led me to Shady Shawn.

Shady Shawn was another soon-to-be junior at my school. He was allegedly a small-time pro (the son of a long line of tattoo artists) and would tattoo anything you wanted for fifty dollars a pop. Unless you wanted something gigantic and ridiculous, then it turned into a by-the-hour thing. Also, if you had to shorten his name, you called him Shady. If you called him just Shawn, he would tell you to GTFO. It was an insult to his legacy. At least, that was the rumor.

Normally, I'd be skeptical of an unlicensed teenage tattoo artist—I'd seen horror stories online of bad tattoos rotting and falling off—but Shady Shawn was a walking portfolio of his own work. He was left-handed, so his entire right arm was covered in his experience, along with a few on the reachable parts of his legs. What his tattoos lacked in symmetry, they more than made up for in artistic vision. You had to hand it to him: He was good.

I found Shady Shawn at his usual location. Even though it was summer, he was leaning against the west wall of school—aka the graffiti wall—blowing voluminous vape clouds into the air as afternoon bled profusely into evening. Shady was a beanpole, wearing way-too-baggy jeans and a black Rancid shirt. His hair was pulled back in a ponytail, which was the only thing visible hair-wise. Everything else was stuffed eyebrow deep in his beanie. As for his face, well, I guess he was kind of hot in a skeezy, backwoods Wyoming, underground-tattoo-scene sort of way.

Shady saw me approaching. He turned his head and blew one last vape cloud. His expression—that of the brooding artist—never changed. He looked at me like this rendezvous had been written in the stars, or he had read about it in his Alpha-Bits cereal or whatever.

"What do you want?" said Shady, pocketing his e-cig.

"I want a tattoo," I said.

Shady rolled his eyes in a way that said "obviously," and he said, "No, I mean, what do you *want*?"

"Oh, uh, something on my right arm? My forearm? I don't know what. I was sort of hoping you could surprise me."

Shady's face pinched into something inscrutable, his eyes narrowed into skeptical slits.

"You want me to *surprise* you," Shady repeated.

I nodded hopefully.

"You do realize," said Shady, "tattoos are forever."

"That's why I can't decide. That's why I may never be able to decide."

Shady stared at me.

"Art, in my opinion, is pure, creative expression," I explained. "I figure you can dream up a better tattoo if you're left to your own imagination, rather than trying to mimic an image I give you or interpret something I tell you to draw. That's not art; that's just a paid commission. I just want you to look at me and *creatively express*. Does that make sense?"

Shady was still staring at me, and I was starting to feel uncomfortable. Maybe this was a bad idea? My first attempt at rebellion was on the cusp of becoming my last. This was what happened when you took Mr. Britton's philosophy class as an elective. Fuck.

"What if you don't like it?" said Shady, finally.

I shrugged. "Then that's my cross to bear. Although I'd

appreciate it if you gave me something badass and not something that objectively sucks."

Over the course of the longest seconds of my life, Shady's face curled into a grin. "I like you. What's your name?"

"Hope."

"You got fifty dollars, Hope?"

I reached into my pocket and ungraciously pulled out a wad of cash I had accumulated, mostly from random babysitting gigs—four tens, a five, four ones, and four quarters. Shady cupped his hands and received it all into his palms. He pocketed it without bothering to count. His artistic purpose had risen above counting.

"Alright, Hope. Let's get you inked."

♩ ♫ ♪

Shady's tattoo parlor was his dad's garage. I was pretty sure it was all his dad's equipment too because it looked expensive, from the reclining leather parlor chair to the adjustable lamps and light fixtures to what was essentially a multitiered toolbox of inks, needles, guns, and so on. The walls were an exotic gallery of pinned-up designs. All in all, not nearly as "shady" as Shady's name might suggest.

We entered through the garage door, which Shady left open. I sat in the parlor chair and fidgeted as Shady assembled his equipment.

"Now, this isn't going to hurt *a lot*—the needle doesn't go deep—but it is going to feel pretty uncomfortable."

"How uncomfortable?"

"There'll be a lot of vibration, and it's going to feel like I'm dragging a needle across your skin. I mean, that's basically what I'm doing."

I cringed.

"Mostly, it'll just feel annoying," he said.

I appreciated his effort to downplay the pain.

But he was right! It was mostly just annoying.

I mean, *really* annoying.

There was a touch of pain, but it was the jarring, intense vibration that had a way of buzzing right down to the root of you, like grazing an active sunburn, making you grit your teeth and want to low-key scream. It might not have been so bad if I didn't have to endure it for over an hour.

"Do you have a cigarette?" I asked, randomly.

Even as I asked the question, I felt my breath quicken and my adrenaline thrum, and I panicked. The tattoo ink must have infected my bloodstream. I had been filled with the spirit of rock and roll. Who knew what I would do next?

If Shady thought this was a weird question to ask in the middle of a tattoo, he didn't let it show.

"Nah, man," he said. He pulled his tattoo gun away—oh, thank God, praise the actual Lord—and removed his e-cig from his pocket, waving it. "Less toxins. You can hit it if you want."

I appreciated the offer. Really, I did. But vaping seemed less like the Strokes and more like Blood on the Dance Floor. Not quite my scene.

"That's okay," I said.

Shady shrugged, pocketed the e-cig, and continued casually maiming my right forearm with his needle gun.

Eventually—after an unknown number of minutes that melted into eternity—the buzzing stopped. The sudden silence and lack of vibration left me unbalanced, reeling. It was post-torture ecstasy. I glanced at Shady as he leaned back, admiring my poor raw forearm, looking immensely pleased with himself.

I took a deep, bracing breath and glanced down.

Starting at my wrist was the profile of a girl's face. A minimalist outline—eyelashes, small upturned nose, lips parted. A series of music notes floated out of her mouth, as if carried by the wind, growing larger as they moved up my arm. The larger they grew, the more they transformed into organic shapes—spiraling, blossoming, becoming living things.

It was beautiful, don't get me wrong. But now that it was a permanent fixture on my body, it was super weird. I didn't know what to think.

I stared at it for such a long time—completely silent—that Shady seemed nervous about my reaction.

He cleared his throat awkwardly. "Here, lemme bandage that."

Shady rolled his swivel stool to a nearby counter, grabbed a narrow box labeled "Saniderm" and a small tub of Vaseline, and rolled back. I surrendered my arm. He applied a thin layer of petroleum jelly and proceeded to wrap it in what essentially looked like plastic wrap. By the time he finished, my arm looked like some cannibal's leftovers.

"So...she's singing?" I asked.

Shady perked up, now that I had finally spoken words, and they weren't horrible criticisms of his art. "Yeah. I mean, sort of. I was inspired by your voice."

Every muscle in my body went taut.

"My voice," I said.

Shady nodded. "Yeah, it's really...unique."

"Unique," I said.

I was trying really hard not to sound hurt, and I was failing. Shady seemed to detect it.

"No no no, it's not a bad thing!" said Shady. "Obviously. I like it. I mean, not to be weird, but it's kind of... *beautiful?* Like, in a bizarre Janis Joplin sort of way."

The highlights I was picking up from this conversation were "bad thing," "bizarre," and "*beautiful?*" with so much emphasis on the question mark, it meant the opposite. I had no idea who Janis Joplin was, but she sounded like a parody of someone's grandma.

The pain in my right forearm felt fresh again. I realized I was clenching my fists.

"I have to go," I said. "Thank you for the... um..."

I was too flustered to figure out how that sentence was supposed to end. So I just left.

Up and out of the chair, marching out of the garage as fast as I could without looking like I was trying to escape. Which I was.

"Whoa, wait." said Shady, confused. "I'm sorry, I... Did I say something?"

It was dark out now, and the streets faded in and out beneath intermittent lampposts. I plunged into the darkness, thinking how nice it would be to just peacefully fade out.

♩ ♫ ♪

But I didn't fade out, and there was certainly no peace in store for me. Mom was waiting. Sitting on the front stoop of our house, perched like a gargoyle. She was holding her watch—a classy Skagen with a silver mesh band—just to let me know that she'd been counting the seconds past curfew.

Curfew was ages ago. Curfew was a distant memory.

Mom stood up dangerously. "Where. Have. You. Been."

As I approached the front door, not bothering to respond, her gaze drifted down to the sheen of my plastic-wrapped arm.

She gasped, clasping her hands over her mouth. "What have you done?"

I walked right past her into the house.

"WHAT HAVE YOU DONE?" she screamed.

I hadn't even made it past the entryway when she grabbed me, not only by my arm but by my actual fucking tattoo.

"Brent, come look what your daughter has done to herself!"

"Ow! Fuck, what the fuck?!" I said, smacking her hand away.

It was purely defensive, but I hit her pretty hard. Between that, saying fuck *twice* (which I generally only did inside my head), and graffitiing a temple of the Holy Spirit (aka my bod, 1 Corinthians 6:19), I had pretty much condemned myself to Hell by all accounts.

Mom's beautiful mouth opened into an appalled chasm. "How dare you? How *dare* you?"

"What are you going to do, kick me out?" I said. I leaned forward until my face was breathlessly close to hers. "I *dare* you."

I turned and walked away.

I think there was a part of me that wanted to be kicked out. Because then I would be left with no choice but to either find Faith, wherever she was, or to die trying. And that only seemed fair.

"If thy right hand offend thee, cut it off!" Mom exclaimed erratically.

I stopped walking.

"—and cast it from thee," she continued, on an incredible roll, "for it is profitable for thee that one of thy members should perish, and not that thy whole body should be cast into hell."

By this point, Dad was in the living room, glancing between the brand-new tattoo on my raw forearm and his wife shouting scripture like an exorcism. Charity was behind him, slightly cowering in the hall.

I whipped around, swelling with rage. "Does my right hand offend you, Mom?"

"Do you really need to ask me that?" she said.

I liked to think of myself as a sane, rational person. But in the face of crazy, it became a personal challenge to be crazier. So I stormed into the kitchen. Slid the biggest knife out of the knife block. Slammed my arm on the kitchen table like a slab of meat and set the blade of the knife delicately above my tattoo, just below the elbow.

"Well, here you go," I said. "Cut it off."

"You are sick," said Mom. She shook her head, disgusted.

"Jesus Christ," said Dad.

"I'm just doing the will of the Lord!" I exclaimed. "My right hand offends you, so cut it off. Come on, have at it!"

"You are a vile, wicked child!" Mom screamed.

"Or is that *my* job?" I continued, undeterred. "Do you want *me* to cut it off?"

I placed just enough pressure on the knife, a line of blood slipped down my arm. Honestly, I didn't feel a thing. All I could feel was the blood pounding in my ears, and the anger and the injustice and the heartbreak. The knife was nothing.

"Jesus Christ!" said Dad. He barreled into the kitchen and carefully pried the knife out of my hand.

"I'm going to Bible study," Mom announced. "I can't handle the evil in this house any longer."

"I guess it's just a metaphor," I said, following after her. "*I'm* the right hand."

Mom grabbed her coat out of the closet, shoved each arm fiercely into its respective sleeve, and veered into hers and Dad's bedroom for her Bible.

"Just like *Faith* was the right hand," I said. "Well, I gotta say, Mom, you cut her off real good."

Mom snatched her open Bible off the nightstand, slammed it shut, and tucked it sternly under her arm. Swiped the car keys off the dresser. I followed her all the way to the front door.

"What happens when you run out of hands?" I said.

Mom turned and slapped me in the face.

I felt that one—physically, emotionally, psychologically, existentially.

Mom's mouth opened to yell at me. It opened wide. And then she just started crying. She dropped her Bible on the floor. She hugged me and sobbed, practically throwing all her weight on top of me. It was like she had lost the ability to stand on her own.

For a long moment, I was in a state of pure, unadulterated shock. I didn't know what to think or feel. And then I started crying too. I didn't want to hug Mom—she didn't deserve it—but I hugged her anyway. I had been forced into this situation, and there was nothing else to do but submit. So I hugged her, and I sobbed, and I realized the old adage "time heals all wounds" was a pervasive lie.

Time was corrosion.

Time was acid.

It ate away at everyone and everything until there was nothing left.

Andromeda should have taken notes. Why didn't she take notes? She knew this would happen. She had seen it—the pain, the confusion, the blindness. Wandering through the Southland Barrens like some idiot stork who couldn't fly. She survived this, obviously, but had it never occurred to her that she might make things easier for herself if she knew exactly how she survived?

Stupid Andromeda, she cursed herself. Stupid, stupid, stupid!

But she knew why. Because that's not how it happened. All this memory had ever been was a rough patch before she met Tanks. And it was so totally eclipsed by their meeting that it never felt like much of a problem.

Well, now, here she was. And it definitely felt like a problem.

For as far as the eye could see, the Southland Barrens were nothing but acid-chewed desert. The sand had condensed and hardened into waves of brown concrete. There was no plant life, and certainly no animal life. The only things she knew for certain lived in these parts were the worms, and they lived deep beneath the surface. Worms were apex predators, but they typically preyed on subterranean life, like roaches. Worms came up for only two things: explosions and dearthquakes. The people who fished for worms were usually hillbillies, and they did so with explosives up the wazoo. You had to have a real hard-on for homemade bombs to get eaten by a worm.

Andromeda was more worried about starving to death. She

hadn't eaten in twenty-four hours as it was. She felt as hungry as those Cardinal Guards looked.

Think, Andromeda, think. What happens next?

Eventually, she would make it to the Dome—Dresdorians called it the Dump—and Southland City. That's where Borgy's Bistro was. That's where she and Tanks would go on their first date.

Andromeda smiled deliriously just thinking about that.

But no, before that. Before that, she got mugged, right? Mugged and kidnapped. Yes. Actually, didn't the mugging-kidnapping happen twice? It felt like it happened twice, but that didn't make sense.

You'd think it'd be easy enough to remember the specifics of being mugged and kidnapped—let alone whether or not it happened twice—but Andromeda tried hard not to dwell on the rough patch. Out of mind, out of sight.

Not that it mattered. Getting kidnapped was actually a good thing because that's when Tanks rescued her. Right?

It was at that moment that she saw a cloud of dust billowing on the horizon. The sand was hard, but it was no match for hover propulsion. A wagon train of frumpy-looking hovercraft was fast approaching. The muggers-kidnappers, if Andromeda's memory was to be trusted.

Andromeda stopped smiling.

Not because of the muggers-kidnappers. That was supposed to happen. It was essential.

No. She stopped smiling because she had just remembered why she called this bit the rough patch.

Tanks was one of them.

—Andromeda and Tanks Through Space and Time,
ÆonQ

—FIVE—

BADASS, MYSTICAL, HUMAN

MOM STOPPED GOING TO CHURCH AFTER THAT.

Technically, she stopped doing *everything* after that—everything from cooking and cleaning and other gender-conforming chores to simply getting out of bed. She rarely left the bedroom, and when she did, she was like some ancient, frail vampire, skirting about in broad daylight, trying to perform some simple, menial task without dying. But not going to church was a startling development. Church was her identity. Church was *who she was*. Without church, I wasn't exactly sure what was left beneath. Maybe nothing. Nothing but this great cloud of depression. Dad was the only one who truly interacted with her. Even Charity seemed slightly afraid of her.

During that first month, my Sunday routine was to hover around the living room in my pajamas, assessing the situation—if this was yet another Sabbath, Mrs. Laura Cassidy would be MIA. Dad would eventually enter the living room, showered but dressed in a sort of limbo—socks, no shoes, Sunday-best slacks, and, like, a Wyoming Cowboys jersey or whatever.

"Where's Mom?" I asked, innocently enough, if not completely genuinely. We all knew damn well that Mom was holed up in her crypt like some Nosferatu.

"She's not feeling well," said Dad, which was what he said every Sunday. "I don't think she'll be making it today."

"Do I have to go then?" I said, which was what I said every Sunday. Asking was only a formality. If Mom wasn't going, I sure as tits wasn't.

Dad pursed his lips into a straight line and shook his head.

In fact, Dad only went the first couple of Sundays. After that, he just... petered out. He kept the Cowboys jersey on and replaced the slacks with something comfier, less fashionable, and practical, like cargo shorts, and slipped sandals over his socks. I was beginning to wonder if he only ever went to church because of Mom.

At this point, Charity—who was too young to drive—decided to find a ride for herself. Dad offered to take her, but she said she didn't want to trouble him.

"That's okay," said Charity, politely and cold as ice. "I called my friend Brianna. She said her family can pick me up."

"Oh," said Dad. "Okay. Hopefully, we can make it with you next Sunday."

Except next Sunday would be the same. It was always the same.

Charity and I only made brief eye contact as she was walking out the door, dressed for worship in something respectfully vogue—today was a cute white top, blush flare skirt, matching blush pumps with bows—while I was slouched easy-sleazy on the couch, unshowered, slightly greasy, wearing Shrek pajama pants and a tank top with a slice of pizza printed on the front. I was observing the Sabbath by watching *Constantine* with Keanu Reeves.

Charity looked at me as if she wanted to say something or rather as if she wanted *me* to say something to *her*, like "You look pretty!" or "Have a nice day at church!" but the only things I really wanted to say to her were swear words. So I intensely returned my focus to the television screen and the badassery of occult detective John Constantine as he exorcised demons back to Hell. Charity frowned at my ironic Sabbath activity.

There was already a wall between us, but every Sunday that Charity went to church and we didn't, the wall grew taller. A slow but sure wall, brick by brick. Charity wasn't the type to say it, but I could see the resentment building in her soft, quiet mannerisms.

In the way she looked at us.

In her silence.

♩ ♫ ♪

Our lack of interaction at home had grown to staggering heights. We tried to not even be in the same room. Calling it "coexistence" would have been praise and a blatant lie. People couldn't coexist in a space filled with this much shame and suffocating disapproval.

So, when I came home from school and discovered Dad sitting on my bed, next to Loafy, holding my ancient, beat-ass iPod, with the noise-canceling headphones stretched strenuously across his big square head, I was understandably flummoxed.

Dad swatted off the headphones, dropped the iPod, and didn't seem to know whether to look at me or avoid eye contact, so he settled on something in between by staring at an invisible point that was floating on and around my face like a fly.

"What are you doing in my room?" I asked.

"Sorry," he said, standing up. "I was just... Um, what I mean to say is... Sorry, I'm going."

He stood up, rigid with embarrassment, and shuffled past me until he was safely outside the door.

"I liked them," he said.

I was inches from closing the door on him, but his words jammed themselves in the way. Less like the stubborn toe of a shoe, and more like a soon-to-be-broken finger.

"Huh?" I said, squinting with supermassive confusion. "Liked them? Liked *who*?"

"The band?" he said. "The, um, Yeah Yeah Yeahs?"

The door just sort of fell open.

"You liked the Yeah Yeah Yeahs," I said.

"Yeah, yeah!" said Dad, nodding, maybe just a little too enthused. "They're great. That Karen O has some killer pipes. Real gentle and powerful at the same time."

I stared at him.

"What's that song called?" he said. " 'Maps'? Yeah, 'Maps.' I really liked 'Maps.' "

"You really liked 'Maps,' " I said.

I wasn't sure how else to proceed with this conversation except to repeat everything he said. And even then, I didn't understand what was happening.

Dad just kept nodding. "Yeah. Yeah."

"What do you want?" I said.

If that sounds mean on paper, I can promise, it sounded even meaner coming out of my mouth.

"I want . . . ," he said. His face flushed, and his eyes grew wet. "I want us to be okay."

"Oh, Daddy," I said, frowning.

♩ ♫ ♪

In our first act of true coexistence in months, Dad and I watched TV together. We somehow settled on *The Great British Baking Show*, which I don't think either of us necessarily *wanted* to watch, but we weren't morally opposed to it either. It was just so goddamned wholesome! All in all, great background noise for two people who were sort of desperate to make amends.

"I like your tattoo," said Dad.

"Whatever, no, you don't," I said. I grabbed a couch pillow and threw it. A big square pillow for his big square lying face.

Dad only barely caught the pillow. "Hey! No, I do! Seriously!"

"You're not allowed to like my tattoo."

"What do you mean, I'm not allowed?"

"Tattoos are only cool as long as they have the utter disapproval of the parents."

"Oh. Well, in that case, I hate it."

"That's better," I said, grinning.

Meanwhile, on *The Great British Baking Show*, American actor John Lithgow had never heard of a Swiss roll, and when the baking began, it was an adorable spiral of self-sabotage.

It was while John Lithgow was whispering "Swiss roll" to himself over and over in a panic that Dad pulled up his shirt sleeve.

He pulled it all the way up, over his shoulder, revealing the scar he had from a biking accident when he was in his early twenties. At least, that was the *story*. I turned and stared at Dad, then at the scar, then Dad, then the scar again.

"No," I said.

"Yeah," said Dad.

"That was a tattoo?"

Dad nodded.

"You lied to us?!" I said.

"Your mother didn't want you kids to know. She thought it would be a bad influence."

"What was it?"

Dad pulled his shirt sleeve down and blushed. "It's embarrassing."

"Oh, nuh-uh," I said, shaking my head. "You don't get to tell me you had a tattoo and then *not* tell me what it was."

Dad sighed. "Do you know who Janis Joplin is?"

For reasons I'm sure you can understand, I stared at Dad, speechless.

"No, of course not," said Dad, chuckling to himself. "She was before your time. Before *my* time, really. She was a rock star from the sixties. One of the best. A real game-changer. She had a short, tragic life, though. Died at twenty-seven of an overdose. Anyway... it was a tattoo of her. I got it before I met your mother, obviously. Back when I thought I'd never settle down."

He rubbed his shoulder self-consciously.

I kept staring. This was one of those coincidences that felt way too fluky for comfort.

"I know, it's weird," said Dad, sort of ashamed.

"No, no, that's not what I—" I said. Then I looked at my own tattoo. "The guy that gave me this. He said he was"—I cringed and air quoted—"'*inspired by my voice*.' He said I sounded *bizarre, like Janis Joplin*."

Dad reared his head back, personally offended. "He said that?"

"I mean...sort of? I think?" Now that I was trying to recall the specifics of what Shady Shawn had said, I wasn't entirely sure.

Dad looked at the tattoo. "Well, it *looks* amazing. It's hard to believe he meant that in a bad way if he drew something like this. This looks like a compliment."

I was silent.

"Also, to be fair," said Dad, "you do sound *a lot* like Janis Joplin. And that is one hundred percent a compliment. Janis had the most beautiful voice in all of rock and roll." Dad looked at me. "Gosh, now that I think about it, you even *look* like her. Wow. Hope, *wow!* You should sing in a rock band!"

"Dad," I said.

"What?"

"Whatever."

"Whatever, *what*? I was in a rock band too, you know." He pointed dramatically to himself with both index fingers and said, "Keyboardist and Minimoog extraordinaire. Me and the Trash Can'ts were the OG garbage band."

I stared at Dad. "You mean *garage* band?"

"What? No, I'm pretty sure it's garbage band." He shook his head. "Whatever. Not important. The important thing is that as a former high school rock star, I think you would kill it in a rock band. You don't believe me?"

"I one hundred percent don't believe you," I said. "I would be the worst singer ever."

"Have you ever even tried singing?"

"As a matter of fact, I have, and I was—" I was about to say "bullied," but I stopped myself. I took a deep breath and said calmly, "I was not that good."

"Well," Dad said thoughtfully, "maybe you just weren't singing the right stuff."

"I'm sorry. Singing *the right stuff*?"

"Yeah."

"What does that even mean?"

"You have a very unique vocal range—"

" 'Unique' is just a nice way of saying 'bad.' "

"WHAT?" exclaimed Dad, outraged. "No, it is not!"

Dad stood up, suddenly on a mission.

"You know what? Follow me."

He charged into the hallway, not bothering to turn off *The Great British Baking Show*.

Meanwhile, John Lithgow's Swiss roll was severely underbaked and looked more like a Fruit Roll-Up. This felt metaphorical: I was the Swiss roll. Except in this metaphor, John Lithgow wholeheartedly believed his Swiss roll was culinary genius and not actual shit.

Dad stopped beneath the cord dangling from the ceiling—the hatch to the attic—and pulled it. The ladder unfolded until it connected with the floor and locked in place.

He shimmied up the ladder with a life in him I hadn't seen in ages.

I climbed softly behind him.

The attic was a dark, claustrophobic space with a low, slanted ceiling and way too many boxes. Dad flipped the light switch on, and a single fluorescent bulb flickered and buzzed, offering a sickly glow.

"Huh," said Dad.

"What?" I asked.

Dad frowned. "I think your mom threw out the Minimoog."

Because he was on a mission, Dad shook his head and moved on quickly, wedging his way into the labyrinthine chaos. Opening boxes, closing them, setting them to the side, and moving on to the next one.

"What exactly are we looking for?" I asked.

"The right stuff, Hope. We're looking for *the right stuff*."

He closed a box, set it aside, and opened the next one.

"Bingo!" he exclaimed.

He pulled out something that looked like a silver brick with buttons. It was attached to headphones.

"What is that?" I asked.

"What do you mean, what is that? It's a Walkman!"

"Does it play CDs?" I asked. But I already knew that was impossible. CDs would not fit inside that brick unless they were tiny GameCube CDs.

"'Does it play CDs,' she says," Dad mocked. "It plays something *better* than CDs." He pulled out a small, plastic rectangle and waved it. "This, my daughter, is called a cassette tape."

Okay. So, like *Thirteen Reasons Why*. Except in *Thirteen Reasons Why*, it was more of a tragic hipster thing, whereas with Dad, it was just an old person thing.

Dad leaned over the box, thumbing frantically through cassettes with a rhythmic *clack-clack-clack*-ing, whispering "Janis" to himself on repeat—not unlike John Lithgow with his Swiss roll. God, I needed to let go of this metaphor already.

"Oh!" Dad exclaimed, pulling a cassette from the stack. "Oh ho ho!"

"Let me guess: Janis?"

"No, but just as good: Joan Jett!"

"Joan Jett?" I repeated. "Janis Joplin? What's with all the J names? Was that a thing?"

"Uh, I don't think so? I think that's just a coincidence. Coincidences happen sometimes."

Ha. Tell me about it.

"These women were like two decades apart from each other," Dad continued. "Joan Jett was my era. She's a mezzo-soprano. I bet you anything that's what you are."

Dad pressed a button that caused the silver box to open with a snap. He inserted the tape, closed the box, and held the headphones to one ear. He pressed a button, listened, pressed another button, and handed the whole bundle to me, Walkman and headphones.

"Here, listen to this. It's called 'Bad Reputation.' "

I slid the headphones on and pressed the Play button.

A violent thrum of guitar anarchy blared, galloping across the soundscape.

"You're living in the past, it's a new generation," Joan Jett yelled. *"A girl can do what she wants to do, and that's what I'm gonna do..."*

Her voice was a serrated blade. It was grungy and jagged and ravenous and perfect. Easily the most badass thing I had ever heard.

And I had spent the past couple of years listening to Karen O, who was the *definition* of badass! But Joan Jett took it up a notch. Joan Jett was as tough as nails made of adamantium and vibranium with a chance of super-tetanus. Joan Jett made me want to punch walls, break expensive things, and start a revolution. Hell, Joan Jett *was* the revolution!

The eeriest thing was that her voice was not all that dissimilar from mine. It was low, and it was husky, and it was not pretty at all. But that's what was so *cool* about it! It was unpretty and dared you to think that it gave a shit. It was like, *fuck your "pretty," motherfuckers!* This voice would bite the cocks off the fucking patriarchy if they got too close.

When the song ended, so did the world, and I'm sorry, T. S. Eliot, but it was a fucking bang.

I stared at Dad, open-mouthed, and he grinned back because yeah, he already knew.

"That was bada—" I started to say, then remembered whom I was talking to, and "badass" turned into, "bada*aaaaauuuuwww-mmph*."

But this stranger who was allegedly my dad only nodded, grinning with excitement, and said, "Oh yeah. Totally *badaauwmph*. Now listen to this."

He was already ejecting Joan and inserting a new cassette.

"Whoa, wait," I said. "Who's this? Is this Janis?"

"Not yet. Haven't found Janis yet. This is Stevie Nicks."

"Stevie Nicks? Who the heck is Stevie Nicks?!"

Dad stole the headphones, again holding them to one ear, rewinding and fast-forwarding, scouring for a specific song.

"The lead singer of Fleetwood Mac. But this song's off her solo album, 'Edge of Seventeen.' Anyway, Stevie's a contralto. Now that I think about it, you're actually probably a contralto."

He handed the headphones to me, and I put them on.

The intro was a chugging guitar riff, oddly reminiscent of "Eye of the Tiger" but somehow cooler. And then Stevie's voice broke the surface of the water, gruff and feathery, ghostly and haunting, and you realized the song was a tragedy. From the imagery of doves, to the echoing loneliness, someone had been irrevocably lost.

Sometimes to be near you
Is to be unable to hear you

There was something mournful in her voice, but not broken. This song was the bridge between life and death. It was mystical. Spun together like a spell. Just pure magic and heartbreak.

And that velvety sandpaper alto of hers sounded eerily similar to my voice.

The song ended. I wanted to have something thoughtful to say, but after listening to the poetry of Stevie Nicks, I was left feeling profoundly inarticulate. So I just removed the headphones and stared at Dad, mind blown.

But Dad was already handing me a third cassette tape.

"Last one, I promise," he said.

On the cover was a black-and-white photo of a woman with a gigantic, pluming mane of rapturous hair. Her perfectly circular glasses were thin rimmed but massive, nearly encompassing her entire smiling face. She adjusted them with a single hand, shackled in an army of bracelets and several fat rings.

Dad was right. She looked *a lot* like me. An older version of me that had approximately 1,000 percent more hair, and every follicle was somehow tripping on LSD.

Once again, Dad commandeered the Walkman, found the song he was looking for, and handed it to me.

"This one's called 'Piece of My Heart.'" He opened his mouth as if to say more, then closed it, and left it at that.

I pressed Play.

The era difference was jarring. A funky, psychedelic intro of guitars and drums wailed, rolling like waves, and then Janis's voice came like a meteor, punching a hole through the sky, only to drop to something slow and soft. With each line, it built in passion and intensity. To call her voice "gravelly" was to be completely blind to its strength and soul, its pain and beautiful realness. It was breathtakingly, blisteringly, devastatingly real. Just dripping with sincerity.

And she sounded Just. Like. Me.

I meant it this time. This was an echo of my voice.

Take another little piece of my heart now, baby
Break another little bit of my heart now, darling,
yeah, yeah, yeah

As Janis charged into the chorus, it was clear that this was a song about being hurt by someone you loved—and forgiving them anyway. Which, at first, made me sort of mad. She was forgiving this guy who was hurting her—probably cheating on her—and her level of forgiveness seemed to be unlimited. Almost as if he could do no wrong. Definitely not the most feminist message.

But then I realized I was sitting on a cardboard box in the attic, listening to songs with my dad. Someone who had hurt Faith. Someone who, in effect, had hurt me. Maybe he didn't hurt Faith directly, but he had failed to stand up for her when she needed it most. And what was this if not forgiveness?

I had always associated forgiveness as a bullet point on the Christian moral agenda. But I wasn't forgiving my dad because he deserved it. Forgiveness was never about *deserving* it.

But I *wanted* to forgive him.

Maybe forgiveness was a selfish thing. Maybe forgiveness was about self-preservation. About personal healing. About allowing yourself to become whole again.

In that sense, "Piece of My Heart" felt like the most human song in the world. It was screaming that love could conquer all. That love was not a weakness but rather the most powerful force of nature. One that could tear down walls, destroy hate, and cripple sadness. Maybe it could.

As for Mom and Charity, well... it was best if I found Faith first. If I found Faith, and *she* forgave them, then that suddenly became a more palatable option for me. Until then, well, at least I had Dad.

But forgiveness aside, I had decided something for myself. Though I would never admit it to Dad, I had been irreversibly inspired.

I wanted to be as badass as Joan.

I wanted to be as mystical as Stevie.

I wanted to be as human as Janis.

♩ ♫ ♪

Late that night, I found myself standing outside Happy's Tavern. I was dressed in all black, with a hoodie pulled over my head, wearing sunglasses, Cole Sprouse style. The only thing that ruined my attempt to become one with the night was my belligerently pink backpack. Mom bought matching ones for me and Charity at the start of the school year, without our permission or approval, perhaps as an absurd subliminal attempt to undermine our sexualities. Neither of us had a boyfriend, and a year ago that would have been any parent's dream come true, but post-Faith, I think it just made her nervous.

On the one hand, this backpack was just the ugliest damn thing. On the other hand, it had mad cargo space, and—barfy pinkness aside—it was practical as all get-out. So I embraced it.

I pulled the shoulder straps tight until it was flat against my back. Took a deep breath, savoring the premonition of rain haunting the night sky with a tangy zing of ozone.

And walked into Happy's Tavern.

Happy's wasn't just any bar. It was a karaoke bar.

Because it was a Monday, the place was desolate. Two dudes sat on opposite ends of the bar—the depressed Monday-night drinkers—with a third dude playing pool by himself. You could just smell the loneliness. So naturally, when the sixteen-year-old girl with the pink backpack and dorky sunglasses came strolling in, I drew all the attention in the room.

The bartender—a short, bald man with a perfectly triangular soul patch—had been taking some sort of inventory. He took one look at me and put down his clipboard, vivified but not surprised, like the Monday-night crazies were right on time.

"I'm just here for the karaoke," I said.

The bartender nodded, but his eyes narrowed, like he could suddenly see through me. I tugged my backpack straps.

"You're one of the Cassidy girls," he said.

"Uh... yeah?" I said, mildly alarmed. "Do I know you?"

The bartender continued to stare at me, and for a moment, I swear to God, he looked genuinely sad. Finally, he snapped out of whatever daze he was in, unfastened the bundle of keys carabinered to his belt loop, and nodded.

"I went to high school with your mom," he said. "Follow me."

I followed him down a short corridor to two adjacent doors painted as red as devils' pajamas. He unlocked the door on the right. The room was small but flashy. Red walls, black-and-white zigzag flooring, black sectional sofa, a small black coffee table. A large flat-screen TV engulfed the wall, hooked up to all the karaoke fixings. The bartender introduced himself as Mack, gave me a brief tutorial on the equipment, pointed out a small food menu on the coffee table in case I got hungry, and started to leave.

"Wait, so do I pay after?" I asked.

Mack shook his head. "Consider tonight on the house."

"Oh. Thank you?" I said, probably sounding more confused than grateful.

It didn't take a genius to realize why he was being nice to me. If he knew Mom, then there was a pretty good chance he knew about Faith. And if he knew about Faith, well... let's just say that everyone's collective gut reaction seemed to be pity—homophobes and allies alike.

Mack quietly—and almost sadly—closed the door.

Welp. I came here looking for a coping mechanism. And now I *reeeeally* needed a coping mechanism. I decided to consider this a convenience.

I scrolled through the music catalog. It leaned on the older side, but in my case, that wasn't necessarily a bad thing. As I scoured the alternative selection, not exactly sure what I was looking for, I stopped dead in front of "Last Nite" by the Strokes.

Maybe you just weren't singing the right stuff, said a version of Dad who lived inside my head.

I pressed Play.

The opening riff was a slow but intense build, placing layer upon layer—guitar, drums, more guitar, bass—like a sexual rhythm. I gripped the mic in my palm, readjusted it, moved with the beat, even threw my head into it, until all the layers climaxed into the silky grind of Julian Casablancas screaming, "LAST NIGHT, SHE SAID, OH BABY I FEEL SO DOWN—"

Only it wasn't Julian's voice; it was mine.

I screamed the words with the pent-up frustration of months spent in hell. I screamed as if this was my one and only chance to say something. I screamed like it was the most ancient, primeval prayer. Like, if I put enough of myself into it, something bigger than myself would hear it—a They or a Them with capital letters. I didn't even care if They did something in response.

I just wanted Them to fucking hear me.

Rotters weren't any particular race or species so much as a collection of people and things from the outer fringe of society. "Rotters" was an ugly word that may have originated phonetically from "marauders," but it also possibly referred to the fact that they were acid-vulnerable beings living in perpetual acid rain. Some people called them Sand Pirates or Dune Raiders, but Rotters was the popular term, at least in Dresdore. Either way, they were criminals because the options were either a life of crime or dying in the desert. They wrapped themselves up tight in spider leather and worm hide, wore blocky UV goggles, and sprayed themselves up and down in generic brand Acid-Off. So from an outsider's perspective, they sort of looked the same, except for the occasional Rotter with six limbs or a tail.

The wagon train slowed to a humming stop in front of Andromeda, antigravs still running. Several Rotters hopped off their respective hovercraft, approaching swiftly.

"Oh, hullo," said Andromeda. She raised her hands as an act of mediation and added, stupidly, "I come in peace!"

The Rotters greeted her at gunpoint. Except for the one who greeted her with the pointy end of a crossbow.

"Oh my," said Andromeda. "Okay. Um."

She raised her hands higher.

The Rotter with the crossbow also had the most feminine build. A build that maybe was—or maybe wasn't—Tanks-like. It was hard to tell beneath the parka made out of giant bug remains. She slung her crossbow over her shoulder and proceeded to frisk

Andromeda for weapons and goods, while the others lazily pointed their blasters. Andromeda blushed.

She maintained her silence for maybe seven seconds.

"Tanks?" Andromeda whispered. "Tanks, is that you?"

The Rotter met Andromeda's eager gaze, visibly confused. Then her gaze drifted up to the severed horn in Andromeda's elevated grasp. Her third eye. It was at least two feet out of this Rotter's grasp.

The Rotter held her hand out, palm up.

"Oh," said Andromeda. She bit her lip, timidly lowered her arms, and squeezed her third eye in both hands like she was trying to wring the spacetime juice out of it. "Okay."

She handed it over.

The Rotter shoved the third eye in her satchel. Then she made an abrupt slicing gesture with her gloved hand.

The other three Rotters holstered their weapons. The four of them started back to their humming wagon train.

Without Andromeda.

"Wait!" said Andromeda. "Wait, what about me?"

She took maybe three steps. The shortest of the Rotters—a husky fellow with only three fat fingers on each hand—unholstered his blaster and pointed it at her sternum, roughly a foot above his head.

"What about you?" he said.

—Andromeda and Tanks Through Space and Time,
ÆonQ

—SIX—

TIME CAPSULE

IT HAD BEEN MONTHS SINCE MY FIRST STOP AT Happy's Tavern, and I had become something of a regular. I usually stopped by on my way home from school, screamed my lungs out for an hour, and went home. The only way I could afford it was because Mack was giving me his "family discount." I appreciated it, but I also felt weird accepting a perpetual discount from someone I barely even knew.

Here was the thing: Mom and Dad went to high school together. They were in the same year. And yet, Mack said he went to high school with my mom?

I was no detective, but I wasn't a dummy.

"Did you and my mom date?" I asked Mack, once, on a particularly nosy afternoon.

Mack just laughed, shook his head in a way that didn't necessarily mean "no," and said, "Go sing your punk songs, you nosy asshole."

I chose to interpret that as a "yes." A hard fucking yes.

But prying further details out of Mack was impossible. He was an impenetrable vault. The Fort Knox of not telling me shit.

But I refused to let this go. So I inconspicuously pressed Dad for clues.

"Did you know a Mack in high school?" I asked him.

"Mack?" said Dad. His gaze drifted, diving deep into his memory banks. "Mack, Mack, Mack. No, I don't know a Mack."

I pursed my lips, disappointed.

"I mean, high school was a long time ago," he continued. "So maybe I knew a Mack then, and I just don't remember now?"

But it was clear from his blank, people-pleasing expression that he had no clue who Mack was, now or ever.

I had a sudden, alarming epiphany about why Mack was giving me the "family discount." What if I *was* family? What if he and Mom, like, I dunno, *banged* back in the day? It sounded absurd—Mom being the puritanical Dracula that she was—but Dad once had a tattoo, so *anything* was possible, right? What if Mom and Mack banged, either before or maybe even while she and Dad were dating, and she got pregnant with me and—

No. Not me. Faith! Mom and Mack banged, and they had *Faith*! Mack was her real father. Meaning when Faith left home with nowhere else to go, maybe Mack, her *father*, was low-key keeping tabs on her, and—

I was suddenly filled with visions of a fugitive Faith lying low at Mack's house.

"Why, who's Mack?" said Dad, gleefully unaware.

"Uh, what? Who? No one. I don't know a Mack."

My poker face was everyone else's I'm-guilty-of-murder face.

"I just remembered I have homework," I said, and ran away.

Out of the house.

All the way to Happy's Tavern.

The place was more crowded than usual—maybe even in the double digits—but I was on a mission. I strolled right up to the bar where Mack was trying to take some trucker-looking dude's order, slapped my hands on the teak wood bartop, and exclaimed, "YOU'RE FAITH'S FATHER, AREN'T YOU?"

"What?" said Mack.

"I figured it all out. *That's* why you're giving me the family discount. You didn't just go to high school with my mom. You *slept* together. But my mom was dating my dad at the time, and she didn't want him to find out—she didn't want *anyone* to find out—so they had a shotgun wedding, and my mom pretended Faith was his. But she's not, is she? She's yours!"

Mack stared at me.

"Faith is living with you, isn't she?!" I said, leaning over the bartop. "Don't lie to me, I know she is!"

I was breathing heavily. I was smiling because I knew I had won. I was going to see Faith again; Mack couldn't hide her from me any longer.

Except Mack's face was all wrong. I was waiting for that jig-is-up sigh. For him to say, "I can explain." Instead, he just had this sad, sad, sad look on his face.

It wasn't himself he looked sad for.

"I don't how else to say this," said Mack. "I try to help young LGBTQ people in the community. I know how hard it can be to be queer in a family that rejects you. My daughter—my *husband's* daughter, from his previous marriage—she told us about Faith. And since I can't help Faith, well...she said you two were very close. Helping you seemed like the next best thing."

The trucker dude didn't even blink an eye. He probably already knew this. Hell, everyone in the bar—all ten of them—probably knew this.

Everyone except me.

"I knew your mom in high school," said Mack. "She was very unkind to people like me. I know it couldn't have been easy for Faith to come out to her."

I felt like a window shattering in slow motion. Every shard was like a synchronized swimmer in an underwater ballet. Spinning slowly, moving outward and away, catching a glint of light, a reflection, and then—suddenly—the pieces fell, and all that was left was a broken, jagged hole in the wall.

♩ ♫ ♪

The first week Faith disappeared, I made missing person flyers—both physical copies that I stapled to telephone poles and digital ones that I tried to make go viral on social media. (They didn't take.)

The first month Faith disappeared, I called and texted everyone in her phone's memory—contacts and anonymous numbers alike. Faith apparently didn't have very many friends. The most frequent number she called was Dungeons and Dugouts in Gillette—basically the most nerd-core store in all of Wyoming—to inquire whether they had a certain manga or figurine or whatever in stock. She called their number even more than she called Mavis. (They tended to text.)

In the months that followed, my M.O. was either to stare blankly at my computer screen and wonder what incredibly brilliant thing I would search for if I was a child detective, or to sit on Faith's bed meditatively and brainstorm until my head hurt. Occasionally, I was even struck with a brilliant idea—one that would lead me like a careening drunk driver into a crushing dead end.

These days, it wasn't unusual for me to wander into Faith's room for no reason whatsoever, lie on her bed, crumple into the fetal position, and just disintegrate. I wish I could tell you that I was going in looking for clues, but by then I felt like a worse detective than Shaggy and Scooby. I mean, at least those doinks *solved* their mysteries! What had I accomplished? Had I solved *anything*?

After making an absolute ass of myself in front of Mack, I gave myself permission to just wander into Faith's room and feel sad for the sake of feeling sad. It was therapeutic. I think.

That's when I accidentally wandered into a time capsule.

All of Faith's belongings—everything that Mom had carted out in a Hefty black trash bag, never to be seen again—had been returned to their rightful places.

Faith's DVDs were all in alphabetical order by title, movies separated from TV boxsets. The mangas were in alphabetical order by author. Her posters and figurines—of Ellen Ripley and Sarah Connor, of Trinity and Furiosa and Alita—occupied their original places on the walls, on the shelves, immortalized in their empowering poses. It left me sort of breathless. I came in to disintegrate, and instead I found myself transported in time.

I don't know how long I stood there in the middle of her

room, wondering which particular episode of *The Twilight Zone* I had wandered into, but eventually I felt someone existing in my periphery. I turned, and there was Mom, filling the doorway like a ghost.

"I think I put everything back right," said Mom.

I opened my mouth but said absolutely nothing. Words were lost to me. I felt like I was in a dream.

"I used some of the pictures she took on her phone for reference," Mom explained. "For when she comes back."

"Oh." I was trying not to fall apart.

I didn't say anything else. She didn't say anything in return. The silence wasn't awkward so much as empty.

Eventually she just left.

So there I was, breathless, emotionally exhausted, transported in time. I found myself sitting on Faith's bed with tender sacredness, like it was holy ground (it was to me), perusing one of Faith's notebooks, one that had been returned to its place, one that appeared to serve no other purpose than to record indecipherable thoughts and drawings. Words like "Henosis," "Nepsis," and "Theoria" with no visible context, sketches of tall alien girls and broken female androids being reassembled from scratch. (I'm sure my mom considered these drawings "inappropriate" at the time.) One page had only seven words on it, and they were written so big, they seized the whole page: *Andromeda and Tanks Through Space and Time.*

I dropped my face into Faith's notebook and started crying.

Time became a fluid, incomprehensible blob in that room, minutes bleeding profusely, whole hours crumbling to dust. I think I might have even fallen asleep.

All I knew was that, suddenly, I heard the rev of the CR-V starting outside. It was also weirdly dark enough that the headlights automatically turned on, flaring through the blinds. I blinked my crusty dried tears away, drunkenly staggered off the bed, and peeked through the window. I discovered Mom behind the steering wheel, backing out of the driveway, driving off into the literal sunset.

It would be *so normal* for me to not give a fuck where she was going. But now that Faith's bedroom had been reassembled like an intricate puzzle, I suddenly *had* to know.

I found Dad in the living room, slumped on the couch watching a *Star Trek*. I don't know which one. One of the *Star Trek*s. Faith would have known which one. There was a bald guy, if that helps. I think he was an internet meme.

"Where did Mom go?" I asked. The question accidentally came out loud and unintentionally aggressive, like the bad cop in a police interrogation.

"Uh," said Dad, blinking, sitting up straight. "Church?"

I looked at my cheapo digital wristwatch. It was 6:51 p.m. on a Tuesday.

"Different church," Dad clarified. "Smaller one, more local."

"Bible study?" I said.

"Therapy."

I stared at Dad.

"It's like a church therapy group for grief sort of thing," Dad explained.

I continued to stare at Dad until he basically started explaining everything from the beginning.

The beginning was, Mom started googling things like "What

do you do when you've lost someone?" Which obviously made it sound like Faith had died, but honestly, that was probably close to the level of grief we were dealing with here. Especially since Faith had disappeared so completely and on such awful, catastrophic terms. Now, everyone else at this grief therapy group *could have been* completely annoyed and unwelcoming of this woman who had essentially chased her daughter out of her own home and who was now dealing with the consequences. But that's not what happened. Instead, they welcomed her with open arms. Including—maybe even *especially*—the pastor who led these group therapy sessions.

The pastor was gay. That seems like a critical detail. And somehow, he loved Jesus just as much as he loved his partner. This was what Mom told Dad.

"So, yeah," said Dad in conclusion. "That's where your mom is."

I continued to stare at Dad. This was one of those weird situations where knowing the full story only made things more confusing, not less.

"You should talk to your mother," said Dad.

If there was one thing in this world I did not want to do, it was talk to my mother.

"Which *Star Trek* is this?" I asked, hard-core deflecting.

Dad both understood why a change of subject was necessary and also didn't seem to mind. In fact, he seemed a little bit elated.

"Um, *The Next Generation*, aka the *best* generation," said Dad matter-of-factly. "If you don't count the first two seasons. Those first two seasons were a bit of a trash fire."

"A trash fire, huh?"

“It always takes a season or two for a new *Star Trek* to stop sucking. That’s just how it is.”

He was not selling me on this show, nor the franchise.

“Sometimes you have to trudge through the bad in order to get to the good,” Dad explained. “There’s something rewarding in that level of perseverance.”

He sounded like a life coach or a motivational speaker, not a person sitting on the couch watching bad television. Was this a metaphor?

“It’s fine!” said Dad, fitting himself back into his indent in the couch, probably in response to the clearly judgmental look on my face. “You don’t have to believe me.”

I didn’t believe him.

“Just know that you’re missing out on a treasure of both science fiction and nineties television. Your loss!”

He was trying to sucker me into watching this bad TV show with him. Not today, Dad. I inched away from the TV toward my bedroom.

“I mean, Faith loved watching it with me, but we’re just a couple of nerds, so what do we know?”

Oh, that sly bastard.

Andromeda panicked. This wagon train could not leave without her. That's not how this was supposed to go.

"My family has money!" Andromeda shouted at the backs of their heads. "You can use me for ransom!"

Three Fingers turned back around. "You're an exiled Dresdorian. Your family doesn't want you."

Fuck, thought Andromeda. Fuck, fuck, fuck.

Andromeda collapsed onto her knees and clasped her hands in front of her. The time for dignity had passed. It was time to beg.

"Please," said Andromeda. "Please take me with you. I have nothing. I have nowhere to go. Please, I'll do whatever you want: cook, clean, fix things—I can fix things! That's not a lie; I'm a good mechanic. Just please, please, please don't leave me here."

She turned desperately to the Rotter who she was 99 percent sure was Tanks.

"You're all outcasts and refugees, aren't you?" said Andromeda. "I'm no different from you. Please."

Three Fingers and Girl Rotter exchanged glances, communicating wordlessly. The sympathy was almost tangible. Finally, Girl Rotter nodded.

"You'll have to wear cuffs until we get to camp," said Three Fingers. "You'll basically be our prisoner until we know we can trust you. No offense."

"None taken!" said Andromeda, just a bit too gleefully.

Girl Rotter pulled a pair of metal rings out of her satchel. Andromeda had never been cuffed before, but she attempted to be as accommodating as possible. Arms out straight, fists balled shut, the soft parts of her wrists exposed. She instructed herself to be cool, but mostly failed. *I'm getting cuffed by Tanks,* she thought. *Oh my God, oh my God!*

Girl Rotter slid the rings over her fists. They shrunk to the shape of her wrists and connected magnetically.

"Ow!" Andromeda yelped. When she realized that might not have sounded very cool, she gave a pained smile. "They're a little tight."

Three Fingers gave a barking laugh. "Good! That means they're working."

The wagon train consisted of three hum bikes, two military-grade Grav-Es, and one hefty Stagecoach 3000 repurposed exclusively for cargo. Well, cargo and prisoners, apparently, because that's exactly where Andromeda ended up. Girl Rotter loaded her in, right next to a pile of bug carcasses sprayed in generic brand Rot-Not. You could tell it was generic brand because now it smelled like chemical and rot. Soon these dead things would be clothes for more Rotters. It was a sad day for fashion.

Girl Rotter took the seat across from her, which, to be fair, was covered in just as much—if not more—dead bug. Not that Andromeda required extra space. She was mostly just long. The real problem was her knees, which were treacherously close to the pointy end of the crossbow resting in Girl Rotter's lap.

All this was forgotten as Girl Rotter began unwrapping her face.

Andromeda immediately unlearned the ability to breathe. It was uninstalled from her brain. She was being strangled by pure excitement.

Girl Rotter removed the last of the wrap, and white hair spilled out. It was cut in a high bang line. Freckles were peppered across her nose. She pulled her goggles up to her scalp, revealing pure black eyes. Because she was a Kelfling. From the planet Kelf, obviously. In other words, not an android. Not an Ixion model anyway. And certainly not Tanks.

"Oh crud," said Andromeda.

—Andromeda and Tanks Through Space and Time,
Æon Q

—SEVEN—

THAT'S DEEP AND ALL, KIERKEGAARD, BUT WHAT DO I SAY TO DANNY?

LIVING WITH CHARITY IN THE MONTHS THAT followed Faith's disappearance was like a social experiment on feel-bad drugs. Like an objectively terrible reality TV show but with no studio to capitalize on our torment.

I say "our" torment because Charity very clearly viewed herself as the martyr of this arrangement. All she ever did was The Will of God, and suddenly, no one was going to church anymore and everyone was depressed. Dad was the only person actively talking to the three remaining members of his family, but he did this in very closed-off, one-on-one conversations. I had no idea what he talked about with Mom or Charity. Frankly, I didn't care. I was just glad *I* had someone to talk to.

God, I was so lonely.

Charity, on the other hand, was making a magnificent demonstration of how not lonely she was.

Breakfast was maybe the one time of day Dad managed to get

more than one member of his family to sit down together to enjoy a meal. By dinner, Charity, Mom, and I were all fully charged in our resentments, disassociations, and antisocialisms, but first thing in the morning, while we were all still groggy and mind-fogged, with the smell of bacon and coffee wafting alluringly from the kitchen, we were like moths to the bug zapper.

So, while I was trying to eat my bacon and eggs in peace (or misery, whatever), there was Charity across the table from me, Bible splayed open beside her breakfast, nourishing herself both physically and spiritually. I was doing my best to pretend she was never born.

Charity read something in the Bible that caused her to laugh.

You know when people laugh at something they're reading on their phone, but you know they're only really laughing because they want you to ask what's so funny? Yeah, this was one of those situations. Except she was reading from the Bible, which made it a thousand times worse.

Charity glanced up at me, grinning like she could barely contain herself, and I made the tragic mistake of making eye contact, which gave her permission to start talking.

"Proverbs," said Charity, knowingly, as if that single word was self-explanatory. And then she started reading: "Let beer be for those who are perishing, wine for those who are in anguish!" She rolled back her head and gave a small chuckle. "Pass the wine, am I right?"

I stood up from the table and pulled on my stupid pink backpack, only catching the briefest glimpse of sadness on Charity's face as I walked right out the door. As if she had a right to be sad about anything.

I would rather laugh at my own funeral than at Charity's stupid jokes.

♩ ♫ ♪

You would think I would have moved on from a prepubescent crush, but nope. The longer I ogled the forbidden fruit, the more infatuated I became. And let me just say, the boy-creature called Danny Roger had aged quite well. Ohhhhhhh mama, he was hot. He had all the right muscles in all the right places. His jawline was sharper than forty-year-old Wisconsin cheddar, and his smile made me want to cry. His family also attended Traditional Family of Christ, and occasionally seeing Danny dappered up in a suit and tie was *almost* motivation for me to become a regular church goer again—but only almost. He was hot. What else do you want me to say?

To that effect, you could also say that Danny's twin brother, Dylan, became less appealing with time. While Danny grew deliciously smart and poetically funny, Dylan became even more annoying and kind of a pig. So, Team Danny for life.

Regardless, Danny and Dylan were a package deal. They tried out for sports together—*all* the sports—of which they were always the star athletes. The Rogers had an impeccable history of dating sisters. (I was pretty sure Dylan the Pig always picked first and forced his brother to date the sister; more on this hypothesis in a second.) They were even in a band together! It was called Roger Roger. Danny was the lead guitarist and songwriter, and Dylan was the lead singer and backup guitarist.

Now, I'm obviously a biased party, but Danny was easily the

more talented of the two. Dylan wasn't a bad singer, don't get me wrong—he sounded obnoxiously like Harry Styles—but it was Danny's lyrics that made those songs shine. He gave it the intellectual and emotional complexity of the Smiths mixed with Slash's ability to shred some fucking guitar. It was an intense roller coaster of jumping up and down and feeling things until your heart exploded.

Everyone in town knew who Roger Roger was. That's because of Sundance High's Battle of the Bands.

Technically, Battle of the Bands was a back-to-back event with prom, held on the first Saturday of May every year. For whatever reason, Sundance High's proms were historically bad—like hot garbage bad, probably due to budget constraints—and, as a result, were poorly attended, which only served to emphasize the staggering level of badness. Tacking Battle of the Bands on to the beginning as a "warm-up event"—with an hour in between to change or freshen up—was meant as a weird, experimental means of driving kids to prom. And you know what? It worked! The Battle of the Bands portion—which *everyone* was invited to, children and adults alike—was the biggest event in Crook County all year.

Last year, Roger Roger won by a vicious landslide. It wasn't a competition; it was a slaughter. It happened just days after Faith disappeared, and was one of the few moments in those early days when music completely overwhelmed my ability to feel sad. I went because waiting for the police to call was killing me, and living under the same roof as my so-called family was like living with my worst enemies. I needed an escape, so I went

Roger Roger's music washed over me like a deep, clean rain over my soul. Over the course of a single song, I felt human again. They were that good.

There was talk that the winner from the previous year shouldn't be eligible to compete the following year, but that talk seemed to be coming exclusively from the other bands who knew they didn't stand a chance. So far there was no such rule, and if Battle of the Bands was judged solely on talent, Roger Roger was sure to win again.

At least, that would have been the case. However, something big was about to happen. Something that was going to turn the town on its motherfucking head.

♩ ♫ ♪

At school, I didn't have any "friends," so to speak. Unless you counted Mr. Britton, the young (late twenties), vaguely humongous (six-foot-something, two-hundred-and-something pounds) teacher of US history and a single philosophy elective class that I had for first period—which most people *wouldn't* count. This made lunch in the cafeteria sort of unbearable. Sitting by myself was just so goddamn lonely, and I didn't dare ask to sit by anyone else. I wasn't sure which fear was greater: the fear of rejection or the fear that they would ask about Faith.

As for sitting with Charity and her friends, well, I'd rather go on a hunger strike.

I sort of pleadingly asked Mr. Britton if I could eat lunch in his classroom. I tried not to sound desperate, even though that's exactly what I was. Mr. Britton said he'd need to ask Principal Reilly.

Principal Reilly said that was okay.

I think everyone low-key knew about what happened with Faith. Not that Faith was popular by any definition of the word—she wasn't—but queerness had a way of popping up in small-town conversation the same way that, say, Satanism and serial killers did. Faith running away from home, never to be heard from again, had sort of turned her into the Lizzie Borden of lesbians. She was almost an urban legend, as fucked up as that sounds. I think that made me what you would call a "special case."

Whatever. As long as I didn't have to eat lunch in the cafeteria.

Mr. Britton's fourth period US history class was in the process of evacuating, and I was entering with my sack lunch, when it happened.

"What the fuck is this?" said Dylan, shoving his phone in Danny's face before he could even stand up from his desk.

Even though Dylan was a carbon copy of Danny, genetically speaking, there were little, self-managed differences. When his shitty personality wasn't a dead giveaway, his hair was. It was just a little bit longer than Danny's and had a tendency of getting in his eyes. Usually because he had a tendency to lose his fucking shit.

"What do you want me to say?" said Danny—surprisingly calm, despite Dylan's phone being inches from his face. He tried to push Dylan's hand away. That didn't go over so well.

"Don't touch me!" Dylan screamed.

I would later find out that the thing on Dylan's phone was a very personal, very long "coming out" post on Danny's social media account. That's right, ladies and gentlemen, my longtime crush of years and years was gay. But don't get me wrong, I wasn't disappointed. In fact, in a weird, backward sort of way, I think I fell just a little bit more in love with him. But not even knowing that quite yet, I was transfixed by (and filled with stomach-twisting anxiety over) the confrontation that was beginning to escalate in front of me.

Apparently, Danny hadn't bothered to come out to Dylan in person, and the reasons why were obvious. Maybe he just wanted to put all the words out there before they could be interrupted and slammed down.

"What do you want me to say?" said Danny. He finally stood up from his desk.

Dylan stepped back and shook his head. "This is fucked up."

"What's fucked up? That I didn't tell you personally, or that I'm gay?"

Danny was trying so hard to remain calm, but his friendly surface was wearing thin.

"THIS IS FUCKED UP," said Dylan, even louder. He sounded so betrayed.

"WHAT'S FUCKED UP?" Danny repeated, matching his volume, the last thread of friendliness breaking. "That you look like me, and I'm gay, so in a sense, you look gay?"

Dylan screamed and lunged at Danny.

It's hard for me to explain what happened next. I'm not a confrontational person—especially not at school. But in that moment, as my brain was scraping for meaning, compartmentalizing images into subtext, Danny became Faith, and Dylan became the rest of my family, and I had to protect Faith at all costs.

I dropped my sack lunch, bolted and weaved through the gawking crowd, planted a foot on the seat of the nearest desk-chair combo, and leaped into the air like I was the Unbeatable fucking Squirrel Girl. Years and years of The Floor Is Lava and Wyoming Ninja Warrior had prepared me for this moment.

I landed on Dylan's back. Wrapped my legs around his waist, my right arm around his throat, and locked him in a choke hold.

His Adam's apple bobbled helplessly in the crook of my arm. I didn't know much about choke holds, but my intent was either to suffocate him to death or to rip his head off his shoulders. I wasn't exactly thinking straight.

"Ughh...glugh...uckkkk!" gurgled Dylan.

Dylan had been grabbing Danny by the throat, but once oxygen stopped circulating into his brain, he started doing something that resembled the Macarena.

"Whoa whoa whoa whoa whoa," said Mr. Britton. "Help, can I get some help?"

Multiple hands were unprying each of my appendages off Dylan, which made me want to punch faces. Then I realized they were also pulling Dylan off Danny, so I finally succumbed. For a moment, I was completely suspended by people holding my limbs. Eventually my feet managed to ungraciously connect with the floor. I wobbled for balance.

Once the three of us were separated, Mr. Britton singled Dylan out. He stepped between us like a mama bear protecting her cubs, but somehow—inexplicably—madder.

"You need to leave," said Mr. Britton.

On any other day, Mr. Britton was a teddy bear. He was, however, roughly the size of an actual bear. And right now, his scruff-covered jowls were rippling. His intimidation factor was as strong and terrible as his Axe body spray.

Dylan rubbed his throat, glancing from Mr. Britton to me like we were annoying but *completely* inconsequential. Less important than flies. He returned his attention to Danny, and the hate was back, and it was cranked to eleven.

"You're out of the band," said Dylan. "I'm kicking you out."

That one touched a nerve.

"I'm lead guitar," said Danny.

"*Fuck* your lead guitar. Fuck *you*. We don't want you, and we don't need you. We'll find someone else. Someone better, who isn't a &%$#@."

Imagine the most offensive thing you've ever heard. Now double it. That's basically what Dylan said.

"Eat shit!" said Danny. "You can't kick me out!"

"Watch me. I'm the lead singer. I can do whatever the hell I want. This is my band. And believe me, once Kaleb and Hunter find out about this, they'll want your gay ass out too. Fuck you, Danny, just fuck you."

Dylan stormed out of the room with such an outrageously wounded look on his face, you'd have thought he was the victim here, and not the shittiest piece of shit ever shat, a total rectal abomination.

"Okay, okay, show's over," said Mr. Britton. He made traffic-directing gestures with his big, beefy arms. "Bye-bye now, so nice of you to stop by, see you later."

The crowd had mostly funneled out of the room when someone shouted a choice slur from the hallway. That caused an appalling ripple of laughter.

At this point, Danny—confident, unbreakable Danny—had his head slumped down like his neck was broken, staring intensely at the floor. He was one of the last ones on his way out the door. Probably hoping to make a quiet, invisible exit.

"Hey, uh, Danny," said Mr. Britton. "If you need a moment to collect yourself... What I mean is"—he gestured at me—"Hope here always joins me for lunch. If you'd like, maybe I can grab you something from the cafeteria, and you can join us? Right, Hope?"

My eyes grew wide and panicky, but I gave a stupid nod.

Coming violently to Danny's rescue was one thing. But having lunch with him? I'm not gonna lie, that sounded terrifying. Just because he was gay didn't change the fact that I'd been crushing on him since about the dawn of time, or at least puberty. It's like, just because Spike Spiegel from *Cowboy Bebop* was an anime character—and therefore, not a viable sexual option—that didn't mean the idea of him didn't make me hot and heavy. Even Faith admitted to being slightly hetero for Spike! What I'm trying to say is, sexual attraction is a self-serving bastard with no interest in what's attainable or even logical.

"I like to think of my classroom as a safe space," Mr. Britton continued when Danny failed to respond. "What just happened was unacceptable. And if I have anything to do with it, it won't happen again. I'm sorry."

"He's not your brother," said Danny, blinking away any trace of sadness. Then he smiled, like everything was perfectly okay. "But sure. Lunch here sounds great."

"Excellent," said Mr. Britton. "Just hang tight, okay? I'll be back in a few."

Mr. Britton gave me a subtle, make-sure-he's-okay look, like I was a qualified person capable of things. I was not, obviously. So naturally, I responded with an unqualified look of unparalleled horror. Mr. Britton then returned a you-can-do-this look, and he was out the door before I could do something embarrassing, like stress puke.

Mr. Britton's absence was even bigger than his presence. It was just my teen heartthrob and I. I sat where I normally sat in first period—the closest desk to Mr. Britton's—and Danny sat where he normally sat, which was the desk right next to mine. I knew this because I was obsessed. The possibility of stress puke was so real.

This was obviously the part where one of us would start a conversation, but Danny, the socialite, wasn't saying anything, so what the hell was I supposed to say? I scoured the classroom for something interesting or thought-provoking to talk about. Unfortunately, it was covered in about one-third US history and two-thirds philosophy (because Mr. Britton *definitely* had a favorite class). A whole section was dedicated to Immanuel Kant, of course. Beside him was a threefold poster of the holy trinity of Greek philosophy: Socrates, Plato, and Aristotle. And in the far back was a pencil sketch of the very first existentialist, Søren Kierkegaard. (Unless, of course, the first existentialist was Friedrich Nietzsche; there was some debate.) To me, Kierkegaard looked more like some young, mad composer. Maybe it was the hair. It was big and wind-swooped back, as it is with all prodigies. Beneath Kierkegaard's face was a giant, obscenely readable quote: "Life can only be understood backwards; but it must be lived forwards."

That's deep and all, Kierkegaard, but what do I say to Danny?

When I finally resigned myself to my fate—that I was a boring, thoughtless person with nothing helpful or meaningful to say—I finally dared to look at Danny. He looked vulnerable. He looked alone. And that's when my heart broke apart again, like it was the very first time. I looked at him, and all I could see was Faith.

"My sister's gay," I said.

Danny looked at me.

"Or lesbian, I mean," I continued. "You know what I mean."

Danny stared silently at me.

Well, the ice was broken. Now what?

But the longer Danny stared at me, the more I saw Faith. I saw her coming out to me for the first time—the vulnerability and the fear of rejection. I saw her in the living room, mortified, as Mom condemned her, just for being who she was.

I looked at Danny, and I saw Faith silently slipping out the door in the middle of the night and never coming back.

I started crying.

"My parents," I said, through the tears and the snot, "they tried to send her away. Tried to send her to one of those camps where they make you, I dunno, *not gay*? So she ran away. That was, like, nine or ten months ago? I think? And I haven't seen her. I haven't even heard from her, not once. I don't even know if she's okay."

That's when I completely lost it. I dropped my face into my hands and just sobbed. I put my whole body into it. This was the sort of crying that was also an ab workout.

I heard desk legs screech across the tile floor—*eeeee... eeeee... eeeee*—and a pair of big, buff arms wrapped around me, gently patting my shoulder in that way that says, *everything is going to be okay*, and somehow makes you believe it.

"Goddamn it!" I said, finally pulling my hands away. "I'm the one that's supposed to be making you feel better!"

"Don't worry," said Danny. "You are."

Andromeda's predestination was in serious jeopardy. Not because she hadn't met Tanks yet. (Not just that, anyway.) It's just that, well, Zaffy was super cute.

Zaffy (short for Zaffyra) was the only Kelfling at camp. She was here because she was in love with another Kelfling girl. (Apparently, this was a no-no?) The Kelf Honor Code authorities took her and her girlfriend into separate rooms, demanding obedience to the law and submission to a rather unforgiving penance process. Zaffy refused. Her exact words were, "Go get a spoon and eat my ass." It was an insult, not an invitation—although her bishop-probation officer was prone to these sorts of misunderstandings and even gave her a look that said, *What, like, right here?* Then he shrugged and leaned in for the kiss. So she punched him in the face. Instant exile.

Her girlfriend submitted. That was the last they saw of each other.

Everyone's stories were similar. Three Fingers—whose name was actually Trog—was a race regarded as little more than vermin where he was from. Everything he owned was repurposed by soldiers for the War. Including his wife. When they resisted, the soldiers killed her and Trog's entire family. They left him alive because they thought his reaction (to the slaughter of his entire family) was funny and a better punishment than a bullet.

Zaffy told Andromeda this. She said it was best not to ask Trog about it. Andromeda agreed that was probably a good idea.

Andromeda adjusted well to life in this small desert village. They called it Henos. Henos was home. Two other Rotter camps (Nepsis and Theoria) surrounded the fringe of Southland City, where they often traded goods and resources.

Oh, by the way: "Rotter" was a superbad word. Andromeda casually used it once, and Zaffy's eyes opened like black holes. Glancing left and right, she leaned into Andromeda's ear. "You definitely shouldn't use that word. It's incredibly offensive."

"Oh." Andromeda had suspected this and felt stupid for letting it slip. "I'm sorry."

"Don't be sorry," said Zaffy. "Just don't do it again."

Andromeda learned that they referred to themselves by their respective camps: Henosans, Nepsians, Theorians. Henos was surprisingly big (population: 104), a circle of mudbrick huts, tents, awnings, and vendors, all protected under a dome force field against acid rain. The force field was portable, dispensed from a central rod and sealed by perimeter stakes. These were religiously maintained because one malfunction could spell certain death.

No one was in charge. Everything was done by vote. In the rare instance there was a tie, they held a camp meeting, allowed everyone to argue their side, and voted again. Nothing was done without a majority vote. It wasn't a perfect system, but it tried to be fair. It mostly succeeded. Andromeda experienced the voting system on her first night. After a warm welcome into camp, and most people greeting her as a friend rather than an enemy, they voted whether or not to uncuff her and accept her into the tribe.

Andromeda received a rare ninety-nine votes in her favor, five votes against. They uncuffed her, and she became the 105th member of Henos. A true Henosan.

Zaffy returned Andromeda's third eye.

"What?" Andromeda glanced from Zaffy to the severed horn in her hands.

"We don't take from our own," Zaffy explained.

Andromeda bit her lip.

"We would've invited you to join us right off the bat," said Zaffy, "but Dresdorians would usually rather eat sand than associate with us. You're sort of a weird case."

Andromeda's eyes welled with cathartic wetness.

"Don't cry," said Zaffy.

"I'm sorry!" said Andromeda, and she started crying. "I'm just happy is all."

—Andromeda and Tanks Through Space and Time,
ÆonQ

—EIGHT—

LOAFY

THE MOST SIGNIFICANT DAY OF MY LIFE—SINCE Faith's disappearance, anyway—started when I woke up from a piping hot dream in which Danny Roger, Julian Casablancas, Spike Spiegel, and I were vacationing together in some South Pacific/French Polynesian paradise. (Like, Tahiti or Bora-Bora or something?) We only had two rooms reserved, so we had to decide who was bunking with whom. I was obviously thrilled with all the options. It was swiftly decided, however, that teenagers should bunk with teenagers, and adults should bunk with adults. So it was me and Danny.

Danny was super bummed.

As it turned out, Julian Casablancas and Spike Spiegel had the hots for each other, so they ditched us and ran away to elope and have a cute little human-anime family together. At this point, Danny told me that he hated me, and I woke up.

It obviously wasn't real, but dreams about rejection have a way of putting you in a weird funk. As I got dressed and went to school, I found myself daydreaming through class about whom

Danny would have gone for: Julian Casablancas or Spike Spiegel. Probably Julian, seeing as he was a real human person, but then I thought how unfair that was to Spike and the vast gayness of animekind—and for the rest of the school day, I had visions of a steamy Yaoi anime starring Danny and Spike. It would take place in outer space, of course. The moment I drew Danny as an anime character in my head, I knew I had gone too far. My engine was revved, and I had nowhere to go but home, where sexual desire goes to die.

While I was cutting across the school parking lot for a long, libidinous walk home, I accidentally found myself walking past Danny Roger. He was sitting alone on a concrete parking bumper at the far end of the B lot. Because I was deliberately trying to avoid eye contact, I found myself paying special attention to both his backpack and a giant, sketchy-looking gym bag beside him. Both appeared fuller than normal. These were strange enough details that I dared to fully look at him.

He looked awful.

His eyes were hollowed out and swollen with darkness. His complexion was drained and sallow. He looked like something that had been stepped on, then scraped off the bottom of someone's shoe, then stepped on again.

Danny didn't see me coming, and he seemed intent on not making eye contact with anyone who came near, choosing instead to stare endlessly at some fascinating speck in the asphalt. I could have walked right past him, and he would have never known.

But that's not what I did.

I stopped.

And then stood there in front of him, saying nothing. Like a dumbass.

Danny couldn't very well ignore the spectator who stopped to stare at the hot mess in the parking lot. He glanced up. Recognition set in, and his countenance even seemed to lift a bit—like, a tiny, infinitesimal bit—although when he opened his mouth, he hesitated, and I was 100 percent certain he had forgotten my name.

That was fine. This wasn't about me.

"Are you okay?" I asked.

"What?" said Danny, flustered—although he very clearly knew *what*. "Um. Yeah. Of course."

He wilted the moment he said it.

"Well, no, not really," he said. "I'm not welcome at home."

"What?" I said—although *I* very clearly knew *what*.

"Yeah," said Danny, offering a sad laugh. "I think my dad's exact words were 'Don't set foot in this house until you've reevaluated your life choices.' Life choices meaning being gay. So I guess I'll be welcome again once I'm less gay.... It's no big deal, really."

He laughed again, but the sadness behind that laugh was gutting. Danny might as well have punched me in the stomach. That's how all these words and sad laughs coming out of his mouth felt. I couldn't speak. The breath was knocked right out of me. Everything hurt, all over, everywhere.

I must have looked like I was on the verge of tears (I was) because Danny immediately looked like he'd overshared and felt the need to console me.

"But hey, it's okay!" said Danny, faking an almost believable smile. "It's really no big deal. I just have to pretend to be straight until I figure out what I'm going to do next. Or graduate and go to college. First-world problems, am I right?"

I started crying.

"Fuck," Danny said to himself, like *he* was somehow the fuckup here. "I'm sorry. TMI. I know you have your own problems. I didn't mean to—"

Stop crying, I said to myself, willing the waterworks to shut off. *Stop crying, stop crying, STOP FUCKING CRYING, HOPE, STOP—*

"We have an extra room!" I blurted out.

That put a definitive halt on the conversation. Danny's mouth was left hanging open. The silence was extraordinary.

But for the first time in months, I felt like I had said something right. Already it felt like every tense, anxiety-filled muscle in my body was depressurizing. I felt it all the way to my core.

"It's Faith's room," I explained. "Obviously. But you can sleep there tonight if you want."

Danny stared at me.

"Actually, I insist," I said. "I'm not letting you go home while there's a no-gay rule."

"But...," Danny sputtered. "Didn't your parents...? Wasn't Faith...?"

Yes, my parents did. And yes, Faith was. But all this was superseded by a bigger, truer fact that I had just learned about myself.

"I honestly don't give a fuck what my parents think," I said. "I will literally battle my mom to the death until she says yes. She *will* say yes, or she will say nothing at all. There is literally no scenario here where you don't have a place to sleep tonight."

Danny appeared mildly alarmed by the idea of battles to the death over his sleeping arrangement.

"But don't worry," I said. "I don't think it will come to that."

♩ ♫ ♪

I offered to carry Danny's backpack while he lugged his giant gym bag. His backpack was heavy as fuck all, but that duffle bag was unquestionably heavier. It was obvious in the fierce tautness of his broad shoulder, in the way his bicep popped, causing the sleeve of his T-shirt to hug the skin, in the *disturbingly* sexy veins throbbing in his forearms—

Sweet baby Jesus in a manger! What was I doing? I had just invited the hottest boy in the history of boys or hotness *to stay the night*. That's fucking what. If Mom or Dad didn't kill me, my sizzling libido surely would.

Nobody was home when we arrived, which was honestly a relief, although God knows it wouldn't stay that way. But that was fine. It was better to get Danny situated, shut the door, and then I could defend it, Helm's Deep style.

Danny reassembled his life around Faith's belongings. The sci-fi nerd paraphernalia. Random fangirl drawings and scribblings, archived in a library of notebooks or pinned all over her walls.

The awkward silence was tangible.

I mean, Danny was silently grateful, and I was silently supportive, but "silent" was the operative word here, and there was too much of it. Do I say something? Do I just walk out of the room and let him get situated? Surely I should say *something* before I just walk out of the room, right? But what?

My gaze scanned the walls meanderingly—but also sort of frantically—for inspiration and fell on a dry-erase board that Faith had turned into a quote board, filled with nothing but iconic sci-fi movie quotes that she had compiled for no discernible reason other than that she was the worst sort of nerd. And yet, desperate for wisdom, I found myself weeding through them for talking points.

"I've been fighting with one arm tied behind my
back, but what happens when I'm finally set free?"
—*Captain Marvel*

"I'm a leaf on the wind." —*Serenity*

"By Grabthar's hammer, by the suns of Warvan,
you shall be avenged." —*Galaxy Quest*

"There is no spoon." —*The Matrix*

"I've seen things you people wouldn't believe.
Attack ships on fire off the shoulder of Orion.
I watched C-beams glitter in the dark near the
Tannhäuser gate. All those moments will be lost in
time like tears in rain. Time to die." —*Blade Runner*

Okay, so that was a magnificent waste of time. All I got out of that was "Time to die." Thanks for nothing, science fiction. WTF, Faith?

"So... I take it your sister likes science fiction?" said Danny.

"Huh?" I said. "What makes you say that?"

Danny laughed.

♩ ♫ ♪

And just like that, the ice was broken. Just completely smashed. What little bits of ice remained, metaphorically speaking, were melting faster than the polar ice caps. But, um, in a good way. (And not in a way that made you fear for the planet and the future of humankind.)

I helped Danny unpack the rest of his belongings. Get situated. And perhaps most importantly, I talked to him—the way one human being talks to another.

"Did you know that climate scientists predict if we don't reduce global carbon emissions by forty percent by the year 2030, the planet will be doomed?" I said.

"Fuck," said Danny, holding a pair of his boxers out in front of him. His intent had been to fold them until I dropped this inconvenient truth. "Seriously?"

I shrugged. "That's what the Intergovernmental Panel on Climate Change says."

I didn't notice Danny's gaze as it shifted ever so slightly—or as he suddenly realized he was holding a pair of his underwear for the world to see, like a proud child holding a work of art. He suddenly seemed deeply horrified.

"But, I mean, it's fine," I said, despite my raging eco-anxiety. "We just have to rally together behind leaders who are taking climate change seriously and kick out the dorks who think it's a hoax. No biggie."

Danny balled up his boxers and cleared his throat conspicuously, and I realized we weren't alone. I rotated slowly, following his gaze, which landed on Mom.

I whipped upright, straight as a board.

The three of us glanced at one another in a *The Good, the Bad, and the Ugly*–style standoff of pure embarrassment before I realized like a dumbass that I was the one who ought to explain.

"Mom, this is Danny," I said. "Danny, Mom."

"Hi, Mom," said Danny. He pocketed his boxers, smiled, and waved nervously.

The standoff continued.

"Danny got kicked out of his house," I explained rather bluntly. "So I told him he could stay the night in Faith's room."

I made very sure to word this as a statement, not a question. I was not asking for her permission. If she wanted to fight me on this, I would fight. But Danny *would* sleep in this bedroom tonight, so help me God. I would die for this cause. I was so ready for a fight. I felt my breath quicken, my fists clenching at my side.

"Danny Roger?" said Mom. "Eric and Cynthia Roger's son?"

Danny was standing so erect, arms flat at his sides. He looked like he should have been standing guard at Buckingham Palace. All he needed was a tall bearskin hat with a dopey chinstrap that didn't fit properly.

"Yes, ma'am," said Danny, the paradigm of politeness.

Mom nodded thoughtfully. She seemed to know exactly who Danny was and why he was here. Sundance was a small town. Word and scandal had a tendency of spreading like the gonorrhea outbreak of 2015.

She glanced down at Faith's bed.

"You probably need new sheets," said Mom. "These ones haven't been changed in"—she almost choked on the words—"in a *long time*. Just give me a moment, and I'll get you all situated."

Mom remade Faith's bed carefully and respectfully, like some holy ritual, a sacrament. She gave Danny a clean towel for the morning and a brand-new toothbrush still in its package. And because Danny specifically requested not to remove Faith's belongings—out of respect for my feelings, I'm sure—Mom helped us rearrange Faith's things, folding her clothes into tighter squares so Danny could claim a drawer or two. Overall, Danny did not require much space.

Finally, Mom stepped out and called Dad (privately) to let him know what was happening. So naturally, I eavesdropped.

I didn't know what Mom and Dad had been talking about lately, but the side of the conversation I heard sounded like the most normal and wholesome conversation I had ever heard. Someone needed help, so they were going to help. The weirdest thing was how they made it sound like Christianity 101. Like this was the fucking basics.

When the phone call ended, Mom came back in, beaming, and said, "Brent can't wait to meet you, Danny."

Everything was pretty much too good to be true. Like the fairy-tale happy endings you're told not to believe in because reality will always disappoint you. And maybe for good reason. Because that's right about the time Charity came home.

Charity's coming home ritual was to kick off her shoes, drop her backpack in the middle of the living room, and to pillage the kitchen for snackage. She did all three of those things. At this point, she must have heard our voices in Faith's room because she appeared in the doorway in purple socks with a Twizzler sticking out of her slightly ajar mouth.

"What's going on?" said Charity, forming words around the licorice.

Danny smiled a pleasant—if emotionally jet-lagged—smile. I smiled in a way that meant the opposite. Like the smile you give someone you don't like in a professional environment.

Mom smiled like someone on a spiritual high.

"Charity, have you met Danny Roger?" said Mom. "He's going to be staying with us for a while."

The Twizzler fell right out of Charity's open mouth.

"Sweetie," said Mom, in a tone that meant WTF.

"Mom," said Charity. "Can we have a word?"

Quietly, Mom followed Charity out of the room, plucked the half-gnawed licorice off the floor, and shut the door behind her. A lot of good that did.

"DO YOU KNOW WHO DANNY ROGER *ISSSS*?" Charity whispered at top volume, hissing on the last word like the world's loudest snake on the other side of the door.

"I just introduced you to him," said Mom's voice, irritated.

"Do you know *what* Danny Roger is?"

In a panic, I fumbled with Faith's old radio alarm clock. We were greeted by BTS's "Dynamite."

"*Shh!* Of course, I know," Mom hissed back, practically speaking Parseltongue. "Keep your voice down."

"You know?" said Charity.

"*Dy-na-na-na, na-na, na-na-na, na-na, life is dynamite!*" said the K-pop gods.

I cranked BTS up as loud as they could go. They were trying their best, I can promise you.

I gave Danny the most embarrassed, apologetic look I could offer. "I'm sorry. Charity's the worst."

"Um, have you met my brother?" said Danny.

Danny cracked a smile, and I couldn't help it. I laughed defenselessly.

"I don't understand," said Charity.

Mom sighed. "I owe you an apology, Charity. I'm not proud of the way I've treated you girls. What I mean to say is... I think I've done some very bad things. Things I might never be forgiven for. But I want to *try*. I want to *do the right thing*. And I mean this from the very bottom of my heart when I say that giving Danny Roger a place to stay *is the right thing*. There's just no question in my mind about that."

That effectively ended the conversation. Ended it like the book of Revelations. Charity literally had no words to wrap around that response.

The silence lasted for eons.

I noticed Danny noticing the ballet of expressions on my face. I didn't know how I looked, but it was probably similar to how people looked when they watched Dr. Pimple Popper videos.

"This doesn't make any sense," said Charity finally.

To be fair, it didn't make any sense to me either. Nothing made sense. I was living in some alternate reality, a parallel universe, where the rules as I knew them suddenly didn't apply anymore.

I heard a pair of footsteps storm away and a door close. There was a moment when nothing happened. Finally, Mom poked her head back into Faith's bedroom.

“How do sloppy joes sound for dinner?” said Mom.

Sloppy joes were Faith’s favorite. There was obviously a running theme here.

“I love sloppy joes,” said Danny. He looked at me—probably to make sure my opinion was being heard.

I simply nodded and tried not to smile too hard.

♩ ♫ ♪

That night, Mom, Dad, Danny, and I had sloppy joes. (Charity insisted on eating in her room, and Mom didn’t push the issue.) All the while, Mom and Dad made conversation with Danny like he was the most esteemed guest and not some unwanted being that had been kicked out of his home.

Right before bed, as I got in my jam-jams and finished brushing my teeth, Danny cornered me outside the bathroom. He looked frail and emotional and completely overwhelmed.

And then he just hugged me. It was physically gentle and emotionally fierce. That hug did the talking.

I felt his body warmth wash over me, his breath on my neck. It caused my heart to stutter and my skin to prickle in cascading waves.

Danny finally let go of me and quickly disappeared into Faith’s room. His room.

I retreated to my room, which was right next door.

I climbed into bed, turned off my bedside lamp, and pulled the covers up to my chin. That’s when my brain—wide awake—made the startling mathematical calculation that my bed was right next to Danny’s bed, and our bodies were maybe three feet away from each other, separated by approximately four and a half inches of wall.

It was under these circumstances that I turned my head ninety degrees, facing the wall, but more specifically facing Loafy, doing his smiley-winky face at me.

It was as if he knew exactly what I was thinking. As if he was telling me it was okay.

He wouldn't judge.

He wouldn't tell.

I grabbed Loafy and shoved him between my legs. I found myself rocking and grinding in the dark, imagining that the wall between us wasn't there, that Danny was slightly less gay than he was—maybe a nice shade of bisexual—and I swear to God. I came so fast, I was shuddering, I forgot how to breathe, and my eyeballs rolled so far back, I should have been able to see my brains.

Andromeda carried her third eye in a satchel that she wore on her person at all times. If anything, it was a token, a severed reminder, of the future she was already beginning to forget. Like a promise ring.

It wasn't working.

Andromeda and Zaffy grew alarmingly close. Andromeda even moved into Zaffy's hut, although it was more of a roommate situation than a lover situation (much to Andromeda's disappointment). Not that the sexual tension wasn't there. Andromeda was bonkers for her, and she was pretty sure Zaffy liked her, but Zaffy also knew about Tanks. More importantly, Zaffy knew that Andromeda had no memory of her, meaning that she must be an incredibly small blip in the timeline of Andromeda. Zaffy wasn't bitter about it. She wasn't, like, holding it over Andromeda's head. She was merely being respectful and diplomatic about Andromeda's timeline. She probably thought Andromeda wanted this. And Andromeda really, truly, seriously did. She loved Tanks, obviously. But she also respectfully and diplomatically wanted Zaffy to get into her pants. Andromeda was just too much of a chickenshit to make the first move.

It's just that every day without her sight felt like a day less in love with Tanks.

—*Andromeda and Tanks Through Space and Time*,
AEon Q

—NINE—

HALF A BAND

I WISH I COULD TELL YOU THAT THINGS GOT better for Danny. That life became a little bit easier for him, knowing he had a bed to sleep in, a roof over his head, food to eat, maybe even a new friend (me). But those were only the most basic physiological needs, my friendship aside. And let's face it: This friendship probably meant more to me than it did to him.

All this was only a patch of solid ground for Danny to stand on while his entire life slid downhill in a fucking landslide. Danny was rejected by his family, sure, but that was only the beginning. The ostracization was soon followed by every single one of his "friends." This included every single person on the sportsball team. (Okay, basketball, whatever.) The name of the sport was truly unimportant, however, because the same cast of dude-bros rotated seasonally from sport to sport. Football in the fall, basketball in the winter, and then came spring, at which point there was a slight division that favored baseball but lost a few brave soldiers to coed track.

I only heard what happened from a third-party source (Mr.

Britton, who overheard it from a flock of jocks, a whole gaggle of them). Apparently when Danny came into the locker room for practice the next day, every single player stopped what they were doing and moved to the exact opposite end of the locker room. A few of them even laughed while it happened.

They had obviously planned this. The message wasn't subtle.

At which point, Danny approached Coach Packer and quit the team. Packer didn't even bat an eye. In fact, Packer suggested he not try out for baseball either.

From that point on, Danny became a regular at lunch with Mr. Britton and me.

Danny wasn't bringing up his exile from the SHS sports scene, and neither of us was sure how to ask about it without making him feel like absolute shit. So mostly, we just danced around the subject like idiots.

"You know, there are some surprisingly exciting extracurricular activities the school hosts," said Mr. Britton. "Did you know the school has a prom planning committee?"

"Oh, really?" I said, feigning interest. Like, it wasn't common knowledge that Sundance High School proms were the fucking worst. I mean, really, Mr. Britton, come on.

"Oh yeah!" Mr. Britton exclaimed, utterly enthused, catastrophically clueless. "As a matter of fact, Ms. Beekman and I were just appointed as the teachers in charge of overseeing it! Kevin Grimes is the teen lead heading the committee—I don't know if you know him—but we're still very actively recruiting enthusiastic young people to blah blah blah blah *blah blah blah*..." I stopped listening. Oh my God, Mr. Britton, SNORE.

"Hmm," said Danny, nodding politely. "I might have to look into that. I have a pretty full load right now, but I'll let you know if something frees up."

He had to know that *we knew* that he was no longer on the basketball team and therefore had more free time than he'd had since elementary school. But he didn't say anything about it, so obviously we didn't dare.

Mr. Britton and I smiled dumbly, and for the rest of lunch, we made listless small talk.

Danny played it off like we were his first choice. He smiled and acted like everything was okay. But during the small moments in between, when I'm sure Danny thought no one was looking, I'd see his face slip into that deep, dark sadness that filled his world like an ocean.

And he'd just sink.

♩ ♫ ♪

That night, as I was hunkered in my bedroom doing homework, I got a text from an unknown number.

> Hey, it's mack. Got your number from the karaoke log-in sheet. I wanna apologize for the other day. Also, I heard what you did for danny roger. I have a surprise for you. Swing by the bar when you get the chance.

This was amusing because Mack had absolutely *nothing* to apologize for. He wasn't the one who accused *me* of mother fucking and harboring one's sister like a fugitive.

However, rather than shift the blame back onto me—where it belonged—I eagerly texted: What is it??

He replied: Lol, what part of surprise don't you understand?

You know me by now. (Tragically.) So at this point in the story, I hope you'll forgive me for automatically assuming this surprise had something to do with Faith. That maybe Faith was standing in his bar *this very second*. Or at the very least, Mack had some clue about her whereabouts. A sighting. An online photo. Anything.

Literally *anything* would have been a fucking treasure to me.

I could have walked right out the front door, and neither Mom nor Dad probably would have stopped me. (I think they viewed me less as a child and more as a tornado at this point in their parenting careers.) However, I didn't dare speak the F-word (Faith) out loud for fear of jinxing her reappearance, and overall, I just didn't want to make a scene. It was under these circumstances that I clandestinely decided to sneak out the window.

I was about halfway through the window—straddling the frame, folded in half, possibly stuck—when Danny knocked on my door and then let himself in.

Danny wasn't a barbarian. My door just wasn't closed all the way. I had this weird thing about closed doors: I hated them, for no reason whatsoever. Unless, of course, the reason was psychological, in which case, it was probably connected to my fear of losing the people I cared about the most and indicated a deep and profound loneliness that was suffocating me from the inside. I dunno. It probably wouldn't kill me to see a therapist. I'd be sure to put that on my mental health to-do list—just as soon as I knew Faith was alive and well.

"Oh, um," said Danny. "Sorry. Bad time?"

"I'm sneaking out," I whispered, in case it wasn't painfully obvious. "Please don't tell anyone."

"Oh, don't worry," Danny whispered back. "I know the rules. Snitches get stitches." He pounded his right fist into his left palm to demonstrate.

I gave a sharp bark of laughter, then silenced myself with a hand over my mouth. The other hand was the only thing keeping me balanced.

"Can I ask where you're going?" he asked.

"There's this bartender I know who has information on where Faith is," I said. "I think. Or something like that. He said he has a surprise for me, so..."

The more I verbalized it, the more desperate and delusional I felt. So I was trying hard not to think about it too much. Or at all. The name of the game was "blind optimism."

"Oh," said Danny, nodding the way you do when you're lost. "Okay? I'll let you get to it then?"

Thank you, I mouthed. I shifted my leg, lost my balance, and fell out the window with a graceless thud. Oof.

"Are you okay—?" Danny started to say. But I was already up and haggardly limping into a very gradual sprint. I gave him a thumbs-up to let him know all the vital organs were intact.

I ran to Happy's Tavern as fast as I could. (Which wasn't very fast.) I was halfway there when Mack texted me an informative disclaimer.

It's come to my attention that I should mention this surprise has nothing to do with Faith.

Ding! Another text:

Sorry for not mentioning that sooner.

Ding!

Or, if that wasn't even a thought in your head, sorry for bringing it up.

I'm not going to lie: I almost cried. I stared at the text, fought back the tears, and repeated to myself this helpful mantra: *It's okay. Everything's okay. Everything is (fuck fuck fuh—no, deep breaths, deeeeeep breaths) okay.* I blinked, and I blinked, until I successfully prevented a sobbing disaster under a streetlamp at the corner of Fifth and Main.

Across the street, I noticed two people sitting quietly at a bus stop, sitting far apart—a tall, beautiful girl of ambiguous age and a frumpy-looking dude with a beard and an overall homeless vibe. They were both watching me like a television drama.

I kept walking. Or limping. I was only now noticing my leg felt not-so-great.

"Well, if it isn't my favorite customer," Mack said as I walked in. His gaze dropped to my wonky limp. "You okay? What happened to your leg?"

"I fell out a window," I said. Mack's eyes grew wide with alarm, so I clarified, "First-floor window."

"Oh," said Mack. "Huh."

He reached into his pocket and removed a small, thin piece of plastic, maybe two inches long, one inch wide. A keychain card,

I realized upon closer examination. It was laminated, with a hole punched in the corner and these words printed on the front:

Free Karaoke
Expires: when you graduate

It had a very—how to put it nicely?—*homemade* vibe? But it was the thought that counted. And it counted a lot.

"I'm proud of you," said Mack. "You did a really good thing for that Roger kid."

I forced a weak smile and looked at my shoes. "It doesn't feel like it."

"How's that?"

I shrugged. "His life is still ruined."

Mack chuckled. "It's not *ruined*. It's just getting started!"

"He doesn't have any friends. They all just ditched him."

"He has you, doesn't he?"

I frowned. I didn't say it, but my immediate thought was *I'm the lucky one to have Danny as a friend, not the other way around.*

"High school's hard," said Mack. "But it's just a teeny tiny sliver of what life's really like. You ever get Chinese food at the mall?"

"What?"

"Chinese food. At the mall. You know how they serve little chunks of chicken on toothpicks? High school's like that. It's just a sample. Maybe it's good. Maybe it isn't. But then you try the real thing, and there's all these options: Beijing beef, orange chicken, Shanghai steak. All I'm saying is, there's a lot more to offer in life than what you're given in high school. Don't go thinking this is all you're ever gonna get."

Mack set the keychain card flat on the bartop and slid it across to me with a single finger.

"As long as there are people like you, Hope, people like Danny will be a-okay."

I smiled and picked up the card. "Is it okay if I cash this in for some free karaoke?"

"Um, yeah," said Mack. He unclipped his big ring of keys from the carabiner on his belt loop. "I'd be offended if you didn't."

♩ ♫ ♪

It was a good, therapeutic, belt-your-throat-raw karaoke sesh, traversing decades and genres. I sang Stevie Nicks. I sang the Strokes. I even made a little room for Gaga ("Bad Romance") because it just felt right. And you know what? I fucking *nailed* it! I don't know why I let those bullies convince me I couldn't sing. It made me think how influential (or damaging) words can be, regardless of whether there's any truth to them.

I sang the way that you wring water out of a wet dishrag. (I would later learn that there was a proper way to train your voice and sing so as not to damage your vocal cords in the long run—but today was not that day.) By the time I was done, I was pretty sure I wouldn't be able to talk tomorrow. I turned everything off, tidied up after myself as a common courtesy, and opened the door.

Danny was standing there.

In fact, he backed up a little bit, like he'd been standing with his ear pressed to the door.

His eyes were so wide they were practically outside his skull.

After I bragged about nailing Lady Gaga, you would *think* I wouldn't be incapacitated with embarrassment. You would also be wrong. I felt like I suddenly had a space heater built inside my face. I could've thawed out a frozen woolly mammoth, just by blushing at it.

"What are you doing here?" I said, eons later.

Danny's face was stunned into submission. He did, however, manage to lift up a keychain card labeled "free karaoke," identical to mine.

I may have been dumb, but I wasn't stupid. I realized Mack probably texted us at the same time. Or he found Danny on social media and messaged him. Explained to Danny that karaoke was a thing I did.

That's why Danny barged into my room.

That's why Mack suddenly texted me, clarifying that the surprise wasn't Faith. Those bastards were "corresponding."

That's why Danny was standing right here, right now, with this card in his hand, and my obituary would read: *Died of embarrassment. Yes, really.*

"YOU CAN *SING*?" said Danny. It was less words, more of an explosion.

I brushed past Danny and made a break for the exit.

"Whoa, hey, where are you going?" said Danny. I heard his footsteps. He was chasing after me.

"Please don't follow me," I mumbled.

"Wait, are you embarrassed?"

No shit, Sherlock. What gave it away? My face turning the color of Mars? (I, of course, wasn't cool enough to say this. I was too busy dying inside.)

I was down the hall, across the bar, and out the front door.

The air was cool and pure, the perfect contrast to the blistering hostility inside of me. I heard the doors *whoosh* open a second time, behind me.

"Hope, don't be embarrassed," said Danny. "You were *amazing*."

It wasn't the word "amazing" that stopped me so much as the way he said it. He said it like—I dunno—how I talked to Faith about the Strokes or how she talked to me about some nerdy sci-fi thing or, better yet, Mavis. Some things were too amazing for words, but you tried anyway and hoped that your raging enthusiasm did the trick when words fell short.

I turned around, tying my arms into a fierce knot. My defensiveness was still cranked up to nine thousand. I was waiting for Danny to laugh, to tease, to make some playful but low-key hurtful joke about my coping mechanism.

Danny's expression was calm and sensitive and concerned.

"You *do* know you're amazing," he asked, "don't you?"

What was I supposed to say to that?

"Hope," said Danny, so serious it was lethal. "You're one of the best singers I've ever heard."

I laughed—a sharp, cynical bark of laughter that revealed I believed he pitied me and nothing else.

"I'm serious!" said Danny. "You're fucking incredible. Your voice is raw, and real, and you capture emotion in a way that doesn't even make *sense* to me! Like when you sang Gaga? Jesus, I got chills! Literal chills, all up and down my body."

I was blushing again, but for all the wrong reasons.

"Hope," said Danny. "You need to start a band with me."

We let those words sit on the silence for a bit. Then I snorted—a ravenous snort of laughter—and dropped my voice the necessary octaves to make it sound dumber. "Yeah, okay."

"I'm *serious*!" said Danny, cartoonishly shrill.

"You want to start a band."

"Yes."

"With me."

"Yes!"

"Why?"

"Aside from *all the reasons* I've stated so far?" said Danny. "How about seeing to it that my brother doesn't win Battle of the Bands? Not to be bitter, but I want him to lose."

I sighed. Tactically speaking, Danny had gone for my Achilles' heel.

"Unless someone stands up to him, he's going to win," said Danny. "You *know* he will. There's not enough musical talent in this town. But I can write lyrics and play guitar, and I'm telling you, *you can sing*. That's half a band, right there!"

I sighed. Danny immediately interpreted that as a yes and pumped his fist. He even made a little victory grunt through his teeth.

I mean, it wasn't not a yes.

"Okay, but," I said, "that's still just half a band. Where are we going to find the other half?"

Danny grinned insidiously, like I'd walked right into his trap. (I did, obviously.) "I'm glad you asked."

"Do you believe in God?" asked Zaffy.

Andromeda made a vague sound of misery, as if struck by a sudden migraine. It was night, the dead-of sort, when living things weren't meant to humor the nagging dread of existentialism. Andromeda and Zaffy slept in separate hammocks slung across opposite ends of the hut, only a small space between them due to the humble size of their living quarters. More space than Andromeda wanted, honestly. But even if they were intimate, Andromeda was unsure it was possible to share a hammock. That seemed risky. Zaffy was hot, but those elbows were pointy. Overall, the place wasn't exactly ideal for sexy time.

A stripe of moonlight poured in, painting a line across Zaffy's wide-awake eyes, her freckled nose, as well as Andromeda's feet since she was facing the opposite direction. She could tell that Zaffy was looking at her, searching for her face in the shadows.

"I mean, your people are religious, aren't they?" said Zaffy.

"You're my people," said Andromeda, flatly. "Henos is my people."

"You know what I mean. Dresdore. The Church of Time. Isn't it an old religion?"

"Just because it's old doesn't mean it's good or right."

"What do you think happens when we die?"

Andromeda stared at Zaffy's face in the stripe of moonlight. She looked scared.

"One malfunction is all it would take for everyone here to die," said Zaffy. "These huts aren't acid proof. If a big enough storm hit, they could collapse right on top of us. I know you're acid proof, and I'm glad you are, but... the rest of us would be toast."

Andromeda chewed on her lip. She hated being invulnerable in a vulnerable community. The only thing worse than dying would be watching everyone die around her.

"It's not even the pain I'm afraid of," said Zaffy. "It's just everything ending. Not knowing if my life meant anything. Not existing in any way, shape, or form. It scares me."

"Do you believe in God?" Andromeda asked politely.

"Trog told me a story," said Zaffy, "about the spirit of Dearth. Her name is Gaea. She lives on top of a mountain in the center of Dearth, somewhere in the planet's core, and she takes many forms: terrestrial beings, animals, plants..."

"Plants?"

"Like, sometimes she's a bush?"

Andromeda snorted.

"Hey!" said Zaffy. "I'm being serious! Trog believes in this."

"Does he? Or was he just telling you a story? Telling you what you want to hear?"

Zaffy became awfully quiet.

"I'm sorry," said Andromeda. "That was a shitty thing to say."

Zaffy said nothing. The silence was like an open, bleeding wound.

"You have every right to believe what you believe," said Andromeda. "I've just had bad experiences with... God. It's always 'holy this' and 'holy that' and 'that's unholy,' and I'm like, 'holy shit, shut the fuck up.'"

Zaffy giggled. That made Andromeda smile. God, it was such a pretty sound.

"You've had bad experiences with people," said Zaffy.

"Huh?" said Andromeda.

"You haven't had bad experiences with God. You've had bad experiences with people who believe in God. You've never actually met God. Unless there are any special divine experiences you've yet to tell me about."

Andromeda sighed. "You're right. I've never met the dude."

"Girl. Gaea's a girl."

"I was using the gender-neutral 'dude.'"

Zaffy giggled again. If God was anywhere, it was in the sound of her laugh.

* * *

—Andromeda and Tanks Through Space and Time,
ÆonQ

—TEN—

HOPE CASSIDY AND THE SUNDANCE KIDS

THE "OTHER HALF" DANNY WAS REFERRING TO called themselves Black Rainbow Infection. That made them sound like a goth-rock thing, or a death-metal thing, or maybe even some synth-y darkwave, electropop thing, which would have been infinitely better than what they were. Black Rainbow Infection was like a Billie Eilish fan club meets a parody of a Paramore cover band meets a bad high school production of *The Rocky Horror Picture Show.*

I know, I know, I know, that makes them sound cool, and I guess they were cool, but not in a way that should be allowed to make music. Not like this anyway. They consisted of:

1. Astrid Nguyen on drums. (Goth-y. Extra. Probably a vampire, but an objectively lovable one. We were instructed to pronounce her last name as "Win" because it was just too embarrassing to watch non-Vietnamese try to pronounce it properly.)

2. Angus Fergusson on bass. (Big, chubby, supergay kid and one of the 1.29 percent Black population of Wyoming. Frequent wearer of fedoras, which was also arguably his greatest and only character flaw.)

3. That was it. They were just drums and bass. All they were really equipped to perform was the *Seinfeld* theme song and not very well, I might add.

By the way, Roger Roger had made a very public display of kicking out their one and only gay member the very *moment* he came out. They announced it on all their social media. They didn't explicitly state *why* they were kicking him out, but if you followed Roger Roger, you probably followed Danny Roger as well and had seen his "coming out" post that very morning.

Black Rainbow Infection organized and signed up for Battle of the Bands the next day.

That's what I liked about them. There was a threat, and so like the Avengers, they fucking assembled. Only this was B-movie Avengers featuring Goth Girl and the Rainbow Fedora—two heroes with not much in common except that they hated the ever-loving *fuck* out of Dylan. Easily his most vocal detractors.

That was the best thing about them. And don't get me wrong, it was a really good thing. But they had no lead guitar and no real melody to speak of, and apparently both of them were lead singer. Except for the parts where they... rapped. That's not to say there wasn't talent here. They each had an incredible grasp of their respective instruments. It was just horribly misdirected.

Danny happened to share AP English with Astrid, which is

where he learned about Black Rainbow Infection and how they signed up for Battle of the Bands as an act of protest. The day after Danny convinced me to join his band, he asked Astrid if we could listen to them perform. Astrid was thrilled at the idea of performing for their first two "fans." She informed Danny they'd be practicing at her place right after school.

They performed an entire set for us in Astrid's guesthouse. Her actual house was a small mansion. In addition to being the county mayor, Astrid's dad, Magnus Nguyen, owned multiple businesses. According to Astrid, he believed in hard work as much as he believed in ultraconservative conspiracy theories, which—tragically—he believed in a lot. The key to Astrid and her dad's successful father-daughter relationship was to smile and not talk about politics, ever.

The living room of the guesthouse was set up like a game room—pool table, foosball table, leather couch, leather love seat, and a wall-mounted TV. All these things were pushed to the sides, however, to make room for Black Rainbow Infection's band shit.

Danny and I sat on the love seat and let ourselves be enfolded by the Black Rainbow Infection experience.

"This first one's called 'At Least Satan Respects Women's Rights,'" said Astrid. "And a one and a two and a..."

Astrid started banging her drums like she was bludgeoning people until they became dead. Angus thrummed his bass so loud that it threatened to rattle the metal fillings out of your molars. Nowhere in this noise did a melody exist.

Astrid sang about a consensual relationship with Lucifer—aka "Lucy"—and aborting the Antichrist at the local clinic.

They were politically charged, for sure. But oof. It wasn't even on-key.

After that, Astrid and Angus shared vocals on "Baby, I Don't Care If It's Cold Outside (You Shoulda Brought a Fuckin' Sweater)." Like the Christmas song. Only in this version, the guy was in the girl's house, and it ended with him getting pepper sprayed in the face. It rhymed things like "go away" with "misogy-nay." I wanted to like it so bad, except that it was *so bad*.

Lastly, Angus Fergusson wrapped it up with "Fuck Ya Chicken Strips." It was about Chick-fil-A.

Again, wanted to love it. But this was when the rapping came in, and Angus was quite possibly the most rhythmless person on the planet. He tripped over syllables like obstacles in an obstacle course.

Near the end of "Fuck Ya Chicken Strips," both of them seemed acutely aware of their audience reception. I couldn't speak for my own facial expression, but Danny was smiling uncomfortably and nodding the way you do when you're trying to leave someone's house, but they're still talking to you.

Angus's bass came to a jagged halt.

"Goddamnit, we suck, don't we?" he said, before he even finished the song.

Angus was the biggest, tallest person in the room. He was wearing a T-shirt that said, "I'm So Gay I Can't Even Spell Striaght!" He was also wearing a fedora. (When was he not?) Today's poison was maroon with an actual feather sticking out of it.

Astrid's drumming petered out like a windup toy at the end of its wind.

"What?" said Astrid. "We don't suck."

Astrid was wearing white jean shorts over leggings and a black sweater with an image of a human ribcage printed on the front.

Her pitch-black hair was pinned in a way that didn't really make sense to me but somehow looked absurdly elegant.

She glanced desperately around the room for positive affirmations, but since Danny and I both appeared to be in various states of paralysis, she turned to Angus. "Right?"

Angus sighed. "What do you want me to say?"

"I want you to say we don't suck!"

"We don't suck."

"Do you mean it? Because you don't sound like you mean—"

"I obviously don't mean it. We sound like a joke."

"Angus!"

"Not even a funny joke."

"ANGUS!"

Angus shrugged. "I tried telling you what you wanted to hear, but you had to go asking questions."

"*Aaanng-guhh-huhh-husssss*," Astrid whine-sobbed. She draped herself over her drums, a final resting place for her. She seemed sure of this.

Angus leaned toward us like a tree in the wind and whispered, "Sorry. She gets like this."

Astrid snapped upright on her drum stool. Glanced between Danny and me like we were her last and only hope. "Do we suck? Tell me the truth. Unless . . . no." She shook her head. "No unless! Just the truth. Nothing but the cold, hard facts."

Angus rolled his eyes. "Don't make them do that. It's embarrassing. For everyone involved."

"I'm sorry, what was that?" said Astrid, cupping her hand over her ear. "I can't hear you over the sound of your bad attitude."

"I don't think you suck," said Danny.

Astrid lit up like a Christmas tree.

"I mean, the songs kind of suck," said Danny. "But you don't."

You know in the movies when two people are embracing, and one of those people stabs the other one in the gut, and you're not quite sure who stabbed whom yet because the camera is zoomed in on their faces, and neither one has quite registered the ramifications of this treacherous act? Okay, well, Danny stabbed Astrid in this scenario. Completely by accident. I think.

"Damn," said Angus.

"Sorry, that came out wrong," said Danny. "What I'm trying to say is, as far as execution goes, the songs could have been better, but I really like your *fighting spirit*—"

"Fighting . . . spirit?" said Angus.

"And as far as playing instruments goes, you're actually surprisingly good."

"Wow," said Angus.

Astrid looked like she might cry. Beneath the whole pagan occult vibe, she was a total Care Bear. If Danny continued at this rate, she might die of a broken heart.

"I feel like I'm fucking this up," said Danny intuitively. "Let me start over."

Oh, dear God.

"We want to join forces," I blurted out.

Everyone stopped talking—Danny included, which was inarguably his greatest contribution so far.

"Join . . . forces," said Angus. He had a real knack for repeating words in a way that made you feel stupid. "What, like, you want to *join our band*?" He said "join our band" like we were talking about a UFO death cult.

"You want to join our band?" said Astrid, lighting up. Her entire self-esteem was riding this unfortunate conversation like a roller coaster.

"Well, actually," said Danny, "I was thinking about the four of us starting a new band together."

"New band? Why does it have to be a new band?"

"Yeah," said Angus. "Aside from the fact that people have seen us perform. And my boyfriend, Kevin, hates us, musically speaking. And my dog buried his head in the couch cushions when we played at my place."

"Okay, okay, I get it," said Astrid. "Jeez, you're vindictive."

"So, what is this new band?" said Angus. "You obviously play guitar." He nodded at Danny.

"You're really good too," said Astrid, pouting.

"*Thank* you, Astrid," said Danny, nodding and smiling like it was *about damn time.* "I write lyrics too."

"Is there something wrong with *our lyrics*?" asked Astrid, more defensively.

"No, I love your lyrics. I love your message. But I think we might want to reevaluate the way we're engaging our audience. I mean, this is Wyoming. We collectively haven't voted Democrat since Lyndon B. Johnson in 1964. But if I know Dylan, now that he's running the message of Roger Roger, he's probably going to steer it in the direction of negativity, and mean-spiritedness, and probably a dash of prejudice-flavored hate. So, what if our message is the opposite of that? What if our message is—"

"What, love?" said Angus with a gaggy look.

"Hope," said Danny. "What if our message is hope?"

Astrid and Angus gave heavy pause for consideration. The

overall reaction seemed to be unanimous agreement. But then Angus blinked, looked at me, and raised an inquisitive finger. "Wait. Isn't her name Hope?"

"Yeah," said Danny. "But that's just a coincidence."

Astrid looked at me. "So, what do you play?"

"Oh, she sings," said Danny. "Hope's our singer."

Well, we had their respect and attention for maybe seven seconds. Now skepticism filled the air like nuclear winter.

"No, believe me," said Danny. "She's good."

"We're not saying she's not," said Astrid.

Angus shrugged in a way that suggested otherwise.

"Don't get us wrong, you *look* trustworthy," Astrid told Danny. "You have the eyes of a Cancer."

If it seemed like this conversation was happening *around* me, rather than *with* me, I can assure you, that's exactly what was happening. I was more of a stage prop than an active participant. And I was supposed to be the front woman of this band?

What little confidence I had was rapidly disintegrating.

Danny's lips were pressed into a hard, contemplative line. He looked at me. "Do you know 'Seven Nation Army'?"

What sort of uncultured rube did he take me for? I nodded emphatically.

Danny looked at Astrid and Angus. He didn't even need to say anything. Astrid grinned and nodded.

And Angus, man. Angus just went for it.

His left hand danced and slid along the neck of his bass, while his right hand strummed with deadly precision. The end result was that sweet, low, seven-note riff.

Technically, Jack White performed it on a semiacoustic that

had been connected to a DigiTech Whammy pedal, lowered an octave to *sound* like a bass. (I read about it in a random issue of *Guitar World* on display at Ralph Records.) But it was absolutely playable on bass, and Angus was owning it.

Astrid jumped in, drumming slow and steady like a heartbeat. Pumping blood and life into the rhythm.

For a second, I panicked. I didn't even have a mic. Danny, however, was one step ahead of me. He had stepped away, and before I even realized where he went, he was planting Angus's mic in front of me.

When I looked into his eyes, I saw enough confidence for the both of us. There wasn't even a hint of doubt.

"You got this?" he whispered.

I nodded. I did now.

I took a deep breath.

And.

"*I'm gonna fight 'em all,*" I sang with slippery coolness. *"A seven-nation army couldn't hold me back. . . ."*

Jack White's vocals were higher—ganglier—than the average male front man, with a slinky sharpness in his delivery. For a stony, porous contralto like myself, I found that he fell comfortably into my range. It was a different sound, for sure, but it fit like my own skin.

I scrubbed each line like a pumice. Grated it gently.

I guess I sort of lost myself. I realized my eyes were closed. When the music fell away, I opened them, and the first thing I saw was Angus. His giant hands had imploded into tiny balls of excitement. He was shaking them like the world's most awkward maracas, directly in front of his rapturous, splitting grin.

I stopped singing, and Astrid finally stopped drumming, despite having already lost her bassist to a random fit of excitement. The sound coming out of Angus's mouth sounded like this: "Eeeeeeeeeeeeeee!"

"Okay, we're in," said Astrid.

♩ ♫ ♪

As we parted ways, we resolved to let things gestate for a bit. Come up with ideas. Figure out exactly *how* we intended to be the antithesis of Dylan Roger. We also needed a band name. Astrid suggested "Pentagram," which got shot down, then she suggested "Sigil of Baphomet," which she kindly explained was the official insignia of the Church of Satan.

"Do you want to get murdered by Bible-thumping cowboys?" said Angus. "Because this is Wyoming, and *that* is how you get murdered by Bible-thumping cowboys."

So the band name was on hold. We exchanged contact info and awkward but excited goodbyes, and Danny and I drove the CR-V home. My head was spinning the entire way.

I was the lead singer of a band.

I was the lead singer of a band?!

And that wasn't even the weirdest part. The weirdest part was that I suddenly had friends. Like, *three of them*, which was three more than I used to have. (Unless you counted Mr. Britton, which—like I said—most people didn't.) You didn't need to be good at math to know why this was a big deal for me.

Within an hour of leaving Astrid's guesthouse, she and Angus added me on social media. Up until now, my social media presence had been kind of sad. Mostly, I used it as a tool to try to track down Faith. Basically internet-stalking anyone who ever knew her, scraping for a lead—which there never was. It was like looking for a ghost.

So it was a little weird that—just like that—the entire concept of social media had suddenly become exciting and alien and unreal. At one point, Astrid started PMing me other band name ideas (Death Bag, Vampire Workday, Scrotum, and so on), and then Angus started texting me, asking what it was like living with THE HOTTEST BOY AT SCHOOL? (His use of all caps, not mine.) He was obviously playing around. However, a part of me thought that it might be nice to talk to someone about the supermassive secret crush that threatened to squash me like a bug. The other part of me—the part that *wasn't* an idiot—realized the catastrophic potential this revelation had to fuck up everything. So I jokingly replied: But what about Dylan? He responded with the barfing emoji and typed: Dylan would MAYBE be hot if his mouth was sewn shut. Then he proceeded to tell me about his boyfriend Kevin's unfortunate obsession with PewDiePie, and the fact that he made fun of Angus for "reading books," and at what point did this become a toxic relationship?

Hope: Who makes fun of their boyfriend for reading books?

Angus: People who binge-watch first person shooter playthroughs on YouTube, that's who.

Angus: He's also fond of telling me I'm fake-gay because my favorite book is a lesbian sci-fi romance.

Hope: YOUR FAVORITE BOOK IS A LESBIAN SCI-FI ROMANCE?

Angus: But I'm not fake-gay!

Angus: I swear to god, I am soooo gay.

Angus: Literary girl love is just so pure.

Hope: Dude, I think that's awesome!

Hope: You would have been best friends with my big sister.

Hope: Her three favorite things were lesbians, sci-fi, and romance.

Meanwhile, I responded to Astrid's "Scrotum" suggestion:

Hope: It's catchy! I only worry that naming ourselves after male genitalia is somehow empowering the patriarchy. Maybe if we stripped the empowerment out of it somehow?

Astrid: crap. you're right.

Astrid: how about "micropenis"?

Hope: I like it! Except, could that be considered body-shaming? Also, I think that's a real medical condition.

Astrid: uggggggh, you're right. dang, this is friggin hard.

Hope: Don't give up. I love your ideas. If anything, they're distracting me from the fact that I'm sleeping three feet away from D

I stopped typing. I also maybe stopped breathing. Carefully—*veeeery* carefully—I pressed my finger on the backspace key until it just said: Don't give up. I love your ideas. I pressed Send, letting out a breath like I had just made it through the other side of a minefield.

This crush on Danny was getting out of hand. I could keep this up for days, weeks, sure—maybe even months. But what if Danny stayed here longer than that? Could I keep this up forever?

Probably not.

Maybe it was best to just come clean with Danny. Tell him that I'd had feelings for him since roughly the Mesozoic era, but I obviously didn't expect anything to come of it. He was gay. I understood that. It was, like, the one and only reason he was here. It was maybe even the only reason we were friends.

I felt my eyes burning, and I blinked, and I realized I was crying. Great. Fucking great, Hope. Real mature. Jesus, why could I never stop crying? Was *this* a medical condition? Did I need to see an optometrist or something?

But it was already decided. I was telling Danny the truth. If this hurt our friendship, well... it's not like I deserved him as a friend anyway.

I exited my bedroom, marched like five feet to the next room, and—like a complete troglodyte—opened his bedroom door without knocking.

I, of course, only realized this after his bedroom door was wide open, and Danny was slamming his laptop closed in the most incriminating way possible. He was lying in bed, shirtless, with his blanket pulled up to his rock-hard pecs.

For several seconds, we stared at each other in unparalleled horror.

I cupped my hands over my mouth and gasped indiscernibly, "oh-my-God-I'm-so-sorry," and ran to my room, unintentionally slamming the door behind me. I threw myself on my bed, buried my face in my pillow, and kicked my feet like I was swimming across the English Channel. What was the cleanest, most efficient way to kill myself in my bedroom? There was that pencil trick the Joker did, but I was bound to fuck that up.

Someone knocked on my bedroom door.

Oh my God oh my God oh my God—

"NO ONE'S HERE, GO AWAY," I shouted into my pillow.

My bedroom door opened cautiously.

Was it possible to smother yourself with your own pillow?

"Hey," said Danny's voice. "I just want to explain... I wasn't doing what you think I was doing."

I pulled my face out of my pillow. Danny was wearing a shirt now. (Thank God.)

"No, hey, it's cool, dude," I said. "I watch porn all the time. I'm not judging."

That was a lie. (About watching porn all the time; I obviously wasn't judging.) I had only *tried* to watch porn once. It wasn't my thing. I was more of a imagine-romantic-scenarios-with-Spike-Spiegel-while-I'm-trying-to-fall-asleep gal. The point was, I was clearly in the wrong here, and Danny had no need to explain himself.

Danny blushed, but shook his head. "No no no, it really wasn't... *that.* I know I reacted weird, but it's nothing like that. You won't believe me if I tell you. Look, it's easier if I just show you."

My mouth was open. I had no idea what was happening.

"Please?" said Danny.

I couldn't very well say no to him. Not after what just happened. So I bit my lip, nodded, and followed him back to his room.

Without any explanation, Danny grabbed his laptop, opened it, and shoved it in my face. He pressed Play. It was... a movie? It had a grainier look than any modern film. The scene was paused on two criminally handsome men with their backs pressed against a wall of rocks, accompanied by the sound of rushing water. Both were dressed for an era I couldn't even begin to guess, but it looked older than the, um, eighties? One of the men had beautiful blond hair, an even prettier mustache, and a cagey look on his face. He was holding a revolver. The other had icy blue eyes, and the most beautiful chin I had ever seen, and he was staring straight ahead with a reckless look on his face. Then he started unbuckling something around his waist, and oh my fucking God, was I about to watch porn with Danny?

BLUE EYES: "I'll jump first."

BLONDIE: "Nope."

BLUE EYES: "Then you jump first."

BLONDIE: "No, I said!"

BLUE EYES: "What's the matter with you?"

BLONDIE: "I can't swim!"

There was a hilariously uncomfortable pause as this revelation settled. The camera angle changed, and they appeared to be on a ledge or cliff, and the sound of rushing water was coming from far below.

Blondie gave a curt nod just to assure Blue Eyes he was serious.

Blue Eyes laughed.

BLUE EYES: "Why, you crazy—the fall'll probably kill ya!"

Blondie glanced back and forth between whatever threat was behind them and the cliff ahead. He put the gun away and gave a tiny shake of his head.

BLONDIE: "OooooOOOooOOOOooo—"

They both leaped forward.

BLONDIE: "—oh SHIT!"

They plunged hundreds of feet to the water below. Blondie held that declaration of "shit" all the way down.

I glanced at Danny, beyond confused.

"*Butch Cassidy and the Sundance Kid*," Danny tried to explain.

"It's a movie?" I asked.

"It's a western."

When that failed to illuminate *anything*, Danny crouched down and reached under the bed. He pulled out his sketchy duffle bag. Unzipped it and dumped the contents all over his bed.

They were DVDs.

They were *westerns.*

More westerns than I had ever seen in one place: *The Good, the Bad, and the Ugly*; *The Searchers*; *Unforgiven*; *Once Upon a Time in the West*; *High Noon*; *The Wild Bunch.* It was just a spread of way too many westerns, splayed in a bargain bin–style heap. Westerns as far as the eye could see. My uncle Gary was a nut for westerns, but this made him seem like only a modest admirer.

Danny looked like a John Wayne–snorting crackhead.

"So . . . you like westerns?" I said.

"I have a problem," said Danny.

"I think it's cool."

I did, in fact.

"Can we watch one together sometime?" I said.

Danny's stare was a lobotomy needle straight into my prefrontal lobe. He was digging deep for some indication that I was bullshitting him, that my offer was some fake courtesy. But it wasn't.

Danny's mouth slowly curled into a smile. "Do you want to watch this one? I can start it over."

"Um, yeah, duh," I said. "Those dudes are hot."

Danny's eyes rolled all the way to the back of his skull and back, grinning pure ecstasy. "Robert Redford and Paul Newman. And yes. One billion degrees Celsius hot."

Danny immediately started sweeping all his DVDs into the duffle bag. That's when I realized I might have made a terrible mistake.

He sat on his bed, back flat against the wall that separated our rooms. Patted the mattress beside him.

My throat was suddenly as dry as the entire Wild West.

I swallowed and crawled across the bed until I was sitting beside him. Stiff as a shot of whiskey straight. We set the laptop between our legs, and Danny started the movie over. The opening credits were juxtaposed with a cute, sepia-toned, silent film–style train robbery. I liked this movie already.

Smooth-talking Butch was the leader of the Hole in the Wall Gang, and man of few words Sundance was his right-hand man. The Hole in the Wall Gang had turned on Butch, however, selecting Harvey Logan as their new leader. Harvey Logan's leadership qualities appeared purely physical because he was an absolute monster of a cowpoke. Just completely gargantuan. Harvey challenged Butch to a knife fight, which was clearly in Harvey's favor. So Butch kicked him in the nads.

Danny leaned his head on my shoulder.

Screw whiskey. I became stiff as fucking absinthe.

"You're the best friend I've ever had," said Danny. "I just want you to know that."

I decided, then and there, that I would never, ever, *ever* tell Danny my secret. I would take that secret to the grave. I would literally rot with it in my coffin.

I didn't know what to say, so I said nothing. Better that than professing my undying love. My gaze wandered, however, landing on the empty DVD case for *Butch Cassidy and the Sundance Kid*. That's when it came to me.

I picked up the DVD case. "I just had a silly idea for a band name," I said.

Danny glanced from the DVD case to me, back to the DVD case, and then his eyeballs inflated out of his skull.

We texted Astrid and Angus only six words: Hope Cassidy and the Sundance Kids. The responses were instantaneous.

Angus: Sweet fuck.

Astrid: YUSSSSSSSS!!!

"So theoretically," said Andromeda, "if I were to journey to the center of Dearth, and climb this geologically impossible mountain in the center of a planet—"

"Nothing's impossible with Gaea," Zaffy explained.

"Right, because Gaea's a subterranean wizard."

Zaffy opened her mouth.

"Gender-neutral wizard," said Andromeda.

Zaffy closed her mouth.

"So, I climb the mountain, and I meet Gaea. What happens next?"

"I think she grants you a wish."

Andromeda snorted ravenously, then composed herself. She didn't want to offend Zaffy. Fortunately, Zaffy appeared to be smirking. She seemed to understand that they respectfully disagreed in matters of spirituality. Maybe she was even joking. This *had* to be a joke, right?

"Only one wish?" said Andromeda. "Not three?"

"You don't want Gaea to think you're greedy."

"Question: Can I wish for more wishes?"

"You *do* want Gaea to think you're greedy, don't you?"

"I'm just saying, omnipotent wishes are hard to come by. You've got to be resourceful."

"If you had one wish, what would it be?"

Andromeda was about to give a joking answer. Then she noticed that Zaffy was sitting upright in her hammock. She'd somehow managed to do this without making a sound.

She was staring at Andromeda so intently—so differently—it made Andromeda's entire body tingle and surge. The entire contents of her body were a chemical reaction to Zaffy's stare.

Andromeda was paralyzed with desire.

A loud bang punctured the sky. It was ultimately what ended Andromeda's paralysis, to say nothing of the incapacitating horniness.

Several bangs followed. Then a scream.

Andromeda bolted upright. Zaffy leaped out of the hammock and scampered to the glassless window. More than moonlight was shining through now. A red, flickering haze danced and glowed. More screams filled the air. Andromeda quickly followed and looked over Zaffy's head. What she saw was fire, and panicked Henosans running in disarray, and others. Black-and-silver-armored others, wearing visored helmets. Wielding guns. Shooting. Sharp lines of blue laser flashed across the night, connecting with bodies, making them drop. The armored others were moving in a slow, predatory formation, devouring Henos like a snake swallows an egg. At their front, a single figure removed her helmet. Her jawline was fierce. Her head was shaved on the left, a swoop of black hair cutting across the right, coming to a devastating point beneath her chin. She was the scariest thing Andromeda had ever seen. Maybe because Andromeda recognized her. But the recognition was only surface level. Beneath the aesthetic was something terrifying and cruel.

"Gather every single Rotter to the center of camp!" she yelled. "I want every last one of them!"

It was Tanks.

It was horror at first sight.

* * *

—Andromeda and Tanks Through Space and Time,
Æon Q

—ELEVEN—

HATE, LOVE, AND TACOS

DANNY STAYED HOME FROM SCHOOL BECAUSE HE wasn't "feeling well." I believed him. Clear until the moment I arrived at school. I wouldn't find out until later that he was online late last night and had stumbled upon something that was about to turn Sundance upside down.

I didn't blame him for staying home. Honestly, I was glad he did. It would have made this ten times worse

There were flyers.

There was viral content.

There was talk. Insidious, juicy talk—the sort that consumes the collective mind. People were buzzing like bumblebees with tinnitus. I got a taste of it on the school bus when one straight white dude-bro (Brock) said to another (Bryce):

"They're called Alt-Right? Isn't that, like, Nazis?"

"No no no, Alt-*Rite*. R-i-t-e. You know, like Rite Aid?"

"What does Rite Aid have to do with anything?"

"Dude, I'm just telling you how it's spelled."

"So they're not Nazis?"

"Have you heard number eight? They hate on basically everything *except* Jews. Pretty sure that means they're not Nazis."

Who could argue with that infallible logic? From the mouths of dude-bros.

I acquired my first flyer because it was taped to my very own locker. I wasn't being singled out. These flyers were everywhere—plastered to walls, doors, columns, to say nothing of the batch that had been crop-dusted across the floor of the main hallway like herbicide. What it lacked in subtlety, it also lacked in taste. And that was before you read the shit they were spewing, at which point you realized they also lacked any sort of human decency. This is what it said:

A POLITICALLY INCORRECT REFORMATION OF ROGER ROGER

PRESENTS

SPECIAL LITTLE SNOWFLAKES

1. *That's So Gay*
2. *It's Okay to Be White*
3. *Feminists (Baby Killers)*
4. *A Comprehensive List of Shithole Countries*
5. *Come and Take It*
6. *Snowflakes Melt in the Bible Belt*
7. *Beware of Target Bathrooms*
8. ______________________
9. *I Find That Offensive!*

Track number eight had a name, mind you, but it was seriously too offensive for me to even share. Really, the whole thing was painful and alarming to look at, but number eight managed the triple threat of being simultaneously racist, sexist, and homophobic all at the same time. It was a long "jokey" title that was clearly meant to provoke.

Well, mission accomplished. I was provoked.

I ripped the paper off my locker and rushed to Mr. Britton's philosophy class. I didn't bother grabbing my textbook.

I was twenty minutes early, so Mr. Britton's classroom was still empty—except for Mr. Britton himself, hunched in front of his computer, listening to what *sounded* like a punk rock song. The look on his face mirrored the sick feeling churning in my gut.

The moment he noticed me, he fumbled to close the window on his computer.

"What are you listening to?" I asked.

"Uh, nothing, it's nothing," said Mr. Britton.

He was sweating like Deadpool in the chimichanga aisle. He might as well have been watching porn.

"Did it have to do with this?"

I stormed up to him and shoved my crumpled-up flyer in his face.

Mr. Britton didn't need to read it. Sundance High was wallpapered in this shit.

He sighed. "You're not going to like it."

"Obviously."

Mr. Britton sighed again—louder and vaguely pleading. This was my chance to change my mind, but fuck that. I was immovable.

He maximized a window, revealing SoundCloud and the title

of Alt-Rite's first two singles. One of them was "That's So Gay." The other was track number eight. The Voldemort of song titles. Henceforth I shall refer to it as It That Shall Not Be Named, or the more abbreviated form, You Know What.

"You're not listening to number eight on my computer," said Mr. Britton.

"Play the other one then."

He hovered the cursor over the Play button for "That's So Gay." Gave me one last look, confirming that I really wanted to do this to myself.

I reached over him, hijacked the mouse, and clicked Play.

A minute into the song—as far as I made it—I had broken its offensiveness into three categories:

1. The song was a personal attack against Danny. Like, it all but mentioned him by name, instead referring to him with every homophobic slur ever invented.

2. As the title suggests, it made gratuitous use of the word "gay" as a general insult.

3. It also included this bit:

   Being lesbian's okay
   As long as you're hot.
   But sorry, Fugly Cassidy,
   You are not.

That was the minute mark. I charged out of Mr. Britton's classroom in a murderous rage.

"Hope, wait!" said Mr. Britton, chasing after me.

My arms were straight, my fists balled at my side. I was digging my fingernails so deep into my palms that I sort of hoped I'd draw blood.

"Wait, Hope, let's talk about this."

"I'm going to kill him!" I screamed.

"There's a way to handle this," said Mr. Britton. "Doing something that'll get you expelled—or worse—is not the way."

I attempted to walk faster. Scoured the busy halls for my murder weapon. All I saw were textbooks. I knew for a fact that Mr. Griffin had *The Yale Shakespeare: The Complete Works* in his classroom. With a high enough velocity—and malintent—it had lethal possibilities.

Outwalking Mr. Britton, however, was a vain attempt. His legs were long, like tree trunks in khakis. He sped in front of me and planted himself like a wall of actual trees.

"Hope," he said. "Stop."

"She's my sister!"

I wanted to sound mad, but the words came out broken and hurt.

"I know," Mr. Britton said calmly.

"Why would they do that? Who is *that evil*?"

"I know," Mr. Britton said softly.

I was crying now.

Mr. Britton let me cry. He waited kindly, patiently, as long as it took, until I had wrung every last drop out of my system.

I took in a deep breath.

Let it out in one great big therapeutic release.

I met Mr. Britton's gaze with all my shit together. A nice little shit package, gift wrapped and tied with a bow.

"What do we do about these assholes?" I asked. "We can't just let this happen."

Mr. Britton said nothing.

"Can we?" I said despairingly.

Mr. Britton sighed. Shook his head. "No. We can't."

♩ ♫ ♪

Mr. Britton and I took our plight to Principal Reilly. Explained that Alt-Rite was nothing short of a hate movement and, therefore, should be barred from having any sort of presence in school. That's when I learned Principal Reilly was a flaming bag of dog shit.

"I appreciate the social activism, guys," said Principal Reilly. "Really, I do. But my hands are tied on this one."

Principal Reilly was a squirrelly guy with a weirdly pointy head, a weak chin, and a neck so thin, it looked like it was barely holding up the infrastructure. All in all, shaped like a football tilted on end for the kickoff. Maybe I only thought this because by the end of this conversation, I wanted to drop-kick it through a fucking field goal.

"What do you mean, your hands are tied?" said Mr. Britton.

Principal Reilly shrugged. "Freedom of speech."

"Freedom of speech," Mr. Britton repeated, unamused.

"This is an institution of learning. We can't just put a cap on what children are able to say or express or think. If we do that, how are we different from Orwell's *Nineteen Eighty-Four*? We'd be the Thought Police!"

"Are you being serious? They're using homophobic slurs, racial slurs—"

"Well, now, hold your horses; they don't use the N-word," said Principal Reilly, like this was an actual counterpoint.

"Are you kidding me?" said Mr. Britton, growing rapidly hysterical. "There are *dozens* of racial slurs out there—for *several* different races—and in a single song, these boys use just about every last one of them! Just because they don't use one *specific* slur doesn't mean they're being *anything* but belligerently racist."

"Look. We live in a time when racial tensions are high. We work in a high school. Teenagers will be teenagers. Race is always going to be an issue—"

"Children aren't born racist!" Mr. Britton exclaimed. "They're taught it. And by refusing to do anything about this, you, Principal Reilly, are teaching it *to* them."

A dense blanket of silence fell over Principal Reilly's office. Mr. Britton was breathing heavy, like social justice was his cardio for the day. Principal Reilly looked like an apple had just been shot off his head. Shots had certainly been fired. Mr. Britton couldn't put the bullet back in his gun.

I'm not saying he wanted to. I'm just saying, time travel is impossible.

Principal Reilly leaned forward, planting his elbows on his desk, fingers interlocked. "What are you saying?"

Mr. Britton said nothing. It was crystal clear what he was "saying."

"You've been with us almost...five years?" said Principal Reilly. "So close to getting tenure."

Mr. Britton's posture shifted, ever so slightly, from offense to defense.

"I like you, Britton. Everyone does. Everyone likes a 'woke

teacher,'" he said, air-quoting. "I'd really hate for something to happen between now and then."

Principal Reilly glanced at me, in case I had anything to add. I, of course, was a speechless idiot. He leaned back in his chair, hands behind his head, cradling his stupid lemon-shaped skull, victorious.

"I feel like this has been a productive meeting," he said. "Thank you—both of you—for coming and expressing your concerns."

Finally, Mr. Britton stood up, silent as death, and started for the door. So I stood up and awkwardly followed. I closed the door softly behind me, afraid to make a sound.

"I have to get to class," said Mr. Britton.

His words snapped me out of my daze. I blinked and looked at him. "Oh. Okay. So, what's the plan?"

Mr. Britton shrugged his husky, bearlike shoulders. "There is no plan."

"What? But what are we going to do?"

He shrugged again, but the weight of his shoulders seemed heavier. "There's nothing I can do."

"What? But—"

"I'm sorry, Hope. We tried. I have to go."

Mr. Britton turned and abandoned me in the empty hallway. A carpet of loose flyers rustled and slipped beneath his footsteps.

The moment he rounded the corner, the bell rang.

♩ ♫ ♪

I couldn't bring myself to have lunch in Mr. Britton's classroom. So I found myself wandering outside, terribly unhungry and a little nauseated, to the graffiti wall. To that tiny inscription, "Faith was here," the final vestige of her existence.

I crouched down and stared at it until my legs hurt. I touched it. When I accidentally smudged the *F*, I jerked my hand away like I'd touched a stove burner. Except it was the opposite. I was the one causing harm.

How like me to ruin everything I touched.

"Hey," said a male voice behind me. It was distinct but soft, firm but gentle, and came from quite a distance behind me. He was apparently taking some serious discretion not to sneak up and startle me.

I turned, and it was Shady Shawn. He was wearing a beanie over shoulder-length hair—no ponytail this time—and a Social Distortion shirt over a thermal long sleeve. His baggy jeans were ripped, practically disintegrating. He was holding a hefty bag of Taco Bell.

"You okay?" he asked.

I obviously wasn't, but I nodded and ran my hand across my face to erase any contrary evidence.

"Are you not eating lunch?" he asked.

"I'm not hungry," I said.

It was at that moment that my traitorous stomach gave me away, unraveling in a squelching gurgle of a roar. Shady Shawn heard it. It was impossible not to hear it within a twenty-foot radius. Shawn and I stared each other down. It was like one of Danny's western showdowns, minus the six shooters. I couldn't speak for Shawn, but I was armed to the teeth with emotional and psychological insecurity.

Shawn drew first—except he was apparently only packing tacos. He raised his Taco Bell bag. "Wanna help me eat this?"

I did. I really did.

♩ ♫ ♪

Shawn and I ate with our backs to the graffiti wall, me beneath the word "DOOM," him beneath "EUPHORIA." He apparently ordered six whole tacos, which was morally incomprehensible to me—who the fuck orders that many tacos?!—and I ended up eating three of them. I didn't realize how hungry I was until I couldn't stop eating. Maybe I was stress-eating? Each time I finished one, Shawn would hand me another, and I would wolf it down like the last one. He tried handing me a fourth taco, at which point I forced myself to exercise a little restraint.

"Nuh-uh," I said, shaking my head and pushing the taco into his chest. "Nope."

"You sure? I think you need another taco."

"I do not *need* another taco. What human being needs a fourth taco?"

"You do, apparently, because you ate those last three tacos in three minutes flat."

"I'm stress-eating. I'm stressed. More tacos will not make me less stressed. They'll just make me gassy, and then I'll be gassy *and* stressed."

"Actually, it's a scientific fact that tacos are the number one reducer of stress."

"You are so full of shit."

"No, I'm full of *science*."

"And from what deeply scientific source did you acquire this breakthrough in the field of tacos?"

"Ummm, William . . . ?"

"William."

"... Nye... the Science Guy."

"You are so full of shit!"

"Science, I'm full of *science*, just like you should be full of tacos."

"Are you trying to plump me up?"

"I'm sorry? *Plump you up?* What am I, the witch in Hansel and Gretel?"

"You're trying to plump me up like a Thanksgiving turkey."

"Okay. Just to be clear. I bought six tacos only because I want to *plump you up*, because I'm actually a cannibal witch. That's our working hypothesis here."

I shrugged. "If the shoe fits."

"The cannibal witch shoe, right, gotcha."

"I'm not going to tell you I'm *not* delicious."

"Oh, I have no doubt."

Shawn was grinning hysterically at me, only barely suppressing a fit of laughter. It was only now that I realized our conversation of "plumping me up" and "cannibalism" had taken on a flirtatious and weirdly sexual tone. I shifted uncomfortably. Not because I wasn't into it. In fact, that was the problem. I was *waaaaay* too into it.

Shawn seemed to notice the change in body language, and fortunately, he read it 100 percent off.

"Sorry, did I say something wrong?" he said.

Some people will say that in a weirdly vindictive manner—like you're the one who's wrong for feeling that way, not them. But that was not the case with Shawn. He seemed entirely apologetic and sincere and worried.

As much worrying as I did for Faith and Danny, it sure felt nice to have someone worry like that for me.

"No," I said, shaking my head. And then I glanced down at my lap. At my right forearm resting there.

At the piece of tattoo peeking out of my long sleeve.

"Actually, I want to apologize," I said.

"Apologize?"

"For running out on you after you gave me this." I pulled up my sleeve and raised my right forearm as an explanation. "It's really cool. I just got confused."

"Confused?"

"I thought you were making fun of me."

"What?" said Shawn. He reared his head back, deeply alarmed. "No! Why would you...? Why would I...? I think you're awesome."

"Oh, um...thanks." I laughed nervously. "I just...People used to make fun of my voice. Which, now that I think about it, was a long time ago, and I hadn't quite grown into it yet. It cracked a lot when I was younger. But anyway, when you started talking about my voice, I guess I just...assumed."

"No," said Shawn, shaking his head. "God, no. I think your voice is fucking gorgeous."

He blushed the moment he said it.

"I mean...not in a weird way. I just think it's...um. I like it. In a normal way. Like, the opposite of weird." Shawn seemed to be growing more panicked the more he talked. "Fuck, what I mean to say is—"

I put my hand over Shawn's mouth. At first, that caused his panic to spike tenfold. Then he realized I was smiling at him.

"Thank you, Shawn," I said. And then it was my turn to panic a little bit. "Sorry, I mean...Shady? I keep forgetting you don't go by Shawn."

Shawn gently grabbed my hand, still covering his mouth, and he pulled it down just enough so I could see he was smiling back at me. "Actually, I like it when you call me Shawn. Don't stop."

The end-of-lunch bell rang, and thank God, because for once in my virgin life, the sexual tension was as blazing hot and two-sided as Darth Maul's light saber. Someone could get hurt with that thing! I reclaimed my hand, and Shawn helped me to my feet, and it was just enough hand-on-hand contact to make me shiver.

I managed a feeble "Okay, Shawn. Bye, Shawn" and hurried inside before I could accidentally say "Shawn" a third time in a row, good lord.

It was only when I was safely inside the school doors, out of Shawn's line of vision, that I allowed myself to smile so hard that my face hurt.

Ixion Inc sold their AI models to military, police, mercenaries, bounty hunters, even criminals. Ixion was based outside the Totality Yielding and therefore was not bound by TY law. Each model had a different visual aesthetic, combat style, and M.O., thanks to an AI system designed to learn and evolve. Some operated as soldiers, damn good ones. Others were the most qualified soldier and were put in charge. Tanks was a leader.

Second in command was an oversized brute name Narls. Narls had four arms with four very visible biceps that he exercised at the gym every day. Narls didn't believe in "leg day." Narls also had two dicks. He was sure to let everyone he encountered know this.

Narls was deeply upset that he'd been passed up for the promotion again. He didn't believe in putting a female machine in charge when there was a very capable nonmachine man to round up Rotters. He had two dicks, for chrissakes! What more could they want?

These soldiers were called FIRE (Federal Immigration and Rim Enforcement). It was on their armored vests. Most people thought the R stood for Rotter. It might as well have. Their mission was to "monitor the refugee threat and prevent invasion." Whatever that meant. The important thing was that it was being taken care of. Munneez G. Schlump—president of the Totality Yielding (aka POTTY)—promised this.

Henosans were dragged out of their homes and gathered like bundles of sticks. Andromeda and Zaffy went willingly, hands in the air. Where could they go?

The good news was that the lasers were the stunning sort. No one had died. (Not yet, anyway.) The bad news? Aside from everything? Zaffy figured it out. Maybe it was because Andromeda couldn't stop staring. Or that she was muttering under her breath, "No, it can't be, no no no." Her disappointment wasn't exactly subtle. Zaffy glanced back and forth between them. And then she did something either terribly clever or incredibly stupid.

"Hey, Tanks!" Zaffy shouted.

Every head turned. But Tanks's head flipped like a switch blade, eyes narrowing, *literally* zooming in. She stormed over in seven swift steps. Andromeda counted them. The way she moved was like poetry. A tragic poem where everyone dies at the end, but still.

"What did you say?" said Tanks.

Andromeda tried to make a subtle slicing gesture across her throat. Tanks noticed.

"How about you, Lightning Rod?" said Tanks, examining Andromeda up and down.

Okay. That hurt Andromeda's feelings.

"She's an exiled Dresdorian," said Zaffy. "She told me your name is Tanks."

Tanks looked at Zaffy. "She told you?"

"You're in her future," Zaffy explained.

"Please don't," Andromeda mumbled as quietly as possible.

Tanks glanced between the two of them, analyzing the situation, converting facts into numbers, crunching them. Then her gaze tilted up. The three of them had garnered a significant amount of attention, from FIRE operatives and Henosans alike.

"Narls," said Tanks. "Finish processing the Rotters. Make sure everyone gets tagged. I'm going to interrogate these two."

Narls was usually too dumb to be anything but compliant. But since he was still sore about the promotion, two of his brain cells accidentally rubbed together, and now he was experiencing a peculiar sensation known as "suspicion."

"Interrogate them about what?" asked Narls.

"About the Rotter threat," Tanks lied. "Obviously. Do your job. No one is paying you to play with your dicks."

Tanks nudged Zaffy and Andromeda with the barrel of her blaster, herding them to the nearest mud hut. It just so happened to be Trog's.

—Andromeda and Tanks Through Space and Time,
ÆonQ

—TWELVE—

YOU ARE FUCKING PERFECT (JUST THE WAY YOU FUCKING ARE)

TWENTY-YEAR-OLD DEJA WILLIAMS WAS WHAT you would call "internet famous." One of those TikTok/YouTube/next-big-video-platform internet sensations, except she was local (she lived in Gillette), which made her pretty much the coolest person in northeast Wyoming. I followed her because, let's be honest, who *wasn't* following her? Her videos were typically humor-based, completely off-the-wall scenarios. But occasionally she got serious. Sometimes her line between humor and seriousness was razor sharp.

The video she posted late last night started off with her trademark laugh-out-loud wit and biting social commentary, accidentally evolved into an incredibly emotional experience, and then escalated into something that belonged in a horror film. By the end, the horror of it all was the only thing that stuck. If I were to pitch the film rights to Blumhouse Productions, I would say it was *The Blair Witch Project* meets *The Wicker Man* meets *The Purge*.

It started with Deja satirically interviewing people coming in and out of Change Through Grace (aka Camp Gay Away).

Change Through Grace wasn't terrible to look at. It was a sprawling, ranchlike facility with fresh-cut green lawns, winding pathways, and a luscious infrastructure of log cabin–style buildings. Very alluring to the parents who could afford it for their young gaylings. It succeeded at drawing your attention away from the security system, which was designed to keep people in, not out.

Not all prisons had bars.

For her impromptu interviews, Deja had dressed up (hilariously) in some Puritan-looking Colonial-era dress that would have looked *great* on a full set of sister-wives. It came with a matching bonnet.

DEJA: "Excuse me! Excuse me, sir. Hi. Hello. My name is Sister Deja Chastity Makegoodchoices Williams. I'm here interviewing the people of this fine establishment to get a sense of the good work of God you are doing here. Are you a doctor? Or a priest? Or a doctor-priest or something? That is a very nice suit, by the way. Did you purchase it at the Salvation Army?"

Deja rotated her camera so that it was focused on both her and an ancient wisp of a man wearing gold-framed aviators and the ugliest suit I had ever seen. It was a double-breasted brown thing, constructed from a vaguely shiny material, with oversized lapels. The whole look screamed: *I was real big in the seventies.*

DOCTOR-PRIEST: "I'm sorry, what is this for again?"

DEJA: "Oh, I'm sorry. I'm homeschooled, and my teacher, Mama Williams, wanted me to write a report on deadly diseases. I hear you're treating a terrible illness known as the gay?"

The doctor-priest lit up, and not in a way that understood this was a joke.

DOCTOR-PRIEST: "You know, it's funny you should say that, because I genuinely believe homosexuality and its appendages—gender dysmorphia, political correctness, et cetera—to be the great plague of this generation. You should count yourself lucky to be homeschooled. It might very well be the most contagious disease out there!"

DEJA: "So is there like a vaccine for it, or . . . ?"

DOCTOR-PREIST: "Oh no, dear, it's not that sort of disease."

DEJA: "Oh good, because my teacher, Mama Williams, always says that vaccines are the devil's heroin."

DOCTOR-PREIST: "I'm sorry, she says what?"

Deja interviewed anyone and everyone coming in and out of the main building—from the highest-ranking ecclesiastical types clear down to the janitor—to hilarious ends. The jig was pretty much up by the time a mother came marching in with her teenage son, who was all packed up and ready to be sorted out like a rogue lock of hair beneath the hot clamp of a hair straightener. He looked like this was maybe the worst day of his life. Then he saw Deja and recognized her in an instant.

BOY: "Oh my gosh, you're Deja Williams!"

DEJA: "Uh, yep. Yes. It is me. Deja Purity Virginityintact Williams. From church."

BOY: "Oh my gosh, Deja, I am such a big fan."

He didn't *mean* to give Deja up. He was simply starstruck. You could see it in the actual stars in his eyes.

MOTHER: "Wait a second. You're not one of those filthy TikTokers, are you?"

DEJA: "Uhhh—"

MOTHER: "I thought the president did away with you people. You ought to be ashamed of yourself. What you are doing is illegal!"

DEJA: "Oh wow. Well, for starters, that orangutan in a business suit isn't president anymore—"

That went over as well as one could expect. The mother marched in, huffing indignantly, clamoring for security. Meanwhile, Deja offered the boy a hug, which he accepted like a treasure. He was in tears when they finally broke apart.

This, of course, only made Deja a teary-eyed mess.

DEJA: "They can't change you."

BOY [sniffling]: "I know."

DEJA: "You are perfect just the way you are."

BOY: "Thank you, Deja."

The boy wiped his eyes with both hands and shuffled inside. Only when he was behind those glass doors did Deja drag her long, voluminous dress sleeve across her eyes. She sniffed violently before daring to look directly into her camera phone.

DEJA: "Welp. I think that's enough shenanigans for one day. Just remember: You are perfect just the way you—"

A figure stepped around the building behind her—and into the camera's view. He was wearing dark jeans, a black hoodie, and a rubber mask that looked like a sheep's head. In the spectrum of scary things, you would not imagine a sheep's head to be up there, but this rubber sheep mask on a strange man's head was the absolute scariest fucking thing you had ever seen.

You could see the horror in Deja's expression.

She turned the camera so that it was exclusively on him.

DEJA: "Hey, buddy. You're a little old for Halloween, aren't you?"

She was *trying* to sound unafraid.

She was not entirely successful.

Sheep Man said nothing.

DEJA: "Okay, well, I don't have any candy, so..." [muttering under her breath] "...fuckin' weirdo."

She turned the phone back on her face, and that's when she—and every single one her followers—saw a *second* masked man, wearing the rubber face of a goat, standing behind her from the opposite side of the building. His hands were behind his back.

When he pulled his hands away, he was holding a baseball bat.

"Fuck," said Deja, and she broke into a frantic sprint. "Fuck fuck fuck fuck fuck."

Her camera swung wildly in her grip, only briefly capturing sight of two masked men chasing her.

She made it to her car, tossing her phone on the passenger seat, and with a lovely view of her car ceiling, we heard her start the car, peel out of the driveway, and make a successful escape.

All the while, she was swearing and sobbing.

♩ ♫ ♪

A version of that video made the evening news. Police were investigating the incident. Although "investigating" seemed to be a loose term, because Chief of Police Daryl Wilkins seemed to have already decided that this was nothing but karma.

CHIEF WILKINS: "We are taking this incident very seriously. I've already spoken with the leadership at Change Through Grace. They are appalled and have ensured their full cooperation in our investigation. With that said, since Deja remains unharmed, I see this as more of a learning experience than a proper police investigation. It should go without saying that when you harass people and their spiritual beliefs, you shouldn't be too incredibly shocked when they retaliate. Let's all just hope that Deja Williams finds more productive ways to spend her time in the future. Get a job, maybe?"

WXYZ 23 News chose not to edit that interview. Hate in all its shades made the evening news. We watched it during "band practice" at Astrid's guesthouse. One might argue that Astrid's giant TV was getting in the way of our productivity, but in this particular instance, it was fuel.

I was livid.

"Oof," said Astrid. "It's like he *wants* people to know he's a homophobe."

"Oh, I'm sure he does," said Angus, deeply unamused.

"We have to do something," I said.

Danny was chewing on his lip, nodding furiously.

"Okay, yes, but . . . what can we even do?" said Astrid.

I shrugged. Glanced around the room for input. "I dunno. What *can* we do?"

Angus raised his hand. I pointed at him. "Yes. You."

"I'm hungry," he said.

Astrid rolled her head back and groaned. Danny clucked his tongue, disappointed.

"Jesus, what?" said Angus. "Am I not allowed to be hungry?"

"Are you not bothered by this?" said Astrid. "This should be personal to you."

Angus was a house built on a foundation of eggshells. Just like that, he cracked.

"Of course, I'm *bothered* by this," he said. "I'm actually *very fucking bothered* by this. But what do you expect me to do about it? Give a fucking soliloquy? Shoot rainbows out of my tummy like a goddamn Care Bear? I've had to put up with this shit my whole life, and I can assure you, I'll have to put up with it until the day I die. I haven't survived this far by asking myself what I can do to make pious old fuckwads accept me for who I am."

Astrid frowned. "I *hope* you don't have to put up with this until the day you die."

Angus's mouth was pinched shut. He shrugged.

"I'm not fighting prejudice for the thrill of it," said Astrid. "I want to *end* it. Maybe that's a lot to hope for, but... that's what I *want.*"

Now Angus was frowning.

"Nobody's asking you to do anything alone," said Astrid. She glanced from Danny to me. "We're all in this together. Right?"

"Hell yeah," I said.

Danny blinked—pretending he wasn't devastatingly touched by Astrid's words—and nodded. "Mm-hmm."

"Goddamn it, guys," said Angus. Now he was emotional. But unlike Danny, he wasn't hiding it. He rolled a beefy fist across his glistening eyes. "Okay. I'm in. Let's do something. But—"

His stomach let out a ferocious gurgle—like some Lovecraftian monster slurping an anaconda like a spaghetti noodle.

"I'm really hungry," said Angus, on the verge of tears.

♩ ♫ ♪

As far as being a band was concerned, we hadn't written any "songs" per se, but we had created a sound. With that said, it wasn't a particularly "rock-y" sound. More like a post-rock sound—an experimental subgenre that explored textures and timbres over chords and riffs. I think all of us wanted to create a sound that made us feel things, and this was what we came up with. It was pure atmosphere. In other words, not the sort of catchy tune that you could easily lay words over.

Battle of the Bands was in about a month. We needed to light a fire under ourselves. I thought that if we scheduled venues, places where we were obligated to play, maybe we could finally create something. I presented this possibility to the gang, and they all agreed that it was probably the kick in the ass we needed. So I called multiple places that seemed like they would be into that sort of thing, offering to play for free—the Auberge, the Boom Boom Bar, Slappy's Pub. Happy's Tavern wasn't a viable option because everyone there liked us, and we could have played "Mary Had a Little Lamb" on the kazoo, and Mack still would have given me a pat on the back. We needed pressure. The sort that turns coal into diamonds. We needed to become a fucking diamond.

The manager of Slappy's—some dude named Russ—was the first person to sound even remotely interested. When he asked what we played, I said, "You know, like feel-good garage-rock peace-punk with a whiff of social commentary? That sort of stuff?" Like that was a thing. He politely asked whether we had some samples he could listen to.

Well, fuck.

I emailed him a digital copy of "At Least Satan Respects Women's Rights," which was debatably the least terrible Black Rainbow Infection song. I claimed that it was just a demo version, that the polished version was waaaaay better. Russ kept me on the line while he listened to it. From what I could make out over the line, it was even worse than I remembered.

When the song ended, Russ cleared his throat with tangible discomfort. "Look. I don't have a problem with your skill level. You're high schoolers, I get it. But your political angle is a problem."

The fact that our "political angle" was the problem here—not our nonexistent skill level—made me want to invent new swear words so vulgar that they would psychokinetically cause heads to explode upon hearing them.

I hung up. No offense, Russ. Or all the offense. Whatever.

All this is to say that we had essentially accomplished nothing.

But now the five of us were at a Hardee's, and we were eating for sustenance, not pleasure, and we were talking proactively about What We Were Going to Do.

Well, four of us were doing that. Danny was impressively ignoring his western bacon cheeseburger, scribbling madly on a napkin. We decided to let him do his thing.

"We're a band," I said. "We obviously have to play something."

"Play what?" said Angus. "We have nothing."

"We have the sound," Astrid offered.

"Yeah, but a sound means nothing without words," said Angus.

I was inclined to disagree with that logic. I believed a sound could *absolutely* mean something without words. But I did agree that it was missing something. A context. A layer. Something that would draw meaning out of it.

And then I had a thought. I proceeded to word it in the dumbest way possible.

"Deja was doing something," I said.

Astrid and Angus paused and looked at me like I was next-level stupid.

"Making a video?" Angus suggested.

"No. I mean, she was doing something *aside* from making a video," I said. "What was the point of her being there?"

"To make people... laugh?" said Astrid, sounding deeply unsure of herself.

"She was protesting," said Angus.

I pointed an overdramatic finger at Angus. "Exactly! She was protesting. She was shining a light on something she obviously believed to be wrong. But it wasn't just about her followers. In fact, I would argue that her followers were only her *secondary* audience. She didn't seem satisfied with her work there until she ran into that boy and his mother. When she hugged him, the words that she said to him. She was giving him..."

I really hated using the word I was about to use, but it was the only word I could think of.

"Hope," I said. "I think the whole point of that video was to give someone *hope*. Someone *there*. You guys, what if *we* did that? What if we...?"

"Played outside Change Through Grace," said Astrid.

"Played for those kids," said Angus.

These weren't questions. They sounded impressed.

"Now we just need a song to play," said Astrid.

I know Astrid meant well. But our enthusiasm deflated like an uncorked air mattress.

Then Danny slid his scribbled-on napkin across the table.

Astrid, Angus, and I all leaned forward, cocking our heads

at awkward angles so that we could decipher Danny's chicken-scratch. What it lacked in legibility, it made up for in staggering levels of mindfucking genius.

"Damn," said Angus, slapping his hands on the table. "Hot fucking damn."

♩ ♫ ♪

Danny, Angus, and I asked permission from the Cassidy and Fergusson parental units if we could stay the night at Astrid's house. Astrid asked her parents if she could host a sleepover in the guesthouse. (The only two boys involved were gay, so...) Unanimous parental approval was granted.

We proceeded to stay up all night slamming energy drinks and iced coffee and hot coffee, and tweaking our instruments, and crafting our sound, and scribbling on an entire tree worth of notebooks and paper, and screaming until our lungs blew out. Fortunately, Astrid's neighborhood was so rich that the neighboring houses were like a zip code away from one another, and we could make all the noise we wanted. By approximately four in the morning, we had crafted the single greatest piece of music written over the course of a single night.

When we finished in a scraggly, caffeine-blazing haze, we debated postponing our performance twenty-four hours for the sake of polishing a very rough draft. (And also sleep.) But then we decided that time was of the essence, and the sooner we dropped this bomb, the better the world would be for it. We loaded all our instruments—and also roughly a mile of extension cord from

Astrid's garage—into Astrid's and Angus's cars, drove the forty-five minutes to Change Through Grace, and proceeded to set up on the front lawn under the civil twilight.

"Have you ever heard of electric drums?" Angus whispered. He was carrying the rack with the cymbals, walking deathly slow, like he was traversing a minefield.

"Have you ever heard of tacky?" Astrid whispered back. "Oh wait."

She grabbed Angus's short-brim straw fedora and planted it on her head.

"Oh, I forgot to tell you, Satan called," said Angus. "You got the job."

"Oh yay!" said Astrid. "Which one?"

"*The* job. Satan's job. He's going into retirement. You're the new Satan. Congratulations."

"Well, it's *about time* a woman ran the place."

"You do realize," Danny said quietly though his teeth, "that this is a *stealth* operation?"

"Astrid and I are the two loudest people on the planet," said Angus. "*You* realize this. It's your fault for inviting us."

"That is an exaggeration," said Astrid.

"Mmm, well," I said, tilting my head side to side.

The amps and guitars were already in position, plugged into a Belkin SurgePlus multioutlet, which was plugged into a dark green, vaguely camouflaged series of extension cords that ran all the way to the facility and an outdoor outlet hidden behind perfectly kempt shrubbery. (We caught the briefest glimpse of a groundskeeper using it during Deja's video.) The sun's rays were just barely beginning to peek beyond the horizon, bleeding orange into the purple sky, which would be all the light we needed.

All that was left were these fucking drums, my God.

Angus set down the cymbal rack, the fifth and final piece.

"Are we ready to rock and roll?" I asked, sort of desperately.

Astrid was wearing a pair of night-vision goggles around her neck. They belonged to her dad, the Crook County mayor. Apparently, an important part of Wyoming politics was being an aggressive part of the hunting scene. She pulled the goggles up, adjusting them over her eyes so that they protruded blockily beneath the brim of Angus's godawful fedora. Tweaked the cymbal rack. Leaned back and observed. Tweaked it again. Leaned back again.

Nodded.

"Let's wake this place up," she said.

"Gimme that," said Angus, snatching the fedora off her head.

The edges of the sky were drenched in the orange of dawn. It was almost 7 a.m., meaning the local ordinance for "quiet hours" was about to end.

And boy, would it end.

♩ ♫ ♪

What we had planned came in two phases. Phase One was that first original piece of music we had created as Hope Cassidy and the Sundance Kids. Now that we had context, we renamed it "The Calm Before the Revolution." It started with Danny, plucking out a lullaby on his guitar. Something soft, and melancholic, and gushing with empathy. Angus joined in, strumming gentle ambiance on his bass. It was less a tune and more like organisms living and growing. Astrid came in on drums like rolling waves, ebbing and flowing, crashing on the shore and drawing away.

I sang.

I didn't sing words. We didn't write words for this part. Instead, I channeled something that at its core resembled "Vocalise," a song composed in 1915 by Sergey Rachmaninoff. It contained no words and was meant to be sung in any one vowel of the singer's choosing. I modernized it with some funky Lady Gaga flare.

Slowly, like something out of *Night of the Living Dead*, sleep-drunk teenagers congregated in the windows. Boys on one side of the facility, girls on the other. For some reason, Change Through Grace was real big on segregating the genders, which was, um, *interesting*, given the circumstances.

As dozens of sleepy bodies pressed against the glass—squinting at four legendary silhouettes making noise on the front lawn—sleepiness dissolved into electric curiosity.

Apparently two staff members were paid to sleep there as well, just in case shit hit the fan: a bearded dude wearing a shirt that said "Let Go and Let God," and some pajamas-wearing Poindexter with a face like a sharp wedge of cheese.

Poindexter, or Pajamas, or Cheese Face—whichever you prefer—marched onto the dewy front lawn in slippers and exclaimed something I could only hear because I had the ears of a fox.

This was part of the plan because Poindexter would have had to disarm the alarm to leave the facility. Passengers were now free to roam about the concert.

That's when we entered Phase Two of our nefarious plot and exploded into a little song we called "You Are Fucking Perfect (Just the Way You Fucking Are)." It was inspired by what Deja said to that boy. (But, you know, spicier.) Every single instrument exploded into the intro like a wild army of snarling rabid unicorns and punk-ass Care Bears shooting white hot rainbow lasers of love and self-acceptance and fucking magic.

And I fucking sang my gushing, bleeding heart out.

They think they can change you,
That they can rearrange you,
Tell you who to like,
Fucking Bellatrix Lestrange you.
But they don't care about you,
Don't know anything about you,
That's why I'm here to say,
What you need to know about yooooooooou

I held that "you" like a pin in a grenade, and when I pulled it, it was pure obliteration. Solid matter came apart, unwritten and undone. I exploded into a fiery, feel-good chorus like an extinction event.

ARE FUCKING PERFECT
Just the way you fucking are!
You're a sensation,
You are a fucking star.
YOU'RE FUCKING PERFECT
Up close and from afar,
And if they can't see that, they are blind,
Blinded by a fucking star.

It was only now that kids were realizing there was nothing keeping them inside. And for that matter, there was nothing keeping them from rocking out. At first, they trickled out—*one, two, three*—and then they poured out—*ten, twenty, thirty!* By the time Hope Cassidy and the Sundance Kids came charging into the second verse, in a sweaty, screaming, blood-pumping blaze, every single teenage resident of Change Through Grace—all sixty-six of them—were moving, bobbing, escalating steadily into a full-on mosh.

"What is happening?" said Bearded Dude.

"You people need to leave!" said Poindexter.

He was trying to sound threatening. *Trying* to be louder than us, which was absurd and majorly futile. His eyes, however, were big and scared, and his chest was heaving beneath those button-up PJs like a paper bag being hyperventilated into.

"I'm going to give you until the count of ten," he continued. "One! Two! You don't want me to get to ten, believe me! Three!"

It hurts to be rejected
They think that you're defected
What you have is a disease,
To be gay's to be infected.

"Six," said Poindexter, nostrils flaring like American flags. "Seven!"

But you're fucking beautiful
You don't have to be so dutiful
If they can't take you as you are
Your life is not the fucking Crucibleeeeee

"Ten!" Poindexter exclaimed anticlimactically. "That's it. Ooh boy. You made me get to ten. That's it."

Danny, Angus, and Astrid banged on their instruments with primal madness, holding those notes before the chorus in a warlike trance. I let go of that syllable—the "uhl" at the end of Crucible—and took a moment to address my audience.

"I need some help singing this chorus," I said. "Your line is 'You're fucking perfect.' I'm not going to sing it. Which means I need all of you to sing it as loud as you humanly can. I want you to sing so loud, your lungs bleed and your hearts explode. Do you think you guys can help me with that?"

"Yesss!" came the resounding, overwhelming response from a wave of moshing teenagers.

"Are you sure?" I asked.

"YESSS!" they screamed with throbbing, pulsating insanity.

I shrugged and offered a slinky smile. "Well, okay then!"

The Sundance Kids detonated into the chorus on a supermassive scale, but even they were no match for the sixty-six voices that joined me on vocals.

"*YOU'RE FUCKING PERFECT!*" they screamed.

> *Just the way you fucking are!*
> *You're a sensation*
> *You are a fucking star.*

Poindexter thrust his fists at his side and declared, "That's it! I'm calling the police!"

"*YOU'RE FUCKING PERFECT!*" all sixty-six teenagers screamed back at him.

Poindexter harrumphed indignantly and then haplessly scampered off to call the police.

Up close and from afar
And if they can't see that, they are blind
Blinded by a fucking star.

"Yes, they're singing!" Poindexter shouted into his phone, covering his ear with his free hand. "No, I don't know why. I dunno, some sort of rock and roll song? There's a lot of swearing in it. Look, I can barely hear you, can you just send the police? This has to be some sort of crime. Okay, thank you. Okay, bye."

The next portion of the song waxed soft and instrumental as we entered the bridge. Here, Danny had given instructions: *Talk to them. Spill your heart out.*

"When I was thirteen years old," I said, "my big sister came out to me. She was fifteen years old at the time, and she was my best friend. She was my whole world. I watched her fall in love—even though it was in secret, and I was the only other person who knew about it. She was afraid of what would happen if people knew, and you know what? She had reason to be afraid! Because last year, someone found out. And that person outed her, and my parents rejected who she was, and they tried to send her here. They tried to send her to Change Through Grace. And you know what she did? She ran—" I choked on a sob. "She ran away from home! And I haven't seen or heard from her since then. This song is dedicated to her. So, when we sing this chorus one more time, I want you to sing so loud that she can hear it, wherever she is. I want you to sing so loud that it reaches every queer kid who has ever been rejected just for being who they are. Do you think you can do that?"

"Yesss!" came the resounding response.

"I'm sorry, what was that? I couldn't hear you."

"YESSS!" they screamed.

"Okay, fine."

We exploded into the chorus one last time, and it was so loud that I could barely hear myself over the poetic calamity of their voices. It was the most beautiful thing I had ever heard. I saw several teenagers in the crowd become teary as they made the most noise they were capable of making. And then I glanced over my left shoulder and then my right shoulder and realized, Danny, Astrid, and Angus were crying as well. Tears streamed down their cheeks as they simultaneously smiled and frowned in that way you do when it's just too much. I sort of stopped singing as I took it all in, but it didn't matter, because the chorus had taken on a life of its own; it had become a living, breathing thing. I became sort of lost and breathless in the transcendental beauty of that moment, seventy teenage voices united as one.

It wasn't until the very end that sirens sliced through us like a scalpel. A disco of red and blue lights flared down I-90 East, and the police arrived to shut down the revolution.

Some people may tell you that this day was not as epic and spectacular as I've made it out to be, and maybe they're right. But where it existed for me, in my heart, it was.

This is my story, and I'm sticking to it.

As Tanks disappeared with the interrogatees, Narls's beady eyes scanned the captive refugees, conscious and unconscious. Some were just now starting to wake up from the stun blast, blinking, twitching, but otherwise paralyzed with neuromuscular incapacitation and, worse, fear. His gaze locked on to an operative whose name he could never remember; too many letters were involved. Instead, Narls called him "Ears." It was because his ears reminded Narls of sails on a boat. He had what Narls liked to call "super hearing."

"Yo, Ears," said Narls. He didn't have to say it loud. Ears looked at him, slightly concerned.

Narls made a get-your-big-eared-ass-over-here gesture with his two right arms. Ears's concern escalated. In general, if Narls wanted Ears specifically for something, it was for something he wouldn't like. He hobbled over reluctantly.

"Yes, Lieutenant Fairweather?" said Ears.

"Ears, I want you to spy on Tanks. Find out what she's talking about with those two Rotters."

"You want me to spy on Captain Tanks?"

"Did I stutter?"

"No, I... it's just that... isn't that insubordination?"

Narls made his angry face, which was identical to his constipated face, and it was horrifying on both accounts.

"I mean, she's our boss," Ears tried to explain.

"I'm your boss, you big-eared doink! What's my name?"

"Uh, Narlson Fairweather?"

"Lieutenant Fairweather. L-O-O-T...N...Look, you know how it's spelled, you giant-eared dummy. How many dicks do I have?"

"You have two dicks, sir," Ears mumbled uncomfortably.

"I have two great big Totality Yielding dicks. And when I give you an order, that's an order from your boss. Do I make myself clear?"

"Yes, sir. Sorry, sir."

"Get those goofy-ass ears out of my sight," said Narls, shooing him away with all four hands. "Don't come back until you have some juicy intel for me."

Ears scuttled away hastily. Dipped into the shadows, crouching low, making a straight line for the glassless window of Trog's hut.

—Andromeda and Tanks Through Space and Time,
ÆonQ

—THIRTEEN—

PUBLIC RELATIONS

THE GOOD NEWS WAS THAT WE DIDN'T GET FINED or arrested. Honestly, surprise gay rock concerts at conversion therapy camps were new legal territory for Sundance PD, so they let us off with a "stern warning" and lots of finger wagging.

That was it. Just good news. Unless you counted our sheer collective level of sleep deprivation. I, for one, was having trouble walking, let alone hauling band equipment back into Astrid's and Angus's cars. But I wore that sleep deprivation proudly, like a battle scar. Danny seemed to be the least sleepy of all of us, so he offered to drive Angus's car because Angus was so sleepy that he couldn't even put words in the correct order in a sentence.

"Thank Danny," said Angus. And then he blinked. "Thank*sssss*. You. Thanks Danny, *you*. Wait. I mean—"

"Get in, buddy," said Danny, clapping him on the shoulder. "You've earned some sleepy time."

Angus giggled hysterically at this, then passed out in the passenger seat a second later.

When we finally arrived at Astrid's guesthouse, we didn't even bother unloading the band equipment. I only had the vaguest memory of wandering dreamlike to one of the two bedrooms, at which point I fell into a great black pool of amnesia.

I dreamed of Faith. I couldn't tell you the exact details of the dream, but I think we were both in elementary school, and I was having nightmares, so Mom and Dad let us camp out in the living room in a fort made of couch cushions with a sheet draped over the top.

Except we weren't *completely* in elementary school because I remembered Faith was queer, and Faith told me how much she liked my tattoo and that she loved my rock band and our performance at Change Through Grace. Then I started sobbing and telling her how much I missed her and asking why she left me. Didn't she love me anymore?

"*Shhhh*, it's okay," said Faith, although her voice sounded weirdly like Danny's. "Everything's going to be okay."

I woke up to midafternoon daylight pouring across my face, and then I realized someone was knocking at the front door of Astrid's guesthouse. I processed all this slowly. Then I realized my arm and leg were draped over warm flesh, and then I realized that flesh belonged to Danny Roger.

In terms of wakefulness, I went from zero to a hundred in one second flat. Danny's back was facing away from me, scooted all the way to the edge of the bed, and yet I was pressed right up against his back, practically in the middle of the bed, big-spooning him like I owned the place. But worst of all, my right arm was wedged comfortably under the nook of his neck, and my fingers were *actually touching* his rock-hard bicep.

The knocking continued.

Ohhhhh boy. *Oooookay.* This was bad. I mean, it was heaven, obviously, and steamy as all get-out—straight up the sexiest scenario I had ever found myself in—but also very bad. If Astrid or Angus walked into this bedroom and found me like this, or worse, *if Danny woke up* and found me spooning him like some of Mary Poppins's sugar to help the medicine go down, I would die.

Some version of the *Mission: Impossible* theme song played in my overworked subconscious as I carefully—very carefully—undraped my left arm and leg from Danny's body. Once I was lying flat on my back, I scooted in subtle, microscopic increments like a starfish across the ocean floor. I pushed my right arm as deep into the mattress as it could go as I attempted to slide it out.

However, now that my body was no longer pressed against Danny's back, his body seemed to realize it had space to move. He barrel-rolled slowly. His beautiful, perfectly shaped head came at me like that boulder in *Raiders of the Lost Ark*.

His face mashed into mine, and then his eyes opened. I'm pretty sure our lips touched, so when we both proceeded to scream, it was practically into each other's mouths.

Just like that, we flew in opposite directions until we were both standing on opposite sides of the bed. I hugged myself awkwardly while Danny rubbed the back of his head and stared everywhere except at me.

"I am so sorry," he said. "I was going to sleep on the couch, but then you started, um, *crying*? When I started to leave the room?"

Oh my God.

"I think you thought I was Faith?" he said. "You kept saying

Faith's name, and you were crying, and I didn't know what to do, so..."

Oh my God, oh my God.

"In conclusion, I'm sorry," he said.

"You have nothing to be sorry for," I said. "I had a dream about Faith, and I think I remember hearing your voice in it, and um... thank you for not leaving me. I obviously have abandonment issues."

Danny's cheeks grew red, but that very well could have been a physiological response to rising temperature in the room because I'm pretty sure my face had inexplicably turned into lava.

Danny *wasn't* bisexual, right? Like, we knew this for a fact. *Right?* I was trying to recall the exact wording of his coming-out post, but the wording as I remembered it seemed just slightly vague and open to interpretation. I suppose I always could have asked Danny myself if he was bi, but I wasn't entirely sure how to execute this very simple task without sounding like the thirsty fool that I was.

The knocking at the front door had grown a little restless.

"I'm gonna go get that," I said, at the exact same moment that Danny said, "I should get that." We both laughed and cringed in unison.

I reached the front door first. Normally, under no circumstance would I have answered someone else's front door, let alone the weird non-front door to someone's guesthouse, but I was sort of desperate for an escape.

Standing on the other side of the door was Deja Williams.

When she wasn't making satirical internet videos, Deja Williams was glam as fuck. Her hair was an elegant tapestry of braids. Her sense of style was like New York hip-hop, California surfskate,

Shibuya street fashion. I dunno, man; she just looked fuckin' cool. She had a nose ring.

Naturally, Astrid and Angus chose now to finally wake up from all that knocking. They crossed paths with Danny in the living room, and then all three of them noticed the internet celebrity standing at the door. They acted like a bunch of janky robots who had just been disabled by some explosive electromagnetic pulse.

"There they are!" said Deja, clapping her hands as all four of us ceased motor function. "There's my band!"

"Deja?" said Angus, finally blinking himself out of a coma. *"Williams?"*

"Oh my God," said Danny. "I am such a huge fan."

Astrid clapped her hands over her mouth as her eyes doubled in size.

I couldn't even do that. I was full-on deer in the headlights.

Somehow, my petrification did not deter Deja at all. Instead, she smiled enormously, exposing her top gums and even her labial frenulum (the little flapper between your upper lip and gums). That makes her smile sound gross, but it was truly a work of art.

"Can I hug you?" Deja said to me specifically. "Is that weird? You know what, I don't care if it's weird. Can I hug you?"

"You should hug her," said Danny.

"Definitely hug her," said Angus.

"I want a hug," Astrid whimpered through her hands.

Deja hugged me, and while I turned into an embarrassing lump of putty in her arms, she said, "Don't worry, Astrid Nguyen, you're next!"

"SHE KNOWS MY NAME," Astrid screamed.

♩ ♫ ♪

Someone had filmed us and posted the video online.

Who did it should have been an incredible mystery. Phones were confiscated before you were admitted into Change Through Grace. But the sneaky little filmmaker outed himself real fast. It was right when we transitioned from "The Calm Before the Revolution" to "You Are Fucking Perfect (Just the Way You Fucking Are)." The camera turned 180 degrees onto Bearded Dude's face.

Oh. My. God, he mouthed.

The camera quickly returned to us because he didn't want to miss another second. He captured the entire song. The whole goddamn shebang. It ended in sirens and red and blue flashing lights as the police rolled in and teenagers scattered.

Deja Williams treated us to some all-day breakfast at Higbee's Café and showed us the whole thing on her phone. It maybe wasn't *quite* as epic as I remembered, watching it later on someone's phone and filmed with a camera of questionable audiovisual quality. But Deja still thought it was cool, and that was all the validation I needed.

The video had nine hundred thousand views. At this rate, it would break a million by dinnertime.

"I hope you don't mind, but I started you guys a GoFundMe page," said Deja.

She opened up a new tab on her phone and showed us the page. And the amount. And holy shit. I'm honestly embarrassed to say the number, but let's just say that it was A Lot of Money.

"That's a lot of money," I verbalized.

"Right?" said Deja.

But I didn't mean it in a good way. "I dunno. I feel weird accepting that."

"Oh, I know. I just wanted to lead with that because I'm afraid I have some, um . . . not-so-great news."

"Uh-oh," said Angus.

Deja pulled up an article on her phone. Passed it around for us to see. "This article just dropped on the *Casper Star-Tribune*."

The article featured a zoomed-in image of Astrid, laughing and pointing finger-guns at an approaching police officer. The image was literally the very last frame of the video. It was accompanied by this headline:

DAUGHTER OF COUNTY MAYOR LEADS RIOT AT CHRISTIAN CAMP

All eyes went from the article to Astrid. Astrid sort of imploded on herself, sinking into her chair, as if to hide behind her massive plate of biscuits and gravy. She seemed deeply uncomfortable that this was suddenly about her and her dad.

Deja took her phone back, typed something else in, and handed the phone back to us. It was the Twitter account of Magnus Nguyen, aka @MagnusWinning. (Crook County Mayor. Christian. Father. American. Nguyen pronounced "Win" as in the opposite of Lose.)

I do NOT support my daughter's riotous behavior. She does NOT exist outside the law. Oh, and as of this moment, her drums are confiscated. They were already loaded up in her car, so I'm driving them to the thrift store as we speak.

And just like that, Astrid was a jack-in-the-box, popping out of her seat, over the table, boldly snatching Deja's phone right out of her hands. Her eyes were like angry balloons.

"LIKE FUCK HE IS," said Astrid. "He can't give my drums to a thrift store. They're SONOR!"

"It's okay," said Deja. "That's why I started the GoFundMe. We can buy you a new drum set."

"But...they were handmade in Germany! From fifteen-hundred-year-old Romanian river oak!"

"What?" said Danny. "Really?"

"They were limited edition," said Astrid, faraway, becoming lost in herself. "Only fifty of them were ever made."

Angus, Danny, and I exchanged sympathetic glances. I'm not saying Astrid wasn't spoiled. But I could understand why this was a crisis.

"How much were they?" asked Deja.

Astrid shook her head. "Don't make me say the number."

"Was it more than what's in the GoFundMe?"

Astrid started crying.

"Okay...," said Deja, nodding, undeterred. "I have an idea."

She took back her phone. Her willowy thumbs danced across the screen.

"There," said Deja. "That ought to do something."

She passed the phone around. Twitter again. She had retweeted Magnus Nguyen with this comment:

Deja Williams ✔ @YaGirlDeej
Currently having a very late breakfast with the four teens who rocked Change Through Grace. Astrid would really like her drums back. Can we keep eyes out at the local thrift stores?

The tweet was collecting likes every second we passed it around. When it reached Astrid, she drew in a deep, collecting breath and let it out. Nodded. She was okay. She was better now.

When the phone circled back to Deja, her eyes doubled in their sockets. "Oh my God. We got a bite. Y'all, we got a bite!"

"WHAT?" said Astrid.

Once again, she snatched Deja's phone right out of her hand. Danny and I leaned in, sandwiching her, while Angus crowded in behind.

Frank @1234frank
This set literally just came in. I work at the thrifty schwifty on san jacinto and davis, across from the taco bell. I'll hide it as long as I can, but you should hurry before my boss finds out.

"Check!" said Deja, waving her hand in the air. "'Scuse me, can we get our check?!"

♩ ♫ ♪

In the spectrum of dumpy thrift stores, Thrifty Schwifty was actually kind of not terrible. It had a bit of a hipster vibe and went well beyond clothes into accessories, decorations, apartment items, thingamabobs, whatchamacallits, doohickies, and a whole corner dedicated to Neat Random Shit. As if Urban Outfitters had shagged the Goodwill.

Frank messaged us to meet him "around back by the dumpster," which was mad sketchy, but what choice did we have?

The moment we rounded the corner, there was the dumpster, and there was Astrid's drum set—gleaming in the sun, shiny and new. Standing conspicuously between them was a man who could only be Frank, looking like the seediest black-market organ dealer.

Frank was a squatty, froglike man, mostly bald except for the unwitting tufts of hair on the sides of his head that had a real "reach for the sky" attitude. I think he rolled out of bed like this. His T-shirt said, "This is what a feminist looks like."

"My baby!" Astrid exclaimed. She was out of the car before Deja even came to a complete stop. She flew past Frank. Draped herself over her drum set, trying her damnedest to hug the whole clunky thing. "I'll never let you go. Never ever."

The rest of us exited the RAV4 and awkwardly observed, but we shared a general collective peace of mind.

"Thank you so much," said Deja, turning her attention to Frank. "Do we owe you anything?"

"No way," said Frank, shaking his head adamantly. "My niece is in that concentration camp you kids rocked out at. My sister and her husband are trying their damnedest to ruin that poor girl's life. You all did a wonderful thing. Thank you, from the bottom of my heart."

Astrid finally stopped hugging her drums, but because she

was emotional and needed to hug something, she ran and hugged Frank. "Thank you, thank you, thank you," she said.

Frank chuckled and gave a lopsided smile. "You kids just do me one favor."

He looked directly at me.

"When this Battle of the Bands comes around?" said Frank. "You put those sleazy Alt-Rite pieces of shit back in their place."

♩ ♫ ♪

We loaded Astrid's drums into the trunk, said goodbye to Frank—a side of Sundance I wasn't even aware existed—and Deja began to drive us home. None of us talked. But not for lack of anything to talk about. I think we were all just processing.

Deja broke the silence. "Random question: Do y'all have a band manager?"

Astrid ended up riding shotgun, which meant that she immediately turned back and looked at us with her eyeballs bulging. Nothing inconspicuous about it. If we were trying to play it cool, we were failing.

"No . . . ?" I said, hoping that wasn't the wrong answer.

"What if I was your band manager?" said Deja. The moment she said it, she seemed to immediately rethink it. "Is that weird? It's weird, isn't it."

Astrid basically didn't budge from her awkward, turned-around position. But she did open her mouth. I could see her retainer on the roof of her mouth. It was kind of gross.

"Look, I'm not trying to make a dime off your minute in the spotlight," said Deja. "When it comes to what you guys are doing—who you *are*—money does not interest me. I don't want to see a cent. What I want is for you guys to succeed. I want this country to succeed. And right now, it's not. Right now, America is rooted in patriarchal dogma, blindness to perspective, and unwillingness to change. If anything has changed, it's empowerment to prejudice and bravery among bigots. But you four... you four are change. You're change, and you're hope, and you're—quite frankly—kind of insane, and I love it. What I'm trying to say is—"

"YES," said Astrid. "A THOUSAND TIMES YES."

"What?" said Deja. "Really?"

"Um, yes please," Angus said, hands pressed flat together, ready to beg.

"You're basically the coolest person that we know," Danny explained.

"If you're our band manager, is it tacky to ask for an autograph?" I asked.

"Okay!" said Deja, nodding overexcitedly. Against all logic, she was acting like *she'd* just been accepted by the cool kids. "First things first, we need to give you guys a social media presence. Do you have a name?"

Trog liked to advertise the fact that he had a bad back. It was his favorite thing to talk about. So, instead of a hammock, his bed was a worm-hide mattress that filled a hollowed-out roach corpse—a thing crafted purely from the workshop of his imagination. Whatever the mattress was stuffed with, it was squishy, adding to the effect of sleeping on a real-life worm. Like a waterbed, but infinitely worse. Andromeda was not a fan.

She and Zaffy were forced to sit side by side at the foot of the bed. (Or was it the abdomen of the bed?) Tanks stood over them, blaster pointed nowhere in particular. Tanks's tongue was moving behind her lips, over her teeth, in a deliberate clockwise motion. It was a habit that grossed Andromeda out, but she was aware that she would grow to love it. (Not until her thirties, but still.) For an AI, Tanks felt devastatingly biotic.

Tanks hadn't asked anything yet, and neither Andromeda nor Zaffy had said anything. The silence did not grow more comfortable with time. The opposite, in fact.

"Tell her," Zaffy said finally. Her tone was indignant, as it is with most traitors.

"There's nothing to tell," Andromeda lied. Surely, the heat emanating off her face would give her away. She felt like a bonfire.

"Tell me what?" said Tanks.

The sound of Tanks's voice—like a firm handshake—unraveled Andromeda from the inside. It made it difficult to breathe. It was a voice she had known for so long, and yet, for no time at all. The truth was, this Tanks was a stranger to Andromeda. This Tanks was a mercenary. This Tanks did horrible things to people. People like Andromeda. Was it possible Andromeda's entire destiny, her entire future, was a fucking sham?

"Just shoot me," said Andromeda.

"What?" said Tanks.

"What?" said Zaffy, eyes wide like whole olives.

"Just shoot me," Andromeda repeated. She finally met Tanks's gaze. Locked on to it like two wrestlers grappling. "Whatever I saw in my future was obviously a mistake. You're here to shoot people, and I'm here to be shot. That's the only future we have."

"What future?" said Tanks. Her jaw was taut, her teeth irately exposed.

Andromeda shook her head. "There is no future."

Zaffy bolted upright, clapped her arms stiffly at her sides, and declared, "The two of you are lovers!"

Just like that, Andromeda died inside. This was objectively worse than being shot.

* * *

—Andromeda and Tanks Through Space and Time,
ÆonQ

—FOURTEEN—

KANT SAYS HELLO

BY NOON THE NEXT DAY, HOPE CASSIDY AND THE Sundance Kids (aka @HCatSK) had six thousand Twitter followers and growing. Rapidly. Our bio:

> The official account of Hope, Danny, Angus, and Astrid. Run by band manager **@YaGirlDeej**. Hope is an act of resistance.

Deja ran our account like Jean-Luc Picard ran the USS *Enterprise*—with diplomacy and scholarship and dignified badassery. (Okay, Dad got me hooked on that dumb show, and he was right.)

Anyway, with our sudden, explosive popularity came an army of internet trolls. Assholes like Joe—aka @proudjoe—whose bio read "proud straight white man."

> figures that the liberal media would promote gay anarchy. **@HCatSK** and **@YaGirlDeej** deserve a jail cell right next to crooked hilary

That tweet had been retweeted and liked more times than I could even wrap my brain around. Obviously, the comments section was a battle between people who were repulsed and people who actually subscribed to this inane bullshit. I stopped reading after the third supportive comment.

Deja, however, was a pro, and her response had received just as many likes and retweets.

> *Hillary. Unless you mean Hilary Duff? In which case, what sort of sick fuck hates on Hilary Duff?

I went to school hoping to separate myself from all this. Not that I didn't love what we had accomplished. The spotlight was just a bit overwhelming. I was so used to being invisible at school that it didn't even occur to me that the paradigm had shifted.

I don't know what I was expecting. But what I got was the attention of Dylan Roger.

I was at my locker, right before first-period philosophy, when someone started slow-clapping behind me. The sort of anti-clap that villains do, right before they reveal their Nefarious Plot to Kill You. I turned, and there was Dylan, pacing like a hyena, starved for attention. Hope Cassidy and the Sundance Kids had sort of usurped it all.

"You've got balls," said Dylan. "I'll give you that. Great big *hairy* balls. That was some stunt you guys pulled."

I wish I could tell you that I was not a confrontational person, but I'm sure you're now well aware that was not true. Something about Dylan's pig face, and the ugly pig words that came out of it, filled me with the limitless courage endowed by associating with pure stupidity. It was the sort of courage that got people killed.

"Why," I said, "are testicles automatically associated with courage? If I kicked you in your stupid little balls, you'd be on the ground crying."

Dylan stopped pacing. He strode right up to me until there was barely a breath between us. Hair in his eyes and staring down at me like I was a light snack, now he looked dangerous.

"You wanna try it?" he said.

Danny appeared out of nowhere—out of literal thin air, it seemed—violently shoving Dylan out of the way.

"You stay the fuck away from her!" said Danny.

Stumbling backward, swaying unsteadily, Dylan nearly lost his balance, then regained it. At first, he looked like a wild animal. A snarling, violent thing capable of who knows what. Then he recognized Danny and what was happening, and he started laughing.

"Look at my brother the queer, defending the damsel in distress!" said Dylan. He started clapping again. "Bravo! Maybe you're not so gay after all."

He glanced me up and down, appraising me like some used thing. He didn't seem impressed.

"You're a little out of her league," Dylan added, "but pussy is pussy, I guess."

If Dylan was looking to push Danny's buttons, he'd found the right one.

"You stay the fuck AWAY FROM HER," Danny repeated. Now *he* looked like the animal. I appreciated Danny helping me...but not like this.

"What if I don't?" said Dylan.

He took a step closer to me. Danny's fists clenched like he was trying to crush coal into diamonds. This was about to get physical real fast.

"If you're not interested, she's free game, right?" said Dylan.

He took another step.

"What if I take her out back," said Dylan, "and fuck her on the graffiti wall?"

What happened next transpired over the course of two, maybe three, sprawling seconds.

Dylan grabbed me by the wrist.

Danny lunged at him.

With my free hand, I slipped my seven-hundred-page philosophy textbook from my locker, swung it like an underhand softball pitch, and launched it spine-first between Dylan's legs, right into his nuts. Kant says hello, you shit-eating fuckface.

That knocked the air right out of Dylan. He dropped to his knees, narrowly missing the receiving end of Danny's wrath.

Danny skidded to an awkward halt—blinking, disoriented—as if waking from a fever dream made of pure rage.

Collapsing at our feet, Dylan coiled into the fetal position, screaming, cursing, sobbing, and cradling his stupid little balls.

♩ ♫ ♪

I waited outside Principal Reilly's office until Mom showed up. It was just me alone, waiting. Dylan was in the nurse's office with a bag of frozen peas on his nads, probably dying, judging from the incredible spectacle he made.

I had no idea where Danny was. I was just glad he wasn't here, being punished for defending me.

"Oh, Hope!" said Mom's voice.

My head snapped up from my sneakers, and there she was, wide-eyed, mouth screwed into a distraught frown, looking me up and down.

"Are you okay?" she asked.

The fact that she opened with "Are you okay?" and not "What have you done?" reminded me that I had no idea who this woman was anymore. Forgive me if my gratitude seemed lost in a haze of skeptical confusion.

Mom looked at me as if asking for permission for what she was about to do next. And then she did it anyway. She hugged me.

My arms floundered awkwardly. Eventually, they settled on her back, patting her reflexively.

"Everything's going to be okay," she said. "We're going to handle this."

I wasn't even sure how to respond to this, so I nodded uncertainly. "Okay?"

"I love you," she said. "I'm here for you."

I couldn't even process that, so I kept nodding absently like I was walking off a concussion. "Yeah, okay."

♩ ♫ ♪

"Hope is expelled," said Principal Reilly.

I received that information like a philosophy textbook to the nuts. But instead of screaming/cursing/sobbing, I went into a sort of stasis. Like a coma but sitting upright.

"Expelled?" said Mom. "W-wh-wha-what do you mean, expelled?"

"What I mean is your daughter will no longer be a student at this school," said Principal Reilly. "I can't make it much clearer than that."

Principal Reilly's fingers were interlocked. He seemed composed, but the corner of his mouth was tweaked slightly upward. He was enjoying this.

"But expelled?" said Mom. "For one fight? That doesn't seem a bit... overboard?"

"Is punishing violence overboard?"

"You know what I mean. You can't just, I dunno, suspend her or something?"

"This isn't an isolated incident," said Principal Reilly. "Need I remind you, your daughter had the police called on her just yesterday. Disturbing the peace, instigating a *riot*, the likes of which Crook County has never seen! And now assault? I'm sorry, but this is a pattern of criminal behavior we simply cannot tolerate at this school. Your daughter's expelled, Mrs. Cassidy, and that's that."

I couldn't speak. I couldn't move. I couldn't even feel my face. They'd have to call an ambulance and haul me out of here on a stretcher because I was basically catatonic.

That's when the door barged open, and in came Mr. Britton, like the world's most outraged teddy bear.

"I OBJECT," he declared, like he was stopping the love of his life from marrying someone else at the end of some deliciously terrible rom-com.

Principal Reilly reeled back in his chair. His weak chin absorbed into the flesh of his neck. "You... you what?"

"Object... I object...," Mr. Britton huffed. He clutched his heart with one hand and the doorframe with the other, breathing like a lawnmower trying, and failing, to start. He was clearly out of breath.

"You can't *object*. You can't even *be in here*! Charles, what the hell do you think you're doing?"

"Dylan was sexually harassing her," said Mr. Britton. He hoisted himself upright, raising several sheets of paper clipped together. "I have an exact transcript of what was said, as well as the signatures of over thirty student eyewitnesses. It's all here."

"You have *what*?"

Mr. Britton, flustered but emboldened by the fires of justice, started reading. "Danny: You stay the fuck away from her—"

"Charles!"

"Dylan: What if I don't? If you're not interested, she's free game, right? What if I take her out back and fuck her on the graffiti wall? Oh my God. My nuts. My fucking nuts. I think my nuts are broken. Oh my God, I think I'm going to throw up. Ugh. Ugghh. My nuts."

Mr. Britton lowered the papers robotically.

"Dylan grabbed Hope by the arm before the bit about the nuts," he clarified. "It goes on, but you get the point."

"I'm sorry," said Principal Reilly, unapologetically. "A transcript? How—*why*—do you have a *transcript* of this? You know what? It doesn't even matter. This is all circumstantial evidence—"

"Circumstantial?" said Mom, outraged. He might as well have used the Lord's name in vain.

"And you don't belong in this meeting anyway, Charles, so with all due respect, get out of here."

"There's a video," said Mr. Britton.

The office went silent.

Mom rotated her head 180 degrees—from Britton to Reilly—like a very smug owl. "Circumstantial evidence, huh?"

The sass emanating off this woman. It was glorious.

"A video," said Principal Reilly.

Mr. Britton nodded. "I can send you a copy. I've already sent one to Kathy in HR"

"You did *what*?"

"I cc'd Superintendent Marshall in the email."

"Charles, are you an idiot? HR deals with EMPLOYEES. *We* deal with students."

"Oh, I know," said Mr. Britton. "But we live in a time when sexual harassment is swept under the rug, just for the sake of job security. Like you said, I've been here almost five years. *So close* to getting tenure."

Principal Reilly's face was turning as red as a suspicious cold sore.

"I'd really hate for something to happen between now and then," said Mr. Britton.

Oh snap. This was like a "cruel irony" thing, wasn't it?

A vein bulging in Principal Reilly's forehead looked like it was about to pop. He was in full-blown nuclear winter from the shade Mr. Britton was throwing. Mr. Britton, meanwhile, was trying *so hard* not to smile. There was sure to be nerve damage from the effort.

Principal Reilly redirected his attention slowly—so slowly—to Mom and me.

"Given the circumstances," he said, placing each word

carefully, "I think we can talk about a *brief suspension* in lieu of expulsion."

Mr. Britton threw his hands up in mind-numbed exasperation, all but releasing the papers into the air like confetti.

"Ha!" said Mom. It came out as a sharp, crazed *bawk*. "That's interesting. I'll think about that." She stood up and pulled her purse over her shoulder. "Come on, Hope."

I stood uncertainly as Mom started for the door.

"Mrs. Cassidy?" said Principal Reilly. "We're not done talking about Hope's punishment."

"Oh, I know. I think this might be a better conversation for me to have with Superintendent Marshall. *Given the circumstances.*"

"Mrs. Cassidy, wait!"

Mom opened the door with no intention of turning around. Principal Reilly jumped out from behind his desk, raced her to it, and—yikes—grabbed her by the elbow.

Nope.

Mom whirled and slapped him in the face.

"Don't you dare touch me, you tiny, *disgusting* little man!" said Mom. "I'll tell you what's going to happen: Hope is going to come back to school tomorrow. And the next day. And the day after that, *every day* until she graduates. And you're going to personally see to it that this piece of trash, Dylan, doesn't touch her ever again because so help me, if he does, I'll sue the pants off this school, and you, and the whole GOSHDAMN DISTRICT. Is that clear?"

Principal Reilly looked like he was about to start crying. He sniffed and nodded urgently.

Mom tugged her blouse straight, adjusted the purse on her shoulder, and nodded. "Good."

♩ ♫ ♪

I decided to walk Mom back to the car. All the ill feelings I had been harboring toward her had been dug up and strewn into a wide-open field. They hadn't disappeared by any means. But they were no longer buried inside me. They could breathe. Faith was still gone, and until I knew where she was—knew that she was *okay*—healing was sort of impossible. But right now, I was too mind blown to feel anything but mind blown.

Shortly after we left Principal Reilly's office, Mr. Britton followed. He trailed behind us—a safe ten feet or so—clutching his papers to his chest with both hands.

Mom leaned into me. "Is that large teacher of yours following us?"

I glanced back. Mr. Britton smiled with all his teeth and waved nervously.

"Yeah, he's following us," I said.

Mom stopped and turned. Mr. Britton screeched to a panicky halt.

"Mr. British, was it?" said Mom.

"Uh, Britton," he said. "Like the Celtic Britons. But with two *T*s."

"Ah. Well. I'm incredibly grateful for what you've done for us. What you've done for Hope."

Mr. Britton shrugged. "Compared to what Hope's done for others lately, it was nothing."

That one hit the spot. Her eyes watered over, and she bit her lip, and she nodded.

"Thank you anyway," she said. "It's good to know Hope has such kind people looking after her."

Before she could break into full waterworks, she grabbed my head like melon in the produce aisle and planted a kiss on my forehead.

"I can make it from here," she said. "Get to class. I love you."

"I love you too, Mom," I said.

It just came out. Like a reflex. Like when a doctor taps your kneecap with that little rubber mallet.

I didn't necessarily *not* mean it. I'm just saying.

The seams of Mom's face unraveled with just too much emotion. She nodded jaggedly, tried (and failed) to suppress a violent sniffle, and left school the way people leave movies designed to make people cry.

When Mr. Britton and I finally made eye contact, I begged him with my eyes to please not ask.

"You guys are going through stuff," he said. "I get it."

I told him thank you, also with my eyes.

Then Mr. Britton got this crazy look on his face—a peculiar starstruck look—as he leaned forward and whispered loudly, "You're friends with *the* Deja Williams?"

I gave myself permission to freak out. Smiled like an idiot, made an embarrassing screeching sound through my teeth, flapped my hands like tiny little chicken wings, the works.

Mr. Britton responded by doing pretty much the exact same thing.

We were only human, you know.

♩ ♫ ♪

Danny went running every night. He wasn't pure lean muscle and zero percent—maybe negative—body fat because he sat on his ass watching John Wayne and Clint Eastwood movies. He did that *after* he ran.

It was a ritual. Every night at 8 p.m., he was out the door wearing sweatpants and Adidas Ultraboosts and a pair of wireless headphones, and he came back at 8:30, drenched in sweat that caused his shirt to cling to his perfect but explosively stinky body. His entrance was always a direct path from the front door to the bathroom, where he immediately showered. I can neither confirm nor deny that I've fantasized what those showers were like. (Oh, what I'd give to be a bar of soap!)

Tonight at 8 p.m., however, I was wearing the closest thing to running shoes I owned (Keds), and a pair of unflattering neon green shorts that looked like they'd been cut from the same material as a safety vest, flagging every passing vehicle's attention to the hugeness of my ass, and a hoodie over a T-shirt that read, "i hate running."

I huffed, and I puffed, and I barely caught up to Danny after he bolted out the door.

Actually, he had to stop for me. I managed to grab his attention by screaming, "Wait! Danny, wait! Danny! *Uhggh!*"

Danny stopped. I hobbled up to him, and then I collapsed with my hands on my knees and tried to breathe without hurling. It was harder than you'd think.

"Are you okay?" said Danny.

Funny he should ask. My legs felt like fire, and my lungs felt like fire, and basically everything felt like fire. At what point did this become a 911 emergency? Needless to say, it had been a long time since my elementary school days of The Floor Is Lava and playground parkour. However, for the sake of not appearing like an unathletic lard, I gave a reassuring thumbs-up.

"I'm cool," I wheezed. "Cool cool cool cool [wheeze] cool."

Danny frowned. "I'm sorry about earlier today."

"*You're* sorry?" I heaved myself upright. "What do you have to be sorry about?"

Danny shrugged. "He's my brother."

"So?"

"So he was harassing you because of me."

"He was harassing me because he's a dick."

"Still. It just makes me sick inside to think that he was using you to bait me. And it worked! I was so mad, I didn't even feel like myself. All I could feel was this rage, and this hate, and I can't help but think, if he really did hurt you, you'd be hurt by someone who looks"—Danny swallowed against a surge of emotion—"who looks *exactly like me*. You'd be hurt by someone who has my face. And I can't bear to think of that. I just can't."

We stood that way for a moment, on the side of the road, saying nothing. The asphalt was wet from a soft rain, glistening dark and infinite beneath a long line of streetlamps.

"You know what Kierkegaard says," I said.

Danny didn't, apparently, because he looked at me like I was speaking in tongues.

"Life can only be understood backwards; but it must be lived forwards," I said.

Danny's confusion only seemed to escalate.

"I don't know where Faith is," I said. "I don't know why your family or your old friends or your stupid coach can't see you the way I see you. *I don't know* why life is so weird or fucking hard for either of us. Maybe someday we'll know, looking back. Maybe we'll even laugh about it! But what I do know, right now, is that *you are not Dylan*. Yeah, he has your face, and your last name, but he doesn't have your heart. That heartless piece of shit does *not* have your heart."

Danny looked like he was about to cry. I felt like I was about to cry. Someone needed to lighten the mood, ASAP.

"Also, that kid is dumb as rocks," I said.

Danny erupted into laughter and tears simultaneously.

"Seriously, did your mom drop him on his head as a baby?" I said. "I think his cognitive development didn't make it past the sucking-on-tits phase."

Danny was crying, but I think we merged safely into "tears of hilarity."

♩ ♫ ♪

It was right before I was getting ready to go to bed that I received the weirdest string of text messages I had ever received in my entire life.

> Hey, Hope. It's Shawn. I just found out what Dylan did/said to you, and I wanted to make sure you were okay.

And then:

> I also found out what YOU did to HIM, and I wanted to give you a high five. Dylan can be a real fucking dick sometimes. Sorry you had to deal with that.

And then:

I'm parked outside your house btw. In case you wanted to talk or receive your high five or whatever.

And then:

Jesus, I keep rereading that last text, and I'm realizing what a psycho I sound like. I'm gonna go, but if you ever do feel like talking or whatever—

There was more to that text, but I didn't finish reading it. Instead, I rushed to my window, flung it open, and shimmied out with significantly more finesse than the last time. It was only when I felt the impact of cold, wet grass between my toes that I remembered I was barefoot. Shit. Fuck. I danced across the Kentucky bluegrass, almost slipped and fell, recovered, and made a mostly straight line to the suspicious, janky-looking Chevy pickup truck idling in front of our house.

I watched Shawn *watch me* do this from his driver's seat, which he did mostly with disbelief but also with just a little bit of elation.

He leaned to the passenger side and opened the door, and I flew inside, like we were about to make some heist-movie getaway.

I only barely managed to close the door behind me as I proceeded to giggle hysterically. What was I doing? This was how people got murdered! I laughed harder.

"You okay there?" he said, grinning.

"Yeah, I just, um," I said, and then I snorted. I actually snorted.

Now Shawn was laughing. There was no way you could not laugh at this.

I raised my hand and announced, "I would like to cash in my five now."

Shawn raised his hand as well, and we high-fived. Well, it *started* as a high five. But then our hands just sort of stayed there, flat against each other.

Have you ever just stopped and *felt* somebody's skin? The warmth, the texture, the little palm creases that outline your destiny or whatever? Because *holy fuck*. Every hair follicle on my body was electric.

I laughed nervously and pulled my hand away—even though it was sort of the last thing on planet Earth I wanted to do.

"How did you even find out where I live?" I said. I was *trying* not to smile, but only because my face was hurting.

Shawn laughed. "Um. Do you know who Mavis Mackley is?"

It suddenly became incredibly easy for me to not smile. I said nothing.

"Anyway, that's who told me," Shawn continued, filling the silence. "Mavis and I go way back. I guess...she was friends with your sister? Or something like that?"

"Something like that," I said, faking a smile.

Shawn seemed to sense that the mood had changed and not in a good way. "Sorry, I know this is probably the creepiest thing ever. Mavis and I just got to talking about what happened, and I told her I felt bad for you, and she's like, 'Well, why don't you tell her that,' and she *just so happened* to have your phone number and home address. So, yeah. Sorry."

"I mean, it's not the *creepiest* thing ever," I said.

"Oh yeah?"

"Oh yeah. Like, my grandma Cassidy collects porcelain dolls? She has a whole room full of them. Sometimes, when we visit and stay the night, I'm the one who has to sleep in that room, and when the moonlight hits just right, you can see a hundred little eyes watching you while you try to sleep. It gives me literal nightmares. That, I would wager, is the creepiest thing ever."

"I'm less creepy than the *nightmare room* full of *terrifying dolls*?" said Shawn, laughing.

"Without a doubt."

"Cool. Cool cool cool."

"I mean, personally, I'm not terribly devastated that you came."

"Oh, well, that's good."

"I would *almost* go so far as to say that I don't mind at all."

"You don't...mind?" said Shawn uncertainly.

I bit my lip and shook my head. Very slowly. And *very* intensely.

Shawn and I stared at each other for a long moment. The air between us was like one of those air lock chambers in a spaceship, and the air had just been sucked out. I couldn't breathe.

And then we kissed.

I don't know who moved first, maybe we reacted in perfect unison, but suddenly, we were all over each other. I grabbed Shawn by the face, weaving my fingers into his long hair, longing to push every inch of my body against him.

It was only when I felt Shawn's body reacting to me—specifically, the *thing in his pants* reacting to me—that I panicked, and sort of backed *all* the way up against the passenger-side door. "Oh. Wow. Um." I gave a laugh that sounded like a sob.

Shawn was still on his side of the truck, in a sort of paralysis.

He barely moved an inch. But when his eyes met mine, he looked vaguely horrified.

"I am so sorry," he said, very quietly.

"No, it's okay," I said, the way people do when they're clearly not. I thought of telling him that this was just my first time feeling someone's dick, even if it was fully clothed, but then I opted not to because basically every inch of my body was screaming that message loud and clear.

"Sorry," said Shawn again.

"I'm gonna go," I said. "But thanks for the, um." I clapped my hands together to mimic our high five.

"Oh yeah," said Shawn, nodding like this was a coherent exchange. "No prob."

I exited Shawn's car, and this time, it was a real-life getaway, but the heist itself mostly consisted of pure embarrassment. I ran barefoot across the lawn, hoisted myself clumsily over the windowsill, and fell inside, flat on my back.

It was only while I was sprawled across my bedroom carpet that a reckless grin splintered across my face.

Tanks looked like someone who'd been told a joke and didn't "get it." Andromeda was trying not to read into it—she was trying not to look at Tanks at all—but Tanks's nonreaction was magnetic. It was like sharing your deepest, darkest secret with someone, who then callously wonders why you even bothered.

"So, what?" said Tanks, deadpan. "Like a fling?"

Zaffy sat down. Directed an expectant look at Andromeda.

Andromeda felt the blood rush to her face. The word "fling" circled inside her head like debris in a whirlpool.

"No," Andromeda said quietly. "Not a fling."

"Then what?" said Tanks, rapidly losing her patience. "Are we married? Because if that's the case, then send the divorce papers already because I am sick and tired of this INANE, POINTLESS, STAR-CROSSED BULLSHIT CONVERSATION."

If Tanks had personally slapped Andromeda in the face, it might have hurt less. The time for cold indifference was over. She was genuinely hurt. She might have felt betrayed by the tears falling down her face—afraid it would convey some silly, childish sign of weakness—but now she didn't care what Tanks thought.

The truth—the ultimate truth—was that Tanks didn't care.

"Shit," said Tanks. She read Andromeda's face like subtitles. "Are we married?"

Andromeda shook her head. "Not anymore."

She started for the door. Her hand stopped inches from the doorknob—but not by choice. Tanks grabbed her wrist.

"Wait," said Tanks. Her hard edge was gone. "Just . . . wait."

"Let go of me," said Andromeda.

"Please, just . . . ," said Tanks. "Just let me figure this out."

Andromeda met Tanks's gaze, confused. "Figure what out?"

Tanks bit her lip, suddenly vulnerable. It was a look Andromeda recognized, and she hated how easily it made her susceptible to forgive.

"I could lose my job over this," said Tanks.

"Your job?" said Andromeda.

"If anyone finds out, I . . . I could be considered a liability."

It had only been an hour, and Andromeda realized something about Tanks: Andromeda hated her.

"You think I give a fuck about your job?" said Andromeda. "Fuck your job. Fuck you. I hope you lose everything."

Andromeda wrested her hand out of Tanks's suddenly flaccid grip and opened the door. There, filling the doorway, was Lieutenant Narls. His meaty jaw was crooked into a lopsided smile. Behind him, a wall of FIRE operatives filled the night, blasters held close, anxiously awaiting command.

"Well, if it ain't Mrs. and Mrs. Tanks," said Narls. "Love sure is funny, innit?"

His beady eyes shifted past Andromeda to the prize: Tanks.

"Men, relieve Captain Tanks of her weapon. If she resists, break her arms."

—*Andromeda and Tanks Through Space and Time*,
AEon Q

—FIFTEEN—

EUPHORIA AND DOOM

YOU COULDN'T BLAME ME FOR NOT DELIBERATELY seeking out information about Alt-Rite. Listening to one minute of one of their songs had told me pretty much everything I needed to know about them. It was almost more than I could handle.

I didn't know shit.

People were wearing Alt-Rite shirts to school, which was a lot of things, if not unexpected. What *was* unexpected was that the back of each T-shirt listed the band members and their roles, and because the hallway was always particularly packed when the five-minute bell rang, I found myself glaring indignantly at the back of an Alt-Rite T-shirt on a particularly refrigerator-shaped jock. I accidentally read it.

DYLAN ROGER – LEAD SINGER, BACKUP GUITAR, LYRICS
SHADY SHAWN – LEAD GUITAR, LYRICS
KALEB CARTER – BASS
MAVIS MACKLEY – DRUMS

There was obviously a lot here to find alarming. I found my eyeballs ping-ponging between Shawn's name and Mavis's name, and I didn't know where to stop—which was worse—until my gaze latched on to "lyrics" attached to Shawn's name, which was *definitely* worse, but then I remembered that Mavis was drumming for a band with lyrics like "*Being lesbian's okay as long as you're hot. But sorry, Fugly Cassidy, you are not*," and suddenly my brain broke. The hallway started spinning, and I didn't know what was real anymore. I couldn't walk straight, let alone stand upright. I veered into the nearest locker, threw all my body weight against it, pressing my forehead against the cool metal, and just focused on breathing. Except I couldn't. I couldn't breathe. It was while I was barely standing, sweaty face against someone else's locker, that I glanced down at my right forearm, at the tattoo that was etched into my skin by the lyricist for a band who threw my sister's name on the ground and stomped on it like a piece of trash.

"Hope?" said Danny's voice, miles away from where I was now. "Hope, are you okay?"

I felt his hand on my shoulder, trying to get me to look at him. When I did, he appeared less as a person than as an abstract concept. I looked at his face, and it was suddenly hard to decipher who was Danny and who was Dylan. What was real?

♩ ♫ ♪

Danny walked me all the way to the nurse's office, and there he refused to leave my side, even when the nurse ordered him to. I was lying on some flat padded surface, a bed-type thing, where the nurse instructed me not to move while she tried to evict Danny from the premises. In the end, she gave up and was about to call my mom to pick me up when Danny told her he'd already called, at which point the nurse dramatically threw her thermometer in the air and stormed out of the nurse's office in a huff. I might have thought it was funny if I didn't feel like absolute horse shit.

Danny finally appeared standing over me, and he was in focus.

"You okay?" he asked.

What a question. I was *better*, but I was definitely not okay. I didn't even know where to start, and to be quite frank, I felt a little uncomfortable talking about Shawn, given my feelings for Danny. I didn't necessarily *not* have feelings for Shawn, but the only one who liked me *in that way* was involved in something that made me literally sick to my stomach.

So I started by telling him about Mavis. Who she once was and who she apparently was now.

Judging from Danny's expression, I was pretty sure nothing I told him was news to him. He knew about Faith, so why wouldn't he know about Mavis? Still, he looked a little sadder with each word I spoke, and by the time I finished, he seemed racked with guilt.

"You knew," I said.

Danny nodded sadly.

I wanted to ask why he didn't tell me. But the reason was so painfully obvious; I just wanted to cry.

"There's something else," I said. I was about to tell him that I kissed Shawn last night—I was so close to saying it—but then I just extended my forearm, tattoo up, and said, "Shawn gave me this."

Danny continued to nod grimly.

"Goddammit, Danny! What else do you know?"

There was a part of me that was suddenly very nervous. Could he have seen me make out with Shawn last night? His bedroom window, like mine, faced the road where Shawn's janky truck had been idling like a pollution machine.

Danny offered a weak laugh. "Way more than I wish I did. For example, I know that Hunter, who was our drummer for Roger Roger, dropped out when Dylan kicked me out of the band. I tried texting and calling him to say thank you, that it meant a lot to me, but he never responded." Danny's smile grew as thin as a soft layer of ice over water. "So, that hurt."

How like me to assume that I was the only one with problems here, while I vented to someone who had been completely rejected and kicked out of his home for being who he was. My frown was as deep and sad as the philosophical pessimism of Arthur Schopenhauer.

"There's something else," said Danny.

Of course there was.

"I mean, it's not really important to anything," said Danny. "I just don't want you to find out about it, and then feel like I was keeping it from you. It has to do with Shawn."

I felt my throat constrict.

"But I don't have to tell you if you don't want to know," said Danny hastily. "Because seriously, it's just one more reason on top of a million reasons why we need to beat Alt-Rite at Battle of the Bands. I wouldn't blame you if you don't want to know—"

"Tell me."

Danny sighed and went on to tell me about Shawn's dad,

Robbie Lee. He was a tattoo artist by day—that much I knew—but apparently by night, he was a renowned conspiracy theorist and the voice of the popular alt-right podcast, *The Armed Patriot*, which was about as controversial and upsetting as you might imagine. He was also the leader of an alleged militant group called STREGA (Sundance Taskforce for the Rise and Emancipation of Great America).

Word on the street was, those two guys in masks that terrorized Deja Williams were STREGA.

As Danny told me all this, I found myself staring at my arm again. At my tattoo.

When I freaked out at my mom and threatened to cut off my arm, I was obviously making a dramatic point. I wasn't *actually* about to cut off my own arm. That was bananas.

But now it didn't sound so bananas. At the very least, I wanted to take a potato peeler to it.

♩ ♫ ♪

During lunch, I found Shawn with his bag of Taco Bell out by the graffiti wall. I stormed up to him with swelling clouds of confrontation billowing up inside me. However, I was only looking at Shawn from the side, and just as I was about to round on him, I noticed he was sitting next to someone—Mavis Mackley.

Seeing Mavis knocked the fight right out of me. Her hair was as pink as ever, dyed fresh to the root, and she was laughing at something Shawn said, smiling the sort of carefree smile that I knew would have made Faith melt. A part of me died inside. I didn't know how I had gone so long without seeing her, checking up on her, talking to her. It was as if the moment Faith disappeared, so had any reason for me to associate with her, and I hated myself for it.

Speaking of hating myself, it was with 100 percent self-loathing that I realized I felt a pang of jealousy at how close Shawn and Mavis were—which was *so stupid* for *so many* reasons.

Shawn finally noticed me in his periphery, and he immediately stood up, as if adhering to that old-fashioned rule to stand when a lady enters the room. He seemed both excited and nervous to see me. "Hope, hey!"

Mavis's reaction was a little more reserved. In retrospect, seeing the little sister of your ex-girlfriend was probably not something that would make you jump out of your seat for joy.

"Hi, Hope," she said, smiling politely.

"Why are you two in that band?" I said, skipping the pleasantry.

"Wow. Okay. Nice to see you too." Mavis was visibly annoyed.

Shawn just looked confused.

"What, Alt-Rite?" he said, like the name itself wasn't incriminating. He shrugged. "I dunno. Probably the same reason you're in your band? We both have things that we believe in. That we're passionate about. I actually really like that about you." He bashfully rubbed the back of his head and didn't quite look me in the eye when he said, "You're really good, by the way."

My heart fluttered a little bit, which in turn made me want to stab myself in the chest with scissors.

"You insulted my sister!" I said.

Shawn's confusion escalated. Mavis's expression, however, remained very much the same. Maybe even a little sympathetic.

"Shawn didn't write that song," she said. "That was all Dylan." She muttered under her breath, "As if the direct references to Danny weren't a dead giveaway."

Shawn, visibly unable to connect the dots, turned to Mavis for clarity, and she said, "Faith Cassidy is her sister."

His eyes widened with realization. "Oh shit." He looked me dead in the eyes and appeared genuinely sorry. "I swear to God, Hope, I had no idea."

I looked at Mavis. "But *you* knew."

Mavis sighed. She shrugged dismissively. "Sure, Hope. I knew. But I didn't write it. I didn't *sing those words*. I just play the drums because playing the drums makes me feel better. What do you want me to say?"

"What do I want you to *say*?"

Mavis's entire facade of being in a good mood snapped like a twig. "You know, Hope, your sister ghosted *us*. She didn't just ghost me. She ghosted you too. I know this because every damn day since, you've looked like the saddest girl who's ever walked the Earth. It's painted all over your face, like some sad Vincent van Gogh. You act like Faith was the victim, but what about you? What about me?"

Mavis was crying now.

"She left us, Hope! Doesn't that make you mad? Because it makes me mad. It makes me fucking furious! I can understand her running away from home, but not talking to us? Not letting us know that she's okay?" Mavis shook her head and wiped a long-sleeved arm across her teary face. "I'm sorry, Hope, but that's just fucking selfish."

Mavis stood up, collected her things, and marched back into the school. Which meant she had to walk right past me. I could feel the heartbreak emanating off her. Or maybe that was just my own. Sometimes separate heartbreaks had a tendency to bleed into each other.

As she disappeared, I was left standing there, staring brokenly at those tiny words on the graffiti wall: "Faith was here."

"Um," said Shawn, awkwardly. He lifted his bag of Taco Bell. "Do you want a taco?"

I started crying.

"Shit," said Shawn. "Fuck. Um."

Shawn dropped his bag of Taco Bell with a heavy, slightly moist *thop*. He approached me, fidgeting, fumbling.

He tried to hug me.

I reacted like his touch was a needle of static electricity. I shook my head and backed away. "I can't do this. I can't. I just—"

And then I just ran inside.

♩ ♫ ♪

That night, Danny sensed that I was off kilter. He also seemed to understand that I didn't want to talk about it. But it's not that I didn't want to talk about it so much as I feared the judgment. I made out with Shawn. Shawn was in Alt-Rite. Was I a bad person? *Probably* not—unless I still *liked* Shawn.

Oh my God, did I still like Shawn? No. Fuck Shawn. I did not like him.

Did I?

The more I thought about it, the more I realized I was indeed a bad person.

I spent the entire afternoon looking up Shawn's dad, Robbie Lee, just to find out how fucked I was. Rest assured, I was fucked.

Robbie Lee's awfulness could be broken into three categories:

1. Racist. (*The Armed Patriot* featured a very prominent Confederate flag on its podcast page.)

2. Sexist. (One of his podcast episodes was titled "Why Feminism Is Destroying Women.")

3. Homophobic. (Another was called "The Gays Won't Be Happy Until Everything Is Gay.")

After all this research, I felt the need to delete my search history, in case my FBI agent used it to somehow figure out that I made out with Robbie Lee's son, and he judged me too. Then I took a shower that was so hot I shouldn't have had skin anymore, but instead I just came out really red. It was while I was coming out of the bathroom with the complexion of a beet, wrapped in towels, that Danny cut me off in the hallway.

"Hey, Hope, I, oh, um, sorry." He averted his gaze between the floor and the ceiling, as if any part of me had sexual power over him. (I sometimes had to remind myself that it didn't.) "Do you want to watch a movie when you get dressed? It's called *In a Valley of Violence*. It stars Ethan Hawke, John Travolta; it's basically the most underrated western of the last decade."

"Sure," I said, probably sounding anything but excited. "Sounds fun."

About halfway through the movie, when Danny was fully aware that I was distracted, he decided we needed popcorn and M&M's. He had this weird thing where he liked to pour a bag of M&M's directly into the bowl of popcorn. It was such a bizarre and cute snack, Mom basically made sure we never ran out of either. I think she was determined to fatten Danny up because he seriously looked like he had starved himself for some ripped, shirtless movie role.

While Danny was cooking the popcorn, his phone blinked with a notification. I didn't have to snoop particularly hard to see that it was a text from Hunter Thorson.

I proceeded to snoop just a little bit harder, leaning conspicuously over the laptop and Danny's side of the bed to read it.

Hunter Thorson

I need you to stop calling and texting me.

Oof. That wasn't even meant for me, and it felt like a personal attack on my heart.

It was at that exact moment that Danny walked in, catching me dead in the act of reading from his phone. I whipped upright.

Danny glanced from me, to his phone, to me, back to his phone. I literally did not have a single word in my defense, so I just sat there, sweating incriminating beads of guilt.

Danny silently approached the bed and picked up his phone. He read it. And kept reading it. His eyes moved back and forth over that single line so many times, it was pure masochism.

I desperately attempted to repair the situation. "Ti West is such an underrated director. Who goes from a filmography composed entirely of horror films and then up and makes a western out of nowhere? I love it."

It was too little too late. Danny didn't even glance up from his phone. He seemed to be disintegrating where he stood.

"Is it okay if we finish the movie tomorrow?" said Danny, not even looking at me.

"Sure," I said. I quietly climbed off the bed and walked out of the room.

I was just in the process of turning around—having just mustered the courage to ask whether he wanted to talk about it—when the door closed abruptly in my face.

Tanks didn't go without a fight.

She kicked Trog's roach-corpse bed on its side, pulling Zaffy and Andromeda behind it. Bug hide was acid proof, so you better believe this shit was laser resistant. She unstrapped her blaster, back pressed flat against the worm hide mattress, unloading a volley of stun blasts blindly over her head. Because the room was flooding with FIRE operatives, like water into the punctured hole of a boat, every shot connected, accuracy be damned.

"AHHHHHHHHHHHH," Tanks screamed, angrily.

If Andromeda wasn't terrified, she might have thought it was incredibly badass and sexy. But alas, Andromeda was scared shitless. Now that she knew her destiny was a sham, her lifespan seemed vastly unpredictable. Holy fuck, was this how she died?

PSHEW-PSHEW-PSHEW-PSHEW-click-click-click-click-click.

Unfortunately, laser energy was not endless. There was a ten-second recharge period. Ten seconds they did not have.

"Sonuvabitch," said Tanks through gritted teeth.

A pile of stunned FIRE operatives had accumulated in the doorway, but that didn't stop the next wave from climbing over their comrades. They, too, knew the ten-second rule.

Tanks stood up. Slung one leg then the other over the upturned bed. Andromeda almost told her to stop. Almost grabbed her hand. But the moment passed.

The first FIRE operative to lay hands on Tanks, she grabbed by the wrist of his blaster hand, pinning it behind his back. A second operative moved in. Tanks kicked him in the face, a straight vertical movement, redirecting his chin to the ceiling. She kicked him again in the chest, sending him into the wall. A third operative fired shots. Tanks was faster, catching every single blast into her living, breathing FIRE operative shield.

The operative Tanks was holding dropped his blaster, and Tanks caught it as he fell. She had been counting the seconds.

"Ten, motherfuckers," said Tanks.

Wielding twin blasters, Tanks unleashed double the chaos. Trog's house became a graveyard of stunned mercenaries piled waist high. The last shot Tanks fired all but sealed the entryway. The operative collapsed on top of the dozen or so bodies he was attempting to crawl over, leaving a sliver of orange fire light at the top of the doorway.

"Your wife is a badass," said Zaffy, mesmerized.

"She's not my wife, you traitor," said Andromeda, also mesmerized.

The wall behind Andromeda and Zaffy exploded. Zaffy screamed. Andromeda couldn't even do that. A pair of arms the size of baby sandworms (meaning they were humongous) wrapped around Andromeda's abdomen and throat, effectively lifting her off the ground. (Barely. Her toes were grazing the floor.) Her eyes rolled to the side, and she saw the meaty outline of Narls's face.

The meathead had smashed a hole through Trog's house. Of course he did. For Narls, every day was bicep day.

"Drop the weapons," said Narls, breathing heavily into Andromeda's face. "Or I make a wish on your wife and snap her in half."

Tanks pointed both blasters at Narls, but she hesitated. In that moment, Tanks and Andromeda made eye contact, and Andromeda swore to fucking God, she saw a glimmer of the woman she grew old with in there. Had all this happened, and Andromeda just forgot?

That moment was all Narls needed. A FIRE operative shot Tanks through the open window, once, twice, three times—just for good measure. Stunning living organisms was one thing. You never knew with androids.

Tanks shuddered with each impact, then collapsed like a wet noodle.

"Tanks!" Andromeda screamed.

—Andromeda and Tanks Through Space and Time,
ÆonQ

—SIXTEEN—

ANDROMEDA AND TANKS THROUGH SPACE AND TIME

YOU WOULD THINK THAT HOT OFF THE SUCCESS AT Change Through Grace, the Sundance Kids and I would be feeling pretty damn unstoppable right about now. Unfortunately, we rode that high like a wave that took us all the way to the shore, and now we were lying belly down on a beach in the middle of nowhere, and it occurred to us: We had no idea what the fuck we were doing.

There were three main factors that led us to this conclusion.

Factor Number One: We were still having trouble writing new music.

This had everything to do with the fact that we had designated Danny as our one and only lyricist. Who wouldn't? He was basically the perfect teenage boy.

Now suddenly he was suffering from a crippling case of writer's block.

"How are the words coming along?" I asked once, feeling brave. Astrid, Angus, and I had practiced the whole hour without him. And let me just say, trying to perform (let alone compose) *anything* without your lead guitar was like trying to perform basic tasks without opposable thumbs.

Danny was hunched over his notebook, surrounded by a graveyard of crumpled-up paper. He was nervously thwapping his pencil on his kneecap.

"Uuuuhhhnng," said Danny in response.

That was literally all he said. So.

Factor Number Two: We didn't have anywhere to play.

None of us realized what a convenience Astrid's guesthouse had been until we didn't have it anymore. County Mayor Magnus Nguyen had made a very public display on Twitter of banning us from the premises. He changed the locks and set up a security system and filmed the whole process, which he shared online; it was ridiculous. So we couldn't even break in (which Astrid knew how to do; an easy-to-climb tree led to the second-floor bedroom window that you could jimmy with a screwdriver) without alerting the police. The last thing we needed was Chief Wilkins taking a great big legal dump all over our illegal band practice. We *could* have brought this problem up with Deja. She obviously wanted to help. But even with all her connections, Deja couldn't find us a free place to practice. And it was an unspoken, hive mind sentiment we all shared that we didn't want her to spend money on us. So now we were taking turns playing at Angus's house and mine. It was the same story at both places.

"Excuse me?" called Dad. "Excuse...um...*excuse me*?"

He politely knocked on the wooden frame of the garage door, as if we could hear it over the bloodthirsty anarchy of our rock and roll. We were playing a song tentatively titled, "Hey Hey Hey Oh Yeah Woo!" It mostly consisted of us making as much noise as possible on our respective instruments and me screaming non-lyrics like "Hey hey hey oh yeah woo!" Look, it was a work in progress, okay? Danny, meanwhile, was curled up in the corner wearing noise-canceling headphones, scribbling cultish ciphers in his notebook. During practice we didn't talk to him, and he didn't talk to us.

As Dad timidly stepped into the garage, everyone's instruments came to a staggered, vaguely annoyed halt. I stopped screaming. The only person who didn't stop was Danny. I don't think he even knew we had been interrupted. I think he was blasting either a TED Talk or Enya on his headphones.

Anyway, this was the third time one of my parents had interrupted us that day. *Just* that day.

"Hey, guys!" said Dad, wearing the overcompensating smile of the proverbial Bearer of Bad News. "I hate to be that guy, but is there a chance y'all could turn it down just a teensy-weensy little bit more?"

It was also the third time my parents had asked us to "turn it down." Like Astrid's drum set had a volume knob.

Dad turned to me with eyes that said, *Please, I'm begging you.*

Astrid, Angus, and I exchanged glances that ranged from exasperated to bleak. We couldn't keep going like this. No one could.

"Sure, Dad," I mumbled.

Danny kept scribbling, off in some distant world separate from ours.

Factor Number Three: Our individual lives were falling apart.

Everyone has their own shit to deal with. We were no exception. Astrid felt that she had let the band down by losing the guesthouse. That text from Hunter was the straw that finally broke Danny. Not hearing from Hunter may have given him some flicker of hope that he hadn't been *completely* rejected by his former life. Now that hope was gone. And me? I was still reeling from the fact that I had accidentally made out with the lead guitarist and lyricist of Alt-Rite. I couldn't tell anyone. Not ever.

At least not until Astrid left band practice more discouraged than ever, Danny retreated to his room like it was a hiding place, and Angus—who was the only one of us with all his shit still together—cornered me like the last cream puff at the buffet.

"Okay, what the fuck is going on with everyone?" said Angus.

"Uhhhhhhhhh," I said, eloquently.

"Scratch that. I know what's going on with Astrid. And I *think* I know what's going on with Danny. You can only pretend to be happy after being rejected by all your friends and family for so long; it was just a matter of time before he broke. But *you*." Angus gave me an Uncle Sam–like point. "Something's up with you. I know it. And I'm going to be *super* annoying until you tell me what it is."

He squinted.

"It's a boy, isn't it?"

Shit sandwiches.

"Don't lie to me, Hope, I can smell boy trouble from a mile away—"

I slapped my hand flat over Angus's mouth, silencing him. "Okay, *shush-shush-shush*, I'll tell you," I whispered, "but you have to swear to God that you won't tell anyone. I'm only telling you because your boyfriend likes PewDiePie."

"Oh mah gahd, isht's tshat bahd?" said Angus's muffled voice through my hand.

"I need you to swear!" I removed my slightly moist hand and wiped it on my pants.

"Okay, I don't believe in God, but I swear on RuPaul, which is basically the same thing," said Angus, panicking.

I took a deep breath.

"Okay, this isn't a *thing*," I said. "I didn't know he was in Alt-Rite when it happened, but I may have sort of accidentally made out with Shawn Lee."

"WHAT?" Angus may have sort of accidentally screamed.

"SHHHHHH!" I howled like the katabatic winds of Antarctica.

"What?" Angus whispered.

"I know, I know!"

"How do you sort of accidentally make out with—" Angus stopped himself. "You know what? Don't answer that. I've done it before. I get it. But *Shady* Shawn Lee? Isn't he like our archnemesis?"

"I mean, I would say Dylan is our archnemesis. Shawn is more like the video game boss you fight right before the Big Boss."

"Do you *like* him?"

"No," I said. "I don't know. I don't *want* to like him."

"No, no, I get it," said Angus, pinching the bridge of his nose. "But look, and I don't mean this in a vindictive way, but you are aware that his dad is like the leader of some far-right militant group? *And* he has a shitty podcast?! Not to cast judgment, but he's sort of objectively a garbage person."

"I've gathered as much," I said bleakly.

"Okay," he said, nodding. He at least seemed glad we were on the same page. "Now I get that people are not the same thing as their parents. You and Astrid and Danny are all proof of that. I somehow lucked out with weirdly supportive parents."

"Your parents are *so* great."

"They are, aren't they?!" said Angus, nodding enthusiastically. "But—okay, we're getting sidetracked. Hope, you need to talk to Shawn."

"What? Why would I do that?"

"You need to find out—for you and you alone—whether or not he subscribes to that bullshit."

"He's in Alt-Rite. Of course, he does."

"Maybe. Maybe not. Does Mavis subscribe to that bullshit?"

I stared at Angus with devastating silence.

"I know about her and Faith," said Angus, shrugging. "Come on, that story is an urban legend around here."

I frowned deeply.

"Look, I know she feels hurt and betrayed by Faith. I know she's coping with it the only terrible way she knows how. Sometimes, when we're damaged, we have to become the bad guy before we heal enough to become something better."

"That's a fucking terrible philosophy."

"It's not a philosophy. That's just how people are sometimes. Most people don't *decide* to be bad. They're just too fucked up to realize that's what they've become."

"What if I just never talk to Shawn again? Just rip the fucking Band-Aid off?"

"I mean, you *could* do that. But what if you still think you like him?"

I made an annoyed sound.

"What if we get all the way to Battle of the Bands, it's us versus them, and everything rides on us defeating Alt-Rite, and you *still* think you like him?"

"Ugh. Okay. Fine. I'll talk to him."

Angus stared at me, unconvinced.

"What? I said I'll do it! What do you want, a blood oath?"

"No, no, I know you will," said Angus, still looking unconvinced. "Can I give you something?"

"Can you *give me something*?"

"A gift. Well, sort of a gift. I'd like it back when you're done with it."

"You want to give me a gift because I accidentally made out with our archnemesis?"

"I want to give you a gift because you're my friend, and I care about you."

I made the face you make when you're trying not to get emotional and failing.

Angus wandered to the corner of the garage, unzipped his backpack, and removed a slim black device that was bigger than a phone but smaller than a tablet. A Kindle? Were those still a thing?

Angus handed it to me.

"Is this a Kindle?"

"I mean, it's an e-reader, not *specifically* a Kindle."

I stared at Angus.

"But yeah, basically it's a Kindle. There's a book I have downloaded called *Andromeda and Tanks Through Space and Time*. I want you to read it."

For reasons I'm sure you can understand, I stared at Angus, speechless.

"I don't want to overhype it or anything," said Angus, "but it will probably change your life."

I was only half-listening to Angus at this point because those weird combination of words in that exact order was causing my head to ring like a bell. The vicious déjà vu of it all threatened to shatter the walls of the simulated reality I was living in.

It *had* to be déjà vu, right? Because there was no fucking way he was talking about what I *thought* he was talking about.

It was at that exact moment that I remembered a separate, seemingly unrelated text conversation with Angus only weeks ago.

"Wait," I said. "Is this the lesbian sci-fi romance?"

"Hope," said Angus. "This. Is. *The*. Lesbian sci-fi romance."

"Who wrote it?" I said, just a little too eagerly. Already, I was fumbling to turn the device on and find out for myself.

Angus laughed.

"What?" I said.

"You're asking the same question that literally the entire queer internet has been asking for months."

"What do you mean?"

"I *mean* no one has even the slightest clue who the author is. Look it up online. You'll see. Hell, look it up on Reddit! It's conspiracy theories for days on Reddit. Believe me, I've read every last thread, and I think I have *less* of an idea who Æon Q is than before I went down that rabbit hole."

"Æon Q?" I said.

Angus chuckled. "Sorry. That's the author's pen name. They/them pronouns. Although there's some pretty heated debate about whether the author is nonbinary or simply *that* anonymous. Look, just look it up, okay? I could go on for hours about it, but if I did, you'd probably be sick of this book before you even read it. Just read it, okay?"

I stared at Angus. *Through* Angus. Was it possible I knew *exactly* who the author of this book was, and I hadn't even read the first page?

"Hope?" said Angus.

I blinked until Angus was back in focus.

"Are you okay?" he said. "You look like you've just seen a ghost."

"Okay," I said.

"Okay?"

"I'll read it."

"Okay!" said Angus, nodding, looking rather pleased with himself. "Dude, you're going to love it."

"Angus?"

"Yeah?"

I hugged Angus. I just sort of threw myself at him. In retrospect, I probably could have given him a little more warning.

"Thank you for being my friend and caring about me," I said.

Once Angus recovered from my sneak hug attack, he hugged me back. "You're too cool for me to not care, Hope."

♩ ♫ ♪

The first thing I did when Angus left was make a straight line to Faith's room, which was (slightly inconveniently) now Danny's room. However, Danny appeared to be in the bathroom, and his bedroom door was open, so I zipped in, snatched one of Faith's notebooks—a very specific notebook—and zipped out, retreating to my room and shutting the door. I was never there.

I opened the notebook and fumbled through the pages until I found seven words filling the entire page: *Andromeda and Tanks Through Space and Time.*

There were suddenly very few things more important to me than reading this book.

But first, I opened up my laptop and did a little internet research for context. What I discovered was that *Andromeda and Tanks Through Space and Time* was a self-published ebook bestseller—technically only a novella in length. It came out only months ago, and it was blowing up the charts. Æon Q was an enigma. There was no social media presence. No author bio. No picture. Not even so much as an email address for fan mail. And yet, here was this book that was tearing up not only the LGBTQ subgenre but the science fiction genre as a whole.

I googled "who is aeon q?"

I was quite unprepared for the mass of information—or disinformation, as the case seemed to be—as it poured in front of me. I skimmed for a basic gist, and the gist seemed to be that nobody had a fucking clue who Æon Q was. Some people suggested the names of similarly voiced known authors—all of which were slammed down and allegedly proven wrong the moment they were thrown into the ring. Other people were treating *Andromeda and Tanks Through Space and Time* like some ancient code, deconstructing the text like it was the *Last Supper.* One person seemed convinced the author was Banksy. I pulled out of the rabbit hole before it could suck me in further. It was relatively easy to do so because not one person was theorizing anything even remotely along the lines of *Æon Q is an eighteen-year-old queer girl from Sundance, Wyoming; first name Faith, last name Cassidy. She ran away from home almost a year ago, and she's been living on the lam ever since.*

I turned my attention from Æon Q to the work itself.

All the reader reviews for *Andromeda and Tanks Through Space and Time* had been five-star praise, saying things like "strange and stunning" and "a weirdo masterpiece" and "This is the best damn story I have ever read in my entire life, fight me." Basically, the book already had a fierce and loyal cult following. Obviously, this was the sort of book that could never live up to the insurmountable hype, and the only thing left to do was to read it and be the one lonely poopy-pants critic on Goodreads. I wasn't trying to be pessimistic. I'm just telling you the way it was. Books like this were never as good as these sorts of reviews told you they would be. Even if—maybe even *especially* if—it was written by someone whom you loved with all your heart.

The book description at the top of the page read:

> Andromeda is a Dresdorian, an alien race of sort-of four-dimensional beings who are also sort of religious assholes. Because they know the "timelines" of all their kind, they know that Andromeda is destined to fall in love with a female android named Tanks, and the Dresdorians are Not Cool with That. They have a facility where they are able to correct "abominable timelines," but Andromeda politely tells them to fuck off, so her third eye is clipped—making her no longer able to see her future—and she is exiled.
>
> Andromeda is forced to wander the walled-off deserts surrounding Dresdore, in a desperate search for the woman

she will fall in love with, whose memory grows fuzzier by the day. But faced against a wasteland inhabited by marauders and giant monster insects and corrupt militants of a tyrannical government, Andromeda is unprepared for the greatest threat to her existence:

What if Tanks is not who Andromeda thinks she is?

Okay, so it *sounded* kind of amazing—and I was already walking in as a somewhat biased party—but I was trying to keep my expectations in check. So I skeptically opened Angus's Kindle, filled with a stunning assortment of high and low literature, and this kooky-looking sci-fi thing I was about to read, and I started reading.

And I *kept* reading.

I didn't know how much time had passed when I reached the halfway point, because my problems and I didn't even exist anymore, because this was *the best damn story I had ever read in my entire life, FIGHT ME*. (Actually, I was a tad upset someone had already used that as the title of their review because it meant I would have to think of something better.) The book was so good, in fact, that I somehow kept forgetting that I was reading something I was almost 100 percent certain was written by Faith. *That's* how good it was.

My desire to finish this book in one sitting—which wouldn't have been incredibly difficult to do—was eclipsed by my desire to savor the moment. Part of me wondered whether there was some clue in it about Faith's whereabouts. If so, shouldn't finishing it right now be my one and only priority? The other part of me—the part that was losing myself in this book like I used to lose myself in Faith's company—wasn't ready for the postbook depression that follows reading a really good book, let alone one that was my sole connection to Faith. I already felt the imminent separation anxiety inching closer with each page.

So I stopped. It was excruciating, but it felt like the right thing to do.

And that's when the depression started to set in.

It wasn't a sudden whoosh of sadness. It didn't come crashing down on me, as it sometimes had in the past. Rather, this was the type that crept in slowly, slurping out of the dark depths of the ocean like some sea monster designed solely for me. Its tentacles coiled around my shoulder, around my waist, and around my neck. It felt comfortable, at least for a moment, maybe only because this felt like what I deserved.

I let this happen. I let myself be strangled.

All I knew was that I now had evidence that Faith was living a life, and it had nothing to do with me.

She had the internet. She had published an entire fucking book on it—even if it was just a novella. She could message me in an instant.

But she was choosing not to.

eavy clouds rolled and rumbled across the jade-tinted sky. A storm was coming. A malignant, slobbering, hungry bastard of a storm that would devour anything that didn't take cover.

Narls dragged Tanks's body to the edge of the force field. He grabbed her by the collar with all four hands. Huffed and puffed, like he was about to jerk a thousand pounds over his head. These types of force fields only neutralized acidic properties, you see. Objects and living things pass through like rays of sunlight.

Narls lifted her and spun. He let go and launched her like a shotput. Her limbs flailed behind her like ribbons. She landed twenty yards away into the hardened sand with a broken clunk.

Andromeda was currently being restrained by three separate FIRE operatives, including the one known as Ears.

Andromeda was losing her motherfucking mind.

"LET ME GO," she screamed. "GET YOUR HANDS OFF ME, YOU FUCKING PIECES OF SHIT, LEMME GO, LET ME THE FUCK GO—"

"Let her go," said Narls.

"Huh?" said Ears, distracted.

Andromeda headbutted Ears, which, admittedly, hurt her as much as it hurt Ears. But Ears was the only one crying.

"My nose!" Ears wailed. "Oh golly, I think she broke my nose!"

The other two operatives wisely let go. Andromeda charged headfirst through the force field, on a direct path to Tanks.

"Dresdorians are acid proof, you know," Ears mumbled, still covering his nose.

"I know," said Narls. "But this'll look better on our report."

"Ah."

Ears was deeply uncomfortable with treachery, mind you. But not nearly as uncomfortable as he was with dying—which seemed to be what happened to people Narls didn't like. Dying was, like, peak discomfort. So treachery it was!

Andromeda ran.

She could already feel the first raindrops. To her, it felt like nothing. Like water. If panic and dread weren't in the equation, it might have felt refreshing.

But Andromeda could see strings of smoke where the raindrops were hitting Tanks's FIRE uniform, singeing the fabric.

Andromeda threw herself on top of Tanks. Already she knew this wasn't going to work. She was long but too thin. She removed her shirt—a worn but expensive thing, spider silk—and wrapped it around Tanks's face. Tanks's beautiful, handcrafted face.

The rain came. Andromeda cradled Tanks beneath her.

Death came down in waves, violently pattering against the bare skin of her back and all around her. Andromeda found herself praying desperately—incoherently—to anything that would listen. If there was a God or a Gaea, it was in their hands now.

If not, Andromeda would have to be enough.

—Andromeda and Tanks Through Space and Time,
ÆonEQ

–SEVENTEEN–

BREAKING POINT

READING *ANDROMEDA AND TANKS THROUGH SPACE and Time* was like trying to do drugs responsibly—only a little at a time, just enough to get by. Just here and there to fend off the feel-bads. First thing in the morning when I was getting ready for school. Before bed. Whenever I walked past a mirror and looked at myself—like, really looked at myself, in the most existential sense imaginable—and hated what I saw. I would hit the fucking brakes on everything (well, everything *except* band practice) and read another chapter. I did this, even though I was fully aware of the approaching withdrawal and depression. But in the moment, it was ecstasy, and that ecstasy was all that mattered.

I was running out of chapters.

Not to mention, the book was getting a little dark too. I was way too invested in these characters, and I wasn't entirely certain all of them would make it to the end. I loved Faith, but I didn't entirely trust her with these characters' well-beings.

All in all, I was in a weird mood. Sure, I was on a good-book high, which must be similar to other highs in the sense that it made you feel enlightened, whether or not you actually were. I was also feeling incredibly brave, which had disastrous potential. But at the root of it all, I was depressed—more depressed than I had felt in months, the tentacles constricting tighter with each passing day—and I think that was making me self-destructive.

That's how I found myself knocking on Shawn Lee's front door one afternoon.

The person who answered was not Shawn. He had a round face and a trimmed black beard, and he was wearing a baseball cap backward.

"Holy shit," said Robbie Lee. "You're that girl from the video."

"Is Shawn home?" I asked.

"Yeah. Yeah yeah yeah. Come on in. Have a seat." He gestured for me to come in, which I did—very, very reluctantly. Fortunately, their living room appeared devoid of any Nazi memorabilia. Mostly, it looked like two boys sharing a place together: big-screen TV, multiple video game consoles with their respective controllers strewn about, and a rather retro collection of DVDs—predictable things like *Predator* and *Death Wish*—stacked haphazardly on the coffee table among pizza boxes and soda cans. This was just one room, but the occasional T-shirt and pair of sweatpants on the floor indicated that it was the same story in every room.

I sat on the side of the black leather sofa that didn't have someone's crusty boxers on it. Robbie hastily snatched those up and literally pocketed them.

"Sorry about the mess," said Robbie. "Can I get you something to drink?"

"I'm okay, thank you."

"Right. I'll go get Shawn." He cranked the volume on his vokes to some ungodly decibel and screamed, "SHAWN. YOU HAVE A GUEST. A *LADY* GUEST."

Fortunately, screaming wasn't Robbie's only method of retrieving Shawn. He disappeared into the man-smelling labyrinth. I heard knocking and Robbie saying something like "the girl from the video" and Shawn screeching something like "She's here? *Now*?" When Robbie returned, he was grinning like this was the best day of his life.

"Shawn's coming," he said. "He just has to make himself look pretty first."

That actually made me smile. Shawn was way prettier than I wanted to admit.

"So," said Robbie, sitting on the sofa where the boxers had been. "You're in a band."

"I'm in a band," I agreed.

"And Shawn's in a band."

"Shawn is indeed in a band."

The obvious conversation starter here was that our bands were the yin and yang of each other; one might say "good versus evil," but that seemed to be opening a can of political worms that Robbie had the good sense not to open. Instead, he and I just sat there nodding at each other. It was so awkward.

"So . . . it's just the two of you here?" I said finally.

"Just us two," said Robbie. "Shawn's mother doesn't like me very much."

I wasn't sure what to say to that, so I just kept nodding.

"Relationships are complicated," said Robbie. "It's sort of a miracle that they work out to begin with. So it shouldn't be too terribly surprising when they fall apart. It always *is* surprising, don't get me wrong. But it shouldn't be."

"Does Shawn stay with his mom at all?"

"Not so much these days. She has a new boyfriend. Him and Shawn don't get along so well."

"Ah."

More awkward silence.

"I realize I'm a biased party," said Robbie, "but Shawn's a really good kid. Way better than I ever was. He has a really good heart."

What even was I supposed to say to that? I just kept nodding. Robbie nodded in response. Cool cool cool cool cool.

Finally—thank God, *finally*—Shawn came out. To his credit, he both looked and smelled very nice. Doc Marten boots, shirt with buttons, the least baggy jeans he had ever worn—actually, they looked like they had *never* been worn—his hair pulled back in a ponytail. No beanie. He was smiling nervously.

"Hey, Hope. Has my dad ruined my reputation yet?"

"I already showed her your naked baby pictures," said Robbie.

Shawn's mouth dropped wide open.

"I'm kidding! Jeez, what the hell sort of monster do you take me for?" Robbie laughed as he stood up and the trauma slowly drained from Shawn's face. "I'm gonna go take a nap. I'll leave you kids to it."

"Actually, Shawn, is it okay if we talk outside?" I asked.

"Yeah. Sure. Of course." He looked like he was about to add a fourth affirmative, like "certainly," but then had the wisdom to stop talking.

He and I walked out the front door. Crossed the front lawn and veered leisurely onto the main road.

I hadn't come unprepared. In fact, I was very aware what direction I was going to take this thing. I figured it was slightly unfair to go for Shawn's dad, so I decided to make this specifically about Shawn.

"I hate your band," I said.

Shawn laughed nervously. "I know."

"Why are you in it?"

Shawn shrugged. "Because I *want* to be in it? Is that bad?"

Well, Shawn, it's not great.

This was when things were bound to get unpleasant. I had done the unthinkable and listened to Alt-Rite. I listened to all their music released up to this point. And because they were very transparent about who and what they were, they credited the lyrics for each song.

With the exception of "That's So Gay," Shawn had written every single one of them.

Including track eight.

The Voldemort of song titles: "It That Shall Not Be Named."

This was not the real name of song. The real name was so much worse.

"You wrote ____ ____________________," I said. I immediately regretted saying the title out loud. It tasted like licking a Nazi flag that Adolf Hitler used to wipe his own ass.

Already, Shawn seemed to know where this conversation was going, and he had that "busted" look that he hid poorly behind a sheepish smile. "Okay, like, yes, that one was all me, but hear me out."

My heart sank, but I said nothing. If he wanted me to hear him out, I would hear him out.

"Okay, so I know it *sounds* offensive..."

Yes, it did.

"...but the song is actually not about any of those things that it's making fun of. In fact, it *supports* liberal belief in its own way. It's about freedom."

"Freedom," I repeated.

"Yeah. It's about fighting censorship, like all the great dystopian novels. For example, um, I believe that Black Lives Matter deserves to exist just as much as I believe the Confederate flag and the KKK deserve to exist—"

I stomped the brakes on this conversation like I was careening ninety miles per hour down a highway that dead-ended at a cliff. "Whoa whoa whoa whoa whoa whoa whoa. You believe the KKK deserves to exist?"

"Well, yeah. Not that I'm going to join it myself, but if you make the KKK illegal, what's to stop someone from making Black Lives Matter illegal?"

"That is not even *remotely* the same thing! The KKK is a hate movement with a history of murdering Black people. Black Lives Matter is about *Black lives mattering*. The opposite of that is saying that Black lives don't matter!"

"Okay, like, I get that's what *you believe*, but there are plenty of people who would argue that Black Lives Matter is *also* a hate movement—"

"Oh my God."

"Yes, that they're antiwhite, and they're only interested in promoting violence and civil disobedience. Some would even argue that they're a form of domestic terrorism—"

"OH MY GOD," I said, rubbing my temples, trying to massage the headache out.

"But that's not what I believe!" said Shawn, urgently. "I believe they have just as much of a right to do what they do as I have a right to hang the Confederate flag in my bedroom. The problem is people telling you what you can't do or say or think—"

"WHOA WHOA WHOA WHOA WHOA WHOA WHOA," I said. "Shawn. Do you have a Confederate flag in your bedroom?"

"See, this is the problem," Shawn said defensively. "It doesn't matter whether or not I have a Confederate flag in my bedroom."

"It matters to *me*!"

"I *like* that you have different beliefs than me! Okay? I *like* that you're the lead singer of a band who is fighting for what you believe in. But what's the point of tolerance if you can't tolerate what I believe in?"

I don't know how bad I imagined this conversation going, but I definitely didn't imagine it going this bad.

"Do you even know what hate is?" I said.

Shawn looked confused, like this was a trick question.

"It's confusing freedom of speech," I said, "with the right to be a hateful asshole without consequences."

"Okay, wait a second—" said Shawn, backtracking.

"It's saying that tolerance should *tolerate* intolerance. That a long history of bigotry, discrimination, and broken dogmatic systems are all rights that deserve to be *protected*. That these things are somehow equivalent to race or gender or sexuality. Do you have any idea how fucked up that is? I mean, obviously you don't, otherwise we wouldn't be having this conversation."

"Look, that's not what I—"

"Everything you believe in—everything that Alt-Rite *is*—is nothing but hate."

"You're right," said Shawn. "I'll quit the band."

Shady Shawn was full of all sorts of surprises. I blinked like I had motes and beams and an entire biblical plague in my eye. There was no way I had heard that correctly.

"I'll quit the band," said Shawn, "if you go out with me."

And there it was.

"No," I said. I didn't even need to think about it. This was nonnegotiable.

"C'mon," said Shawn.

I wasn't getting through to him. I needed to try harder. "No no no no NONONO."

"You want to defeat Alt-Rite, right?" said Shawn. "That's the whole reason you started this band to begin with, isn't it?"

That one hit where it was supposed to. I opened my mouth but had nothing. He wasn't wrong.

"If Alt-Rite loses me, they lose Battle of the Bands," said Shawn. "Danny Roger and I are literally the only two guitarists at our school who can pull off Alt-Rite's set list. If they bring in someone from outside our school, they're disqualified from the competition. Plus, if I drop out, there's a fifty percent chance Mavis will drop out too. She only joined because she and I are friends, and I asked her to. Don't you want that? Can you imagine Alt-Rite losing both their lead guitar *and* their drummer?"

I *did* want that. And I *couldn't* imagine it. It all seemed too good to be true, and worst of all, I believed him.

"You've painted me into something I'm not," said Shawn. "Go out with me. Just for a little bit. Battle of the Bands is in less than two weeks. Once it's over, you're free to break up with me. There'll be nothing to stop you. Just give me a chance. I think you'll find we have more in common than you want to believe."

"Like what?"

There were so many not-terrible answers he could have given. We both liked punk rock. We both liked tattoo art. We both had an appreciation for a Roger twin (even though, like their bands, Danny and Dylan were the yin and yang of siblings born from the same zygote). But Shawn didn't lead with any of those.

"Like, we're both white, we're both straight," said Shawn. "We just have different political views is all."

Remember what I said about wanting to peel the skin off my right arm? Well, now you could apply that to my entire body. I wanted to take a shower in hydrochloric acid. I hated that I was somehow "appealing" to a vile, disgusting creature like this.

I started screaming.

"Whoa, what the . . . ?" said Shawn.

I kept screaming, and I started shoving him in the chest. I didn't want him to fall. I just wanted him to get far far *faaaaaar* away from me. My goal was to be as "unappealing" as possible.

"What's wrong with you?" said Shawn.

I screamed louder. I shoved harder. I think I even started slobbering a little bit.

The last shove almost tipped Shawn over. He staggered wildly, barely caught his balance, and then just kept walking away.

"You're fucking crazy," he muttered.

I watched as he retreated back the way he came, disappeared back into his house, back to his "freedom" and the Confederate flag that may or may not have been hanging from his bedroom wall.

I pulled my gaze away and stared down at my hands. They were trembling.

I rotated my right arm slightly. The tattoo on my forearm stared back at me.

That's when I started disassociating.

Andromeda could not be Tanks's umbrella, no matter how hard she tried. She could feel Tanks eroding beneath her, her synthetic exterior dissolving, frame warping. Andromeda could hear the sizzle, like peroxide on a wound. It was a traumatic, soul-fucking experience. It wasn't supposed to end like this. They grew old together!

"Tell me about our future," said Tanks, beneath the fabric of Andromeda's shirt.

"Tanks?" said Andromeda, horrified. "Oh my God, you're awake?" She did not want to be alone—but not at the expense of Tanks being awake for this. This was barbaric.

"I don't want to die. If I have a future, I want to hear it. Even if it's just a story."

Andromeda blinked the tears out of her eyes. "I don't know where to start."

"Since I'm dissolving, maybe tell me about a time I looked nice?"

Andromeda started sobbing.

"It's okay," said Tanks. "You don't have to—"

"No, no," said Andromeda, shaking her head, sniffing ferociously. "Um. It's cliché, but on our wedding day? You wore the prettiest dress."

"A dress," said Tanks. "Huh. I was sure I would've worn a tux."

"I begged you to wear it. I wore the tux."

"That makes sense. I love a tall girl in a suit."

"You mean a Lightning Rod in a suit?" Andromeda tried to sound bitter but failed.

Tanks gave a broken laugh. "Sorry about that. So, I look pretty in the dress, huh?"

Andromeda smiled, and it hurt. "You were the most beautiful thing I'd ever seen."

"What do I do in this future? I assume I don't work for FIRE?"

"You teach martial arts to kids at a dojo."

"You're shitting me. Does it pay well?"

"Not especially. But you love it. You would die for these kids."

"Oof," said Tanks. "I'm pretty selfless, aren't I?"

She meant it as a joke, but she had no idea. "You really are," said Andromeda.

"What's the most selfless thing I ever did?" said Tanks. "Aside from teaching snot-nosed brats how to beat each other up?"

"Six years from now, you have a procedure. It syncs us. It allows you to aesthetically age with me. We grow old together. And when I die, it allows us to . . . to . . ."

"Wow," said Tanks. "I must really love you, huh?"

Andromeda gave a helpless shrug. "You must."

"Unwrap my face."

"What?" said Andromeda, alarmed. "No!"

"Do you love me?"

Andromeda shook her head fiercely. "Don't do that."

"I just want to see your face."

"This stupid shirt is the only thing protecting your stupid brain!"

"Your shirt can't save me. The acid's already eaten through the back of my head."

"What? No!" Andromeda curled her fingers around the back of Tanks's head. They were met by a gaping hole and a soggy mess of exposed wires and chips. "No no no no!"

"I've already died for you once," said Tanks. "Let me do this on my own terms."

Who was Andromeda to refuse? She peeled away the wet layers of her shirt like a burial shroud. Beneath it all was Tanks's decaying face, blinking away wetness and light.

"You have kind eyes," said Tanks, smiling. Her voice was glitchy. Breaking apart.

Andromeda's frown was crippling her.

"Take care—*kzzt!*—Andy," said Tanks. Andy was Tanks's pet name for Andromeda. Neither of them knew that this was where it started. "Maybe we'll—*fzzt!*—meet again."

Her voice powered down—growing slow and heavy and deep—and she died.

—Andromeda and Tanks Through Space and Time,
ÆonQ

—EIGHTEEN—

A LONG, FIERCE KNIFE

I ENDED UP CALLING DANNY FOR A RIDE HOME from Shawn's neighborhood, which he did, no questions asked. He asked Mom if he could borrow the CR-V, which she said yes to because Danny was her new favorite member of the family, and he was there in less than ten minutes.

It's not that I *needed* a ride. I think I just didn't want to be alone with my thoughts.

That feeling of needing to take a scalding-hot shower returned. I felt gross. Tainted. The fact that I checked all the boxes on Shawn's Nazi-friendly dating wish list made me feel queasy about my very existence.

I needed to talk to someone.

I *thought* about talking to Danny throughout the entire drive home. In the end, I didn't. Even though he was my best friend. For some reason, I just couldn't get the words out.

"Are you okay?" said Danny. "You seem . . . bothered."

Considering we had a lot to be bothered about—losing Astrid's guesthouse, experiencing a creative crisis as a band, that fucking text message from Hunter Thorson that Danny and I *still* had yet to talk about—it was easy enough to deflect.

"I am," I said. "But not by you."

"Do you want to talk about it?"

"Maybe later? Over a western? Or running? I'll try not to die this time."

Danny grinned and placed a sincere hand over his heart. "You know me so well."

We exited the car together. Entered the house together. Walked to our individual bedroom doors together. He went inside.

I didn't.

Instead, I veered into the kitchen.

I stopped in front of the knife block.

In particular I found myself staring at the handle of that long, fierce knife I grabbed the night I got my tattoo. The horrible screaming and fighting between my mom and me.

The line of blood I drew when I placed just a little bit of pressure on my skin.

When that image in my head transformed into something else entirely, I took a deep, staggering breath and retreated to my bedroom.

The image of the knife was still in my head. The things it could do.

I glanced down at my right forearm. At my tattoo. At a piece of Shawn permanently etched into my skin.

It would never fade away.

I called Astrid. She answered on the second ring.

"Hey," she said bleakly, because that seemed to be the default setting of Hope Cassidy and the Sundance Kids these days. "What's up?"

I told Astrid everything. No icebreaker, no buildup. I just spilled it all out, like my actual guts if I was a character in a *Saw* movie. Astrid listened with a silence usually reserved for outer space.

"Ew," Astrid said when I finished. "Oh my God. Are you okay?"

"Yeah?" I said, which was a lie and not a very good one. "I just feel gross is all."

"Yeah, no kidding. Man, what a skuz bucket."

I nodded, which I knew was unhelpful during phone conversations. It was just difficult to talk about what I was feeling.

"Do you think I made a mistake?" I said.

"What?" said Astrid. "Mistake how?"

"Shawn said he would quit the band if I went out with him."

"No."

"Just until Battle of the Bands. Less than two weeks from now. Then I could break up with him. And then Alt-Rite wouldn't have a lead guitar. Maybe not even a drummer."

"No no no."

"That would cripple them, wouldn't it? There's no way they'd be able to find a replacement guitar before Battle of the Bands. That would mean we won."

"That's not winning," said Astrid. "That's dehumanizing. I'd rather eat my own drum kit than let you be Shawn's trophy romantic hostage."

"But—"

"No fucking *buts*, Hope. Either we win the right way, or we don't win at all. *You're* better than that, *we're* better than that, and by fucking golly, *feminism* is better than that. Shawn can stick his Nazi dick in a steaming pile of sauerkraut."

Astrid didn't take pep talks lightly. Everything she was saying should have made me feel better. But it didn't.

My gaze shifted to the tattoo on my right arm.

I hadn't told her *everything*.

"You know my tattoo?" I said nervously.

"Um, yeah, duh," said Astrid. "It's badass."

"Shawn gave it to me."

"What?"

I didn't say anything. I'd already said too much.

"Shawn Lee?" said Astrid.

"Mm-hmm."

"Shady Shawn Lee gave you that tattoo."

"Mm-hmm."

Now Astrid was quiet. A stronger *What the fuck?* seemed to be the question she was looking for, but she couldn't find it.

"It was before Alt-Rite," I said. "Before I knew who he was. *What* he was. I just heard that he did tattoos, and I wanted a tattoo, so . . ."

I didn't know why I was telling Astrid this. It was obviously a cry for help, but I don't know what I expected her to do about it. Like I said, this fucker was permanent.

"Do you know who Roman Polanski is?" said Astrid.

"Huh?" I said. This successfully translated across the phoneline as a resounding "no."

"He's a filmmaker. One of the greatest horror filmmakers of all time. He directed *Rosemary's Baby*, *Repulsion*, *The Tenant*—some truly revolutionary shit. I discovered his films before I found out who he really was."

"Who he really was?"

"He was a rapist pedophile."

"Oh."

"He was arrested and charged with six offenses against a thirteen-year-old girl. I'd go into the details, but it's, like, truly horrific. He eventually accepted a plea bargain. Then he fled the country. I think he lives in France now."

"Wow."

"Wow is right. And I found this out *after* I was basically in love with his films. So naturally, I had a crisis. I was in love with a bunch of movies made by a horrible human being. Did that make *me* a horrible human being? I owned several of his movies on Blu-ray, and I threw them all in the trash after I found about this. But even then, I was still in love with these movies. Even though I hated what Polanski *was*, I couldn't bring myself to *hate his movies*. And that's when I realized something: These movies were a part of me. They had shaped me into who I am. And you can't throw that in the trash. Do you understand what I'm saying?"

I think I did. But I still wanted her to explain it to me. It felt like something I needed to hear out of someone else's mouth.

"Art means nothing without the people who experience it," said Astrid. "The experience is what truly means something. My experience with *Rosemary's Baby*, with *Repulsion*... that means something. And that meaning has absolutely nothing to do with a sick man who raped a girl. Not to mention, it undermines all the other incredible people who contributed to those films. What I'm trying to say is, that tattoo is not Shawn. It's you. It's a part of who you are. Personally, I think it's badass. I think it'll be a nice reminder of that one time we kicked Nazi ass at Battle of the Bands."

I laughed. A laugh that was on the verge of tears.

"But if you want to remove it professionally, I understand," said Astrid. "Hell, I'll go with you, just for support. It's your choice. I love you either way."

It almost seemed like she was going to stop there. And it wouldn't have been a terrible note to end on. But then she took that extra step.

"Just, whatever you do," said Astrid, "don't hurt yourself over it. That's the only wrong choice you can make here."

I started crying.

"Fuck," said Astrid. "Hey, tell ya what: Do you wanna have a sleepover? My place, your place, it's your call."

I was nodding my head pointlessly. Sobbing uncontrollably.

"Fuck it," said Astrid. "I'm coming to your place. Is Danny home?"

"Y-ye-yes?"

"Can you hand the phone to him?"

"Uh-uh-uh-uh-huh?"

"Just put him on for a sec, then I'll have him pass it right back to you. I swear to God, I'm spending the night, so you better get ready for some baller mani-pedis."

My crying reached the point of violent hiccupping. I exited my room, took three whole steps, and knocked on Danny's door. He opened it to my ugly-sobbing face. He looked understandably confused. His confusion only escalated when I held the phone out to him. Without saying a word, he took it.

"Hello?" he said.

I heard Astrid's voice, but the words were a low blur. Slowly, his eyes locked on to mine. They seemed to bloom with a strange sadness. He nodded. "Yeah. Yeah, for sure. Okay, hold on."

Danny lowered the phone to his chest.

"Hope, do you wanna hang in my room for a sec? I've just got a quick question for your mom, then I'll be right back. You can talk to Astrid."

"Oh-oh-oh-okay," I said.

Danny stepped aside and graciously guided me into his (Faith's) room and sat me down on his (Faith's) bed. He lifted the phone to his ear. "Okay, here she is. See you in a few. Okay, bye."

Danny handed the phone back to me. I hiccuped into the receiver.

"Okay, so," said Astrid. "What's your favorite movie?"

"Uh," I said. "*Shrek*?"

Danny took a couple steps backward, offered two very enthusiastic thumbs-up at *Shrek*, slipped out the door, and closed it behind him.

"Dude," said Astrid. "I love *Shrek*. It's a classic. We are so watching *Shrek* tonight."

♩ ♫ ♪

I wasn't a dummy. I knew this had turned into a low-key self-harm intervention. But no one pried into my psychological state. (It was fragile, very fragile.)

Instead, everyone was just there for me.

That night, we all watched *Shrek*—Astrid, Danny, Mom, Dad, and me. (Charity was holed up in her room, as per usual.) Mom notoriously hated *Shrek*, but tonight, it had suddenly become her favorite movie, right up there with *Ben-Hur*. She laughed at every single one of Donkey's jokes.

Mom and Astrid sandwiched me on the sofa, all three of us snuggling under Faith's old comforter. Personal space did not exist. I loved it. Dad and Danny recognized I was in good hands and relinquished themselves to the recliners.

Shrek profoundly explained to Donkey that ogres were like onions.

Mom seemed to think this was an ideal time to interrupt.

"Remember when you were little, and you had nightmares?" Mom whispered into my ear. "Or it was raining outside, and you were scared of the thunder? So you would sneak into our bedroom and sleep with us?"

I looked at Mom.

"If you're ever having a bad night," said Mom, "or you just don't want to be alone . . . I'm just saying, the offer still stands. Your father will sleep on the couch if he has to."

My lips bunched together helplessly. A monsoon swelled beneath my face. I forced a feeble nod.

Mom kissed me on the forehead. Leaned her head against mine.

"Oh, you both have layers," said Donkey. "Oh. You know, not everybody like onions. Cake! Everybody loves cakes. Cakes have layers!"

Mom snorted and laughed.

Narls observed Andromeda's body, sprawled flat across the desert floor twenty yards away, with growing unease.

Here was the sitch: He hadn't exactly done things "by the book." And FIRE was a very by-the-book organization. Exiled Dresdorian memory connections as they related to active-duty FIRE operatives were to be reported to HQ. Both parties would then be brought in for questioning, blah blah blah; Narls didn't give a dick.

FIRE was aware of the "turncoat situation." Trackers were implanted in operatives, monitoring movement, vital signs, and so on. When half the taskforce was incapacitated, explanation was needed. Also, why wasn't Tanks answering her goddamned radio? Narls was forced to give a revised version of What Happened: Tanks discovered an exiled Dresdorian was her future wife; they fell in love and ran off together. But not before taking down half of FIRE. Then it rained acid, so Narls added that Tanks was "hopefully dead."

"This sounds uncharacteristic of Tanks," said Admiral Phawn over the receiver.

"Well, you know," said Narls. "Women, am I right?" He laughed at his own joke.

"I'm a woman," said Admiral Phawn.

Narls's laugh died like everything did in the acid, a slow disintegration.

"I'm sending over a team to investigate," said Admiral Phawn. "Lock things down and prepare for their arrival. They'll be there within the hour. Don't touch anything, don't tamper with anything, don't piss without first asking my permission. Out of either one of your penises. God, why would you even tell me that?" The transmission ended.

Narls snorted. Telling everyone about his dicks didn't always work in his favor.

"So basically, you're my accomplice," Narls informed Ears.

"Sorry, I'm your what?" said Ears, panicking.

"I mean, I only acted because you told me Tanks was planning a coup."

"I did no such thing!" Ears shrieked.

"But it's fine, it's fine, because we're not going to get caught."

"We're not?"

"Just, I need you to tell me how we're going to not get caught."

"Oh God," said Ears. "Mother told me I should have gone into accounting."

"I'm the brawns, you're the brains, Ears. Now use that big, stupid brain of yours. How do we not get caught?"

"My name's not even Ears!"

"Okay, then. What is your name?"

"It's Errol Elwin Egbert."

Narls squinted his beady eyes into irritated specks. Shook his head. "Yeah, I'm not calling you that. Think fast, Ears, we ain't got all day."

Ears sighed. "Well, the Dresdorian girl being alive is a problem."

"Right. So how do we eliminate the problem, if you catch my drift?"

"You mean, how do we murder the possibly underage Dresdorian girl?"

"Yes, Ears. That was my drift. Thank you."

"Okay, well... hypothetically speaking... if Tanks died in the acid..."

"Uh-huh, hypothermally speaking," said Narls, nodding.

"FIRE might believe a story where the Dresdorian kills herself in distress."

"Ooh, that's good, that's good," said Narls, nodding faster.

"But framing a gunshot wound is tricky. Modern forensic ballistics and such. We need something messier. Something that destroys the evidence. Something like a..."

"A bomb?" said Narls. He had that kid-in-the-candy-store look in his eyes.

Ears's gaze wandered off. "Yeah.... If the girl stole one of our, say, proton grenades... and Tanks died right in front of her eyes.... Yeah. Blowing herself up with a proton grenade? That's actually kind of poetic." Ears blinked. Narls was nowhere in sight.

—Andromeda and Tanks Through Space and Time,
AEon Q

—NINETEEN—

MY VAG

DANNY, ASTRID, AND I WERE CARPOOLING TO school in Astrid's car when we discovered she had Awkwafina's *Yellow Ranger* album on her phone, which resulted in us blasting "My Vag (Vag Redux Edition)" with the windows down, rapping along at the top of our lungs. It was far and away the most normal part of our day.

We were pulling into the SHS parking lot when my phone chimed, and I received a supremely weird text: What did you say to shawn?

Before I could even fathom a response, it was followed by: Nvmd. I don't want to know. This is mavis btw.

And then: Sorry if that came across as passive-aggressive. I just know you guys talked the other day and now he's being a dick.

We were then treated to a brief intermission by a group text from Angus: GUYS. DID YOU SEE THE VIDEO?

Mavis continued: I'm sure that has nothing to do with you and everything to do with Shawn.

And then: Sorry for what I said about Faith. I obviously still care about her otherwise I wouldn't be such a heartbroken asshole about it.

Lastly: I quit alt-rite but don't get too excited. It's definitely too little too late.

At this point, Awkwafina was just repeating "better than a penis" like a mantra, in case that statement was not clear at this point in the song. Astrid, who was driving, and Danny, in the back seat, both seemed acutely aware of each new text as it popped up with a noisy buzz in front of the last one. I don't think they could read anything, except maybe the look of alarm on my face.

When Astrid parked, I sighed and simply handed the phone over. There was too much for me to unpack on my own. Naturally, Danny lunged forward, reading ravenously over Astrid's shoulder.

We were provided context the moment we set foot in school. Angus was lying in wait, and we stepped right into his ambush.

"Guys guys guys guys guys," said Angus. "Did you see the video? Did you see the *fucking video*?" He then seemed to find it suspicious that the three of us entered school in such close proximity. "Wait, did you traitors carpool without me?"

"Uhhhhhh," said Astrid, like she'd just been caught cheating.

"Never mind, just, ugh." Angus snatched my phone right out of my hands, which the three of us had been sanctimoniously clustered around, pulled up a very upsetting video, and shoved it in our faces. "Watch this, stat."

♩ ♫ ♪

Brianna Lopez was someone I had never spoken a single word to, and yet I had spent the past year hating her out of sheer principle.

You might remember her more distinctly as "Charity's friend Brianna." The same one who saw Faith making out with Mavis in the window of Ralph Records, who told Charity what she saw—the first dominoes in a cascading, spiraling chain of destruction.

Brianna was the star of this new TikTok video making the rounds at Sundance High School.

She wasn't *in it*, per se. But her full name was very clearly printed on a piece of paper, along with a *very specific* date and time (tomorrow afternoon), being held by a mysterious hand. The paper lowered, revealing a building that had probably once been a house but had since been recently repurposed as a business, clear from the small, makeshift parking lot with fresh yellow lines. The walls were painted a mossy, aquatic blue-green, and a trapezoid-shaped sign fit neatly into the triangle of the wall above the front door where it met the lip of the shingled roof.

The person holding the camera phone approached the sign above the door until the words became painstakingly clear.

WOMEN'S RESOURCE CENTER
OF NORTHEAST WYOMING

The video abruptly ended in the blazing, guitar-screaming miasma of Alt-Rite's "Feminists (Baby Killers)" and a very short, fast roll of film credits:

Written and Directed by Alt-Rite
Starring
Dylan Roger's left hand
Brianna Lopez's poor life choices

The abortion clinic in Gillette
Premeditated murder?

The video ended, and so did every conceivable limit to the depths to which Alt-Rite would stoop.

Danny, Astrid, and I just stood there, completely mindfucked, while Angus existed in our periphery, waiting for some sort of reaction.

My phone buzzed, notifying me of another text from Mavis. I opened it.

It's fucked up, yeah?

And then:

Boo

Danny, Astrid, myself, and even Angus reacted to this text like characters in a horror film—backing up, whipping around, fully expecting some killer in a mask to jump out and start stabbing someone.

There was no masked killer, but there *was* Mavis, and she was standing behind us, grabbing a wad of her oversized sweater with one hand, apologetically tucking a lock of pink hair behind her ear with the hand holding her phone. She was smiling the way you do when you are very sad.

"I'm sorry," she said. "Alt-Rite is the fucking worst. Forgive me?"

I think she was talking specifically to me.

I couldn't move.

"I love Faith," said Mavis. Wetness brimmed across her indestructible eyeliner. "I miss her so much. And I am *so sorry—*"

I powerwalked into Mavis and body-slammed her with a savage hug, and then we just started crying into each other.

"Okay, *what* is going on?" said Angus. "Isn't she Alt-Rite's drummer?"

"She quit," Astrid whispered.

"Oh shit," said Angus. And then, slightly louder, "Oh *shit.*"

After Mavis and I got the hugging and crying out of our system, Mavis sniffed monstrously and pulled back. "Okay, but like seriously though, what the fuck happened with you and Shawn?"

I told Mavis what the fuck happened. If she was surprised by a single thing, it didn't show. Instead, she just looked sadder and sadder with every detail. By the time I finished, she looked like the saddest emo song ever written.

"He wasn't always like this," said Mavis. "He used to be so nice. I mean, he still is, sometimes, but you know what I mean. He can be super nice and super fucked up at the same time. Which almost makes it worse."

I hated that I knew exactly what she meant.

♩ ♫ ♪

By the time lunch rolled around, Mavis finally had the chance to sit with us and haphazardly explain what was going on. It was terribly uncomplicated. But I also had a feeling Mavis was omitting key details.

"For *Dylan-related reasons,*" said Mavis, "Dylan was dead set on shaming Brianna Lopez—a fifteen-year-old—for wanting a very responsible, private medical procedure, at which point I sort of put my foot down and told him, look, dude, you do this, and I'm out. And he did it anyway. So, I'm out. But that hardly does them any damage because they asked Hunter Thorson to replace me, and for *Hunter-related reasons*, Hunter said yes, and I'd be lying if I said he wasn't a better drummer than me."

I looked at Danny, and Danny looked like the saddest country song ever written, filled with the tragedies of a thousand cowboys.

"Why does Dylan want to shame Brianna so bad?" asked Astrid.

"Why would Hunter *quit* Roger Roger, and then *join* Alt-Rite?" asked Angus.

"Dylan-related reasons?" I asked. "Hunter-related reasons? What aren't you telling us?"

"Look, I've already said too much," said Mavis. "I can promise you, I'm not protecting Alt-Rite secrets. There are just certain things that I don't have the right to talk about. You just have to trust me."

"We trust you," said Danny, a little too quickly. "We appreciate you telling us this much."

I harrumphed dubiously but let it rest.

"None of that is important anyway," said Mavis. "The important thing is that I think Alt-Rite is planning something big, and awful, and you guys need to be ready for it."

"What could they *possibly* be planning that is worse than that video?" said Astrid.

None of us had a response to that. It was the sort of dread-filled silence that was the exact opposite of reassuring. You know that scripture "With God, all things are possible"? I had a feeling the same was true for Alt-Rite.

But, you know, in a bad way.

♩ ♫ ♪

Brianna was basically the shorter brunette version of the Charity Cassidy "Good Christian Girl"™ model. Meaning she had bangs for days, was just way too pretty, and wore deceivingly hipster-ish glasses to distract you from the fact that she was blind as a hate crime without them. I knew this because she had spent more sleepovers at our house than any non-Cassidy human being. Poor eyesight aside, I think Brianna and Charity mimicked each other's style. I think they even used to swap clothes until Charity experienced a Jack and the Beanstalk–level growth spurt.

Brianna did *not* tell Charity that she was planning on getting an abortion after school tomorrow. Nor did she tell Charity she was knocked up. The reasons for this secrecy should not be surprising.

I learned this when I accidentally eavesdropped on their entire conversation from the bathroom stall.

It was between sixth and seventh period, and the bathroom was empty because the tardy bell was about to ring. However, it was That Time of Month, so. You know. That's when Brianna walked in. I think she was deliberately taking advantage of everyone's desire to not be tardy.

Tardiness was the absolute least of her concerns.

Through the crack in the stall, I watched her walk up to the bathroom mirror, stare at her reflection for a solid ten seconds, and then break down sobbing.

I heard the bathroom door open a second time. Brianna frantically whipped upright and attempted to pull herself together, but no amount of togetherness could have prepared her for her best friend.

"What the heck?" said a voice that was unmistakably Charity.

I caught only the briefest glimpse of the look on Brianna's face from the reflection in the mirror, and it was the sort of look that even the best horror director couldn't pull out of their leading actress.

"You're pregnant?" said Charity. "Why didn't you tell me?"

"You know why I didn't tell you," said Brianna brokenly.

"Why? Because you knew I would be *against murder*?"

"Charity, I can't have a baby! I'm fifteen! *Barely!*"

"Well, maybe you should have thought about that before you... you... Who did you even...?"

"It doesn't matter," said Brianna quietly. "It was a one-time thing."

"A one-time thing," Charity repeated. "Do you have any idea how slutty that makes you sound?"

My stomach clenched like a fist. I hated that for someone like Charity there was no right answer. Pretty sure if Brianna had sex *more than once* with a single person, Charity's response would have been exactly the same.

"It's not like that," said Brianna. "You have no idea how *not like that* it is."

"Then tell me! Please, I *want* to understand."

"Do you, really? Because I feel like all you're *really* here for is to make me feel worse on what is already the worst day of my life."

Brianna tried to walk past Charity, but Charity blocked her.

"Wait," said Charity. "Just . . . wait."

"What?" Brianna said angrily.

"You don't have to *keep it*," said Charity. "There are other options! Do you know how many good couples aren't able to have a child of their own? Who would *die* to be able to adopt and raise yours as their own?"

"My dad doesn't even know about it! He can't. Charity, if he finds out, my life will be over. It will *literally* be over. Even my mom told me it's best he doesn't find out."

Something about that statement connected, made impact. It seemed to hit Charity in a spot that never fully recovered from the last time a life was ruined.

"Your life won't be over," Charity said softly. But even as the words came out, she didn't seem to believe them, not fully.

Brianna took a step away from her.

"Please, just . . . leave me alone," said Brianna.

Brianna brushed past Charity, storming out of the bathroom in a terrible hurry.

The tardy bell rang.

Charity did not leave. Not right away. She leaned against the nearest sink, head down, seemingly staring into the drain.

When she did leave, it was very slowly.

Only then did I dare to pull my pants up and flush and release the jagged breath I'd been holding like a grenade handle with the pin removed.

Narls ransacked the munitions cache of his government-issued Grav-E. He had never used a proton grenade in the field. This was about to be the happiest day of his life.

He returned to Ears with an entire belt of proton grenades slung over his shoulder.

"Oh wow," said Ears. "Okay. So we only need one of those puppies—"

"Nonsense." Narls made long strides to the force field perimeter. "What if I miss?"

"No, see, that's the thing, we're going to plant the grenade, not throw it."

"In acid rain, are you out of your goddamned mind?"

"That's why we have to wait for the rain to stop."

"FIRE will be here within the hour!" said Narls. All this thinking was giving him a migraine. Fuck it. He plucked the proton grenade off the belt like a piece of fruit.

"No, listen to me, Narls. You can't throw a FUCKING PROTON GRENADE..."

Narls pulled the pin out with his teeth.

"...IN ACID."

Narls pitched it in a slicing horizontal line. It might as well have gone right into the spinning teeth of a woodchipper. The blast painted everything in white.

It incinerated Narls's right arms (his pitching arms) and his right dick (his fucking dick), and he died instantly. It also short-circuited the force field. The dome warped and dissolved, from the damaged west perimeter stakes to the central rod, then glitched out of existence.

Everyone saw this. And everyone screamed.

Ears dove on his belly and screamed like it was the last sound he would make. Yet all he could hear was a sharp ring. That's because the proton blast blew off his right ear.

After a few agonizing seconds Ears realized that death was terribly slow. Also painless—except for his right ear, which felt like he'd gotten a very punk piercing. Was he dead? Ears (Ear?) opened his eyes to a jarring blip of blue sky. The rain had stopped.

He looked at the Rotters tied together in easy-to-manage clumps. All unharmed. He found himself staring at a particular Rotter known as Trog. Trog was yelling at Ears. Ears realized this because his hearing was coming back.

"Untie us!" said Trog. "We need the force field up before it rains again. Do you hear me?"

Ears blinked. Hearing was one thing. Processing was something else entirely.

"DO YOU WANT TO DIE?" yelled Trog.

Ears could process that question. And no, he didn't. Ears staggered to his feet.

"Second Lieutenant Egbert?" said some rando FIRE operative (Snakes, he believed?) slithering around camp. "Does anyone know who Second Lieutenant Egbert is?"

Ears, limping, raised a hand. It felt like he'd repeatedly kicked a brick wall barefoot.

"You?" said Snakes. "Ears, you know Second Lieutenant Egbert?"

"Yes," said Ears. "That would be me."

Snakes eyed him skeptically.

"Why's everyone always so surprised I'm second lieutenant?" said Ears, pouting.

"Hey, Ears!" Trog shouted. "We got a storm cloud on our three o'clock!"

"Right. Fuck." Ears cupped his hands over his mouth. "Attention, everyone! Hi. I'm Second Lieutenant Egbert. I need operatives to retrieve Tanks and the girl. See that they get medical attention. Everyone else, cut the refugees loose. We need this force field up!"

"Cut them loose?" said Snakes. "But I heard from Buzzy over in Comms that Admiral Phawn said to not even piss without—"

"Do you see these ears?" said Ears, pointing to both ears. (He didn't realize he was missing one.) "Because I hear every fucking thing that everyone says. So cut these refugees loose and fix this force field because it's in all of our best interest THAT WE NOT DIE."

Snakes nodded quietly and slithered off to free the refugees.

"God, I should have been an accountant," said Ears.

—Andromeda and Tanks Through Space and Time,
AEon Q

—TWENTY—

HEY HEY HEY OH YEAH WOO! (WHATCHA GONNA DO?)

IN TERMS OF BEING A "BAND MANAGER," DEJA hadn't done a whole lot. We couldn't really blame her. She was an internet celebrity. We were a high school band. She helped us maintain our social media presence, and, sure, she got Astrid's drums back, but outside of that, there wasn't really much else for her to do.

Twenty-four hours after Alt-Rite's TikTok video dropped, however, that changed.

Deja became a machine of action.

During first period, Mr. Britton was discussing the Kantian philosophy of "autonomy." In other words, the ability to make informed, uncoerced decisions for oneself. Kant believed that for there to be morality, there must first be autonomy. In his *Groundwork of the Metaphysics of Morals*, autonomy coincided with both human dignity and personhood. Kant believed that autonomy and rationality were the two benchmarks for a meaningful life. A life without them would not be worth living. According to Kant, it would be equivalent to the life of an insect or a plant.

My phone buzzed. I casually slipped it out of my pocket, glancing at it under my desk.

It was a text from Deja: Call me.

And then the text vanished because my phone was vibrating with an incoming call from Deja Williams.

"Hope, that better be an emergency call from you mother," said Mr. Britton, only vaguely annoyed.

"I have to go to the bathroom," I lied. And then, because I was the worst liar ever—and also because I was sitting at the front of the class—I discreetly held my phone in front of my chest so that he could see the incoming call.

Mr. Britton leaned forward and squinted.

Then his eyes ballooned in their sockets.

"Yes, Hope, you may go to the bathroom," Mr. Britton said loudly and awkwardly, like a bad Shakespearean actor. "Far be it from me to deny you of your God-given, um . . . bathroom rights."

Oh my God, I take it back—Mr. Britton was the worst liar ever. I shielded my face uncomfortably as I made a quick exit.

The moment the classroom door closed behind me, I answered the phone. My voice cracked with stress. "Hi, Deja."

"Hope, I need you to get everyone together. We need to have a band meeting ASAP."

"Uh, okay. I'm in school right now, but—"

"I got another tip from Frank. You know, from the Thrifty Schwifty? Apparently, Alt-Rite is planning an impromptu performance this afternoon at the Women's Resource Center in Gillette."

"The women's clinic?" I said, feeling sick.

"From what I understand, they're stealing a page out of the

Sundance Kids' handbook and intend to play 'Feminists (Baby Killers)' over and over until they either drive everyone away or they get the police called on them or whatever. Apparently, they're planning it in conjunction with one of your classmate's appointments? Some girl named Brittney or Brenda or . . . ?"

"Brianna," I said, breathless.

"Yes. Brianna. So, not to advocate truancy or anything, but—"

"Jesus. No, I got it. I'll get everyone together. Where should we meet you?"

"Already on my way over. I'll pick you up."

Danny was the only one whose schedule I had memorized by heart. I group texted the band: Alt-Rite emergency. Leave class now, and high-tailed it to Ms. Beekman's AP Bio class. I barged in like I owned the place. Like I was holding an actual fucking deed in my hand.

"Excuse me, but I need to borrow Danny Roger right now!" I proclaimed. "It's a family emergency!"

Sundance High wasn't a big school, so basically everyone knew Danny and his current living situation. And absolutely *no one* knew what constituted a "family emergency" when you weren't welcome at home.

"Oh," said Ms. Beekman. She seemed genuinely alarmed. "Okay? Go ahead then."

Danny was just now examining his phone, noticing my text. Judging from his face alone, you'd have thought the "family emergency" was all four of his grandparents being held at gunpoint by German terrorists in a hostage situation at Nakatomi Plaza. He collected his things in one mighty sweep of his arms, and we were outta there.

As soon as the door closed behind us, Danny screamed calmly, "Okay, what the HELL IS ALT-RITE DOING THIS TIME?"

Right as I opened my mouth, my phone buzzed. An incoming call from Angus. I answered.

"Astrid and I are over by the trophies," said Angus. "So, if you don't mind my asking, what the fuck?"

"Meet me out front," I said. "Deja's picking us up. We'll explain on the way."

"On the way *where*, Hope? I have a test in AP Calculus today! And not to be the responsible one, but so does Astri—"

At least that's what Angus started to say, but I heard a struggle as the phone apparently was wrested out of his hands.

"Deja's picking us up?!" Astrid exclaimed, breathing heavily.

"No, Astrid, we have a test!" Angus said in the background. "Think of college applications!"

"But! But Deja!" Astrid protested.

"Astrid, can you put Angus back on?" I said.

Astrid handed the phone over, no questions asked. "What, Hope? What could possibly be so pressing it can't wait until after school?"

"Do you trust me, Angus?"

"Oh my God, Aladdin, please don't."

"Angus. Do you trust me?"

"*Ugghhhhhh*. Fine. I trust you. But I'm very unhappy about it."

"I call shotgun," Astrid yelled in the background.

"What? You can't call shotgun until the car is in sight!"

"Says who?"

"Says the rules of shotgun!"

"That sounds like a made-up rule."

♩ ♫ ♪

The four of us packed into Deja's RAV4. Angus took shotgun this time. Meanwhile, Deja explained everything, which was basically the exact same thing she told me over the phone. After all, she was relaying secondhand information from @1234frank. Not that we needed more information. There was plenty of outrage to be shared over our secondhand take on the situation. By the end of it, Angus seemed to have completely forgotten about tests and calculus and college applications.

"Those mother*fuckers*," Angus adequately summarized.

"What is even the point of them doing this?" said Astrid. "Is it, like, payback for Change Through Grace or what? I mean, it doesn't even make sense."

"A band like Alt-Rite doesn't do things to make sense," said Danny. "They do it because they can. Because they think it's their *right* or some shit."

I couldn't help but think of Shawn and wonder where Brianna fit into his fucked-up definition of freedom.

"Honestly, I don't care what their motivation is," said Deja. "At the end of the day, it's just four teenage misogynists shaming every woman coming in and out of that clinic. We can't let them do that."

"So what do we do?" said Angus. "How do we fight this?"

"I'm glad you asked. What have you got?"

A deathly silence fell over the back seat.

"I mean, what songs have you written so far?" said Deja. "Way I see it, the best way for bands to battle is to outplay each other.

If Alt-Rite is spreading their hate with music, then we kick their asses with music."

Our collective silence and the incriminating shame on our faces spoke way more than words ever could.

"You haven't written anything?" said Deja.

Deja's disappointment wasn't mean-spirited or condescending. But disappointing your hero on *any* level was mortifying. Like we were horses she had put all her money on, and we turned out to be jackasses.

Danny, our alleged songwriter, looked the most debased of all.

Deja noticed our shame. How could she not? It looked and smelled like a trash fire. She immediately backtracked.

"That's okay," said Deja. "That's fine! I'm sure there are other ways we can . . . um . . . You guys are just high school kids. You have a lot going on. I obviously don't expect you to be songwriting *machines*."

I couldn't speak for everyone else, but the more Deja tried to make us feel better, the more I personally felt like a massive loaf of shit that couldn't even flush down the toilet properly.

"Wait," said Danny.

We all turned and looked at Danny who had this wild and distant look in his eyes, which meant he was experiencing either a stroke of genius of some sort or simply a stroke. With Danny, it could go either way.

"We do have *something*," said Danny, stroke-of-geniusly.

"We do?" said Astrid.

"What?" I said. "You don't mean, 'Hey Hey Hey Oh Yeah Woo!', do you?"

"Oh no, we definitely *do not*," said Angus. "That's not a song; it's a crisis."

"Well, sort of," said Danny. "But the melody is actually really good. It's got the energy. It just needs a little meat on the bone. Here, check this out."

Danny unzipped his backpack and removed a notebook—one of the very same notebooks he'd been scribbling in for days, like some consumed conspiracy theorist. He frantically flipped through pages, stared at one for a hot second or two, then nodded, each one nod more enthused than the last. "Yeah. Yeah, this could work!"

He handed the notebook to me.

"Keep that melody in your head. Pay attention to the time signature. Maybe keep a 'hey hey hey oh yeah woo' at the beginning of each stanza. Think of it in layers."

I looked at the words on the page, and Astrid leaned in, reading along. Several lines were scratched out erratically, but what appeared as mere gibberish from a distance suddenly came together. It just popped out at you like a revelation. The more Astrid and I read, the more our jaws slowly dropped like a pair of drawbridges.

"Sweet fuck," I said.

"What, let me see!" said Angus.

"This could work," said Astrid. "This could really work!"

"I wanna *seeeeee*!" Angus pleaded.

We passed the notebook up to Angus, and he read quietly, clear until the moment that he wasn't reading quietly.

"Oh shit," said Angus. "Oh shit, you guys. OH SHIT."

Danny smiled his first real smile in days.

♩ ♫ ♪

We spent the next several hours practicing at Angus's house.

What our previous practices lacked in direction and substantial output, they made up for in sharpening our instrumental and vocal skills and finding our synergy, not to mention creating a melody we now realized was actually *pretty damn good.* In those few short hours, we were performing this spliced-up new song composed of the unworking pieces of old songs as if it was an appendage of ourselves. We were the Dr. Frankensteins of reanimating songs out of the pieces of dead ones, and it was *alive!*

Meanwhile, Deja had an idea about our entrance and proceeded to call in a favor or two with the locals. As it turned out, a local bar owner had in his possession the very thing she was looking for and *also* happened to be Hope Cassidy and the Sundance Kids's self-proclaimed "biggest fan."

His name was Ulysses Mackintosh, but everyone called him Mack.

♩ ♫ ♪

The Women's Resource Center on West Eighth Street was a small, unsuspecting little thing. Sure, the deep blue-green paint job was a bit loud, giving it that small-business boutique look, and it had two very pretty raised boxes of planted flowers out front—vibrant splashes of white, blue, and yellow—but you had to be really looking for the place to find it. The small sign above the door was all but unreadable from the street. You would never guess the purpose of this house-turned-clinic just by looking at it.

Well, you *wouldn't* have been able to guess, I should say, were it not for the protesters. And no, I'm not talking about Alt-Rite.

They were there too, but this was something different.

There were four of them, all teenagers, all wearing matching neon green shirts that read "Traditional Family of Christ." A youth group. They were marching, yelling, waving signs that read "Pro-Murder" and "Respect Religious Freedom!" and one with a great big picture of a very Caucasian Jesus and this caption:

BEFORE I FORMED YOU IN THE WOMB,
I KNEW YOU. —GOD

Well, three of them were doing this. The fourth was standing a visible distance behind them, leaning against the wall of the clinic, her arms folded into the world's tightest knot, wilting. She stood there despite a very open and available outdoor bench parked right beside her. It was easy for me to overly focus on this fourth protester—reason being, she was Charity.

She looked like she was going to be sick.

Loathsome tallness aside, she was a neon green blip in the background while her church friends waved their signs like war flags. Every once in a while, they would start a chant: "Thou shalt not kill! Thou shalt not kill!"

Meanwhile, Dylan Roger, Hunter Thorson, Kaleb Carter, and Shawn Lee were off to the side, lackadaisically setting up their equipment. It was late in the afternoon, an hour after school ended, when they arrived to set up their band shit. They arrived with the sort of jet-lagged look you get after a long layover in

Dallas–Fort Worth. I think they were low-key annoyed—by their fellow protesters or that they didn't have a cooler audience waiting for them. Hunter, in particular, looked especially sour, like he was being blackmailed to be there. I found myself paying special attention to him, maybe because he was the cause of so much of Danny's anguish. He was easily the tallest of the four, with a strong, unshaved jawline and hair pulled back in a bun. He seemed the antithesis of Kaleb Carter, who was the shortest and thickest and hillbilliest of the bunch, wearing a camo jacket and American flag shorts.

Now that I was taking a moment to study Hunter, I realized that he was actually majorly hot. I wondered, Did Danny maybe have a thing for him? If Danny had the courage to come out, it didn't seem like a terrible leap that maybe it was because there was someone specific that he really liked.

I observed this from the bed of a flatbed truck parked about a block away.

The back window of the truck's cab slid open to reveal Mack behind the steering wheel and Deja in the passenger seat.

"You kids ready to rock and roll?" He was looking at me specifically, grinning like some sort of proud parent.

An hour earlier we had secured Astrid's drums to the flatbed with ratchet straps, along with my mic, all our amps, and a gas-powered generator. The moment we arrived in Gillette and found a clandestine place to park and spy on the women's clinic, the Sundance Kids and I climbed aboard. Danny and Angus were holding their guitars with one hand, and all four of us were hanging on to the cab for dear life—although we weren't even moving yet. Mack promised to go slow. Apparently, he used this very same truck as a float in the Lighted Parade, which he participated in annually, but I dunno. This seemed like a solid way to die.

I swallowed hard against the knot in my throat and croaked, "Let's rock and roll."

♩ ♫ ♪

We rolled slowly down Eighth Street, and Mack was right: He was going *so slow* that it was almost impossible to fall. Once we gathered our courage, I grabbed my mic and took front and center. Danny and Angus took their places at my left and right, and Astrid settled into her drum set like a pilot in her cockpit. We jammed leisurely, the sort of jam sesh that is less a song than a striptease of what's to come, a warm-up. And believe me, since we technically just wrote this song mere hours ago, we needed all the warm-up we could get.

We didn't have to drive far. Our, shall we say, "conspicuous" presence—rock-and-roll on wheels—sucked the yelling, marching, and overall life out of the protest across the street. "Thou shalt not kill! Thou shalt not— What the?"

Hunter Thorson had nearly assembled his drum set when he saw us. He managed to tip over his cymbals, which gave a glorious crash.

"What the fuck?" said Dylan.

Mack slowed to a graceful halt directly in front of the Women's Resource Center, and that's when our impromptu camera crew assembled: Mack and Deja with camcorders, Frank rushing from behind the clinic with a boom mic—oh, and Mr. Britton.

Mr. Britton all but died of a lethal dose of happiness when

my text invited him to camp out in the back alley of an abortion clinic after school with Frank and a pair of boom mics. I made him promise not to ask for Deja's signature. Made him swear on Kant's *Critique of Pure Reason*.

Cameras and boom mics converged around us in stunning unison. At that exact moment, Astrid kicked us off with a torrent of drumbeats like gunshots, and Danny and Angus grinded noisily into a grungy guitar intro, while on vocals I leaned violently into the riot grrrl scene, mostly channeling Kathleen Hanna of Bikini Kill.

> *Hey hey hey oh yeah woo!*
> *You think you own this body; tell me whatcha gonna do?*
> *Gonna desecrate this temple? Buddy, I got news for you.*
> *I'm the motherfucking goddess, run the place like Xanadu!*

"Shit," said Dylan. "This is a *battle*. Their *battling* us!"

All four members of Alt-Rite were suddenly fire ants in a mound that had just been stomped on. They madly scrambled to pull their shit together.

> *Hey hey hey oh yeah* [sarcastic] *wow.*
> *You think you're in charge? Well, baby, look at me now.*
> *I built my kingdom on your ruins. You're burnt toast, you're chow.*

I'm the queen of this castle, the fuckin' thunder in
the clouds!

The Caucasian Jesus sign fell right out of the hands of the boy holding it. Charity's mouth was wide open. If I had binoculars, I swear, I could've seen her tonsils.

"Mother*fucker*!" said Dylan. "Where's my mic?"

"*So tell me,*" I sang.

Who's laughing
Now?

"Kaleb, where the *fuck* is my mic?" Dylan screamed. Or tried to scream. I was louder.

Cause she is meeeeeee;
I'm gonna fix her crown.
And we are weeeeeee;
You can't tear us down.
It's my bodyyyyyyy,
You stupid fucking clown.
You can't touch us;
We're gonna make a sound.

"Seriously?" said Kaleb. "You're blaming me? It's *your* mic, dumbass!"

"And we drove here in *your* truck, you dumb shit."

"So *what*?!" said Kaleb, hysterical.

"Hey . . . my dudes . . . ," Shawn interjected as awkwardly as possible, "this probably isn't the most productive way to—"

"SHUT THE FUCK UP," Dylan and Kaleb yelled in miraculous unison.

Shawn turned and walked away with both hands in the air.

Hunter, meanwhile, clearly uninterested in Alt-Rite's problems, had become hilariously invested in Astrid's infectious beat and was silently mirroring it with his own drumsticks.

Hey hey hey oh yeah WHAT?
These heels ain't just for show, I'm gonna kick your butt.
You tried to call me a slut, 'cause you don't like my strut.
You think you're the king? Well, baby, I'm the Tut!
Hey hey hey hey oh yeah woo!
You think you make the rules? A fuckin' woman made you!
Without her you're nothin'; you're fuckin' gum on my shoe.
You try to fuck with my rights, and I will FUCK. WITH. YOU.
So tell me watcha
Gonna
Do?

It took a little longer this time—no doubt because of the Jesus-y protesters and the vaguely Nazi band camped out front—but as we soared into the chorus for a second time, and people realized what we were all about, we finally began to accumulate an audience. Women and men from the clinic, in street clothes, scrubs, and lab coats. People from surrounding businesses—a Jimmy John's, a frozen yogurt place, even a maternity store! One pregnant woman came out, ripe as a watermelon, holding her belly with one hand and waving her phone's flashlight with the other.

"Hunter, are you fucking kidding me?" said Dylan. "Are you fucking *drumming along* with them?"

He wasn't drumming along with us—only pretending to. But like Kaleb and Shawn, he seemed to have had his fill of Dylan's shit for one day. He casually flipped Dylan off while continuing to make drumming motions.

"That's it," said Dylan. "I tried giving you a chance. I'm telling EVERYONE about you and Brianna. I'm telling EVERYONE about you and Danny. I'm telling EVERYONE about EVERYTHING."

Danny missed a note on his guitar.

I momentarily forgot the words to the chorus.

We quickly recovered, and it went enormously unnoticed in the ebb and flow of the pulsing crowd. But when I looked at Danny, his face was white, and in that moment I knew everything.

♩ ♫ ♪

I wouldn't read it until later—much later—but late that night, a conversation transpired between two users on an aggressively Christian social media site. Those users were CharityMeansLove and netflix&dyl, the latter of whom would soon be flagged for having a "suggestive username." But it didn't matter. Not to netflix&dyl. He had only subscribed to the site fifteen minutes earlier for the sole purpose of having this conversation.

netflix&dyl: hey, ur charity cassidy, rite?

CharityMeansLove: Hi. Do I know you?

netflix&dyl: dylan roger.
netflix&dyl: aka dannys brother
netflix&dyl: aka the brother of the gay kid living in ur house

CharityMeansLove: Oh!

netflix&dyl: good oh or bad oh?

CharityMeansLove: Lol, I know who you are, Dylan Roger.

netflix&dyl: uh-oh. bad oh?

CharityMeansLove: No, I mean everyone knows who you are! You're kind of a celebrity.

netflix&dyl: good oh!!
netflix&dyl: u a fan of the band?

CharityMeansLove: I mean, it's kind of crude for my taste. No offense.

netflix&dyl: none taken (;
netflix&dyl: can i tell you a secret?
netflix&dyl: you have to swear an oath of secrecy. if you tell anyone, i'll have to kill you

CharityMeansLove: Um, maybe you shouldn't...

netflix&dyl: i actually really miss danny and i want him to come home
netflix&dyl: shit
netflix&dyl: is that weird?
netflix&dyl: don't answer. i know it's weird.

CharityMeansLove: I don't think that's weird at all.

netflix&dyl: okay ur turn

CharityMeansLove: My turn?

netflix&dyl: I just told you my deepest darkest secret, and since you didn't swear an oath of secrecy, i now need you to share your deepest darkest secret, so if either of us spills the beans, we can expose the other to the world for the weirdo that they truly are
netflix&dyl: so
netflix&dyl: ur deepest darkest secret please

netflix&dyl: i'm just kidding

CharityMeansLove: Okay. Here it is...

netflix&dyl: oh shit

CharityMeansLove: I love EDM.
CharityMeansLove: And electronica.
CharityMeansLove: Basically all electronic music ever.
CharityMeansLove: I stole my dad's Minimoog out of the attic, and I've been composing some of my own stuff and downloading it to SoundCloud.
CharityMeansLove: I snuck out of the house and went to a rave once. I danced all night with complete strangers and glow sticks. It was the greatest night of my life.
CharityMeansLove: I think something's wrong with me.

netflix&dyl: what? why is that a secret?
netflix&dyl: what the heck is a minimoog? sounds cool.

CharityMeansLove: Sorry, I guess that was kind of weird. A Minimoog is a keyboard. And yes, it's cool.

netflix&dyl: i mean you strike me more as the taylor swift type, but you can like edm! i think that's cool.

CharityMeansLove: That means a lot (:

netflix&dyl: u know, our music is crude for a reason

netflix&dyl: alt-rite's music, i mean

CharityMeansLove: What do you mean?

netflix&dyl: it's all about making a point. shedding a light on TRUE evil: socialists and pervs and baby killers and stuff. politics these days is all about believing what the media tells you to believe. they hate god, they hate religion, they even hated the president of the united states! and now, it's suddenly "cool" to be gay, which is really messed up. if somebody doesn't speak up against this shit, who will? so being crude is like the lesser of two evils.

netflix&dyl: sorry for swearing btw

netflix&dyl: my dad says not to swear in front of pretty girls (;

CharityMeansLove: No, it's okay!!

CharityMeansLove: I agree with you (:

CharityMeansLove: About the other stuff, not me being pretty.

CharityMeansLove: I mean, I don't think I'm ugly.

CharityMeansLove: Ugh. Words.

CharityMeansLove: [inserts foot in mouth]

netflix&dyl: LOL

netflix&dyl: can i ask a weird question?

CharityMeansLove: Okay . . .

netflix&dyl: how old u are?

CharityMeansLove: Almost 15

netflix&dyl: really? you look older.
netflix&dyl: in a good way

CharityMeansLove: Aw shucks. I'm just tall.
CharityMeansLove: And also legally blind without my glasses.

netflix&dyl: what are u doing rite now?

CharityMeansLove: Homework. It's super fun.
CharityMeansLove: I'm lying. It's not.

netflix&dyl: u wanna go to sonic and grab some tots?

CharityMeansLove: Tots?

netflix&dyl: tater tots
netflix&dyl: you can order whatever you want. i just fuckin love their tots.
netflix&dyl: sorry for swearing.

CharityMeansLove: You don't have to apologize.
CharityMeansLove: I can't though. It's a school night):

netflix&dyl: awwww, c'mon! sneak out ur window!

CharityMeansLove: I would get in sooooo much trouble.

netflix&dyl: ur sister had the police called on her not long ago.

netflix&dyl: pretty sure sneaking out the window and grabbing tots with me is the lesser evil here.

netflix&dyl: you still there??

CharityMeansLove: Okay.

netflix&dyl: okay??!?

CharityMeansLove: Let's get some tots.

Zaffy was in the first group of refugees cut loose. She broke free in a sprint, in a straight line for the edge of camp, and the long, thin blur on the sand that was Andromeda and Tanks.

She had only taken a step or two past the edge, where the perimeter stakes were fried, when the ground shook beneath her.

Zaffy stopped. Everyone stopped. But the ground did not stop shaking.

This was not a dearthquake.

"Zaffy, get away from there!" Trog hollered.

Explosions drew them out of the ground.

Zaffy was frozen in place as the biggest living thing she had ever seen exploded out of the ground like a tower made of flesh. Ribbed and segmented and throbbing. It emerged maybe fifty yards west of Andromeda, but fifty yards was nothing when you were roughly the size of a solar flare.

The tip of the tower curled downward, and its mouth peeled open five ways. It didn't have teeth so much as a jugular of endless spikes.

"WORM!" someone screamed.

Zaffy ran for Andromeda.

The worm nosedived. A flesh-colored rainbow from hell. It came down like a world-ending comet, tail and all, with no intention of slowing for impact.

The monster came down directly on top of Andromeda and Tanks. Swallowed them, as well as at least ten feet of sand in every direction, burrowing downward.

Zaffy skidded to a broken halt as hundreds of feet of flesh—meat as wide as camp—plunged into the ground like it was diving into water. Lastly, its tail whipped and slurped, smacking the ground like a felled tree, leaving a short, dry ravine behind it, ending in a bottomless crater that disappeared deep, deep, deep down into the center of Dearth.

—Andromeda and Tanks Through Space and Time,
ÆonEQ

—TWENTY-ONE—

CHERRY GARCIA

OUR PERFORMANCE AT THE WOMEN'S RESOURCE Center was an unmitigated success. The *video* of that performance was even better. Directed and edited by Deja, it was of unquestionably higher visual and audio quality than the Change Through Grace video. It already had five million views, making it dictionary-definition viral. Our Twitter following doubled. We now had about as many followers as the Earth had McDonald's. We should have been on top of the world.

Except that Danny was depressed.

I still hadn't confronted him about Hunter. And he didn't tell me. I'd be lying if I said that didn't hurt my feelings just a little bit. But what could I do? After Danny caught me reading his phone, I felt that I had inadvertently forfeited certain privileges, such as confidentiality and trust.

These days, Mom gave us free rein to use the CR-V, which Danny usually ended up driving. I think she hoped that Charity would ask us for a ride, and we'd have to give her one. Then everything would slowly patch itself together.

But Charity never asked us for a ride. I had *no idea* how Charity was getting to and from school—especially after her friendship with Brianna seemed to have imploded—but I was about to find out in a big way.

It happened one particularly quiet drive home from school. Shortly after we pulled onto my street Danny stomped barbarically on the brakes like we entered a school zone with a cop pulled off to the side.

He flipped a u-ey.

"You know what?" said Danny. "Let's grab ice cream. My treat."

"Wait, what?" I asked.

"I just figure we deserve to celebrate, you know, with all the good stuff that's been happening lately. With the band, I mean. Have you been to Big Spoon?"

Something was obviously wrong. First of all, this was the most he had spoken to me all day. Second, he looked nervous.

I glanced in the passenger-side mirror and saw an unfamiliar car parked in my driveway.

And... people inside?

Christ, were they making out?

"Turn around," I said.

"What?" said Danny, panicking. "But what about ice cream?"

I unbuckled the seat belt and opened my door.

I wasn't going to *jump*, per se. But I wasn't going to *not jump* either. This was what you call an ultimatum.

"Okayokayokay!" said Danny. As he turned the car back around, he muttered under his breath, "Sweet merciful fuck."

The car looked eerily similar to Danny's car before he got disowned, possibly the same make, model, and year, and then I realized the fucker in the driver's seat was Dylan Roger. His profile was unmistakable, even as it was pressed fiercely into the face of some blond in the passenger seat. Christ almighty. What reason did Dylan *possibly* have to be parked in our driveway making out with some random blonde—

Dylan's mouth traveled down her jaw to her throat, where he started sucking like a parasite. The girl rolled her head back, mouth open, and she was wearing thick-framed glasses. Her eyes met mine, and for the literal love of Christ, it was Charity.

I jumped out of the car. Danny was driving slow enough that I could do this and stay on my feet—let alone not die.

"Hope, wait," said Danny, but it was too late. I was storming the Dylmobile.

Charity reacted exactly how I thought she would: pushed Dylan's face away, straightened herself, adjusted her top and her hair, even glanced at herself in the mirror. Dylan, meanwhile, was not upset at all at being cockblocked. He was grinning. He had already won. He would take this psychological victory to his bedroom later and wank off to it.

I slammed the palm of my hand against her window and didn't stop until she rolled the window down.

Then she seemed to realize the radio was blasting "Levels" by Avicii, and for some reason she panicked, fumbling with the knobs until it was playing something that sounded vaguely Christian.

"Excuse you," said Charity, visibly irritated.

"Excuse me?" I said, losing my absolute shit. *"Excuse... me?"*

"Excuse us," Charity mumbled to Dylan. She climbed out.

That was my chance.

I forced my way into the passenger seat.

"HEY, YOU STAY THE HELL AWAY FROM MY SISTER, YOU DOUCHEY PIECE OF FUCK," I said, pointing a dangerous finger at Dylan.

Dylan was smiling *so wide*. He was thrilled. This was the happiest day of his life. Some kids had Disney World; Dylan had this.

"Hope!" Charity screamed.

The unthinkable happened. A pair of arms grabbed me from behind, one around my abdomen, the other around my throat, wrestling me out. I tried to fight it, but this person was stronger. For a second—a brief instant—I thought it was Danny. He had finally turned on me. Someone like him was too good to be true. I felt the air cut out from my lungs. From my brain. I started seeing little black holes, slowly inhaling everything in sight.

I was thrown aside. I only barely caught my balance. It should have been a miracle but instead turned out to be the opposite. The moment I regained my bearings, I saw Charity, and she was red-faced, teary-eyed, and *furious*.

She slapped me in the face.

That slap rang through my skull like the bang that jump-started the universe. It was pure déjà vu. It was exactly how Mom slapped me after the tattoo. The sort of slap that deconstructs you as a human being.

I gaped haplessly. Touched my face, which felt like frozen ground beef thawed out in the microwave—sizzling and raw. I glanced from my hand to Charity. What was even happening?

"You stay away from him!" said Charity. "You stay *the hell* away from him!"

"What the...?" I said, blinking. "Charity...he doesn't care about you."

"No." Charity shook her head.

"He's just trying to get back at me!" I said, getting riled up all over again. "He doesn't give a *shit* about you!"

"No, Hope!" Charity snapped. "*You* don't give a shit about me."

"Wha...?" I started to say. Already, it felt like a lie in my throat.

"You've *never* given a shit about me. Not once, not ever. Faith was the only one you ever gave a shit about, and I'm *sorry* I was never good enough for you, but I am so tired of trying. I'm done."

"Charity, I—"

"No!" she cut me off. "Don't even *pretend* you're my friend. You're not even my sister."

It was the word "sister" that connected. It hurt worse than the slap.

Charity climbed back into Dylan's car, all but slamming the door shut.

"Get me out of here," she said.

"Where?" said Dylan, faux-sympathetically.

"Literally *anywhere* is better than here."

Dylan started the engine, and again I caught a glimpse of that unrestrained glee. He peeled out, narrowly missing the CR-V—which was stopped in the middle of the street like a parade float—and he floored it. His tires were keening savagely, bansheelike death wails. They rounded the corner *Tokyo Drift* style and disappeared.

I don't know how long I stood there staring at the empty street. I don't know how long I *would have* stood there if Danny hadn't said anything. Possibly forever.

"Hope?" said Danny.

I looked at Danny in a psychologically concussed daze.

"Do you still want to get that ice cream?" he said. "My treat?"

I just stared at him until tears glided freely down my face, accumulated at the bob of my chin, and fell to my shoes.

♩ ♫ ♪

Since I was in no state to make public appearances, Danny opted for individual pints at the local Decker's Market. I went in wearing oversized sunglasses and a Batman hoodie with the hood pulled over my head and the drawstrings pulled tight. Yes, it had Bat ears. Danny got chocolate-chip cookie dough, and I got Cherry Garcia, which we ate in the CR-V. We had brought our own spoons.

And there we ate in a vacuum of silence. This was interrupted only by my occasional whimpering (existential misery), moaning (ice cream–related ecstasy), and the sound of my cold spoon clinking against my teeth.

"How old was Charity when she outed Faith?" Danny asked.

"Um," I said, blinking. I was trying to think past the horrible brain freeze I was deliberately giving myself. "Thirteen?"

Danny nodded. Inserted another spoonful of chocolate-chip cookie dough in his mouth. Swallowed.

"When I was thirteen," said Danny, "Dylan, Kaleb, and I were at this very Decker's. We saw this old man, maybe in his sixties, wearing high heels and makeup, just strolling around the produce aisle. Dylan and Kaleb thought it was hilarious. They just kept snickering and joking about it. They couldn't get over it. And then they noticed that I wasn't joining in, and . . . I dunno, I panicked. It was like I thought they could see right through me. I had a crush on Hunter at the time. No need to act surprised. I know you know."

I shrank into my Batman hoodie and shoved another spoonful of Cherry Garcia into my mouth.

"Anyway, in that moment, I could think of nothing worse than them making fun of me the way they were making fun of him. So I shouted at the top of my lungs, 'Hey, fag.' I hated myself, but I also felt . . . relief? Relief that my secret was still a secret? But that old man walked right up to me, and he said, 'I am a human being.' Dylan and Kaleb, of course, just made fun of the way he talked. They thought the whole thing was fucking hilarious. But it's haunted me. Haunted me that I was the very thing that makes coming out—being queer—terrifying."

Danny looked at me. A harrowing look of incubated grief.

"I'm not saying what I did is justifiable because I was thirteen. I'm not saying what Charity did is justifiable because she was thirteen. But we're all products of our environment. My family was prejudiced, and from everything you've told me, it sounds like your mom was too, and your dad just let it happen. You can blame Charity for a lot of things. But you can't blame her for how she was raised."

"It would be a lot easier to forgive her if I knew where Faith was," I mumbled.

"Forgiveness isn't even in the equation. All I'm saying is, if you care about Charity, now is the time to let her know—before it's too late. I never knew Faith but—judging from everything you've told me about her—I think she would have wanted that."

Danny was right.

God fucking damnit, he was right.

The Dresdorian religion, the Church of Time, was a spirituality that shared a lot in common with other Dearth religions. Religious overlap was inevitable, no matter what corner of the universe you worshipped in. (But don't tell a Dresdorian that.) Like Trog's faith, the Dresdorians believed in a God that lived at the center of Dearth. But this God didn't grant wishes. Rather, this God was the binding force of space and time and thus called the God of Space and Time. This God was genderless, not because They didn't have a dick or a vagina, but because They didn't have a body at all. The God of Space and Time was everywhere and nowhere. But primarily, its everywhere-and-nowhere-ness existed in the center of Dearth. (Don't question it; it made sense if you had enough faith.) The God of Space and Time had blessed Dresdorians with their "four-dimensional" natures—not because the God of Space and Time loved Dresdorians more than other beings, but because the Dresdorians were the only beings that mattered. Everyone else was fodder (according to the Church or Time). If they weren't, why hadn't they been blessed with what the Dresdorians had?

Some Dresdorians claimed to feel the God of Space and Time beneath their feet, pulsing, feeding their third eye. It wasn't an uncommon phenomenon—even Andromeda had felt it—and it only served to testify of the "irrefutable truth" of the Church of Time. It was why the church and the state were one and the same. Why men like Allfather Odyss were both mayor and minister.

Dearth was not without science, however. And science had an explanation for the "God" that Dresdorians claimed to feel beneath their feet. By observing and mapping the magnetic field of Dearth, they theorized that a primordial low-mass black hole existed at the center of the planet. They believed that in the moment of the Super Spark (the explosion that jump-started the universe), these primordial black holes were created and they had been there ever since. It was possibly the reason Dearth was even a planet to begin with.

It was believed that a Dresdorian's third eye was merely an antenna to the black hole at the center of the planet.

Dresdorians had terrific reception.

The good news was that Andromeda missed all those sharp teeth on the trip down the worm's esophagus. Probably the only good news to be found in a situation where one is being eaten by a worm. To the worm, Andromeda was not a meal. She wasn't even a snack. She was too small. She was more like an herb or spice. Her being eaten was purely by chance—a wrong-place-at-the-wrong-time situation. The worm was coming down, and she and Tanks were in the trajectory of its open mouth, and down the hole they went. Nobody wants to eat a fly, but sometimes it happens.

The worm made a straight shot downward. Down, down, down, to wherever it is that worms go. Even for Dearth scientists, the jury was still out on that one. But as the worm descended at breakneck speed, the scar on Andromeda's forehead pulsed. Then it began to throb. She could almost feel her third eye—like, physically feel it, like it was still mounted to her forehead, a regal extension of her mind. It resembled that prickling sensation of blood returning to an appendage, less needles, more like the Sands of Time trickling in, filling the ever-elusive hourglass of one's existence.

It was in that moment—the first since her third eye was clipped—that Andromeda saw a memory.

* * *

—Andromeda and Tanks Through Space and Time,
ÆonQ

—TWENTY-TWO—

HOPELESS

REPAIRING MY RELATIONSHIP WITH CHARITY WAS already a daunting, next-to-impossible task. At least that's how it felt to me.

Then she moved in with the Rogers.

She didn't tell us she was moving. She just did. She'd left early that morning for school, before the rest of us were even up, and she was nowhere to be found at dinnertime that night. Not that she would have eaten dinner with us anyway—she had sentenced herself to solitary confinement indefinitely, choosing to eat in her bedroom instead—but Mom always popped in to let her know that dinner was ready.

Today's poison was meatloaf. And...

Charity was not in her room.

She wasn't anywhere in the house.

She wasn't anywhere, period.

Finally, after Mom went bedroom to bedroom yelling Charity's name, she called Charity. Charity didn't pick up. She *texted* Charity.

Charity texted back: I'm at Dylan's house.

Mom made the angriest face imaginable but managed to exercise restraint in her text back: Well dinner's ready. Come back home please.

Charity texted back: I'm not coming home.

Mom texted back: Excuse me? What do you mean you're not coming home?

Charity texted back: I guess you could say I'm "pulling a Faith."

Mom stared at that text for a long time, unable to fathom a response.

Charity texted back: The Rogers already said I could stay here as long as I need to.

Mom snapped out of her daze and texted back a firestorm: NO!!! You do not get to do this to me. You will come back home this instant or I will come over there and drag you out of their house with my bare hands. I LOVE YOU but you are making me VERY ANGRY RIGHT NOW. Come home. Come home right now and I will pretend this conversation never happened. Your meatloaf is getting cold.

There was a significant delay—in which Mom had time to put on shoes and a coat, and she snatched the car keys from the dish by the door. She was all but strangling the keys when Charity's response finally came: I'm not coming home. If you come over, the Rogers will not answer the door. If you try to break in, they will call the police. I'm turning off my phone now. We're having chicken alfredo which I like a lot more than meatloaf.

Mom's physical response to this text was to scream.

Then she dug up an old phone book—a relic of a bygone era—and rang up the Rogers on their landline.

The Rogers were, of course, prodigiously Christian. So why in the holy name of fuck would they let their horny-ass son's fourteen-year-old girlfriend move in with them? Wasn't this, like, chastity 101?

Well, it turned out that Eric and Cynthia Roger were schemers too. Even though they wanted nothing to do with Danny—not until he "reevaluated his life choices"—they also didn't want him living with people who would simply support his gayness. According to them, we were "undermining their parental authority" by letting Danny live with us. They were also maybe a tiny bit upset about me hitting Dylan in the nads with a seven-hundred-page philosophy textbook.

Inviting Charity to live with them was what you call a "power move."

Mom called the police.

Dad, meanwhile, hovered nearby, pacing in tight circles, either mumbling indiscernibly or just making disgruntled gibberish sounds. It was hard to tell the difference.

When Sundance PD found out who was calling and what this was about, they forwarded Mom to Chief Daryl Wilkins. At this point in the story, you should know that was the worst thing that could happen. Mom put him on speaker. She did this because Dad's proximity and overall neuroticism were getting on her nerves.

"Hello, Mrs. Cassidy. I understand you're unhappy with your daughter's current living situation?"

"'Unhappy' is not the word I would use. 'Pissed' is getting

close, but it's not quite vulgar enough. I want to use *swear words*, Chief Wilkins, and Lord help me, I'm trying not to."

"I see."

"You *see*? Do you see that Charity does not have our permission to live with her boyfriend who SEXUALLY HARRASSED MY OTHER DAUGHTER? Why is every officer I talk to giving me the runaround?"

"You mean your daughter who physically assaulted Dylan the day after she started a riot and had the police called on her?"

"Are you kidding me? You too?"

"What this is, Mrs. Cassidy, is a classic he-said, she-said situation."

"Actually, Chief Wilkins, it is nothing of the sort. There is video proof—"

"Mrs. Cassidy, are you calling to talk about Charity, or are we just going to talk about Dylan? Because if you want to talk about Dylan, I'm going to have to forward you to someone else."

Mom's wide mouth was spread thin. She was gritting her teeth to dust. "Fine. Charity. Let's talk about Charity. I want her home immediately."

"I'm afraid I can't do that."

"I beg your pardon? I'm her *parent slash legal guardian*. It is the *law* that she lives with me."

"Just as Mr. and Mrs. Roger are the *parent slash legal guardian*, so to speak, of Danny. You see, what we have here is a bit of a switcheroo. Sure, I can obey the letter of the law and bring Charity home. But if I do that, I'll have to stop by your house and pick up Danny too. Fair is fair. What they do with him at that point is their business, not mine, but I hear they were looking into that place your daughter turned into a rock concert. Er, not the abortion clinic. The other one."

Danny was, unfortunately, present for this conversation. We were all hovering around the phone on the kitchen counter. Mom was actually leaning over and clutching the edge of the counter like she intended to break it off.

She looked at Danny.

Danny looked dead inside.

I opened my mouth to interject, but Mom beat me to it.

"Nope," she said. "Pass. *Hard* pass."

Shit. When did Mom become so fucking cool?

I could almost feel Daryl Wilkins's smug face leering on the other line. "Okay. That's what I thought."

"Let's talk about Dylan now," said Mom, undeterred. "You forward me to *whoever* you need to."

♩ ♫ ♪

At the end of the day, Dylan hadn't done anything "punishable by the law."

Punishable by the *school district*, however, was a different story.

With police inquiring into a video that had been sitting in Superintendent Deborah Marshall's email for almost three weeks now, a disciplinary meeting was in order. The best part was that this could very well disrupt Dylan's involvement in the Battle of the Bands.

Unfortunately, Superintendent Marshall put it on Principal Reilly's shoulders to schedule the disciplinary meeting.

He scheduled it for the day after Battle of the Bands.

♩ ♫ ♪

Speaking of Battle of the Bands, it was in three days. This also meant that prom was in three days. Angus was the only one of us who "had a date," but I also had it on good information from Astrid that he and Kevin were fighting, which had *everything* to do with Angus's sudden preoccupation with the band and his unexpected career in social activism.

But whatever. Prom was a luxury we couldn't afford. Battle of the Bands was the one true thing that mattered to us, and fortunately, we had our choice of *two* killer songs to slay the competition. And not to get cocky, but we had kicked Alt-Rite's ass once already with "Hey Hey Hey Oh Yeah Woo! (Whatcha Gonna Do?)" History was smiling in our favor.

Or so we thought.

"You can't play viral songs," said Mr. Britton. "That means any song over five million views on YouTube. Anything over that will be automatically disqualified."

Danny, Astrid, Angus, and I were eating lunch in Mr. Britton's classroom when he dropped this rather unfortunate amendment to the Battle of the Band rules. He was wearing a purple cable-knit sweater that matched the purple bags under his eyes. I don't think that was intentional. He didn't seem to be sleeping well.

Danny set his fork down with a heavy, dread-filled *clack*. "What? That's not a rule! Since when is that a rule?"

"Since today. Since Principal Reilly learned that *both* of your songs have just over five million views on YouTube. According to him, it's an 'unfair advantage,'" Mr. Britton said with air quotes.

Danny, Astrid, Angus, and I stared at Mr. Britton, appalled. We were fucked. *Royally* fucked. By order of Her Highness the Queen.

Mr. Britton leaned forward heavily, cupped a hand to his bearded jowl, and loud-whispered, "Don't tell him I told you this, but Principal Reilly doesn't want you to win."

Mr. Britton was trying to be funny. It was a noble attempt.

"He finds your progressiveness and forward-thinking offensive," he continued to explain with no shortage of sarcasm, leaning back and adjusting his sweater. "So maybe if you toned the human rights down a bit, maybe reeled things back to the Dark Ages, you'll stand a fighting chance."

He was still trying to be funny. I think he was upset.

Danny looked worse. Danny looked like he might be sick.

It wasn't unwarranted. We all seemed to understand that Battle of the Bands represented something. Something important. It was like a microcosm for humankind.

If Battle of the Bands was fucked, what did that say for humanity as a whole?

The bell rang, and we all dispersed to our individual classes, in individual states of despair.

♪ ♫ ♪

After school, Danny sent a group text to the Sundance Kids and me.

> I resign as band lyricist. My head is just not in the game right now. Looking forward to everyone else's ideas. 😌

The smiley emoji seemed like one of those things you tack on to a message to seem less miserable than you really are. Take away the smiley emoji, and all I saw was a boy who was hurting.

The responses were vague and despondent.

Astrid: Maybe we should all take the day off to gestate. Let things settle and see if we come up with any ideas on our own.

Angus: I don't think that's a bad idea.

On the drive home, Danny turned the radio way up, which seemed to be his way of saying, *I don't want to talk about it.*

I tried anyway.

"About that text—" I said.

"Let's not talk about it," said Danny. "We can talk about *your* lyric ideas, if you have any, or *anyone else's* lyric ideas, but I don't want to talk about me or my ideas or how I feel right now. Please, just... not right now."

I gave a broken nod. Sank into the passenger seat. Didn't say a word for the rest of the ride home.

♩ ♫ ♪

I stayed up late that night reading *Andromeda and Tanks Through Space and Time*, and I was gearing up for the end—or what I could only assume was the end since everyone was *in the process of dying*! God, if Faith really did write this (innocent until proven guilty, I suppose), she had some explaining to do.

I was reading to get my mind off things but somehow accidentally did the opposite. I couldn't stop thinking. My mind was a supercollider.

I thought about Newton's Third Law of Motion, which I learned about in Ms. Beekman's physical science class—how every action is met by an equal and opposite reaction. But could it apply to social events? The entire history of civil rights, for example, was riddled with actions and reactions.

I thought about the Civil War and the American civil rights movement, which I learned about in Mr. Britton's US history class last year. How they were met by the respective assassinations of Abraham Lincoln and Martin Luther King Jr.

I thought about the 1969 riots after the police raided the Stonewall Inn gay bar. They were instrumental in gay liberation, but hardly ended LGBTQ discrimination. If anything, the fight had only just begun.

The fact of the matter was that every push for progress was always met by a violent shove backward.

I guess it was only natural that Hope Cassidy and the Sundance Kids were finally about to reap the consequences for their fight against hate.

Andromeda was making love to Tanks.

The initial sensation was warmth. Andromeda tried managing her expectations, making love to an android, and it was unnecessary. Tanks felt more biological than Andromeda did in her own skin. And instead of feeling vulnerable like Andromeda thought she would, she felt like she was home. Tanks was home.

Another memory eclipsed this one: their first date at Borgy's Bistro, which they could barely afford. They went because she had *told* Tanks this was where they had their first date. Now Tanks had to go and make it a reality. Andromeda felt sick, wondering how they were going to make rent. She scoured the menu for the cheapest item that wouldn't be a complete embarrassment to order. A breadstick? Could she order a single breadstick?

Tanks seemed to know that money was on Andromeda's mind. So she did what any good girlfriend would do: She inserted a pair of straws in her mouth like tusks, dangled her hands limply in from of her chest like fins, and began clapping them together.

"Arf arf!" she said. "I'm an aquatic mammal!"

Andromeda had been sipping quietly at her water (which cost money, mind you), but swallowing had suddenly become impossible. She tried not to spew, and instead, dribbled water down her chin and all over the table. She was choking, laughing, and crying.

A waiter inconveniently appeared at the table as Andromeda was attempting to mop herself up with a cloth napkin. "Would you two like more time with the menu?"

Tanks directed a meaningful look at the waiter. Both straws were still in her mouth.

Andromeda covered her entire face with the damp cloth napkin, a real-life burial shroud, because she was dying of laughter. This was it. This was how she died.

But this wasn't how she died, because that's what she saw next: her death.

It wasn't sad. Quite the opposite. It was happy, beautiful, maybe the most meaningful moment of her existence—waiting patiently as the light flickered out. Because she wasn't alone. Their clocks were synced. She was leaving this world with her best friend. Tanks's hard edges had softened considerably over the years, but her beauty had not. Andromeda adored every wrinkle on her face. She wished she could trace her finger between every single one. Was that weird? It was weird, wasn't it?

"It's not weird," Tanks told her, smiling so very gently.

Tanks had chosen to go like this, and somehow, inexplicably, she was emanating joy. Whether this was the end of her journey, or the beginning of a new one, she was ready.

More memories came, each one appearing faster than the last. Their wedding, quiet walks through Southland Park, Andromeda's first job (entry-level robotics and automation), spooning (Tanks shamelessly loved to be little spoon), their first dog, their first child, a boy, whom they adopted. His name was Garland, and he grew up to be so kind, so gentle. Surely, he got that from Tanks. The memories layered upon one another like art on acrylic pages, adding depth, becoming three-dimensional. No. Four-dimensional. Her memories were forming a tesseract into the future.

A third eye was merely an antenna to the true machine, the Dresdorian brain. Those three beating hearts in Andromeda's chest were pumping her pineal gland full of blood—fuel—so that it could receive a signal from the singularity at the center of the planet, where tidal gravitational forces become infinite and the singularity said, Here Is Everything.

Andromeda was now close enough. She didn't need an antenna. She had the signal.

Something clicked. Memories transitioned from a flip-book of moving pictures to animation as pure and flawless as organic life. Her consciousness shot through time. She knew what was going to happen next because it had already happened (in the future). Tanks may have died, but she wasn't *dead* dead. She was a machine, and machines could be fixed.

Andromeda could fix things. That's not a lie; she was a good mechanic.

—Andromeda and Tanks Through Space and Time,
Æon Q

—TWENTY-THREE—

ALT—PROM

WORD ON THE STREET WAS THAT A SERIES OF obscenely generous donations had come from the likes of Eric and Cynthia Roger, County Mayor Magnus Nguyen, and, most generous of all, tax-exempt megachurch Traditional Family of Christ (although the check was personally made out by its owner, Pastor Raines), in favor of a privately owned prom. It would be like any other prom, except bigger, better, and more exclusive. Same-sex couples were prohibited. If you and your date were not a boy and a girl, the bouncer would turn you away.

They "rented out" both Sundance High School's gymnasium *and* the football stadium for this event. So *regular* prom and Battle of the Bands would have to happen somewhere else. Chuck E. Cheese, perhaps?

They claimed this wasn't discrimination because they invited and encouraged *all* to attend, gay or straight alike! But it was sort of like inviting your queer adult child to the family reunion and then forcing them and their partner to sleep in different rooms. You can be gay, sure, just so long as you're not gay *under my roof.* That sort of thing.

Thanks to their lavish donations, they were pouring thousands of dollars into decorations. The theme was unstated, but the *color theme* would either be black and white or blue and pink. The decision was a difficult one, only because they couldn't seem to figure out which color the straight pride flag was. They didn't outright say this, but google "straight pride flag" and tell me that's not what they were thinking.

The football stadium—which was normally reserved for Battle of the Bands—was now a venue with a fresh slate and only one band currently signed up to perform: Alt-Rite.

That's right, folks. Alt-Rite was bowing out of Battle of the Bands. Although "bowing out" was putting it modestly, because what they were really doing was attempting to swallow Battle of the Bands whole. They were encouraging all the other competing bands to drop out and compete with them at this "new venue"—aka the *only venue* that could host an event of this scale. Alt-Rite still wanted to battle, apparently. They just wanted to do it in a place where gays weren't welcome.

They were calling this shitshow Alt-Prom.

♩ ♫ ♪

By the end of school, every single band except Hope Cassidy and the Sundance Kids had dropped out of Battle of the Bands and signed up for the new "competing bands" event being hosted by Alt-Prom. They were calling it—drumroll, please—Battle of the Bands! It was basically the exact same event but without us because we refused to be complicit. No one seemed to know what this meant for normal prom and Battle of the Bands, and no one seemed to care, especially not Principal Reilly. The man appeared to be walking on pure sunshine through the halls. I had a feeling he was somehow instrumental in orchestrating all this.

So, depending on your perspective, you could say that we won Battle of the Bands by default. (Yay?) But you had to be terribly optimistic to see it that way because what *really* happened was Alt-Rite and their adult constituents had subverted the whole process and beat us in the most slimy, evil way possible.

The worst part was that the whole school was buzzing about how prom was *actually* going to be cool for once. No one seemed to mind its insidious, exclusionary nature. If it didn't affect them, why should they mind?

It was the straw that broke the camel's back—the camel, in this particular instance, being Angus's and Kevin's relationship.

Apparently, Kevin was so into the idea of this baller new prom, he cornered Angus at his locker, suggesting he and Angus go to Alt-Prom as a "double date." Except their dates would technically be girls.

"By the way," said Kevin, "I already asked Cyndi Keebler to be my date, and she said yes."

He said this so casually. So coolly. Like he fully expected this to go over well.

"I figure you can ask either Astrid or Hope," Kevin continued, when Angus's silence was starting to become uncomfortable. "If you ask Astrid, then maybe Hope can go with Danny, and it can be a triple date! It'll be great."

Danny, Astrid, and I were literally in the vicinity as this conversation happened. We could hear every word, and Kevin knew. I think he was hoping we would somehow be supportive.

"Are you fucking with me right now?" said Angus.

"I mean, you don't *have* to ask Astrid or Hope; you can ask whoever you want," Kevin backtracked.

"Astrid and Hope aren't the problem. Why do you want to go to Homophobe Prom?"

"Okay, for starters, it's not 'Homophobe Prom,'" said Kevin, weirdly agitated. "They actually went out of their way to state that gay people are welcome!"

"As long as they have a straight date," said Angus. "How very inclusive of them."

"Why does everything always have to be political with you? Can't you just have fun?"

"I'm sorry?"

"This is going to be *fun*," Kevin reiterated. "Just do this one thing for me, just this once."

"I'm not going to this skeezy-ass prom with you, Kevin! I want to go to prom *with you*."

"Well, I'm going to Alt-Prom, so . . ." Kevin trailed off. The ultimatum was laid.

"So . . . what?" said Angus. "Are you breaking up with me?"

"I think you're the one who's breaking up with me," said Kevin.

They stayed that way for a long moment, saying nothing.

"Okay," said Angus, finally.

"Okay," said Kevin.

"Okay then."

"Okay then, well, bye."

"Oh, bye *yourself*, Kevin!" Angus snapped. He slammed his locker door like it might somehow separate him from Kevin, but Kevin was still there, so Angus stormed off.

He didn't go far. In fact, he appeared to have just stalled in the middle of the hallway, in a stasis, while the flow of end-of-school traffic broke and reconnected around him. He was offered a significantly wide berth, but I think this was less about politeness and more about the discomfort of being around a large person having a mental breakdown.

Danny, Astrid, and I finally came out of the woodwork to try to console him.

"Angus, I'm so sorry . . . ," I said.

"Leave me alone," Angus mumbled.

"C'mon, man, we're here for you," said Danny. He touched Angus's shoulder.

"LEAVE ME ALONE," Angus screamed. "DON'T TOUCH ME, JUST LEAVE ME THE FUCK ALONE."

Danny recoiled, looking thoroughly hurt, cradling his hand like he'd touched a hot burner.

"Just go," said Angus. "Just go away, just go."

Astrid was weeping. She was in full empath mode, and she was crying all of Angus's tears for him.

She turned to Danny and me.

"You two go on ahead," she whispered. "I'll talk to him."

It wasn't an unreasonable thing for her to say. She'd known Angus way longer than us. It made sense that she'd be able to get through where we couldn't.

That didn't make it hurt any less.

Danny and I drove home, not even able to comfort each other. All I could think about was that I had finally found friends whom I cared about and who cared about me, and I only realized it now, as it was all falling apart.

Maybe that was the default state of the universe. Maybe that was the only reason things existed.

So they could fall apart.

♩ ♫ ♪

With everything crumbling between my fingertips, trying to talk to Charity suddenly didn't seem any less impossible than any other problem in my life. In fact, it almost seemed like the most approachable one. She was my sister. How hard could it be to fix things with my sister?

I tried to find her at school, but either she had mastered the art of avoiding me, or she wasn't there. I really didn't want to have to call or text her. This wasn't that sort of conversation. I needed to communicate with her in the most human means possible, no barriers between us, because, so help me, if Dylan slithered his tentacles any tighter around her, I was afraid I'd never get her back.

It was under these circumstances that I walked to the Rogers' house, unannounced. I didn't tell Danny where I was going, and he didn't ask.

The Rogers' house was lush. A sumptuous, castlelike, European-style two story, with white cobblestone brick walls, a running theme of arches, and a curved wall housing a wide circular staircase, visible through a series of staggered windows.

I knocked on the Rogers' front door. It opened immediately. There, standing in the doorway, was Dylan Roger, grinning like a clown soaked in a vat of Ace chemicals. I was pretty sure he'd seen me through the window, walking up the street.

"Looks like you won Battle of the Bands," said Dylan, emanating smugness like a bad cologne. "Congrats."

God, when it came to being an insidious low-life piece of shit, Dylan was genuinely at the top of the food chain.

"I need to speak to Charity," I said. And then, because I was desperate, "Please."

"Yeah. Okay. For sure." Dylan nodded, unnervingly receptive. He leaned backward, craning past the door, and yelled, "Charity, it's for you!"

"Who is it?" Charity's voice called back.

"Your sister."

A long, terrible pause followed.

"Not the lesbian," Dylan clarified.

Every muscle in my body tensed. Hearing Dylan refer to Faith so dismissively filled me with a pantheon of vengeful gods. I took in a deep breath and held it. Like a dam holding a flood. I just needed to talk to Charity. That was all. *Just let it slide, Hope.*

"Tell her to go away," said Charity.

I should have expected as much, but that didn't make it feel like any less of a gut punch. However, I barely had a moment to process it.

"Don't be a bitch!" Dylan shouted. "Talk to your fucking sister, you worthless."

My mouth fell open. I didn't know which was more shocking, more offensive: "bitch" or "worthless" as a noun. Maybe it was intended as an adjective, and Dylan and his stunted vocabulary couldn't thing think of a good noun to modify, so he left it. But I didn't think so. I think that was the official title he intended: *you worthless*. The longer it sat, the more it felt like Dylan's brand of hate.

An epoch later, Charity arrived silently at the doorway, and Dylan stepped away. The tension in their body language spoke volumes: Dylan was in control, and Charity was doing as she was told. Such submissiveness—from someone as headstrong as Charity, no less—was alarming.

Charity stepped outside and closed the door behind her. She folded her arms quietly.

"What do you want?" she said, since I wasn't starting the conversation.

"You let him *talk to you* like that?" I asked.

"Is that what you want? To talk about Dylan?"

"That's what I want to talk about *right now*, sure! In what version of Christianity is it okay for your boyfriend to call you a 'bitch' and 'worthless'?"

"He's just... Dylan. He does that sometimes. He doesn't mean it."

I literally had no words in response to that.

"Dylan's good," Charity mumbled. She didn't even sound like she believed it.

I shook my head. "Dylan is a lot of things, but good is the exact opposite of what he is."

Charity shrugged. "I have to go."

She started for the doorknob, and I panicked. The door opened maybe an inch before I pushed it shut.

"What the hell?" said Charity.

"Don't go in," I said. "Please."

Charity stared at me like I was a complete stranger. In a way, I guess we were strangers.

"What do you want from me?" she said.

"I want you to come home."

"No, you don't."

"Yes, I *do*!"

"No, you DON'T." Charity was mad now.

"Charity!" I said. Her name practically crumbled out of my mouth. "I love you."

Charity shook her head, her face sculpted out of cold stone. There wasn't an inch of her that believed me.

"If there's anyone who *doesn't* love you, it's fucking Dylan," I said. "From the sound of it, he doesn't even *like* you."

"Oh, fuck you, Hope," said Charity.

"No, seriously," I said. "The only reason he's dating you is because of *me*. This is his way of *getting at me*. I have his brother, so he gets to take my sister as romantical hostage. You are *nothing* to Dylan!"

Something in that line connected. But not the right way. Not how it was supposed to. Charity's skewed glare splintered, like a crack in ice.

I tried backtracking. "You are a lovely, wonderful person, Charity, and you deserve—"

"You really think the whole world revolves around you," said Charity. "It just grinds your nerves that someone might actually like me for me."

"What? No! Charity, that has nothing to do with—"

"The only person I mean *nothing* to is you, Hope. Where have you been for the past *year*? Because I can promise you, I've been hurting for all three hundred and sixty-five days of it. I don't know or care what sort of coping mechanism you're looking for on her anniversary, but it's not going to be me. You can't just try to swoop in here when I move in with my boyfriend and pretend that you have anything but your own interests in mind."

I stared at Charity blankly.

She saw it right in my face. She even had the gall to smile, even though zero percent of her appeared happy about anything. "You didn't remember, did you?"

No.

"May the Fourth be with you?" said Charity, smilingly bitterly.

No no no.

I pulled my phone out of my pocket—even as the facts as I knew them were crashing down on me. Prom was in two days.

My phone displayed the date as clear and final as if they were carved on a headstone: May 4.

It had been a year. A whole year.

"Happy Anniversary," said Charity. "I hope you feel as alone as I do."

The words had been spoken. They couldn't be unspoken. There was no taking something like that back, and even if she could, I didn't think Charity would. She really, truly, genuinely hated me.

Maybe I deserved to be hated.

Charity thrust the door open and walked inside—a hollow shell of a person, but a victorious one—and slammed the door behind her.

And I?

I came undone.

♩ ♫ ♪

I wandered in limbo for an indecipherable amount of time. I felt my phone vibrate in my pocket, but I didn't even pull it out to check who was calling. I could tell you who *wasn't* calling: Faith.

Muscle memory brought me into the general vicinity of home. Danny met me the rest of the way. Not on purpose, mind you. His evening run had brought him into my path. I was only vaguely aware of the oncoming silhouette. He slowed as he approached and plucked his headphones out. He absorbed me in all my glory—a martyr of my own self-destruction. The Jesus Christ of fucking things up. My kingdom was chaos; my throne was disorder.

I was crying and shaking *so hard*. I shouldn't have had tears left, but they were still coming.

"Jesus Christ," said Danny. "Hope, are you okay?"

I was, in fact, not okay. I was a million red flags waving.

"What's wrong?" said Danny.

What *wasn't* wrong? Charity was choosing to live with her abuser over me, and Faith had disappeared without a trace exactly a year ago today and hadn't even attempted to reach out to me, not once, not to let me know she was okay, not even to let me know that she didn't hate me, and the reason why was becoming devastatingly clear: She probably *did* hate me.

"I think she hates me," I weeped.

"What? Who, Charity?"

Charity obviously hated me, and I wasn't any happier about that. But that wasn't whom I meant.

"Faith," I said. "I think Faith hates me."

Danny stared at me, perplexed, confounded. He shook his head. "No. That's not true."

"It's been *a year*," I wheezed. "May the Fourth be with you!

How could she run away for a year and *not* hate me? She'd have to be dead!"

Now I was spiraling.

"What if she *didn't* write *Andromeda and Tanks*?" I said. "What if I'm just so delusional that I've convinced myself she wrote it, but she didn't because she's dead!"

"What?" said Danny. I had officially lost him.

"Either she hates me or she's dead. Which is worse? For someone you love to *die* or for them to hate you? I can't decide which is worse. Is that horrible? I can't decide which is worse!"

I was panicking. I was forcing myself to pick between two hells. This was some real *Sophie's Choice* bullshit. I couldn't breathe.

"Calm down," said Danny. "Breathe. Deep breaths. In and out. Just focus on breathing."

I was neither calming down nor breathing. The world was on fire. Fire devours oxygen. The only thing I could breathe was flames.

"I'm all alone," I said, and I meant that in the most existential sense possible.

"No," said Danny, shaking his head. "That's not true."

"I've *always* been alone. I will always *be alone*."

"That's not true!" Danny grabbed my face. "Look at me. Hope, please, look at me."

I looked at him. He was crying. The unstoppable, unbreakable Danny Roger was crying.

"You have me," he said. "You will always have me."

A breathless moment passed between us. It sucked the breath right out my lungs. All I could do was stare into those kind, beautiful, compassionate eyes, like whole worlds of hope. It was the sort of look that made you feel like you were the most important person in the world, and I'll be honest—no one had ever looked at me quite like that. I lost myself in those eyes. *Truly* lost myself.

That's when I kissed him.

I grabbed his face, I grabbed his hair, and I kissed him like it was the most basic survival instinct. Like that first breath you take after you've been holding your breath underwater. And for a moment—just a moment—I felt whole again. I felt human. I felt like maybe, just maybe, I would survive this. We could survive this together.

Our lips broke apart. Pulled away. I opened my eyes.

Danny looked horrified.

I was still holding Danny's face in my left hand, cupping his jaw, a clump of his hair in my right. I let go of him like he was burning hot and I had scalded myself. Jumped back, staggered a safe distance away.

Danny was petrified in place, a fossil. He couldn't even blink. I had bludgeoned him into a state of paralysis with my reckless, stupid love. I realized in the most painful way that everything I felt was completely one sided. I had Danny *as a friend.* I would always have Danny AS A FRIEND. How like me, to ruin everything I touched.

Charity hated me. Faith hated me. The jury was still out on Danny, but I knew one thing for certain now: I hated myself.

I ran away.

♩ ♫ ♪

I never stopped running.

I ran through neighborhoods, down long roads, across empty

lots, through fields of tall grass. I ran until I reached the northern edge of town, and I kept running, on a vague uphill trajectory into the Bearlodge Mountains, Wyoming's small slice of the Black Hills. I ran until every trace of sunlight had dissolved into night.

I ran into the forest.

My legs hurt, and my lungs hurt, but more than that, my heart hurt. It was my heart that kept me running. I had to get far away from everyone and everything. I couldn't do this anymore. It hurt too much. Faith ran away, so I would run away too.

I guess, in a sense, I was running away from myself, which was impossible, so my plan was to run until I died or I became Forrest Gump. One or the other.

The trees parted for a moment, their tall bodies and long limbs giving way to a universe of stars. My gaze was a reverse free fall into endless space. It looked like a child had spilled glitter across black construction paper; some kindergarten craft project gone awry. That didn't mean it wasn't beautiful. It was stunning chaos. Maybe there was a God, but he was just a fucking child. Some great, omnipotent baby. He was up there wreaking chaos, spitting up the Milky Way galaxy, shitting universes and life, sticking whatever galactic carpet trash he could find into his mouth like culinary treasures, crying bloody murder for no reason whatsoever, and then falling asleep in his own shit. That would have made so much sense to me. I could believe in a God like that.

I don't remember the running ever stopping. I only vaguely remember puking from physical and psychological exhaustion, but even then, I think I kept running.

I ran until I ceased being.

Andromeda may have gone down like a fly, but she settled like food poisoning.

The worm's gastric acid was trying—and failing—to dissolve this tiny Dresdorian spice that had slipped past its lower esophageal sphincter. Instead of doing what digestive systems do, it was bubbling and burbling, frothing and foaming, in a chemical reaction of volcanic proportions. In effect, Andromeda was giving this worm some nasty-ass indigestion.

This was maybe the first time in recorded history that a worm had had the misfortune of eating a Dresdorian. Worms didn't like to resurface. They liked the blankety, womblike comfort of impacted dirt hugging their long noodle bodies. This worm, however, was having heartburn in all five of its hearts. This acid reflux was a son of a bitch. Animal instinct had a way of improvising, and it was telling this massive tube of flesh to go back up (above ground) and regurgitate like a motherfucker. This worm was gonna be sick no matter what.

The worm flipped a vicious u-ey, turning on a dime, and jettisoned to the surface like the scariest fucking geyser you'd ever seen. Up or down, gravity didn't matter much when you were a thousand feet of muscle with a tummy ache. It cut the time of its ascent in half.

The worm exploded from the surface, ushered in by a ravenous mushroom cloud of sand and dust, devouring whole dunes like raviolis. Its long body unspooled from the ground like a rope of puss from a zit, first up, then down, hitting the hard acid-crusted sand like a derailed train. Every life-form for miles would feel it.

It then proceeded to writhe and squirm like a, well, like a worm in the sun, which it was, but that's not what this was about. This worm's SPF was infinity—it could do laps on the sun if it wanted. No, what was really happening was the universal concept of dry heaving. The five flaps of its oral cavity peeled open and back, way back, baring teeth and gums and way too much of its insides. It almost looked like it was folding itself inside out, or perhaps doing something sexual, like ejaculating its own esophagus. But there was nothing sexual about it. This worm had never been less pleasured.

Finally, in a fondue of the purest revulsion, the worm barfed. Vomit, half-digested roaches, and bile poured out of it in a steaming, stinking landslide. The worm heaved and retched until everything on its insides (that wasn't a vital organ) was safely on its outside.

Nestled cozily amid the goo and the muck, her face barely above the surface, was a tiny, unconscious Andromeda. The fumes of the worm's digestive tract had knocked her out in seconds. Everything she had seen was fuguelike, no more than a fever dream.

Some dreams were easily forgotten. Others were like profound ideas, dancing on the edge of enlightenment. Once thought, they could never be unthunk.

Clutched fiercely in Andromeda's arms, never to be let go, was what remained of Tanks.

The worm rolled sluggishly—all three million tons of it—like a very large teenager into bed after a shit day in the public education system. Then it slurped lazily into the ground like that last bit of water down a drain, a slow, soft gurgle.

Last time this worm ever ate foreign food, guaranteed. Fucking intestinal parasites.

* * *

—Andromeda and Tanks Through Space and Time,
AEon Q

—TWENTY-FOUR—

GOD'S TOWER

OKAY, I DIDN'T CEASE *BEING*. BUT I DID STOP being conscious.

I know this because I woke up, and it was morning.

I was propped vaguely upright, back leaning against a flat smooth outcropping of bedrock. The heels of my dust-covered Keds were inches from a steep drop, but I was less focused on the danger and more on the staggering, picturesque beauty it opened onto. Rollicking hills carpeted in a rich blanket of trees. Grapefruit-flavored dawn washing across a sloping horizon. And at the center of it all, a tiny but jarring butte of igneous rock sprouting from the earth like a pale tooth set against the higher, darker, pointier Missouri Buttes behind it.

"Beautiful, isn't it?" said Angus, who was apparently sitting right beside me.

My head rotated slowly, like the hidden door in some ancient stone temple riddled with booby traps and death. I stared at Angus, trying to make sense of what was going on. Angus didn't meet my gaze, opting instead to inhale the view. He wasn't smiling, per se. But he seemed happy. Or at the very least, content. The last time I saw Angus, he was the exact *opposite* of content. Was I hallucinating? Was I . . . ?

"Am I dead?" I asked.

Angus reared his head back slightly, smiling in that sarcastic way you do when someone has said something magnificently stupid. "No. That would mean *I'm* dead. Why would *I* be dead?"

That was a solid point.

"Unless you think I'm like the Magical Negro in your life story," said Angus.

"What?" I said, panicking. "Angus, I—"

"I'm fucking with you," said Angus, smirking. "Kevin once took me hiking on the trail that leads here. I found you face down in the middle of it in a pool of your own vomit. I cleaned you up a little bit with some wet wipes and carried you over here."

"You carry wet wipes with you when you hike?" I said.

"Really? That's what you're taking from that?"

"Sorry," I said, blinking groggily. "Still waking up."

"I get sweaty. Wet wipes are hygienic. You should be *thanking* me. You were wearing barf like it was in season."

"How far did you carry me?"

Angus pointed his thumb backward. I wasn't sure how I was supposed to interpret that, but when I turned around, peering past the wall of bedrock, a line of vomit visibly traced the dirt path like a slimy snail trail, until it abruptly ended in a vaguely human outline and Angus's heavy footprints, barely ten feet away.

"Psh," I said, leaning back against the bedrock. "You barely carried me at all."

"Oh my God, you ungrateful turd," said Angus. He was laughing.

I said nothing. I let his laughter peter out into a cathartic sigh.

"Do you believe in serendipity?" he asked.

"The John Cusack–Kate Beckinsale movie? Nope."

"Oh, shut your mouth. That was a damn near perfect movie."

"If by perfect you mean schmaltzy and ridiculous, then sure, it was perfect."

Angus opened his mouth wide with hysterical disbelief, trying so hard not to smile. He shoved me playfully. "I hate you. I literally hate you."

I laughed. "Serendipity? Isn't that basically the same thing as synchronicity? Meaningful coincidences?"

"Sort of?" said Angus, uncertainly. "I think synchronicity is the philosophical version. Serendipity is more like a pleasant surprise."

"So, luck?"

"Yeah. I guess luck," said Angus. "I just think it's funny that I came out here to get over my breakup with Kevin, and I found you."

"Yeah," I said, distantly. "Funny, huh?"

"I literally never go hiking, Hope. Literally. *Never.* I only went with Kevin because he was hot. You have to understand that this is a once-in-a-lifetime coincidence."

I said nothing.

"You see that weird-looking rock formation all the way out there?" said Angus. He was pointing at the butte that looked like a pale tooth. "That's Devils Tower."

"What?" I said, sitting erect. "Are you for real?"

I knew a few things about Devils Tower. For one, it was the first United States national monument, established in 1906 by

President Theodore Roosevelt. For two, that dumb rock was, like, a weird obsession of Faith's. I think this had everything to do with Devils Tower playing a climactic role in the finale of Steven Spielberg's underrated sci-fi masterpiece, *Close Encounters of the Third Kind*. It's where the aliens and scientists meet and essentially had a very synth-y 1970s rock concert, complete with laser show. I mean, *technically* the aliens were trying to teach the humans their basic tonal vocabulary, which consisted of light and sound. But c'mon. It was basically a concert.

It planted a completely absurd idea in my head for how we might still win Battle of the Bands. Like *really* win, in the most meaningful way possible.

"How can we see that thing from here?" I asked. "Isn't Devils Tower like thirty miles away?"

Angus shrugged. "We're pretty high up."

Who all knew about this view? Did *anyone* else know you could see Devils Tower so close to Sundance? This was yet one more thing I absolutely had to show Faith whenever I found her.

If I ever found her.

"There's an old Native American legend," said Angus. "The Lakota, Kiowa, Cheyenne, and Crow each seem to have their own version of it. But in the version I heard, a group of seven girls were playing together when they were spotted by a giant bear named Mato, with claws the size of tipi poles. Mato chased them, and in an effort to escape, the girls climbed on top of a rock and prayed to the Great Spirit to be saved. It's said that their faith was so great, the rock rose high out of the earth, up to the heavens, safely out of Mato's reach. Mato scraped and clawed to get up, leaving those giant lines you see all around Devils Tower, but he couldn't reach them. The Great Spirit was so impressed by the faith of these seven girls that he brought them up to the heavens so they could live forever in peace, and the seven stars, the Pleiades, appeared as a symbol of hope, to remind all who saw them that no matter how bad or scary things get, you have the power within you to face the thing that threatens to harm you and the ones you love."

Angus pointed directly above Devils Tower, into the pink of dawn breaking across the sky.

"When Kevin told me that story, the Pleiades were directly over Devils Tower. He pointed them out to me. It was stupidly romantic."

Angus lowered his hand, leaned back, and sighed.

"Devils Tower actually got its name from a translation screwup. The Lakota called it something along the lines of Black Bear Tower, but the word for 'black bear' is *wahanksica*, whereas *wakansica* is 'bad god' or 'evil spirit.' But to the Lakota, Devils Tower is like the exact opposite of bad or evil. It's a holy place to them. More like a God's tower than anything else."

I stared at Angus, saying nothing.

"This is where Kevin and I first came out to each other," said Angus. "So, even though it's marred by the, you know, the *Kevin part*—it's still where I first came out to another human being, you know? I guess it's still got that spiritual connection for me."

I couldn't help but think of Danny. And that stupid kiss. And how I'd probably fucked up the greatest friendship I'd ever had.

"And what do I find here but you?" said Angus, studying me. "Hope...what are you even *doing* out here anyway?"

His voice was way kinder and more sympathetic than I deserved. It made me feel sick.

"Danny called us," said Angus. "Me and Astrid. He's *worried* about you. Your *parents* are worried about you. Not to state the obvious, but you just sort of ran off in the middle of the night—on the *anniversary of your sister's disappearance*, apparently—and never came home. I hope I don't have to explain why that would make your family freak out."

That just made me feel shittier. Not only did I put Danny in the awful situation I put him in, but then I had to go and disappear and make a spectacle of it all. But what was I *supposed* to do? I couldn't very well show my face in Danny's presence ever again. This was obviously the part where I moved to South Dakota and adopted a new identity, witness protection style. My new name was Jane Schmane; I liked piña coladas, as virgin as myself, and dancing in the rain.

"Danny didn't tell you?" I said.

Angus shrugged cluelessly. "Tell us what?"

I sighed. I couldn't run away from this. I had tried to run away from this, *literally*, and Angus's being here was irrefutable proof that I couldn't.

"I kissed Danny," I said.

Angus laughed.

He laughed until he realized I wasn't laughing along.

"Oh, you're serious," he said.

My mouth became the smallest orifice in my face. I nodded timidly.

"Do you, um, have feelings for...?"

I nodded violently, recklessly, like a metaphor for my actual love for him.

"For how long?" said Angus.

"Oh, let's see," I said, pretending to count my fingers for no reason whatsoever. "Third grade, I think? Maybe fourth grade."

Angus's jaw was hanging like a swing.

"The weird thing is, it was always Danny. Never Dylan. I could always tell them apart, and I always thought Dylan was an obnoxious putz. But Danny? Danny was perfect."

"Hope," said Angus, measuring his words. "You live with him."

"OH MY GOD, TELL ME ABOUT IT," I said, somewhere between laughing and having a nervous breakdown. "Our rooms are right next to each other. Our beds are on opposite sides of the same wall. When we sleep, our bodies are maybe three feet away from each other, separated by about four and a half inches of wall. Believe me, I've done the math."

Angus didn't look like he didn't believe me. Whether or not that was a good thing was anyone's guess.

"And just to be clear," I said, "yes, I know it's stupid."

"It's not stupid," said Angus.

"It is so stupid."

"No, really, it's not."

"C'mon, Angus. You don't need to make me feel better about it. It wouldn't be stupid for *you* to have a crush on him because you are actually in the demographic of genders he's interested in. I'm not. You have a chance with him. I don't."

"Do you know how many straight boys I've had crushes on?" said Angus.

His question caught me off guard.

"Eleven," said Angus. And then, as if to prove a point: "In elementary school: Charlie Danson. In middle school: Lewis Sarno, Doug de Castro, Neal Karpouzes. High school: Brady Dorsey, Lucas Alondra, Jerry Choi, Todd Korsmo, Jordan Wiley, um... Micah Harper... oh, and Cameron Hodges."

I stared at Angus.

"I follow up on them sometimes," Angus continued. "And by follow up, I mean stalk them on the internet. None of them have come out. Honestly, I've never had a reason to suspect any of them were gay. I just liked them. Some of them, I liked *a lot.* One of them, I even thought I was in love with, and I maybe exchanged, like, a hundred words with him the entire time I knew him."

I frowned again. Not sad frowning. Angus was just making me emotional.

"Love is weird," said Angus. "People need people. Gay or straight, boy or girl, or any of the in-betweens. I'm not saying it always works out. It usually doesn't. Life isn't a rom-com. It's maybe stupid to expect someone to love you when they just don't feel the same way. But it's never stupid to love someone. All I know is, you've probably done more for Danny than maybe any human being on this planet. And in the end, that's the kind of love that means the most. Maybe Danny doesn't need romance right now. Maybe he just needs friends. People like you and me. But on a side note, speaking as a very gay boy... I think you're fucking great, Hope. I wouldn't change a thing about you."

I was weeping silently on a cliffside overlooking the most beautiful landscape I had ever seen. I was not okay.

"Not to give unwanted hugs," said Angus, "but if you need a hug..."

I lunged into Angus and hugged him fiercely.

Angus smiled. "We're gonna be okay, Hope."

I nodded, blinking away the tears, fully believing him.

"With that said," said Angus, "you need to talk to Danny. Clear this whole thing up with him."

I made immature grumbling sounds into Angus's shirt.

"Hope, Danny probably thinks he's homeless again."

I snapped upright. "What the fuck?"

"Think about it: You gave him a place to live. You gave it to him after he had nowhere else to go. Then, this girl who has given him everything, who he cares for deeply but NOT LIKE THAT, kisses him, then freaks out in embarrassment, and runs away. How is he supposed to think that will turn out for him?"

"Jesus fucking Christ," I said. "I would never kick him out. My *parents* would never—"

"*You* know that. But he doesn't. He's probably more scared how this will turn out than you."

"Oh my God. Oh my God oh-my-God-ohmy—"

Angus snapped his fingers in front of my face. I blinked.

"Focus, Hope."

I nodded.

"Let him know that everything's okay. That is your number one immediate goal. Literally nothing else matters—not prom, not Alt-Rite, not Battle of the Bands—until our lead guitar slash lyricist knows he still has a place to live. If we're gonna fight, we need all our warriors."

I nodded furiously.

"Once you've done that, I need to show you something," said Angus.

"Show me something?"

"I'd tell you now, but honestly, it's going to be a bit of a distraction, and I think you and I can both agree there's only one thing you need to be focusing on right now."

I nodded, feeling determined, and emotional, and fierce, and emotional, and empowered, and *way too fucking emotional*, but strong enough to fight.

♩ ♫ ♪

The very first thing I did when I arrived home—after repeatedly reassuring Mom and Dad that I was okay—was knock on Danny's door.

He opened it with a sort of dread, like he was expecting to find Death himself on the other side, scythe and all.

"I'm sorry," I said.

"Me too," said Danny, instantly, like it was the first breath he had taken in minutes. "I'm really sorry if I gave you the wrong idea or impression or... you're just my best friend is all."

"Please don't apologize. You have nothing to apologize for. I'm the one who violated a sacred trust."

"Sacred trust?"

"Between a girl and her best friend."

Danny gave a painfully sincere smile.

"I hope you're not so weirded out that you feel like you have to find somewhere else to live," I said. "I want you to live with us as long as you want or need to. I love you in the most gushingly platonic sense possible. It's truly disgusting—"

Danny hugged me. "I love you too, Hope."

He didn't feel the need to cheapen it with a disclaimer. Danny's love was too pure for that.

A very loud, very distraught sniffle caused us both to lean back and peer down the length of the hall. I already knew who it was, even though I told these traitors to wait in the car. (Battle of the Bands was tomorrow, and we hadn't given up the fight, not yet.)

Angus was cradling his hands over his heart, beaming. Astrid was crying—great big gumdrop-sized tears, cupping her face in both hands.

"Are you guys kidding me with this right now?" I said. I was trying—and failing—to scowl. "What part of *wait in the car* don't you understand?"

"I'm sorry, it's just so beautiful!" said Astrid, weeping.

"Do you need a gay hug?" said Angus.

"Don't ask me if I *need* a gay hug!" Astrid exclaimed. "Just give me the gay hug already! As much gay as you can put into it!"

Angus hugged Astrid. Then Danny and I did too, and Astrid just lost her fucking shit.

"I'm so *happyyy*," she wailed.

Andromeda woke up with only a hazy recollection of events. A struggle in the desert. She got mugged, right?

Mugged and kidnapped. Yes. Actually, didn't the mugging-kidnapping happen twice? It felt like it happened twice, but that didn't make sense.

Whatever the case, she distinctly remembered that Tanks—whom she had been cradling in her arms, half-eaten by acid—was one of the bad guys. But not anymore. For whatever reason, they were past that. Tanks was good. Andromeda knew that, better than she knew her own reflection in the mirror.

And Andromeda knew that she could rebuild her.

She was supposed to rebuild her. She already had rebuilt her (in the future).

All that was left was for her to do it in the here and now.

Fortunately for her, the mysterious pool of dried, crusty slime she woke up in was within walking distance of a vast, shimmery dome of light, washing over the east like a colorless rainbow, one with impressive depth. It was the Dome—the biggest acid-proof force field on the planet Dearth.

And beneath it, a speckle of meager skyscrapers. A rundown metropolis: Southland City.

To Andromeda, it looked like hope.

—*Andromeda and Tanks Through Space and Time*,
ÆonQ

—TWENTY-FIVE—

THAT SWEET SPOT BETWEEN INSANE AND GENIUS

WE HAD ROUGHLY THIRTY-SIX HOURS UNTIL prom and Battle of the Bands. The only gay-friendly version of both was looking to be very empty, seeing as we were the only participating band. Fortunately, because Sundance High School students had a history of skipping school in mass numbers the Friday before their hot-garbage prom, the district decided to make it official and cancel school on Friday altogether. We all would have skipped anyway because, look, we had shit to do. And I wasn't kidding when I said that Devils Tower had planted an idea in my head.

But I barely got started spilling the beans on my nefarious, semiformed plot when Astrid interrupted me.

"Okay, Hope, I think this is a super-duper good plan, but first, please tell me you've read *Andromeda and Tanks Through Space and Time* already!"

"*Ash-shtrid*," said Angus conspicuously through his teeth.

"What?" I said. "Wait, have *you* read it?"

"Yes!" Astrid exclaimed. "I *had* to once Angus told me Faith was the one who wrote it!"

Those words deconstructed into unfathomable ciphers before my ears. I was rendered incapable of processing them.

"Oh shit," said Danny. This was apparently the first he'd heard of it.

"ASTRID!" said Angus.

"What?" said Astrid. And then her eyes went big. "Wait, did you not tell her?"

Before Angus could even respond, Astrid slapped her hands over her own mouth.

"Okay, first of all," said Angus, "I don't know *for certain* that it's Faith. But I do *think* it's Faith. I would say that I'm, like, ninety-five percent sure it's Faith. I didn't outright say it before because I have no proof, but there's been some recent developments online that seem rather incriminating. In a good way. Good incriminating. The best part is that we have a way to contact her!"

I had to sit down, which happened to be in the middle of the hallway floor, because we never quite moved from our congregation in Danny's open doorway.

"Cool," said Angus, flopping his hands to his side.

"Hope, sweetie," said Astrid, crouching in front of me. She waved her hand in my face. "Can you tell me how many fingers I'm holding up?"

"Can't," I mumbled incoherently. I was shaking my head.

Astrid stared at her hand, where she held up three fingers, mildly alarmed. "She isn't having a stroke, is she?"

"No, I mean . . . I already know Æon Q is Faith," I said. "But I can't—"

"You *do*?" said Danny.

"*What?*" Angus squawked.

"I mean, I've at least been pretty sure for a while now," I said. "But it doesn't matter if I can't talk to her."

Astrid, Angus, and Danny stared at me in a vacuum of silence.

"What do you mean, you can't talk to her?" said Angus.

Danny just looked sad. Technically, he and I had already had this conversation—even if I was a mostly incoherent, babbling mess.

"I don't think she wants to talk to me," I said quietly, trying not to sound sorry for myself. And then even quieter: "I don't think she likes me anymore."

"Oh my God. FALSE!" Angus proclaimed so loudly that Astrid, Danny, and I jumped. "Somebody get me a computer, stat."

♩ ♫ ♪

When we had relocated to my bedroom with my laptop, Angus proceeded to spill all the contrary evidence he had accumulated thus far. For starters, there was the dedication for *Andromeda and Tanks Through Space and Time*, which I had stupidly missed because Angus's e-reader automatically skipped past all the introductory stuff: title page, copyright page, table of contents, and so on. Angus, of course, always scrolled back to read this stuff, or so he claimed, and therefore had stumbled across this before he had even met me:

To my Homegirl, my Best Friend, my Rock,
Hope,
Because without her, what the hell have we got?

I'm not going to lie, reading that turned me into a weepy mess.

But I had to move on quickly because Angus was already opening my laptop and pulling up Æon Q's incredibly recent online presence, including a Twitter account. The first thing I noticed was the header photo of Æon Q's profile: Devils Tower—a very Faith choice indeed.

The second thing I noticed, which was the main thing Angus wanted to show me, was that Æon Q was apparently the internet's biggest fan of Hope Cassidy and the Sundance Kids.

The first video Æon Q shared was of our performance at Change Through Grace with this comment: Oh my god, have you SEEN this? I am in tears. Literal bleeding-heart tears. I KNOW this girl.

When several of Æon Q's followers begged to know how Æon Q knew this so-called Hope Cassidy, they replied: Hope was my best friend growing up.

Someone responded: Wait. Is THAT the "Hope" you dedicated AaTTSaT to??!?

Æon Q replied: MY LIPS ARE SEALED, I'VE SAID TOO MUCH!!!

Aching curiosity aside, Æon Q's followers seemed incredibly respectful of the writer's super-secret identity.

Immediately after the video, Æon Q shared the GoFundMe page Deja had set up to buy back Astrid's drum set. It was prefaced by this comment: Just donated my rent this month to this cause. Okay, jk, but if you have to choose between buying my book and donating to this band, you should definitely donate to this band. GET THIS GIRL HER DRUMS BACK!!!

"Awwww!" said Astrid weepily, holding her hands over her heart.

The second video Æon Q shared was our performance at the Women's Resource Center, accompanied by this comment: FUCK FUCK FUCK YEAH. EAT MY SHORTS, PATRIARCHY. HOPE CASSIDY AND HER SUNDANCE KIDDOS ARE MY LIFE.

Æon Q's most recent post was a retweet of Deja Williams: The Gillette megachurch, Traditional Family of Christ, has funded an expensive anti-LGBTQ Prom (no same-sex dates) in protest of Hope Cassidy and the Sundance Kids' performance at Change Through Grace. Alt-Rite is headlining, and they're dragging the entire Battle of the Bands competition over with them. Land of the free, huh?

Æon Q's comment that accompanied it was simply a frowny face and a broken heart emoji.

I had seen enough. Danny, Angus, and Astrid just stared, open-mouthed, as I clicked the DM button, marked by an envelope icon, and composed this message: Is that you, Faith? It's me, Hope.

I hit Send.

And then I kept typing.

I miss you so much. I love you to the fucking moon and back.

I hit Send.

And then I kept typing.

I don't have a date to our gay-friendly prom tomorrow night, but if you aren't doing anything, wanna go with me?

I hit Send.

And then I quickly closed the laptop and stood up. If, for whatever reason, Æon Q wasn't Faith and I had just asked a total rando to prom, best to just step away and wait for a reply at this point, either way.

Besides, we still had to fix prom, write a killer new song, and win Battle of the Bands.

"We need to sign up for Homophobe Battle of the Bands," I said.

"What?" asked Astrid.

"We do?" asked Angus.

"Why?" asked Danny.

"We're not actually going to show up," I said. "But we need Hope Cassidy and the Sundance Kids on that roster. Think of it more like throwing a stick in someone's bicycle spokes. The best part is, we're still going to win. Trust me."

Angus giggled at this thought. "I'm all for throwing sticks." He pulled out his phone to commit the act. "Signing us up!"

"I admire your confidence," said Danny. "But how are we going to win?"

"We're going to beat these bastards at their own game," I said. "Through the art of subversion."

Danny, Angus, and Astrid stared at me like I was either a genius or insane. I wasn't claiming to be either, but I had probably found that sweet spot right in between.

"I'll explain later. First, who's in charge of prom? *Inclusive* prom, I mean, who's in charge of Inclusive Prom?"

"Hold on, I'm looking it up," said Astrid, thumbing her phone. "I think I saw it on the school website."

"I think it rotates between teachers every year," said Angus. And then muttered under his breath, "Partly why it sucks so hard every year."

"I think it's Ms. Beekman from AP Bio?" said Danny. "Ms. Beekman and um . . . someone else, maybe? Wait a sec—"

"Mr. Britton!" Astrid exclaimed.

"WHAT?" said Angus.

"Oh shit, he is, huh," I said, remembering.

There was also a student lead in charge of the prom planning committee, who was, technically, bureaucratically in charge of prom, theme-wise, and it was a troubling name indeed. Astrid shoved her phone forward, and the three of us huddled in, around, and over her like a series of disconcerting growths on her back.

"Kevin!" Angus screamed. "Are you fucking . . . *fucking* me?"

I wasn't claiming to take Kevin's side on anything. But then again, I could also see why Kevin was upset about Angus spending too much time with the band if he didn't even know *his own boyfriend* was on the prom planning committee. Like, how?

Just like that, I feared my entire plan was about to implode on itself, and we hadn't even started.

But then Angus pulled his phone out of his pocket and pressed Dial on what appeared to be the first name that showed up. We all stared at him in varying states of crisis.

"Hello, *Kevin*," said Angus. "What's this about you being in charge of the prom planning committee? Because last I heard, you weren't even *going* to that prom."

There was a pause.

"No, it's not *canceled*! Just because everyone jumps ship doesn't mean the ship doesn't exist! Are you fucking kidding me with this right now?"

Another pause.

"Well, I want it. I want you to crown me king of the prom planning committee. No, I don't *care* what the position is actually called, I just want you to give it to me. Crown me as king. No, Kevin, say the words. Crown me king. CROWN ME KING! Okay. Thank you. Now email Britton and Beekman, certifying your crowning of me as king. I'll know if you don't."

Angus hung up and stared at us all, deadpan. "Guys, I'm king of the prom planning committee."

All of us exploded into a hysterical screaming fit, jumping and flailing. Danny even lifted him into the air and spun him.

"ALL HAIL ME, KING OF THE PROM PLANNING COMMITTEE," Angus proclaimed.

"Angus, will you go to prom with me?" asked Danny.

"Wait, wot?" said Angus.

While Danny asked Angus to prom, I turned my attention to Astrid. We were on *such* a time crunch, there was literally just no time for us to dillydally on beautiful little moments like this. Still, Astrid and I tried not to smile too hard as this happened in our periphery.

"Astrid, can you call Deja and find out if she still has access to that GoFundMe money, and if we can legally and morally redirect it to funding Inclusive Prom instead? If she says yes, get her together with Mr. Britton. We're literally going to need every last cent for what we have planned."

"OH MY GOD, CAN I CALL DEJA," said Astrid in a state of pure ecstasy.

"Do you need her numb—"

"I have it on speed dial," said Astrid. The phone was already to her ear as she strolled leisurely from my bedroom like some hotshot Hollywood thing. "*Heyyyy*, Deja, babe, I've got a hella big favor to ask of you—"

At that point, Angus was grabbing me by the shoulders, shaking me and squealing, "I just got asked to prom!"

I grinned deliriously and squeezed Angus in the mother of all hugs.

"Oh my God," said Angus, snapping upright. "I've got a prom to plan!"

I was one step ahead of him, with Mr. Britton's number already pulled up on my phone. Angus dialed it on his own phone and pressed Call as he raced out of my room. His voice reverberated down the hallway. "Mr. Britton, Mr. Britton, Mr. Britton, did you hear? You did?! Yes, I'm the king! Wow, Kevin's response time was never this fast when we were together."

I turned specifically to Danny.

"I know you said you resign as our lyricist," I said. "But I respectfully reject your resignation. You're the only one of us who can write lyrics for shit, and you always write your best stuff under pressure anyway. So, what do you say? Will you accept my rejection and help us save Inclusive Prom?"

Danny's smile was as wide and bright as a slice of the moon. It sparkled like the Pleiades. "How can I say no to Inclusive Prom?"

My phone buzzed annoyingly in my pocket, regardless of the fact that Danny and I were having a moment. I gave a disgruntled little huff and pulled it out, then said "fuck" when I saw the name on the screen.

I didn't know it, but it was about to become the most important phone call Hope Cassidy and the Sundance Kids would ever receive.

nce upon a time, Southland City must have been pretty neat. The flashy hologram ads. The multitiered air traffic.

Those overly jagged high-rise buildings with pagan-looking logos riddled with symbolism and an overall "evil corporation" vibe going on. But the holograms were outdated—glitchy and flickering. Traffic was a mess because airspace had been under construction for the past decade. Even the evil corporations looked exhausted, absentmindedly abandoning their villainy to the back burner, set to a mild simmer.

Andromeda wandered in, caked in bile, barely carrying half an android, pivoting the weight of it on her hip like some tragic psychological replacement for a lost baby. Not one person batted an eye or an eyestalk. Welcome to Southland City. They had seen worse.

Her first stop was the public library. The librarian gave Andromeda a bit of stink eye—not unwarranted, as there was a very real stink to consider. Andromeda found a computer in a quiet corner, propped Tanks against the table leg, and proceeded to research. She sifted through sketchy, possibly illegal sites that claimed to have blueprints for individual Ixion androids. They even went so far as to list individual parts and components.

That's when she stumbled on a rather damning piece of information. The primary processor of Tanks's cognition was made out of a purportedly illegal substance known as dresdorium.

Dresdorium was made out of Dresdorian third eyes.

Andromeda fell down the rabbit hole that was the inhumane practice of "clipping Dresdorian exiles." Dresdore was its own independent state within the Totality Yielding. The selling and purchasing of dresdorium was illegal, which was why Ixion existed lawlessly outside TY borders. However, there was a thriving black market. Sketchy buyers purchased third eyes from starving exiles for disgustingly low prices. Because they could.

Andromeda unfastened her satchel and removed a severed, spire-shaped horn. She opened her fingers, allowing it to roll in her palm. She had planned on purchasing parts and materials with the money she would get from selling it. Now there was the question of whether she'd get enough, to say nothing of the moral dilemma of selling herself to reassemble her dead future wife. Who was made from the suffering of exiled Dresdorians.

Andromeda clutched her third eye to her chest and sobbed. Why was this so *hard*? Was life only a never-ending struggle? Maybe this was why people believed in God. The only way to cope was to believe there was something better than this. Andromeda would have believed anything, just to entertain the lie that everything was going to be okay.

"Excuse me," said an older female voice. "Miss, are you okay? Do you need help?"

Andromeda choked down the last sob that wanted to escape. Swallowed it like a dry pill. She blinked until she could see past the tears and turned her head. Standing a safe but concerned distance away was a woman with moon-white hair and black eyes, frowning. A Kelfling. She was small, except for her very pregnant belly. Her hand rested on top of it.

Andromeda didn't know why, but something about this woman felt familiar. Reminded her of someone. But who? Her memory turned up nothing.

Andromeda was still holding her third eye in very plain sight. The woman had noticed. It was painfully obvious who and what Andromeda was.

"Do you know where I can sell this?" Andromeda's voice broke on the last word.

The woman's frown deepened. "I don't think you should do that," she said.

"Sorry," Andromeda mumbled. Stupid Andromeda. She stashed her third eye away and collected Tanks from the floor. "I'm going to go. Please don't call the police."

"No, I... what I meant is, there are other ways for you to get the help that you need."

Andromeda wasn't listening. She had to get away. She lifted Tanks off the floor. That's when Tanks's head broke off her torso, a clean snap, landing with a heavy thud.

And then it had the audacity to roll deep under the table.

—Andromeda and Tanks Through Space and Time,
ÆON Q

—TWENTY-SIX—

LOVE CAN SEE

SUNDANCE HIGH WAS LIKE EVERY OTHER American high school in the sticks. Teachers underpaid. Arts programs cut. Buildings falling into disrepair. Overall underfunded.

The football stadium, however, was fucking *lit*.

It seated four thousand. It was glossy and clean and white and loudly utopian—or dystopian—depending on how you felt about football. How much did it cost? Are you sitting down? Fourteen *million*. It was technically called Ford Stadium because I guess the Ford Motor Company paid for it, but that just made me think of Aldous Huxley's *Brave New World*, and how Huxley hated Fordism (mass production, consumerism, technocracy) almost as much as the modern civilized world hated Facebook, post–Cambridge Analytica.

Tonight, Ford Stadium was a rock concert.

The stage was a massive black monolith of raging badassery. Arches of metal framework held up hulking lights and hidden lasers and who knew what the fuck else. At the very back was a projector screen for added visual stimulation because what's a rock concert without the risk of a seizure? Amps were stacked high on either side like totem poles, but with less symbolism and more health concerns. Anyone moshing in front of those bad boys would lose their hearing by age forty-five. The whole thing was a Pandora's box of sensory overload.

The stadium lights flooded the arena, illuminating hundreds of heads and bodies filling the bleachers, packing the field, some battling to get to the front like an apocalyptic Black Friday scenario. It was like they *wanted* to go deaf.

Seven bands were listed on the roster being handed out at the entrance: Hangry Hangry Hipsters, the What, Super Blue Blood Moon, Narwhalcotics, Princess Leia's Buns, Hope Cassidy and the Sundance Kids, and—in a slightly bigger font than everyone else because apparently they were headlining—Alt-Rite.

It was like the winner had already been decided. Like it was predetermined.

Maybe it was.

But honestly, if we were judging by band name alone, any one of these bands could have beaten us. (Princess Leia's Buns had my vote.)

There was, however, a strong color theme in the crowd: red and pink, worn by very separate people. The colors did not mix well together, but maybe there was something to be said for that. The red was Alt-Rite merch: mostly shirts and hats. They all read "Alt-Rite" in white letters, except for the stylized anarchy *A*, which was blue and circled and bleeding like fresh spray paint. It looked American in the way that makes you cringe.

The pink shirts were Hope Cassidy and the Sundance Kids

shirts. The *n* in "Sundance" was a rainbow. There were hundreds of these shirts. If Deja wasn't responsible for making them, she at least *knew* who was responsible for making them. I knew this from the conspiratorial smile on her face when we all first saw them and our jaws dropped. Fortunately, Alt-Prom—set to begin an hour after Battle of the Bands ended—had opted for the black-and-white color theme, like the dystopian metaphor for repressed sexuality that it was, so we weren't in any way contributing to their straight pride motif. I think they made the decision when they learned the trans flag was *also* pink and blue. Heaven help them.

First up was Hangry Hangry Hipsters. They looked like a band that had studied for hours what Arcade Fire *looked like*. There were eleven of them, and they wore things like suspenders and jean jackets and neon jumpsuits and dresses made of feathers, and they played instruments that included (but were not limited to) the sitar, panpipes, the omnichord, a musical saw, gadulka, xylophone, and a digital ukulele made out of an iPad and iPhone hooked together. Tragically, they didn't understand what music was.

"Hi, we're Hangry Hangry Hipsters," said a boy wearing an actual Christmas sweater with blinking lights and tinsel and everything. "This one's called, 'Splenda Will Kill Ya; Oh, Hey, Mind If I Bum a Smoke?' "

Okay, so they were hilarious, more of a hipster parody than anything else. But God, the sound they proceeded to make was like every sound-making toy in a toy store being slowly run over by a construction steamroller.

Next up was the What. They were admirably inspired by the Who, and even more admirably attempted to perform a song that wanted to be "Baba O'Riley," which they didn't even *try* to disguise, calling it "Teenage Wasteland."

I say attempted because they tanked. It was bad. Even worse than the hipsters.

Super Blue Blood Moon was pure death metal. Easily the most metal thing I'd heard since Cannibal Corpse's "Hammer Smashed Face." They looked scary too. As if KISS and Slipknot had settled down and had kids. Makeup and masks and fake blood. I wasn't nearly hard-core enough to know whether it was good metal or bad metal, but the lead singer sounded like the Cookie Monster, here to eat cookies and kick ass. (And he was all outta cookies.)

Narwhalcotics sounded like the Pixies. A little grungy, a little surfy, with a neat loud-quiet shift in the song structure. Pretty damn good!

Princess Leia's Buns was the game-changer—a pair of girls cosplaying as *Star Wars* characters Kylo Ren and Lando Calrissian. Kylo was looking especially emo, lips puckered as she brooded; meanwhile, Lando was dapper as fuck in blue velvet, smiling and waving and playing with her cape. Their hair was fabulous. Lando was on guitar, while Kylo manned a keyboard and laptop set up on a folding table. They both had mics.

"Hi, I'm Lando Calrissian."

"And I'm Kylo Ren. But my dad calls me Ben. At least he did... until I killed him."

Laughter and cheers and boos filled Ford Stadium, a moment of unmitigated life.

"We like *Star Wars*," said Lando. "Even the prequels. Even *Phantom Menace*."

"Especially *Phantom Menace*," said Kylo.

"This one's called 'Falling in Love at the Speed of Light,' aka—"

"Aka 'It Could Have Made the Kessel Run in Less Than Twelve Parsecs.'"

What followed was a peppy, electric sound like Tegan and Sara at their most heartfelt. They sang in a back-and-forth-and-together duet fashion. It was only a dorky *Star Wars* song on the most surface level. At its soft, gooey core, it was a love song to each other—whether they were best friends or sisters or lovers. In the end, I suppose it didn't matter. Their love for each other was the purest kind: genuinely liking someone for who they are, and their feeling the same way about you.

Princess Leia's Buns ended to rapturous, shattering applause, like endless waves crashing on a cliff face.

As Princess Leia's Buns packed up their gear and exited the stage to ravenous audience ecstasy, a single figure took their place on the stage, wearing a big brown alpaca wool sweater: Sundance High's very own US history (and one period of philosophy) teacher, Mr. Britton.

The overall sense of euphoria—the cheering, the applause, the ear-bleeding, drum-shattering breakneck decibel of uncategorized noise—plummeted.

Mr. Britton shuffled up to the main mic. Adjusted it to his unanticipated height, at which point it gave a testy screech of feedback, sharp as a lobotomy needle, causing everyone to recoil and cringe.

Mr. Britton opened his mouth.

Then he closed it, removed a folded sheet of paper from his pocket, and started reading straight from the page.

"Hi, my name is Mr. Britton," said Mr. Britton. "I regret to inform you that Hope Cassidy and the Sundance Kids will not be here tonight, seeing as they have a prior engagement."

"WHAT?" screamed the loudest singular voice from the crowd.

This was followed by the whole stadium losing its motherfucking shit. The mood ranged from confusion to outrage to curiosity to amusement. Some people seemed to be expressing all these things simultaneously.

"With that said," Mr. Britton continued, "they've left a message to their faithful and loyal fan base, as a way of saying thank you for all your enormous love and support."

Mr. Britton gave a thumbs-up, which could have meant anything, but was specifically meant for Frank (aka @1234frank from the Thrifty Schwifty), who was haggling with the man in charge of the projector. Whatever the argument was about, the projector dude finally relented.

The massive screen filled with live video footage of the monolithic Devils Tower, floodlights emphasizing the hexagonal columns that made up its ribbed texture—the "claw marks" of Mato the Bear. Behind it, a shotgun blast of stars glittered in the pale night sky. It was a sight of pure wonder. Even the floodlights couldn't drown them out.

The camera lowered onto an empty outdoor prom composed of rainbow colors—from clusters of balloons to tablecloths to streamers strung from the nearest trees. A portable dance floor had been pieced together at the center of it all. It was humble but also extraordinary, in the way that small, intimate things are.

Behind it all was a considerable stage—just big enough to require stairs on the side.

And a band.

Us.

Hope Cassidy and the Sundance Kids.

We were surrounded by amps stacked on top of amps, about to make some noise in these hills, the likes of which hadn't been heard since Steven Spielberg, John Williams, and company back in 1977.

We knew what was happening at Battle of the Bands because Mack was there, live streaming the whole thing for us via FaceTime.

Of course, our being here required a Special Use Permit (for events, weddings, gatherings, and so on), which typically needed to be applied for thirty days in advance. However, the superintendent of Devils Tower National Monument happened to be a hard-core Hope Cassidy and the Sundance Kids fan, and Deja had managed to secure us a "fast pass," so to speak.

Deja had also hired a film crew to capture our performance here at Inclusive Prom—or *tried* to anyway. When she attempted to pay them, most turned the money down, opting to volunteer instead.

The first thing you might have noticed, as the camera crew zoomed in on us, was the fifth and final member of Hope Cassidy and the Sundance Kids. She was new to the group.

And she was wearing a custom-made, robot-looking EDM helmet that covered her entire face with a black visor.

Let's back up a bit to give this new member a proper introduction.

THIRTY HOURS EARLIER

"So, what do you say?" I said. "Will you accept my rejection and help us save Inclusive Prom?"

Danny's smile was as wide and bright as a slice of the moon. It sparkled like the Pleiades. "How can I say no to Inclusive Prom?"

My phone buzzed annoyingly in my pocket, regardless of the fact that Danny and I were having a moment. I gave a disgruntled little huff and pulled it out, then said "fuck" when I saw the name on the screen.

It was Charity.

I showed it to Danny, whose eyes got bigger when he saw it. "What are you waiting for? Answer it!"

I answered it. "Helghhh." Fuck. I cleared my throat awkwardly, like I was raking gunk out of a dirty alley gutter. "Huh-hello?"

Charity sniffed loudly. "Can you pick me up?"

For the record, I was literally the last person I expected Charity to call to pick her up from *anywhere*. If we were to make a comprehensive list, I expected my name would come in front of Satan himself, but literally behind everyone else, complete strangers and potential axe murderers included.

"Uh, sure?" I said. "Where are you?"

"Dylan's house."

I guess I sort of forgot how to speak because I said nothing for a long moment.

"This was a bad idea," said Charity. "I'll call someone else."

I quickly snapped out of my stupor. "No no no no no! I'm coming, okay? Charity, I'm coming. *Okay*?"

This time, there was a long pause on Charity's end. "Okay," she said finally. "I'll be out front. Come quick."

"Yeah. Of course."

"And Hope?"

"Yeah?"

There was a formidable pause.

"I'm sorry about yesterday," she said.

"Oh," I said. "Okay."

Neither of us seemed to know how to continue the conversation at that point, and so we hung up. It felt like an unspoken agreement.

I looked at Danny in a mind-melted daze. "I guess I'm picking up Charity?"

Danny was grinning at me. "You got this."

I was about to argue with him, but—no. He was right. I *did* have this. There was literally nothing more important in the world than picking up Charity from that steaming shitbag's house.

♩ ♫ ♪

When I rolled onto the Rogers' street in the CR-V, I spotted Charity sitting on the curb. She had a backpack on her shoulders, a purse in her lap, and appeared to be wearing multiple layers of clothing. Before I even came to a proper stop in front of the house, Charity was already up and darting for the passenger-side door. I came to a jarring halt, just so she could climb in without dying. When she shut the door behind her, she was deliberately hiding her face from me. But there was no hiding the red, swollen sadness in her eyes.

That's when I noticed Dylan, visible from one of the staggered windows on the staircase. He was pressing a blood-soaked wad of tissues to his nose with one hand and a frozen bag of vegetables to his eye with the other.

"Holy crap, what happened to Dylan?" I said. And then my eyes got a little bigger when I realized Dylan almost certainly wasn't the victim. "What *happened*?"

"Just go, please," said Charity.

I nursed the gas, and we slowly veered out of the Rogers' neighborhood.

The silence between Charity and me was an ocean. I wanted so badly to say something, but what?

"I know how this looks," said Charity. "Dylan didn't do anything. He *wanted* to but...he didn't."

I nodded slowly.

"I mean, he tried to, a little bit, but I punched him in the face."

I said nothing.

"Then, when he followed me into the kitchen, I hit him in the face with a waffle maker."

In any other context, I might have found that hilarious. But given the circumstance, it was just horrifying.

"Are you okay?" I asked.

Charity started to nod her head but broke halfway, and she shook her head instead, eyes brimming with tears.

"We might have done it eventually," said Charity. "I liked him, I really did! But he just *had* to do it before Battle of the Bands. He kept saying it was 'for good luck,'" she air quoted, "whatever that's supposed to mean. But then I realized it had nothing to do with me. He's obsessed with *you*. All he cares about is getting even with you! For humiliating him at the abortion clinic, for becoming so popular, for... for taking his brother away?"

Charity erupted into horrible, choking sobs.

"Why does he think he can hurt you so much by what he does with me?" said Charity, weeping. "That would mean you *care* about me, doesn't it? How does Dylan know that, and I don't?"

Now I was crying. I had no words in response, only tears.

"I miss Faith," said Charity. "I don't think you know that, but I miss her so much. My biggest fear is that I'll never be able to tell her how much I love her. Sometimes I wake up in the middle of the night in a panic, and that's the only thing I think about. You know?"

I knew.

"All I ever wanted was for you two to accept me," said Charity, "and I realize you probably never let me into your Cool Sister Club or whatever because you thought I would do the very thing I ended up doing, but... I didn't *want* that! I didn't want Faith to go anywhere! I just told Mom what Brianna told me, and the whole thing just exploded. I just wanted Faith to notice me. I wanted *you* to notice me. And I realize that's stupid, and I'm the reason everything got ruined, but... I didn't *mean* to ruin everything!"

"You didn't ruin everything," I said softly.

"But I did!" said Charity, crying. "That's all I ever do! I want to think that things might have turned out differently if Faith never left, but then Danny moved in and... and I... I've been nothing but awful to him!"

Charity dropped her face in her hands, heaving with tears.

"And Danny's never been anything but nice to me!" she said. "Did you know that he helped me with my math homework? I was on the couch, and I was just staring at this one problem for the longest time, and I couldn't get past it, and Danny's like, 'Oh, you need to multiply the numerator and the denominator by the conjugate,' and he just goes and walks me through the whole problem. And I just stared at him like a complete idiot. I wanted to say thank you, but I didn't even know how!"

I didn't know about that, but it sounded like a very Danny thing to do. *That guy.*

"I feel like everything I've been taught to believe is all mixed up in my head," said Charity, "and I don't know what I'm supposed to do, or who to be, or what I even *am* anymore. I wish I could take back everything and start over, but when you've ruined everything, where do you even start?"

"Now," I said.

"What?"

"You asked where do you even start? You start now."

"But *how*?" said Charity, despairingly.

"There are two proms tomorrow. One of them is going to tell queer kids everywhere, in or out of the closet, that it's okay to be who they are. The other one is just candy-coated prejudice. If you want to tell Faith you love her—if you want to say sorry to Danny, or like, thank you for the help with the math problem or whatever—there's one specific prom you should be a part of."

Charity's eyes lit up in a way that I did not expect. But it was *nothing* compared to the words that spilled out of her mouth.

"Can I join your band?" she asked, just way too excited. Her eyes were huge, sparkling like gold doubloons.

"Oh," I said. "Um."

Charity already seemed to sense that she had overstepped, and she was trying hard not to sound too mortally wounded. "I mean. I obviously don't expect you to make me an *official* member of the band. Not after everything. Just for prom. Just to do my part to make things right."

"I really appreciate the offer," I said. "Honestly, I do. But no offense, I don't know if we have a room for a piano in the band. I think that's more of a Billy Joel thing."

"Not a piano," said Charity, undeterred. "Something else."

♩ ♫ ♪

Charity opened her bedroom closet, shedding daylight on Dad's long lost Minimoog. Its Appalachian hardwood exterior gleamed like a ballroom floor. (Charity had surely polished it since the last time I saw it, years ago.) And it wasn't the only thing in there. There were also studio monitors, midi controllers, audio interface, microphones, outboard gear, and instruments I couldn't even begin to describe, but if I was to try, I'd say it looked like the BBC had a garage sale after the original *Doctor Who* was canceled back in 1989.

The cherry on top was a custom-made, robot-looking space helmet. It was black and gold and walked a treacherous line between dorky and badass.

I pulled out the space helmet. "What is this?"

Charity grabbed the helmet and popped it on her head with a smooth *plunk!*

"Every EDM DJ needs a helmet," said Charity's muffled voice.

I had no words. What do you even say to something like that?

"EDM stands for electronic dance music," Charity clarified.

"Okay, this is all really cool, but..." I trailed off because I wasn't sure how to process all this. The revelation itself was head-spinning, but even if I had time to absorb it properly—which I *didn't*—I hadn't the slightest fucking clue how to properly utilize her.

"You said Inclusive Prom's happening at Devils Tower, right?" said Charity.

"Yes?"

"And that's where the climax of *Close Encounters* happens, right? Like, Faith's *favorite movie of all time*?"

"Yes?" I said, eyes widening with realization. I still hadn't told Charity about Faith yet. I think I was just planning on letting that unfold naturally.

Charity raised a single finger and tapped out the iconic five musical tones—D, E, C, C (octave lower), G—from *Close Encounters of the Third Kind*.

"Oh shit," I said.

♩ ♫ ♪

And that's how, thirty hours later, Charity was on stage with us, manning a DJ control center with Dad's Minimoog at its core. She was wearing a black skeleton-printed jumpsuit and about a dozen glow-stick bracelets, and—because apparently she had the time—she had dyed her hair neon green on a razor-sharp whim. Although it probably only *seemed* spontaneous to us, the people living outside Charity's head. I had a feeling Charity had been wanting to do that for a *long* time. It might have seemed pointless, considering it was mostly hidden beneath her EDM helmet, but I liked to think it was the symbolism that was important.

Charity was the singular exception to our dress code. The rest of us were dressed halfway between punk and prom, meaning lots of fishnet, skinny ties, and the coolest assortment of blazers we could find at the Thrifty Schwifty.

Charity kicked things off by tapping out *Close Encounters'* five tones. She pressed a button on her control center that caused the tones to repeat, then played variations on top of them, weaving it all together in a tapestry of galvanizing sound.

My voice pierced the fray like a needle with thread, slowly weaving together fabric made of pure electricity.

> *They say love is blind,*
> *That the only thing I see*
> *Is the thing that I want to see, that my eyes are closed, sewn shut by naivety,*
> *Even though you're in front of me.*

Danny's fingers danced like ballet on his Gibson. Angus carried the mystic soul of our beat with his purring bass, a deep-breathing rhythm. Astrid pattered her drums like rain against window glass.

> *They say you and I,*
> *That we're not meant to be.*
> *They say we're just fireflies flying aimlessly in the dark, that our love is wrong,*
> *So why do you feel so right to me?*

Up until this point, the sheer intricacy of Charity's beat was a web of woven chaos. That's when the beat dropped, and our laser show exploded behind us (a last-minute purchase thanks to Deja and our generous GoFundMe donors, all of whom were *all about* supporting Inclusive Prom). A strobe of neon lines and colors thrashed and pulsed across Devils Tower, turning us into silhouettes. Meanwhile, I sailed into a chorus that may or may not have had lines ripped straight from the pages of *Andromeda and Tanks Through Space and Time*. So I hope you'll forgive me because I sort of lost my mind.

You better believe that you're the only thing that I need
Because you are you
And I am me
I say you better believe that they don't know what the hell I need
Because hate is blind
Only love can see.
Because you are you
Baby, I am me
Because hate is blind
Baby, love can see

As we sailed into the second verse, everyone on their respective instruments reeled it back in, soft and subdued.

I'm an alien
On a planet of nothing
But I've known you my whole life, I feel you in every part of me

It's like we were meant to be.
I have been cast out
They don't want no part of me
But that's okay because I have you, my machine girl, and you're everything I need
You were made just for me.

As we launched into the chorus for a second time, my voice danced across Charity's blanket of electric sound. The laser-filled air was carpeted in it. Pulsing. Throbbing. Danny proceeded to shred and slay so hard that his guitar should have miraculously transformed into a battle-ax with strings. Angus was the god of thunder on his bass; he caused the Earth to shake and tremble. Astrid bashed and thrashed her drums like she was committing a Class A felony. And Charity—oh man, Charity—she did things to those keys that hadn't been done since Sir Elton John. It was obscene. It was fucking ridiculous. It was *totally* hard-core.

By the time we finished, there were only ten teenagers in attendance at Inclusive Prom.

And none of them were Faith.

♩ ♫ ♪

The night was wild, full of stars and sweat and a surprisingly brisk cold front. We were surely on the cusp of a storm. I was overdosed on my own adrenaline, and I wasn't alone. We were still loitering/screaming/dancing at Inclusive Prom, a vast, mostly empty party in the middle of Black Hills nowhere. It didn't matter. My blood was pure electricity.

"WHAT THE SHIT WAS THAT, CHARITY?" Danny screamed at her, utterly delighted.

"I DON'T KNOW," Charity replied. She was smiling so hard I felt my own face cramping *for her*. But maybe that was just my own smiling crisis. The overall feeling was a contagious cloud of ecstasy.

Angus was simply screaming. No words, just sounds.

"*Wub wub wub*," said Astrid, moving her arms robotically. I think she was pretending to be Charity's bass drop.

We parted ways with the film crew Deja found for us, thanking them for their help, to which one of them replied, "No, thank *you*." He said that was, no shit, the best live band performance he'd seen since Queen at Live Aid. Okay, guy, thank you for lying and inflating our fragile little egos. I'll save that compliment for every rainy day for *the rest of my life*, maybe monsoon season in Mumbai while we're at it.

That's when we heard something odd in the distance. A heavy, charged sound.

"Do you hear that?" said Charity.

We did, but none of us had quite pieced together what it was. Thunder? The wind? A train? We were anticipating a storm, but this was some next-level auditory buzz, like...

...like a hundred cars rolling single file down 110 West...

...every single one of them on a direct trajectory to Devils Tower...

...filled with hundreds of teenagers dressed for prom, screaming and hollering at the tops of their lungs.

"Oh. My. God." said Angus. He glanced from Astrid, to me, to Danny.

Astrid and I were speechless.

Danny was smiling and crying simultaneously. Silent tears streamed down his face. In that moment, it became clear: all the hardship, the trauma, the rejection, the doubt, everything he had suffered through for the past few months.

It was all worth it for this one moment.

♩ ♫ ♪

The news reached us right about the time that the mass exodus did. It was all over social media. Princess Leia's Buns won Battle of the Bands. They allegedly won by *a lot*. The word "landslide" was being used.

But Princess Leia's Buns was only a fraction of what everyone was talking about.

Everyone was talking about us.

A video of our performance was making the rounds. It was pointless to tell you how many views it had, because the numbers were skyrocketing by the second. And the comments! Oh my God, the comments.

glowwyvern

has anyone seen my breath? because hope cassidy took it away.

reply

Hermione Stranger

Pretty sure the two guys in Daft Punk had a baby together, and she just joined my favorite local band. That bass drop, my god. \m/ >_< \m/

reply

CliffLovesPoptarts

Holy fucking shit. I just shit my pants. I'm STILL shitting.

reply

Lando Calrissian—whose name was actually Vanessa Patel—had this to say:

@HCatSK

kylo and i will not sleep until we hunt down hope cassidy and her sundance kids and they take this stupid trophy off our hands. if we had a trophy for all of humanity, we'd give you that instead, but we don't, so you'll have to settle for the one that almost went to the nazis. WE'RE COMING FOR YOU!!! >:D

reply

So, what happened with Alt-Rite?

Apparently, they wrote a new song exclusively for Battle of the Bands. And by "they," I mean Dylan. It was the second song he was the sole writer of. It was called "Hopeless Cassidy and the Suckass C*nts."

That's right. Their *one* song—the final performance of the night, the culmination of months of anticipation—was a petty shot at us.

Everyone hated it. Even the hard-core Alt-Rite fans. According to them, the very cesspool of humanity, it just "wasn't that good."

Even Kaleb and Shawn publicly admitted to hating it.

Word on the street was that Dylan insisted that this was their Battle of the Bands song, and Shawn, Kaleb, and Hunter had all said no. So Dylan threatened them. If they didn't play this song, he was walking out. They had to find a new lead singer. He could find a better band than these pieces of shit anyway; fuck these guys.

Hunter flat out walked out on them.

Alt-Rite was forced to play without a drummer.

According to Shawn and Kaleb, not having drums wasn't even the worst part. The song was already that bad.

♩ ♫ ♪

Inclusive Prom may have been small and intimate on a decorative scale, but the sheer volume of people who filled it was apocalyptic in scope, like a dance party at the end of the world. The borders of what was considered "dance floor" expanded by default. People danced in the backs of pickup trucks. Some were even dancing on top of their own cars! This was partly because Charity was currently DJing a personally remixed version of the Jonas Brothers song "Sucker." At this point, the Sundance Kids and I were 100 percent content letting Charity run the show, musically speaking.

Danny and Angus and Astrid and I danced together, and Danny and Angus danced together, and Angus and Astrid danced together, at which point Danny asked me if he could have this dance.

It was a slow song, but it wasn't weird for us. Not anymore.

Maybe it was because I was trying hard to ignore the absence of the one person I was hoping the most to find here. Maybe not. All I knew was that I missed her, and I was trying hard to not let that one disappointment spoil this moment.

"You okay?" asked Danny.

I nodded, even though it felt just a little bit like a lie.

"She loves you," said Danny.

I nodded, even though the feeling of a lie never went away. It was becoming hard to maintain eye contact.

"Have I ever told you how cool you are?" said Danny.

I looked at Danny and rolled my eyes. "C'mon, do you even know me? I'm the exact opposite of cool. Just because I'm in a band doesn't mean jack shit—"

"The band isn't what makes you cool," said Danny. "You're cool because you're yourself—gleefully, recklessly, one hundred percent yourself. And if that isn't cool, then fuck. I don't know what is."

Not a word of that sounded like a lie coming out of his mouth.

It was at that moment that Lando Calrissian and Kylo Ren—or the girls cosplaying them, at least—took the stage and, with Charity's blessing, commandeered the mic.

"HOPE CASSIDY AND THE SUNDANCE KIDS," said Lando. "COME TAKE THIS G.D. TROPHY OFF OUR HANDS."

Kylo Ren waved a gold-colored trophy shaped like a guitar over her head, screaming.

Just like that, the energy of Inclusive Prom became a rock concert all over again. All of it was pulsing, throbbing, hundreds of hands and fingers unraveling in the air. Somehow, everyone seemed to know exactly where we were, and against the laws of physics, the crowd occupying the dance floor compressed and parted, forming a path down the middle—a straight line all the way to the stage. It was unreal. Almost biblical. Danny, Angus, Astrid, and I jogged down the path, arms out, because everyone (respectfully) wanted a piece of us. I, alone, probably gave a hundred passing high-fives before reaching the stage.

The five of us tottered up the stage stairs. I barely had a moment to find balance when Lando tackled me in a hug. When she finally let go, she took a couple of embarrassed steps backward, attempting to tie her own hands in a knot.

"You were *so great*," she said. "Not that you need me to tell you that."

"MY TURN," Kylo squawked. She butted herself in between us, holding the trophy in front of her chest. She squealed and gave the trophy a little shake.

I glanced at Danny beside me. Gave a little sideways nod his way and winked. "Give it to him. He's the mastermind."

"Wait, what?" said Danny, going rigid. "No, Hope, I didn't even—"

But it was too late. Kylo pushed the trophy into his chest. And then she hugged both of us, one in each arm.

"I'm hugging all of you, don't think you're getting out of this!" Kylo declared.

"You should say something," said Lando, looking directly at me. "They've already heard our nonacceptance speech. We all want to hear from you."

I looked at Danny, but he was already shaking his head. "No way. I'm not saying a word. This is all you, Hope."

"Speech! Speech! Speech!" Lando chanted, pumping her hands in the air. It caught fire.

"Speech! Speech! Speech!" the crowd began to roar in jagged waves.

I took a deep breath. Let it out like it was a century's worth of collected dust.

Stepped toward the nearest mic.

The crowd lost it. The structured chant obliterated itself in wild screams and manic applause. It continued this way until I reached the mic, at which point, an unsettling quiet fell over the stadium. The silence was heavy and disorienting.

I accidentally breathed into the mic, causing a rumble of staticky thunder.

What was I supposed to say? What *could* I say? I wasn't special. Not any more special than Danny or Astrid or Angus or Charity. I *certainly* wasn't more special than Deja. Or Mr. Britton, or even Frank. We couldn't have done this without any of them.

Who the fuck was I? Beneath the lyrics and the punk rock and the spectacle of it all, who was I? I was just someone who lost something. I was...

...staring hopelessly into a restless crowd when I saw her.

Faith.

I *saw* Faith.

She was maybe twenty yards into the field, inconspicuously trying to move closer—like she might have just arrived. One face in the middle of a hundred faces. And like every single one of those faces, she was looking directly at me.

I might have thought I was hallucinating—that I was projecting Faith's face onto some lookalike—but standing right next to her was Mavis Mackley.

Mavis looked emotionally worn, like she had spent the better part of a century sobbing and smiling simultaneously.

"Faith?" I said. My broken voice crumbled against the amplifying force of the microphone.

Faith's eyes went wide. She clearly hadn't expected herself to be spotted, Where's Waldo like, in a crowd of this size. She covered her mouth with her hand.

"Faith!" I screamed.

I couldn't do stairs. In this moment, I didn't even know what stairs were, let alone where they were. I dashed to the edge of the stage, high enough off the ground to fuck up my ankle if I landed like an idiot. So I hoisted myself down, dangling my feet over the edge. I was going to jump.

I expected everyone to get out of the way, but that's the exact opposite of what happened. Instead, they pooled beneath me, arms raised, palms flat, ready to catch me.

No. Ready to *carry* me.

Oh. Um. Okay. This was happening.

I was in too much of a hurry to fight it, so I went with it. Slid off the edge of the stage, landing securely into a bed of hands.

"Over there!" I ordered, pointing into the crowd. "Take me over there!"

It wasn't light speed, but it was shockingly efficient. I rotated onto my belly for a better view, surfing deeper into the crowd. Where was she?

For a second—a brief, eternal, heartbeat of a moment—I thought I lost her. I could almost feel my heart breaking inside my chest. Just bursting with blood and gore.

"Faith!" I screamed. "Faith, where are you?"

And then I saw a single pair of hands wave like scissor blades.

Between them, jumping into view, was her face. I thought I might have a cardiac event.

"Right here, Hope!" she called out. "I'm right here!"

The crowd knew what to do. They parted like she was the single most important person in the world. (She was.) The hands beneath me carried me faster, as if propelled by the urgency inside me. My hands reached for hers and they clasped together, our fingers interlocking. The hands controlling my legs and lower body readjusted, tilting me upright, setting me gently onto the grass.

Her hair was dirty brown, shoulder length, neat and clean. A dash of sprinkles peppered her nose. She was wearing a plaid button-up shirt, tucked into high-waist jeans, and a yellow braided belt. To top it all off: penny loafers. It was such a Faith outfit, it hurt to look at it. It was beautiful.

"Faith!" I cried, plowing into her. I hugged her around the neck, rubbing my face all over her, all but blowing my nose in her hair. "Oh my God, is it you? Is this real?"

I had to take half a step back, just so I could take her all in. I grabbed her face, massaging her cheeks between my fingers like Play-Doh. I swear, I just wanted to make sure I wasn't dreaming this.

"It's me," said Faith, laughing and trying not to cry. "It's real."

"Hi, everyone," said Danny's magnified voice from the microphone. "So, Hope hasn't seen her sister in a year, so maybe we can give them some space? Thank you. I think, um, Angus and Astrid have some words for us."

Astrid and Angus, the world's two greatest talkers—or *talkiest* talkers, at least—commandeered the microphone, and proceeded to give our acceptance speech. I wouldn't have had it any other way.

When I looked back at Faith, her gaze flitted sideways for a second, then returned to me.

"Wanna meet my girlfriend?" she said, nervously.

"Who, Mavis?" I said, stupidly. Even though I already knew for a *fact* that Mavis hadn't seen or heard from Faith in over a year.

Mavis laughed.

Faith smiled nervously, but her focus shifted to a very definite presence behind me. She raised her hand like a karate chop, slicing down in a dorky robotic gesture: "Hope... meet Deja Williams. My girlfriend."

That announcement completely debilitated my ability to turn around. My brain shifted violently to spin cycle, and Deja's name flattened against the inner wall, suspended by sheer velocity.

By the time I finally turned, a slow penguin shuffle, there was Deja Williams.

She looked the most nervous of all. Maybe the only time I had ever seen Deja nervous.

"I don't... um," I couldn't even process what was happening, let alone how to respond. "What? I'm confused."

"I saw your video," said Faith. She stepped beside Deja, and their fingers cautiously interlocked. "You know, the first one? I saw what you did at Change Through Grace. I was... speechless." She raised her hand to her chest, and her lip quivered. "Seriously. So touched. And I wanted to reach out, to say thank you, to... *help* somehow. But I wasn't ready to show my face in Sundance. I *certainly* wasn't ready to see Mom and Dad again. But Deja and I had been dating for a bit, and she was . . . you know . . . *Deja fucking Williams*. So I asked if she'd help you guys out."

"She didn't need to convince me," said Deja. "I've basically been your number one fan since day one."

"Um, number *two* fan," said Faith, smirking.

Deja playfully shook her head, pretending to be discreet. She held up a single finger, pointed to herself, and mouthed: *I'm number one.*

This was all too much. I felt the weight of everything crashing down, washing over me, sweeping me away.

"You've been watching me?" I said. "This whole time?"

"Oh, Hope," she said, blinking back tears. "I never stopped watching you."

I couldn't even stand anymore. I collapsed into her arms and sobbed uncontrollably. A year's worth of suffering, all at once. The floodgates opened, and it all came rushing out of me. There was no stopping it.

And I finally felt release.

I was choking on tears, and yet, I felt like I could finally breathe for the very first time.

I thought *I* was crying, but Deja was off on the sidelines, bawling the whole fucking Nile. Both hands were covering her face, trying to hold it all in, but mostly, she was just falling apart.

"Can I hug you guys?" she asked politely.

We both tackled Deja in a Cassidy hug sandwich.

"Gahh, my sister is dating Deja Williams!" I exclaimed, flinging my head back, cackling deliriously.

Faith was no longer trying not to cry. She was just crying.

"You know I love you, right?" I said.

Faith gave a fragile laugh. "Of course, I know."

"I love you *so fucking much.* I missed you so bad, I thought I might die—"

Faith hugged me before I could finish. "It's okay. I'm here now."

We stayed that way for a long moment, not moving, not speaking, not doing anything except being there, which was all either of us ever really needed.

Then Faith locked up. Every muscle in her body went rigid. That's when I remembered I wasn't the only Cassidy girl up on that stage.

We slowly untethered, and I turned around.

There was Charity in her skeleton jumpsuit, standing no more than ten feet away, cradling her helmet like she was the Headless Horseman. Her eyes were hard as marbles behind her thick-framed glasses and acid green waterfall of hair. She stood perfectly, calamitously still.

I glanced between them, grasping for a read, but they were both unreadable. I wasn't even sure if they were breathing. Was *I* breathing? I don't think I was breathing.

Finally, Faith's mouth tweaked into a delicate, forgiving smile. "Hi, Charity."

Charity's face crumpled like a paper bag. Her mouth screwed into a terrible shape, and her eyes bled tears.

She ran shamelessly into her big sister's arms, wrapped around her, and broke down sobbing.

"I'm sorry, Faith; I'm so sorry, I'm sorry!"

I watched my sisters hold each other. Heal each other.

Maybe time, itself, didn't heal all wounds. Maybe, in the end, it was people who healed those wounds. Nobody wants to hurt.

Maybe, deep down, all we want is to forgive and be forgiven.

That was the last straw. Andromeda collapsed onto her knees and elbows and fell apart. Her chest heaved, and her eyes burned, and it just hurt too much to hold it all in.

"I have to fix her!" Andromeda cried. "I have to, and this is all that I have!"

"What if I can get you a job?" said the woman.

Andromeda sniffled loudly and looked up. "Hugnghh?"

The woman shifted her weight from one leg to the other. She traded hands too, resting her left on her pregnant belly and using the right hand to gesture to herself.

"My husband and I own a casino hotel," she explained. "There are lots of jobs—cooking, cleaning, waiting. A few of the hires live in the hotel, rent-free. If that's, um..."

Andromeda stared at the woman. The woman glanced at the spreadsheet of parts on the computer. Then lowered her gaze to Tanks. (What was left of her.) "We have a robotics department," she said. Andromeda's stare intensified.

"Most of our games are droid-officiated. The robotics department oversees routine maintenance. Our robotics director has been clamoring for an assistant for ages. She might be able to help you with your friend. If you'd be more interested in a job like...that."

"What are you doing?" said Andromeda.

"I'm sorry?"

"You're offering me a job? And a place to live? And someone

who might be able to help me to . . . ?" Andromeda glanced hopelessly at Tanks. (What was left of her.) "Why?"

"You remind me of my daughter," said the woman.

Andromeda gave a weak laugh. "Jeez. She must be a real shitshow."

It was only after she said it that she realized how callous that probably sounded.

"I'm sorry," said Andromeda. "I didn't mean it like—"

"You are not . . . ," said the woman, cutting her off, suddenly emotionally overwhelmed. "You are a beautiful girl who has been terribly wronged."

Her black eyes grew glassy and wet.

"I'm not a good person," said the woman. "I'm no better than the people who did that to you. Because of what I've done, I might never see my little girl again."

For a fleeting instant, Andromeda could see this woman's daughter. Wintery hair cut in a high line across her forehead. Freckles peppered across her nose. It was a charming image that filled Andromeda with a flutter of joy. She felt like a friend from a different life.

"She was exiled to Dearth," said the woman quietly. "Thanks to Dresdore, this planet has turned into an exile hub."

Andromeda wasn't sure what to say to that, so she said, "Have you tried putting out flyers?" Like an idiot. Good God, Andromeda.

"Oh yes," said the woman. Nodding. Laughing. Weeping. "Big, expensive flyers. That's actually why I'm here. She loved to read, you know. I could buy her all the books in the world, and she'd still come to the library. I think she came just for the smell of it."

"She sounds lovely," said Andromeda. Seeing someone else's sadness didn't make Andromeda feel better, but it did make her feel less alone.

"She was. I can't atone for my actions, but I can help you. It's maybe the only thing I can do. So please: Let me help you."

Andromeda sniffled. In the process, she inadvertently caught a whiff of herself. She smelled like fermented death. "I could really use a shower," Andromeda confessed.

"We have those," said the woman, smiling vulnerably.

Together, they retrieved Tanks's head from underneath the table. The woman carried it as gently as she carried the dear thing growing deliberately inside of her. Andromeda carried Tank's torso. They walked slowly, serenely, like the breath released at the end of a long, hard day.

They exited the Zaffyra Public Library.

Andromeda never saw the small statue in the lobby, a young Zaffy, nor the plaque beneath it. Zaffy had kept a book of quotes in her bedroom, and the one inscribed on the plaque was her favorite:

You are you
And I am me
And hate is blind
But love can see.

ACKNOWLEDGMENTS

Of all my novels, *Hopepunk* traveled the longest journey. If I'm to thank people, the person I have to start with is my (first) editor, Laura Schreiber, who first acquired *Hopepunk*. She was responsible for some important, early-game creative decisions that challenged me as an author more than anything I've written to date, such as the idea that Hope Cassidy and the Sundance Kids should perform original songs, not covers. That seems like such an obvious choice to make, especially at this point in the book, but at the time, my thought process was, how the fuck do you write original songs IN A BOOK? Thank you, Laura, for challenging me in the best ways.

Secondly, and perhaps most importantly, I have to thank my (second) editor, Liz Kossnar, who saw *Hopepunk* safely to its end. Thank you, Liz, for doing your damnedest to preserve the creative integrity of this story, and also for being responsible for one of the most important character rewrites in the story, Deja Williams. Both Faith and Hope might not have ended up with their happiest ending in a different version of this story, so readers, thank your lucky fucking stars for Liz!

Thank you, Caitlyn Averett, for your editing contributions before the Big Shift, and especially for all the pictures of that damn cute cat of yours.

Thank you, Hannah Milton, for your editing contributions

after the Big Shift, as well as for taking care of my previous works at their new home at LBYR.

Thank you, Adams Carvalho, for drawing a more badass version of Hope than I ever could have imagined.

Thank you, Mary Claire Cruz, and to the entire design team, for thinking up that gorgeous rainbow outline in the title design. (That was you, right??) Fucking brilliant!

Thank you, Elizabeth Degenhard, and the copyediting team, for the subtle brilliance of the work you do.

Thank you, Jenny Bent, for being the best agent an author could ask for.

Thank you to my life partner, Erin Rene, for loving me. I don't know why you keep doing it (I mean, have you met me?!), but thank you for doing it anyway.

And lastly, thank you to every queer kid who has ever lived and had the courage to hope for a happy ending to their story. I love you more than you will ever know.